S0-BJM-553

The Secret Sister

Center Point
Large Print

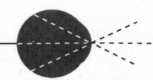

**This Large Print Book carries the
Seal of Approval of N.A.V.H.**

The
Secret Sister

Brenda Novak

CENTER POINT LARGE PRINT
THORNDIKE, MAINE

This Center Point Large Print edition is published in the year 2015 by arrangement with Harlequin Books S.A.

The text of this Large Print edition is unabridged. In other aspects, this book may vary from the original edition. Printed in the United States of America on permanent paper. Set in 16-point Times New Roman type.

ISBN: 978-1-62899-728-6

Library of Congress Cataloging-in-Publication Data

Novak, Brenda.
  The secret sister / Brenda Novak. — Center Point Large Print edition.
    pages cm
  Summary: "After a painful divorce, Maisey Lazarow returns to Fairham, the small island off the North Carolina coast where she grew up, to heal and to help her troubled brother. Her tenuous relationship with her mother is further strained when Maisey tries to discover what really happened to their older sister whom her mother claims never existed"—Provided by publisher.
  ISBN 978-1-62899-728-6 (library binding : alk. paper)
  1. Divorced women—Fiction. 2. Family secrets—Fiction.
    3. Large type books. I. Title.
  PS3614.O926S43 2015
  813'.6—dc23
                                                    2015028956

To my nephew, Travis. I loved having you come and stay with us so often as a boy. Some of my very best memories are of you, which makes it even more of a joy to see that you have grown into a man we can all be proud of.

1

Maisey Lazarow's brother met her at the ferry—alone. Part of her, a big part, was grateful her mother wasn't with him. Even after ten years, Maisey wasn't ready to confront the autocratic and all-powerful "queen" of Fairham, South Carolina. The fact that Josephine hadn't deigned to come with Keith made it clear Maisey would not be easily forgiven. Only after her mother had punished her sufficiently would she be welcomed back into Josephine's good graces.

Although Maisey had expected as much, coming up against that reality nearly made her balk. What was she doing here? She'd sworn she'd never return to the small island where she'd been raised, that she'd never again subject herself to Josephine's manipulation and control.

But that was before, when she'd set off to build her shiny new life. And this was now, when that shiny new life had imploded on her. She was coming back to Fairham because her brother needed her but, truth be told, she needed Keith, too.

At least her mother wasn't currently married. The men Josephine chose were almost as bad as she was, just in different ways.

What Maisey needed most was her father, she

realized as she stood at the railing, peering through the passengers crowding the gangway. Breathing in the island air, smelling the salty ocean and wet wood of the wharf, it all reminded her of him. But Malcolm had died in a boating accident when she was ten. That was when her mother had grown even more over-bearing. Without Malcolm, there was no one to soften Josephine's sharper edges, no one to hold her in check. Not that the buffer he'd provided was the only reason, or even the primary reason, she missed him . . .

"There you are!" Keith called across the distance, waving to make sure he had her attention.

Grabbing the handles of her two suitcases, which contained everything she hadn't shipped to the island in boxes, she stepped into the flow of people so she could disembark. It was too late to change her mind about moving home. She'd given up her apartment in Manhattan and depleted most of her savings, thanks to the exorbitant fees of the divorce attorney she'd had to hire.

"You look great," Keith told her as she moved closer.

Maisey conjured up her best approximation of a smile—she seemed unable to smile spon-taneously these days—and embraced him. "Thanks." She was wearing an expensive white tunic with Jimmy Choo shoes and Chanel jewelry, but she'd never looked worse and she knew it. She hadn't been sleeping or eating well—not since *that* day two years ago, the worst day of her life. It didn't help that her brother was also going through a difficult time. Once she'd learned about his suicide attempt, she'd been so manic about selling her furniture and what she could sacrifice of her other belongings so she could return to Fairham to be with him that she hadn't bothered to do much shopping or cooking, which had caused her to lose even more weight. Her color wasn't good, either.

But her brother didn't look much better. Nearly six-foot-six with a set of broad shoulders that gave him a nice frame, he could stand to gain some weight, too. And he had dark circles under his eyes—the same blue-green eyes she possessed that always drew so much attention.

"You look good, too," she lied, and suppressed a wry chuckle. She was home, all right. The pretense was already starting. Her ex-husband's frank honesty was one of the things that had attracted her to him, which made his actions at the end of their marriage seem especially ironic.

"How was your trip?" Keith pulled her thoughts away from the past, where they resided far too frequently.

"Not bad," she replied. No way did she want to regale him with stories of how difficult she found it just to walk out of her apartment building. She'd spent weeks at a time holed up in bed, but he didn't need to know that only the urgency of his situation had been sufficient motivation to get her on her feet again. "How's Mom?"

He shot her a look that acknowledged the tension any reference to Josephine created. "The same. She might not act like it, but she's excited to have you home. She's had a room in the east wing prepared for you."

The *guest* wing? The significance of that didn't escape Maisey. If there'd been any doubt that she was to be treated with cool disdain until she'd done her penance, this proved it.

The anger that flared up, making her stiffen, surprised Maisey. Apparently she wasn't *completely* cowed and broken. The idea of walking into Coldiron House—named after Josephine's father, Henry Coldiron, who'd owned most of the island before Josephine inherited it—brought back a hint of her old defiance. She couldn't cope with living there, couldn't submit, as she would have to submit, in order to regain her mother's approval.

"I won't be staying at Mom's," she said.

Keith had started to reach for her suitcases. At this, he straightened. "What do you mean?"

"I mean I have to find somewhere else."

He measured her with his eyes, and she found them so hollow she grew frightened for him all over again. Was he doing as well as he claimed? He didn't seem to be particularly robust—in body or spirit.

"I understand it'll be a bit uncomfortable for you at first." He glanced away as if he could tell she was trying to see behind the front he was putting on. "But trust me. Mom will come around. You'll piss her off if you don't stay at the house, and that'll only make matters worse. After a few weeks . . ."

"No." She broke in before he could get any further into his appeal. "I can't do it."

He stared at her. "You're serious. You've barely arrived, and you're going to make her angry? She has too much pride to put up with the rejection."

"She rejected me first. And I don't have a relationship with her, anyway," Maisey said. "We communicate through email or her house-keeper, for crying out loud. I've spoken to her only a handful of times over the past decade." And when they *had* talked, there'd been more silence than anything. There'd even been silence when Maisey had desperately craved consolation.

"You need her," he said. "We both do. And that means we'll always be under her thumb."

Although she was secretly frightened that might be true, Maisey scoffed at it. "No. I'll help you, stand by you. I just need to . . . to get back on my feet, and she can only hurt my ability to do that." The thought of walking through those heavy doors, dragging her belongings behind her, almost gave her a panic attack. At least, if she didn't stay at Coldiron House, she'd retain some autonomy, some independence. She had to protect the little peace of mind she had left.

He rubbed his gaunt face. "So where will you stay?"

"I could rent a room from someone in town." She had enough money for that, didn't she? Her reserves would last six months or so . . .

"Here on Fairham?" Her brother shook his head, adamant. "That would provoke an all-out war."

He was right. To maintain *some* semblance of peace, she couldn't cross certain lines. She couldn't embarrass her mother by revealing that there was any strain inside the family. Appearances were everything to Josephine. They were Coldirons, even though their surname was technically Lazarow, and they needed to comport themselves as such.

How many times had she heard *that* lecture?

"What if I got an apartment in Charleston?" she asked, but decided against it almost as soon as the words passed her lips. Charleston would cost too much and, left on her own, she wouldn't recover. Being sequestered in a cheap, unfamiliar apartment would be worse than living alone in New York with the furniture Jack hadn't taken.

"I don't see . . ." he started, but she cut him off again.

"Wait." The solution had occurred to her, and it was so obvious she couldn't believe she hadn't thought of it before. "Why couldn't I stay in one of the bungalows?"

"The *vacation rentals?* They're on the far side of the island!"

"So?" Going back and forth to Coldiron House wouldn't require a ferry, like it would from Charleston. And it was September, when the small influx of vacationers who visited Fairham each summer returned to their regular lives. *One* of the nine units should be available. "We're talking ten miles if I take the bike path. I'll buy a bike and ride over whenever you want me to. Or you can come hang out at my place."

Maisey felt that would be even better. Not only would living in Smuggler's Cove enable her to avoid their mother, it would provide *Keith* a place to go occasionally, a place where he wouldn't have to deal with Josephine—meaning he wouldn't have to resort to drugs as his escape.

"Most of them haven't been refurbished since Hurricane Lorna last fall," he said.

"I could've sworn you told me months ago that Mom was hiring a contractor." That was well before Keith's last big blowup with Josephine, when he'd stormed off to "live his own life." He'd disappeared for several months before ending up on another drug binge, which had culminated in the black moment that had brought him home again—the same black moment that had ultimately brought her home, too.

"She *has* hired a contractor," he said, "but she didn't get around to it until I got back a couple of weeks ago. Construction's just begun."

Her mother had waited a *year* to rebuild? "Why'd she wait so long?"

He took her suitcase, and walked toward the sleek gray Mercedes he'd parked in the lot. It was their mother's car. He no longer owned anything to speak of. Although he'd turned thirty-six in February, an age by which most people had managed to accumulate a vehicle and some furniture or other personal property, he'd sold everything for drug money. What he hadn't sold, he'd given away while he was high or destroyed out of anger and frustration.

"She was in another relationship with some off-islander, so she couldn't be bothered," he said in response to her question. "But I'm sure she'll tell you the delay was all my fault. As you know, I haven't made things easy on her—or anyone else."

Including himself . . . Keith had caused nothing but heartache. But it disturbed Maisey that her mother always had to assign blame. "The future doesn't have to be a reflection of the past." She touched his arm for encouragement. "We'll get through the coming months together. It'll be okay now that we have each other."

When he didn't respond, Maisey wished she hadn't questioned him about the delay in construction, hadn't made him accept responsibility for it. He needed to look ahead—not behind. "I'm sure the bungalows will be ready by next summer, which means we only missed one tourist season."

He was putting her suitcases in the trunk, so she couldn't read his expression. "That's the goal," he said.

"Have you been out to see them recently?" she asked as they slid into the sun-warmed interior of the Mercedes and buckled their seat belts.

"Mom's sent me over once or twice, yeah."

"How bad are they?"

"Pretty bad."

She cringed. *"Structurally?"*

"Units 1 to 4 need structural repairs."

"What about 5 to 9?" They were set back off the beach, in the trees. Maisey assumed the wind hadn't hit them as hard.

"They're sound, but they still need a lot of work."

Maisey hated that the bungalows had been damaged. Since the eighties, when her father'd had them built, Smuggler's Cove had been a magical place for her, a place where she could find him, or some essence of him, even after he

15

was gone. She had so many fond memories of tagging along to the rentals that, when he died, she'd wanted to scatter his ashes there on the beach. But her mother retained control of his remains, like she did everything else. His ashes were kept in a decorative urn on the mantel of the formal living room at Coldiron House. Not for any sentimental reason. But because it allowed Josephine to pretend he was her one great love, since she hadn't been able to get along with anyone else—not for long, anyway. Every other relationship had fallen apart within two or three years.

"I don't mind helping with the cleanup and repairs, maybe doing some painting, that sort of thing." There was a period when she and Jack, her ex-husband, had watched almost every do-it-yourself show on TV, and used much of what they'd learned to improve their small cabin in the Catskill Mountains. It had been sold, as stipulated by the divorce decree, but she'd always loved it there.

Keith backed out of the parking space. "I'm not sure the contractor's going to like having you in the middle of everything."

"I'll stay out of his way." She tucked her dark hair behind her ears. It was getting too long; she needed to have it trimmed. "Who'd Mom hire? Anyone from around here?"

"Raphael Something. Can't remember his last

16

name. I didn't ask where he was from. I know he's done other work on the island, though, because I've seen his sign—High Tide Construction."

Maisey had never met anyone by that name or heard of the company. But then, plenty could've changed since she'd been gone. "Can we go to Smuggler's Cove now, see if it's even a possibility?"

He hit the brake, stopping before they could exit the lot. "You're not thinking of moving in without asking Mom . . ."

Knowing that she had a viable alternative—if she *did* have one—would help her get through that daunting first encounter. "I can't imagine she'd refuse to let me live in one of Dad's bungalows. He'd turn over in his grave if she did." They were something her father had created and paid for with the money *he'd* brought into the relationship. "Besides, I'm supposed to inherit the development, remember?"

"*If* she follows his wishes."

Maisey had to acknowledge that the future of the cottages rested in her mother's hands, since Josephine had inherited them first. "Well, you've heard the cliché—it's easier to ask forgiveness than permission."

He pursed his lips. "Not with her."

The complexity of Keith's relationship with Josephine accounted for a lot of his problems. Maisey wished he could get out on his own so he wouldn't need Josephine's help. Then he could also reject her advice and any unwanted intrusions into his life. But, so far, that hadn't happened; he and Josephine were mutually dependent on each other. She provided financial support, and since she couldn't be satisfied with any of her romances, he gave her companionship—when he wasn't acting out. They loved each other but hated each other, too. But because Maisey was coming home with almost nothing, she wasn't exactly the perfect example of how to get away, so she hesitated to say too much.

"Come on, I'm on her shit list, anyway," she said, pretending more indifference than she felt.

He released a sigh. "Fine. Then why not really piss her off, huh?"

2

Keys Crossing was the island's only town. It was also the only land not owned by her mother. As the marina, and the downtown streets with their various municipal services and private businesses—the small town hall with adjoining police station, the fire house for the even smaller volunteer fire department, the Sugar Shack, the Drift Inn, the various gift shops and the one grocery store in town, not to mention Love's in

Bloom, her mother's flower shop—gave way to swaying palm trees, sandy beaches and lush vegetation, Maisey felt her heart begin to lighten. She'd been right to come here. She could sense it deep in her bones—now that she wasn't heading directly to her childhood home.

She closed her eyes, enjoying the hot sun beating down on her through the windshield. This summer she hadn't spent nearly enough time outdoors . . .

Keith interrupted her moment of tranquility. "Do you ever hear from Jack?"

She and her brother hadn't talked about the divorce for months. There'd been too many more dire things to focus on, most recently his attempt to take his own life with a bottle of sleeping pills. If the manager at the dumpy motel where he'd been staying in New Orleans hadn't come into his room to kick him out for nonpayment, he'd probably be dead.

"No, not a word," she said. "He has no reason to contact me. Why?"

"Just curious."

"Maybe the situation would be different if we still had Ellie," she added, "but . . . now that she's gone, our divorce really is goodbye."

Her brother didn't say anything about her child. Like most people, he shied away from the grief a loss like that inspired. "What *happened?*" he asked instead. "Why'd he cheat?"

She'd asked herself the same question so many times—and didn't like any of the answers. She couldn't help blaming herself for being unable to recover from Ellie's death as quickly as he could, for being less of a woman than he wanted, for needing him when he wasn't capable of giving her any solace. "He said he wasn't fulfilled in our marriage. Whatever that means."

Keith shifted in the driver's seat. "Have you met your replacement?"

"Once. We ran into her on Fifth Avenue." It was difficult not to hate Jack's new girlfriend. She wasn't particularly attractive, and didn't seem to have anything else that should've been hard for Jack to refuse, which only made Maisey feel more inadequate.

"After he left?" Keith asked.

"Before. They went to high school together, so they'd known each other in the past. I believe that accidental run-in on Fifth Avenue is where the affair started. She must've contacted him on Facebook or emailed him afterward—or he contacted her, and . . . their relationship grew from there."

"Does it hurt to talk about it?"

It hurt to even *think* about Jack. Maisey wasn't sure she'd ever get over him. Her marriage was supposed to last forever. But Keith was fighting enough battles. She couldn't expect him to prop *her* up. "No, I've put it behind me."

Her brother shook his head. "How'd we miss that he was such a douchebag?"

Grateful for his attempt to lighten the conversation, she smiled ruefully. "You mean how did *I* miss it? If I remember right, you were never too fond of him."

"He hated me."

Jack hadn't understood Keith's volatile nature, and had no patience with it. "The funny thing is that I can't blame Mom for the collapse of my marriage. I moved away so she couldn't turn me into the person I become when I'm around her. I thought that would make it easier to be successful in a relationship, but even that didn't change the ending."

"You gave it your best shot." He gripped the steering wheel with both hands. "Believe me, there are no answers for some things."

"How are *you* doing?" she asked. "Okay?"

"Taking it minute by minute."

"Have you been working at the flower shop?" Josephine had started the business four years after Malcolm died, following the demise of her next marriage.

"Almost every morning."

"Is Mom there very often?"

"Only when she's lonely or bored. Lately that amounts to about three days a week, for an hour here or an hour there. She has Nancy now, who manages it for her."

"So you spend your afternoons . . ."

"Going to my NA meetings. I hate having to catch the ferry for those. It all takes up so much time."

She could believe that. But they were an important part of his recovery. He wouldn't want to spend *all* day at the flower shop, anyway. And it wasn't as if he could find other work. The island had a population of only 2,500, so jobs weren't easy to come by. His temper and drug use would preclude him from maintaining a steady job, no matter where he lived. He'd proven that in the past.

"I'll go to the meetings with you," she said. "Give you some company."

"You don't want to come." He grimaced. " 'Hi, I'm Keith Lazarow, and I'm an addict.' Why would you want to listen to that bullshit?"

"Because I care about *you,* and I'm hoping that having a companion will make attending those meetings more . . . tolerable."

"What about your career? Don't you have a new children's book under contract?"

Feigning preoccupation with the scenery flying past, she turned her face to the window. "My career's on hold for the time being."

"On hold? You haven't said anything about that before."

"Because it's not a big deal. I'm just taking a break." She couldn't bring herself to tell him that she couldn't do it anymore. That the drawing, the ideas, the words, the enthusiasm . . . it was all gone. She couldn't come up with another Little Molly Brimble book, had no idea how she'd created her other books, since that kind of creativity seemed so out of reach to her now. To make it official and to escape the pressure she'd felt, she'd even fired her agent. "For the next few months, I'm going to figure out something else I can do."

He pushed aside the hank of dark hair that fell across his forehead. "Sounds to me like you're giving it up."

"Not necessarily."

"You can't quit creating, Maisey—not because of Ellie or Jack or me. You love what you do. You're good at it. And famous!"

She rolled her eyes. "I'm *not* famous."

"You were making a name for yourself. You were on your way."

Acutely conscious of the absence of her wedding ring, which had represented an important part of her identity for nine of the past ten years, she laced her fingers together in her lap. "Doesn't matter. Molly Brimble is on an indefinite leave of absence." She sounded more absolute than she'd intended. She didn't want him to continue prodding her since she was suddenly struggling to ward off tears. Lazarows didn't cry, especially in front of other people, and that included family. She'd only embarrass herself and make Keith uncomfortable.

"It was Ellie who died, Maisey," he said softly.

Her child's life had been so short, only six weeks . . . "You think I don't know that?" she said. "You think I haven't missed her every minute of every day since that terrible morning when I found her?"

He set his jaw. "My point is that it was two years ago. You have to figure out a way to get beyond it."

She couldn't look at him, not without losing her battle with those tears. Because of her relationship with Josephine, she'd let Jack talk her into burying Ellie not far from where he'd been raised in Philadelphia. But since she'd never lived there, and he was now out of her life, that felt so strange and far away. She wished she'd insisted on burying Ellie on the island, as she'd initially requested. "Get *beyond* it?" she repeated as if that was impossible.

"Yes. Unless, of course, that only applies to me." He was throwing her own words back at her.

"No, of course not. I *am* getting beyond it in the only way I believe someone can get beyond something like that. I told you, I'll do something else until I'm ready to start writing again." She couldn't fall apart after all the encouragement and advice she'd offered him. She couldn't even admit how close to despair she really was. She

24

had to stand tall and lead the way, set an example for him.

They turned onto the narrow dirt road that led into Smuggler's Cove and, about a quarter of a mile ahead, spotted a black pickup with a High Tide Construction placard on the door. It was parked outside the first bungalow on the back row—Unit 5. Maisey knew because of her familiarity with the cove; she couldn't see the house through the trees that'd grown so much since she'd last been on the island.

"Looks like Mom's contractor's hard at work," she said.

"Actually, he must be at lunch."

"How do you know?"

Keith shrugged as he slowed to navigate the various potholes. "He lives there."

Maisey gaped at him. "Only for the duration of the project, though, right?"

"Permanently—unless he decides to move. He told Mom he'd give her a heck of a deal on refurbishing the others if she'd sell him one. So she did."

A wave of resentment washed over Maisey. Her mother had mentioned other interested parties through the years but Josephine had always refused them. "The bungalows aren't for sale. They never have been." And if it was up to her, they never would be. Her father had told her they'd belong to *her*.

"Since Dad's gone, Mom's in charge, and I have to admit that selling made sense."

As soon as they passed the black truck, which was loaded with lumber, and the curved drive came into view, Keith pulled to the far side of the road.

"How do you figure?" she asked.

"He's going to maintain and manage the properties once he's finished with the refurbishing. Maybe you'll wind up with one less house, but they'll be in good shape when you take over."

"And what does he get for staying on? Will he become one of her employees?"

"Not really. He just won't have to make house payments."

"That's generous, considering the winter months are so quiet around here. Once he gets all the cottages fixed up, he won't have much to keep him busy."

Keith put the transmission in Park but didn't turn off the engine. "If I had to guess, I'd say it's about cash flow. What she would've had to pay for the repairs she keeps as the down payment. What she would've had to pay for an on-site manager she keeps in lieu of a mortgage payment."

"She's sacrificed a valuable asset!"

"*Sacrificed?* It's not a sacrifice if she receives fair compensation."

"Is she *that* tight for money?" Would she sell the others? Maisey wouldn't put it past her. What her father had brought to the marriage paled in comparison to what Josephine had contributed, so she wouldn't hesitate to do whatever she wanted, despite his promises to Maisey.

"Not necessarily. It's about being strategic." He ducked his head to peer out her window. "Even if she was in financial trouble, unless it became so obvious we couldn't miss it, we'd never know. She's very private about her finances, as you know. Not only that, but she acts as if I'm too stupid to understand business."

He'd never shown any aptitude. Maisey couldn't fault Josephine there. So she pretended to be too preoccupied to respond to that comment. "Why'd Raphael pick Unit 5?"

"Mother wouldn't let him have any of the first four. They're closer to the sea, more in demand during the summer."

Thank God for small favors! Maisey glared at the contractor's truck. She'd never shopped for a Ford F-250, but it looked big, rugged and costly. "A mortgage is only part of the cost of living. He'll have other bills to pay." She'd learned all about those other bills when they'd quickly drained her bank account . . .

"I'm sure he's got income. He still has his business, and Mom doesn't care what he does as long as he keeps everything up around here. He probably plans to fold Smuggler's Cove in with his regular work."

"I see," she said, but gripped her purse tightly—as if she wanted to fling it out the window at that truck, which was impeding the limited view through the trees.

"That's okay, isn't it?" Keith asked.

"It's not what *I* would've done."

"You're sentimental. Mom is . . . less so. And that still leaves you with eight units."

She was upset that he didn't seem to care, because she knew how he'd react if it'd been *his* inheritance Josephine had diminished. What if she'd sold the flower shop, which they'd both been told would go to him?

He shifted the transmission and began to drive away.

"Whoa, what are you doing?" Maisey asked. "We're not going to talk to the contractor?"

"I don't want to interrupt the poor guy at home. I figure you should see what you're getting into before we bother anybody."

"Won't we need keys?"

"Not to poke around a bit. You might take one look at the other bungalows and tell me to drive straight to Coldiron House."

"They'd have to be a lot worse than this. The little I can see looks fine." What if this guy had his sights set on owning the whole development one day? And if she ever tried to make the property complete again, what if he refused to sell and she couldn't get the bungalow back?

"Unit 5 is in decent shape because he finished it right away, so he could move in," Keith explained. "Now he's starting on the seaside units. They have the highest priority since they go for the highest rents."

She peered through the trees, craning her neck to see the next unit. "I don't like that he's here—or that he might become a permanent fixture." She didn't want *anything* to change, not in this place.

"You haven't even met him."

"I don't need to meet him."

When they turned in at Unit 6, she cursed under her breath. "*Look* at that."

"Told you. Not quite what you saw at the last cottage, is it? And it's the best of the ones that are left." This time he cut the engine, but she didn't get out. She stayed in her seat, gazing at the buckled porch, the sagging and missing shutters and the all-too-obvious water damage, which had left a mark halfway up the walls.

"Is it completely empty inside?" She hadn't considered that . . .

"Everything's been gutted, so Raphael can do what he needs to do."

She began to worry that she wouldn't be able to stay here, after all. "Where's the furniture? Was it ruined?"

"Not all of it. Mom had me help move everything. She insisted we throw out the drapes, bedding and towels, stuff like that. They needed to be replaced, anyway. Most of the furniture, even some of the mattresses, were salvageable, though. What's left has been stacked in the last unit."

That was good news. Depending on what had been saved, Maisey could furnish whatever unit she chose. She could always buy bedding. Perhaps she'd make her own drapes—or order them online if she couldn't come by a sewing machine.

But there was no denying that the bungalows looked worse than she'd expected. She'd been living in New York, newly single, when the hurricane hit, but she'd heard it was the worst Fairham had ever endured.

Now she could see that was true.

Keith opened his door. "Should we check the inside?"

She nodded, and they got out. But the bungalow was locked, as she'd predicted. They were trying to look through the windows when they heard the sound of an engine and turned to see the same pickup they'd noticed in front of Unit 5.

The driver parked behind the Mercedes. Maisey couldn't see much of him, though, until he started toward them.

Then her breath caught in her throat. Not only did she recognize this man, she'd once had sex with him!

3

"Oh, God, that's Rafe," she breathed, her voice low enough that the man approaching wouldn't hear.

"Who?" Keith said, but there was no time to explain.

"Rafe" Romero wasn't just someone she'd once slept with. At sixteen, she'd lost her virginity to him, rather unceremoniously, in the back bedroom of a party she'd been forbidden to attend (because there would be riffraff like him there), and she'd done it to spite her mother. She might've continued to sleep with him. The fact that he was four years older, reckless and without "prospects," as Josephine would say, made him an appealing choice for her purposes—especially since all that "unsuitable" came in such an appealing package. But once he'd learned she wasn't eighteen, like she'd said, he wouldn't have any more to do with her. Even when she'd told him she was a Lazarow, thinking that might make the difference, he'd narrowed his eyes as if he had no respect for her family name or her money. He'd said that just meant she wouldn't understand anything about the real world. She could *still* hear him laughing when she'd stomped off.

As he closed the distance between them, Maisey hoped he wouldn't remember her. She'd had eighteen years to realize how self-destructive and ridiculous her behavior had been, and was embarrassed by it. Particularly when she recalled how brazen she'd been . . .

Pretend you don't have a clue who he is and maybe he won't recognize you, she told herself. He'd been so drunk that night she thought she had a chance—until their eyes connected and he hesitated midstride.

He definitely recognized her. *Shit* . . . "Something I can help you with?" he asked.

"There is if you have the key." Grateful that he didn't immediately give away their previous involvement, she pointed at the door.

"You're Josephine Lazarow's daughter," he said.

She nodded politely but indifferently. "Yes. My name's Maisey. And I'd like to see this unit."

He smiled at Keith. "Good to see you again."

"You, too. Sorry to come by out of the blue. We didn't want you to think there was anything going on when we passed your place. It's just that my sister's considering moving into one of the bungalows for—"

Maisey felt certain he was about to say "for some strange reason," and jumped in to finish the sentence for him. "The next few months."

When Rafe's golden-brown eyes returned to

32

her, Maisey noticed that the acne he'd had as a teenager was gone. Other than a five-o'clock shadow, his skin was smooth and clear and almost as golden as his eyes. He'd also added quite a bit of muscle, mainly in the arms and shoulders, which made him look powerful. His dark hair, although shorter, retained a bit of curl at the ends, and thick black lashes framed his eyes.

The years had been kind to him, and he'd had more in the looks department than most men to start with.

"You mean after they're rehabbed?" he said.

"No. Now," she clarified. "I understand they need work. But as long as the place isn't going to fall off its stilts or give way under my feet, I can make do. Or would you suggest another unit?"

"This one's in the best shape," he said. "I'd say you're in the right place as far as that goes. But there's nothing inside any of them."

She ignored his bemused expression. "Keith tells me there's furniture in the end unit. He'll help me retrieve what I need. The utilities are on, aren't they?"

"They were off until I had them turned back on last week. I figured I'd need power and water for the construction work. But—" Rafe motioned toward his own bungalow, even though they couldn't see it for the distance and the trees "—it only took me two weeks to fix mine up.

Wouldn't you rather give me a chance to get this ready for you?"

"That's okay. My mother wouldn't want me to distract you from the seaside cottages. And I'd prefer not to wait. As long as you don't mind a slight change of plans, I'd be happy to do some of the work myself—cleaning and painting and small repairs. None of which will affect your contract."

He seemed at a loss as to why she'd be willing to do that. "If it's what you want."

He had to be wondering why she wasn't moving into Coldiron House. Most people would expect her to stay in her family home. There was a certain cachet that went along with being a Lazarow and living in the mansion her grandfather had built. But the townspeople who envied her didn't realize how difficult Josephine was, and that money and family history could only make up for so much.

Fortunately, Rafe didn't come right out and ask why she preferred a water-damaged bungalow. He seemed to be a man who knew when to keep his mouth shut.

She gestured at Unit 6. "Would you mind letting us in?"

"Not at all." He withdrew a ring of keys from his pocket and led them up the steps to the front porch, where they waited while he unlocked the door and swung it open. "Here you go."

The turpentine and other chemicals that'd been

used so far wafted out. "Smells clean," she said.

"I sprayed for mold and mildew."

"Clean?" Keith wrinkled his nose as he walked in. "It stinks. Are you sure you wouldn't be more comfortable at the house?"

Maisey followed her brother. "Positive."

Rafe brought up the rear, then stood off to one side while they wandered around. It wasn't until Keith went down the hall to the bedroom, and she was in the kitchen taking stock of the appliances she'd need and whether the stove and microwave still worked, that he approached her. And then, thank God, he lowered his voice.

"You've grown up." His smile reached his eyes, which suggested romantic interest and took her off guard. She hadn't had a man smile at her in quite that way for some time. Or maybe she'd just been too caught up in the pain caused by her divorce to notice.

"And I've learned a few things along the way." She stepped into the opening to make sure Keith wasn't coming back yet. Then she took a deep breath. "Look, I'm sorry for how I behaved when we met. I was . . . unbelievably forward."

"I'm not holding that against you," he said. "We've all done things we wish we hadn't."

She let her breath out slowly. "Thank you for understanding."

"Of course." His expression turned to one of chagrin as he rubbed his neck. "I was a little out

35

of control myself back then. Being a punk and rebelling against the world."

"You seem to have recovered nicely."

His smile slanted to one side. "I like to think I've matured."

"That makes two of us who've matured. We're different people these days. So . . . if you're willing, I say we forget the past. Agreed?"

"The *way* we met might be hard to forget," he teased. "But I understand you have a reputation to uphold. I won't breathe a word of it. I'd never do that to you, anyway."

She smoothed her tunic. "I'm grateful."

"No problem. Maybe we can just . . . start over."

What did *that* mean? Start over how? "Excuse me?" she said.

He slid his hands in his pockets and leaned against the counter. "You're not with someone, are you? I don't see a ring . . ."

Once again, she felt the absence of the gold band that had resided on her wedding finger for so many years. "No, not anymore."

"Then will you let me take you to dinner sometime?"

The way his shoulders lifted slightly seemed endearingly boyish, as if he really didn't want her to say no. But she hadn't expected this and wasn't prepared for it. "That would be impossible," she said. "I appreciate the offer, though."

When she rejected him so quickly and

unequivocally, he looked a little deflated. "Are you *that* sure you won't like me?"

She scowled. She'd been "off the market" for so long. Even after Jack had moved out, she'd been sequestered in her own home, working—or trying to work—for over a year. That left her feeling socially clumsy. She almost gave in just to avoid sounding like a bitch, but she wasn't ready to start dating, especially someone like Rafe. "I'm not going to be your next conquest," she said.

He raised a hand. "Whoa! I said *dinner*."

After checking the hall again, she decided her brother must be in the bathroom. "I heard you, but let's be honest. No man wants to make an investment without some kind of return."

When he realized she was serious, his playfulness evaporated. "I wasn't asking for a commitment to sleep with me, for God's sake. Dinner's . . . dinner. How else am I supposed to get to know you?"

He'd lost that rangy, lone wolf aura that had made him seem so unpredictable and dangerous when he was a younger man. It'd been replaced with a strong sense of purpose but, in some ways, that made him *more* of a threat. There weren't many men who had the confidence to go after a woman so directly, and that scared the hell out of her. "Trust me, we wouldn't be well-suited. I'm doing you a favor."

"I can look out for myself."

"There's no need to waste any time or money. Like I said, I'd be a bad investment."

He hesitated for a second. Then he said, "Are you afraid I can't afford it? I don't come from money so I'm not good enough for you?"

"Stop it! No. Of course not."

"Because we never really got to know each other," he said. "And, for the record, I'm embarrassed about that night, too. If I'm remembering correctly, it wasn't my best performance."

Sex with Rafe had lasted all of about thirty seconds. There'd been a brief flash of pain as he'd pushed inside her, some frantic movement while she'd stared at the water stain on the ceiling and a moan as he'd climaxed. Then he'd rolled off her and passed out. She'd had no idea why the other girls talked as if he was so good in bed. She hadn't been impressed. But she could hardly blame *him* for the disappointment she'd experienced. She'd offered herself up to be used; it wasn't as though *he'd* come on to *her*.

"It has nothing to do with your . . . performance. I deserved what I got."

He winced.

"It wouldn't have been so bad if I'd had any clue about sex," she clarified, "but you know how the movies romanticize everything. My expectations were too high, that's all."

"Wait a second." He stepped closer, close enough that she could smell his cologne. "Are

38

you serious?" he whispered. *"That was your first time?"*

"We're talking about the distant past," she said. "None of it matters anymore."

He raked his fingers through his hair. "I honestly don't remember you telling me you were a virgin."

Why were they even discussing this? "Because I *didn't*," she said, her voice as hushed as his. "I was too busy trying to act experienced—like I was eighteen. Anyway, you were so drunk I'm surprised you remembered me at all. I was actually hoping you wouldn't."

"Well, shit," he said. "Now I wish you didn't remember me, either. I don't want to be the guy who ruined your first time. No wonder you won't go out with me."

"*I* ruined my first time. I was hoping for too much."

"Somehow that only makes it worse," he said dryly.

The toilet flushed, and she sent him a warning look. "Keith's coming back."

"Am I doing something wrong?"

She shook her head. "I don't want him badgering me about getting out and dating again. I'm not interested in . . . in a relationship," she said, and went back to inspecting the kitchen.

After that, Rafe seemed pensive, but he waited patiently for her to finish roaming through the house.

"This isn't *too* bad," she told Keith when she returned to the living room where he'd been chatting with Rafe. "I'm sure I'll be fine." There'd be *real* peace here and not the memories she'd experience in her mother's home. She needed a "cave" to crawl into, a neutral place to call her own. Even better if that place had the positive associations of Smuggler's Cove.

"Maisey, come on," Keith said. "You can't be serious."

"I'm absolutely serious. I could throw a few rugs on the floor, use the bar near the kitchen window to eat and put a mattress and a chest of drawers in the bedroom. I won't need much to get by."

Keith rolled his eyes. "Just come home and get it over with. You won't last two weeks here. Why would you want to be by yourself, anyway, after everything you've been through? You were by yourself in New York. If that's what you wanted, you could've stayed there."

She preferred not to include Rafe in anything too personal, but Keith didn't seem to have the same reservations. "This is different from the city. I can hear the sea, which reminds me of all the times I played here as a child. And, despite the hurricane damage, Smuggler's Cove seems . . . safe in a way no other place does." She turned to Rafe. "Mr. Romero, would *you* mind if I moved in? I could fix it up to the best of my

40

ability until you're ready to start on it. And then I could relocate to a different unit."

"I'm sure we can work something out," he said, but his words were clipped and he was no longer smiling.

"See?" She looked at Keith. "Mr. . . ."

"At least call me Rafe," he broke in.

"Okay." Thanks to the humidity, she was beginning to perspire. She pulled her hair up to get it off her neck. "Rafe here says he can work around me. So . . . Mom won't be able to launch *that* argument."

"She can launch any argument," Keith grumbled. "Watch her."

When her brother walked out onto the porch and leaned on the railing, Maisey glanced at Rafe. "I really won't be any trouble," she murmured.

"I'm sure you won't," he said, but she couldn't tell if he was being facetious.

"As soon as you tell me you need to be in here, I'll get out."

"Right. If we're careful, we can avoid each other indefinitely."

She wanted to tell him that wouldn't be necessary. She saw no reason they couldn't continue to be civil if they happened to bump into each other. But she was afraid to start another conversation along those lines with Keith in such close proximity. "I'll grab my bags from the car. I might as well leave them here while we go over to the house."

Keith watched from his spot on the porch as she wrestled her heaviest suitcase out of the trunk and dragged it over to the porch steps. He wasn't happy she was staying, so he didn't offer to help. Instead, Rafe came down and insisted on carrying her luggage into the cottage. She kept trying to tell him she could manage. It didn't seem polite to let him do her a favor on the heels of her refusal to go out with him. But he acted as if he didn't hear her.

"That's it, then," she said to Keith when her things were stowed in the otherwise empty bedroom. "We might as well head over to see Mom." She couldn't put it off any longer.

"Fun," he muttered, and started for the car.

She stood on the porch, watching her brother's retreating back as Rafe locked up.

"Should I bring over a mattress and a few other necessities, like a fridge, and have them here for when you get back?" he asked.

"No, I'll do that myself." She had no idea how she'd move something as heavy as a fridge. But she hoped that, between Keith and her, they'd manage. She didn't want to be a nuisance to Rafe Romero, didn't want him complaining to her mother. Having to take that into consideration at all bothered her. It was part of the reason she resented the fact that he was living here. She didn't feel she should have to answer to any-one—not at Smuggler's Cove.

"It could be dark when you get back to this side of the island," he said.

She checked her phone—nearly two. "The sun won't set for another five hours." She certainly hoped she wouldn't have to stay at Coldiron House *that* long.

"I was under the impression you've been gone from Fairham for quite a long time."

"I'm afraid it hasn't been long enough."

His expression was inscrutable as he removed a key from his ring and handed it to her. "This will get you in here. Stop by later, and I'll take you over to Unit 9."

"Why don't you give me that key, too? I can put it under your mat when I'm done, if it's too late to disturb you."

"Sorry, I'll need it this afternoon. I've stored a lot of my construction materials there."

"I see."

"But I'll slip the key under *your* mat when I finish up if you'd rather not come to my place."

"That'll be ideal. Then I won't have to interrupt your evening."

"You wouldn't want to *need* anyone," he said, and went down the stairs before she could respond.

Maisey followed more slowly and joined her brother in the Mercedes.

"What was *that* all about?" Keith had the air on—thank goodness, because the humidity was even more oppressive than usual for this time of year.

"What?" she replied, preoccupied with Rafe's last comment. She *didn't* want to need anyone. Everyone she'd known had let her down. Her mother had never been someone she could lean on, not emotionally. Her brother didn't have the strength to keep *himself* on a productive path, never mind anyone else. Her father had died. And her husband had abandoned her when she needed him most.

"Oh, God, that's Rafe," Keith said, mimicking her words from before.

As Rafe's truck disappeared around the bend, she said, "I've met Mom's contractor before. At a party a long time ago. I didn't recognize his name because we called him Rafe and not Raphael."

"Did he remember you?"

"Once I reminded him, yeah."

"That's it? You met him at a party years ago and you were *that* distressed to see him again?"

"I wasn't *distressed,*" she lied. "I was surprised."

Keith looked at her more closely. "Were you two friends?"

"Not at all. He's four years older. I barely knew him."

"Did he go to Fairham High?"

"He did. If you hadn't been away at boarding school, you would've been a freshman when he was a junior and probably would've known him a lot better than I ever did. He seems nice enough now, though. Is he a good contractor?"

Their tires crunched over the pebbles in the road. "Mom checked him out pretty thoroughly. He comes highly recommended." He turned onto the paved street. "Speaking of Mom, are you nervous about seeing her?"

She shrugged, pretending she wasn't, but her heart began to pound faster and faster with each passing mile.

It seemed like only seconds later that they were winding their way to the highest point on the island.

"Pippa's still there, isn't she?" Maisey asked.

"I doubt Mom'll ever let Pippa go," Keith replied. "She needs her too badly, and they get along quite well. But we have a new grounds-keeper."

"Since when?"

"Since Jorge retired and moved to San Diego three years ago. The new guy's name is Tyrone."

She hadn't kept up. Three years ago, she'd been too busy, if not too happy, to stay in touch. And once she'd lost her family and her ability to write and illustrate, she'd been too miserable.

They stopped outside the decorative iron gates surrounding Coldiron House. Then Keith pushed the button that made those gates grind open, and she saw the mansion where she'd grown up—with its columns and double-story verandas, hanging flowerpots and carpet-like lawn—for the first time in ten years.

Nostalgia warred with anxiety.

So much for her great escape, she thought. She'd just made a perfect circle.

4

Her mother, dressed in a highly tailored burnt-orange skirt and jacket with matching pumps, was expertly made up and coifed. She was even wearing lip-liner with her lipstick. But just because she appeared to be on her way to Love's in Bloom, or somewhere even fancier, didn't mean she'd be leaving the house. Josephine always looked as if she belonged in the pages of a fashion magazine, and she never seemed to age. She did everything she could to prevent it.

As a child, Maisey had been proud of her. When Josephine walked into a room, people noticed, especially men. And the way she carried herself, so regally, helped her win over anyone her beauty might not have captivated.

It wasn't until Maisey grew older that she began to perceive her mother's vanity—and the many hours she spent getting Botox and other treatments—as more desperate and self-indulgent than admirable. But she didn't *want* to see through that carefully prepared veneer. She wished she could still be under Josephine's spell, like almost everyone else.

"Hello, Mother." She nodded respectfully as she stood at the threshold of the drawing room where her mother waited to receive them. She wished she was one of those daughters who could fall into her mother's arms and sob out her pain, but she knew Josephine wouldn't truly welcome her.

"You've arrived." Although her mother put down the small dog she'd been holding in her lap and got to her feet, her smile was cool. "Come in. You must be hungry and tired. I've ordered tea."

Maisey was grateful when her brother preceded her. She needed another moment to compose herself, another moment to prepare that aching, empty spot inside her for a fresh jolt of life as a Lazarow.

Here we go, she thought.

Focusing on the dog, which looked like a Yorkie, she gathered her courage, marched toward her mother and gave her the requisite air kiss on each cheek. She knew she'd be criticized if she didn't perform this family ritual, although it meant nothing.

When she breathed in the scent of her mother's perfume, the memories of her childhood began to assault her. "You look lovely, as always."

"If only I could lose a few pounds," her mother responded with an air of lamentation.

Josephine murmured something similar whenever she received a compliment. Not because she truly believed she needed to lose weight; she considered it gauche not to avoid the appearance of conceit.

Annoyed by the pretense, Maisey nearly grimaced. She felt as if she was playing the magic mirror in *Snow White*.

Magic mirror, in my hand, who's the fairest in the land?

My queen, you are the fairest in the land.

"What a beautiful outfit," her mother said.

Maisey was tempted to indulge in the same game her mother did by saying, "What, this old thing?" But knowing Josephine would easily figure out that she was the brunt of that joke, Maisey overrode the impulse. "I'm glad you like it."

"Keith's been so excited about your arrival. How was the trip?"

They hadn't seen each other for ten *years,* and yet it was *Keith* who was excited? Keith had visited her several times in New York. He'd last seen her at Ellie's funeral. Fortunately, he'd also come earlier, when she was born, or no one in Maisey's family would ever have met her baby.

But Josephine could never admit to needing or missing anyone who'd dared to question or criticize her. Or maybe she really hadn't missed Maisey . . . "Not too bad. Still, I'm glad it's over."

Josephine scooped up her little dog. "This is Athena."

"She's darling."

Cuddling her dog, Josephine stepped to one side and peered into the entry. "Where's your luggage?"

Maisey hadn't wanted to break the news that she'd be staying elsewhere so soon. But now that the question had been posed, she had no choice except to answer it. "I, um, stowed it over at Smuggler's Cove."

Her mother's eyes flashed with an emotion she quickly suppressed, and she put her dog down again. "Why would you leave it there?"

"I've decided to move into one of the bungalows. I like the idea of being so close to the beach." She mustered a smile as if she couldn't feel the torrent of her mother's displeasure. "It reminds me of Dad."

The mention of her father didn't distract Josephine for a second. "But the bungalows aren't ready for occupancy."

"Unit 6 isn't so bad," Keith said, obviously trying to smooth the way.

"And I can manage until your contractor gets around to the rehab," Maisey added.

There was a protracted silence. As a child, Maisey would've caved in and said something to relieve the tension, something like, "But I'll stay here, if you'd rather." She'd always been a pleaser. Even as an adult, it required determination not to succumb to her mother's powerful will.

"You'd rather move into a damaged shack than return to Coldiron House?" her mother asked.

"I'd hardly call the bungalows *shacks,* Mother," she said, choosing to skirt the real issue. "They're structurally sound and will be quite cozy once they're restored. In all honesty, I'd like to assist with the restoration if I can. I enjoy do-it-yourself projects."

"Since *when?*" Josephine demanded.

"Since I married Jack," she replied coolly.

There was a slight pause. "Yes, Jack brought out a lot of things in you I didn't know existed."

Maisey almost reacted to her sarcasm by saying, "You mean like a backbone?" But her mother was still talking. And, determined to maintain the peace, Maisey stifled that rejoinder.

"You're no contractor," Josephine was saying. "And I'm already paying Raphael Romero. Why would *you* get involved?"

"Because I think I'd find it . . . therapeutic."

Her mother waved her words away. "Therapeutic how?"

Was she serious? "It'll give me something to concentrate on to get my mind off . . . the recent changes in my life."

"Surely you have better things to do," her mother said. "Why impinge on your writing time?"

Now wasn't the ideal moment—if there could ever be an ideal moment—to tell Josephine that she hadn't been able to produce more than a few words, which she'd edited right off the page. She hadn't been able to draw, either. Not for months. "I'm sure I can fit everything in." These days she had nothing *but* time.

"At least you get paid for writing. You'll get nothing in exchange for working on the bungalows."

"I'm not expecting anything."

Josephine's chin went up as she sank back into her seat. "Except free rent."

She just *had* to make Maisey acknowledge the financial help she'd be receiving. Her mother had inherited a fortune from her father, who'd inherited it from *his* father. Yet she acted as though she'd earned every penny. "I'm willing to pay rent," Maisey said. "How much would you like to charge me?"

Josephine grimaced. "Stop."

"You're the one who mentioned it."

"It doesn't make any sense to go there when you could stay here for free. That's all."

"How could my moving into the damaged bungalows cost you any more than having me move here? They're empty, aren't they?" Maisey regarded her mother expectantly. Putting

Josephine in a position where she'd have to *state* her objection in order to get her way was the only effective tool Maisey possessed.

"If that's what you want, it's of no consequence to me," she said, right on cue.

After a quick glance at Keith, who was standing by the hearth, Maisey sat down and pretended to take Josephine's words at face value. But she was more convinced than ever that staying at Smuggler's Cove, even with Rafe Romero living next door, might just save her sanity.

There was a slight clatter in the doorway, and a girl in her late teens carried in a tray of small sandwiches, deviled eggs, cookies and tea.

"Thank you, Clarissa." Josephine slid forward to pour.

Maisey waited until Clarissa had left to question the girl's identity. "I see you have someone new on staff."

"Clarissa is Pippa's niece. She's helping out until Pippa's well enough to resume her duties."

Maisey shot Keith another look. If Pippa was sick, why hadn't he told her in the car? Pippa, her mother's most recent housekeeper, had started the year Maisey left, so they didn't know each other well. They had, however, communicated now and then over the past decade—usually when Pippa sent out invitations to Josephine's annual Christmas party and Maisey replied with a note expressing her "regret" at being unable to attend.

Pippa would invariably follow up with a Christmas card and an interesting summary of all that'd happened on Fairham that year. Although Pippa never revealed anything Josephine wouldn't want her to, Maisey had always considered that update a kind gesture. Pippa had even sent a gift when Ellie was born. "She's ill?"

"Not seriously," Josephine replied. "She has a bronchial infection, so, for the past week, Clarissa's been filling in." She put down the teapot. "I might keep the girl on. There are times Pippa could use the extra help."

"I'm sure Clarissa would be grateful for the work." Because there was so much that stood between them, and Maisey had lost faith that they'd ever be able to breach the gap, she felt it was better to discuss the daily running of the estate than anything personal.

"She should be. She has no other prospects," Josephine said.

Maisey twisted around to make sure Clarissa wasn't in the hall, but her mother didn't seem to care whether she heard or not. In the rare moments when Josephine chose to be honest, she could be brutally so.

"Tea?" Her mother gestured at the tray.

As Maisey picked up her cup and saucer, Keith walked over and popped two cucumber sandwiches into his mouth, one right after the other.

"At least put your food on a plate!" Josephine snapped at him, her voice harsh enough to send Athena skittering backward. "Or did you do that just to upset me?"

"I did it because I'm hungry," he replied, sounding equally irritated. "And who else is here to see me? I'm supposed to impress you and Maisey? *She* doesn't care."

Maisey opened her mouth to agree. She didn't want something as minor as eating cucumber sandwiches the wrong way to make this tea more uncomfortable than it already was. It didn't take much to set off either her mother or her brother. But Josephine didn't give her the opportunity to react.

"*I* care!" she cried. "Have some respect." Josephine turned back to Maisey, but now there were pink stains on her cheeks. "Since you're here, I take it you and Jack haven't reconciled," she said.

Those words proved that Josephine was no longer on her best behavior. Had she thought about it for even a second, she would've known that Maisey didn't want to talk about Jack. But whether or not the recipient would be pleased by the topic she chose had never stopped Josephine before.

"No."

"You don't think you will?"

Maisey clenched her jaw but forced it to relax

so she could answer politely. "He's with some-one else."

"Already?"

Josephine knew this. She *had* to know it. Maisey had kept in touch with Keith and, more loosely, Pippa, even if she hadn't maintained direct contact with her mother. No doubt they'd shared the basic facts of her life—and more information had probably come from Keith than Pippa. As close as Maisey felt to Keith, as loyal as he tried to be, he'd never been particularly adept at keeping his mouth shut. The fact that Josephine claimed *not* to know about Jack strained the bounds of credulity, but allowed her to act innocent while Maisey writhed.

"Jack was involved with another woman before he moved out," Maisey explained. Was that what she wanted to hear? Did Josephine enjoy making her say it?

"I see." Her mother had warned her that Jack, who'd been working as a lifeguard at the public beach in Keys Crossing when she met him, would be unlikely to support her "in the life-style to which she was accustomed." He came from decent, middle-class folk and had a business degree but no connections to help him get a start in the world of finance, which was his goal. Ironically, once they'd moved to New York, he'd managed to land a good job at Merrill Lynch simply by interviewing and had turned out to be quite talented with money.

Josephine must've been aware of that, too. It was something she would've questioned Keith about whenever he came back from New York. *Where do they live? What kind of rent do they pay? Is their apartment big?* Yet those two words—*I see*—sounded suspiciously like, *So I was right. And you dared question me* . . .

"Then your marriage is really over," Josephine added, driving the knife deeper still.

"Yes." Maisey wanted to point out that Jack had failed in a completely different area than the one Josephine had predicted. But, once again, she bit her tongue. What did it matter? Jack was out of her life.

Josephine's cup clinked as she returned it to her saucer. "What's on the horizon for you now?"

Maisey didn't have any official plans. She just wanted to help support Keith's recovery. *Someone* had to step in. He couldn't continue the downward spiral that had led him to attempt suicide. And why not come here? She hadn't been doing anyone any good in Manhattan—including herself. "Maybe I'll change things up, get a job."

She had to create *some* income unless she wanted to fall into the same vulnerable position as Keith and be dependent on Josephine for everything. It wasn't as if she was getting any alimony. She'd been making as much as Jack when they split. Granted, there were still some royalties coming in, but that wouldn't happen for another few months—and wouldn't amount to all that much.

Josephine paused with her cup halfway to her mouth. "What do you mean? What kind of job? There's nothing on the island that would suit you—nothing but menial labor."

"Menial labor would keep me busy at least." Even washing dishes would demand she maintain a schedule. She needed structure, some reason to keep moving so she could escape the inertia that had struck her down in New York.

"Writing and illustrating will do that, won't they?"

Following Josephine's cucumber-sandwich rebuke, Keith had gone back to his place by the mantel. Maisey could feel the weight of his stare. He was probably wondering if she'd tell their mother what she'd told him in the car, but she couldn't face the backlash the truth would create. "I'll put in a few hours here and there." Or make the attempt, if and when she could bear to try.

"That's the beauty of what you do." Josephine brought her cup to her lips. "You can work from almost anywhere."

Maisey realized she'd been drinking her tea without any sweetener and added a sugar cube with the silver tongs that had been in the family since before her grandfather had emigrated from France and purchased the island. Selling her children's books to a traditional, well-known publisher was one of the few things she'd done right, according to Josephine. Josephine liked the respectability that went with being successfully published, and she liked the accolades Maisey's books had received. That was what Keith had told her, anyway. Her first book was published when she was twenty-seven, married and living in New York.

"That's *one* of the benefits," she agreed. "But, at the moment, I don't have any pressing deadlines. So . . . for the next few weeks, until I can find a job, I'll concentrate on fixing up my little bungalow."

Her mother wrinkled her perfectly formed nose. "As I said, doing anything with the bungalows makes no sense. My contractor can handle it."

"I know. I met Raphael while we were there—" she certainly wasn't about to mention that she'd met him before "—inspecting the damage caused by the hurricane. He seems perfectly capable, but he said he wouldn't mind my help."

"You don't think you should've asked *me* what I thought of the idea first?"

Maisey took a sip of her tea. "I didn't want to bother you with something so . . . trivial."

"Maisey's going to my NA meetings with me," Keith piped up. "That should make the ferry ride a bit more pleasant, wouldn't you say?"

"I'm grateful for anything that'll keep *you* on track," Josephine said. "Good Lord, what you've put me through!" She clicked her tongue. "Maybe she'll spend a few hours at the flower shop with you every week, too, so you can *finally* grasp the art of arranging. She was the best arranger I had when she was in high school. But you only ever do one-tenth of what I need."

When the color drained from Keith's face, Maisey flinched. He could've used some encouragement instead of yet another insult.

"It's been so long since I worked at the flower shop, I'm sure he'd have to teach *me* a thing or two." Maisey could tell her brother was offended by what their mother had said. She could feel his dark mood from where she sat. But at that point, the conversation took a less emotional turn, giving her hope that they'd weathered the worst of this meeting, and that she'd be able to cajole him out of his resentment after it was over.

They talked about Josephine's many cousins, who mostly lived in Charleston these days, and how they were coping with the death of Josephine's half-brother on her mother's side; he had been the patriarch of that part of the family. Then they discussed the renovation of the east wing, following which her mother mentioned that Maisey was too thin (of course!) and needed to have her hair trimmed (which she already knew). As the minutes passed, Maisey grew more convinced that the worst was behind her. Her mother had pointed out every flaw, touched on almost every sensitive subject. What could be left?

But just as Maisey was beginning to feel less anxious, Josephine looked up with a hint of challenge in her eyes.

"And what about little Ellie?" she asked, drawing her eyebrows together and lowering her voice as if she was trying to be gentle with the razor-sharp sword of her mouth.

Apparently there *was* one subject left. But it was *so* sensitive Maisey hadn't expected *anyone* to bring it up—not even her mother.

"What about her?" Maisey held her teacup so tightly she thought it might shatter. "Ellie's dead. I called you when it happened."

"You said it was SIDS . . ."

"It *was* SIDS."

"The doctors are convinced? They've confirmed it?"

"I wouldn't have told you so otherwise."

"But . . . it's hard to believe a perfectly healthy baby can go to sleep at night and . . . and not wake up in the morning with nothing occurring in between."

Maisey hated that she was beginning to tremble. "It happens. It happened to Ellie."

"I'd think there would've been *some* sign, that's all."

Some sign *she'd* missed? As usual, her mother was trying to assign blame, make her feel responsible for every bad thing that had occurred in her life. "I have no idea what you're getting at."

Josephine's lips pursed. "It's strange. That's all," she repeated.

"Why are we even discussing it?" Maisey asked.

Hearing the rancor in her voice, Josephine bristled. "Well, if you want me to be frank, I'm merely letting you know that the way you handled the whole thing—keeping me out of her life—wasn't right. I never even got to meet my grandchild!"

Placing her cup on the tray in a very deliberate movement, Maisey came to her feet. "You're not going to blame *me* for the fact that you never got to meet Ellie, Mother. We contacted you when she was born. You could've come then. Keith did. But you were too busy trying to punish me for marrying Jack without your blessing, for leaving Fairham and daring to live a life that didn't include you."

Her mother set her chin—an expression Maisey knew all too well, and used to fear as a child. "That's. Not. True!"

Maisey would not let her revise history like this. "It *is* true," she insisted. "You barely spoke to us when we called. You didn't ask one question, not how much Ellie weighed or how my labor went or whether she was healthy."

"You informed me you'd just had a child, and then you hung up. You gave me no chance to say anything!"

Rage welled up, dark and forbidding and threatening—and yet somehow welcome as an outlet for all the pain. "Forgive me. I thought dead silence suggested you weren't interested. You could've called back but you didn't. We emailed you a picture and got no response."

"I was supposed to thank you for taunting me with what I was missing? I wasn't going to force my way into your life if I wasn't wanted. I know Jack never liked me."

Conscious of her brother's unrest, Maisey felt a brief desire to rein in her emotions for his sake. But she was too far gone to stop. "For good reason!" she cried. "You didn't want me to marry Jack, and you made your opinion very plain."

Josephine sneered at her. "Now that he's shown his true colors, it's funny you should bring *that* up. You could've avoided a lot of heartache had you listened to me."

Maisey wasn't willing to tolerate any more. "Don't *ever* mention Jack or Ellie to me again," she said, and stalked out.

"Maisey!" Keith hurried after her, but she refused to stop or turn around until she was well clear of the house. And by then she was breathing so hard she had to bend over to keep from passing out.

She heard Keith behind her, but he didn't speak again. He stood there as if he didn't know what to do.

Once she'd overcome her dizziness and straightened, he kicked at the tufts of grass on the lawn. Had they been like most families, he might've gathered her in his arms. That was what she needed. Maybe *he* needed it, too. But neither one of them knew how to reach out for that kind of comfort.

"I'm okay." She took a deep breath. "I'm sorry. I didn't mean to get into it with Mom, didn't mean to put you through that." What good would she do him if she only caused more upset and pain?

"It's not *your fault*," he said. "She had no business saying half the things she did, especially about Ellie."

Maisey wiped the sweat from her upper lip. "She always has to place blame—but never accepts responsibility for her own actions."

"It's that damn pride of hers," he said. "Are you sorry you came back?"

She shook her head. "I knew what to expect." She might've *hoped* for more, but past experience had never allowed that hope to fully blossom. "Will you tell me something?"

"Of course."

"Why haven't *you* said anything about Ellie? I mean, other than telling me I need to get beyond it. You came to her funeral but you never asked about her death. You never asked what it was like for me to find her, either."

He shrugged helplessly. "Because I know how much you loved her. And I know how hard it was to lose her. There's nothing anyone can say to make that better."

"God, I miss her." Squeezing her eyes shut, Maisey wished she could go back in time. She missed Jack, too, but she would never admit it. So maybe she'd inherited more of her mother's "damn" pride than she cared to acknowledge.

Fortunately, Keith didn't try to compensate for his inability to comfort her with the typical clichés—that she'd get over Ellie's death, that time heals all wounds, that the loss of her baby was no one's fault. She'd told herself those things plenty of times, and he was right. They were a waste of breath. The pain she felt didn't respond to logic.

"Will you give me a ride back to Smuggler's Cove?" she asked.

"I'll need to get the truck. You can't stay there without furniture, and we can't fit a fridge in the back of the Mercedes."

Maisey nodded and he went to grab the keys. But he didn't have good news when he returned.

"Tyrone's in town with the truck. He's getting some fertilizer and trees he plans to replace. We'll have to wait until he's back."

"I *can't* wait." It was too hot and humid to

stand outside, and she wasn't going back into the house. "Can you take me now, in the car? And bring the truck over whenever it's available?"

He rubbed his forehead. "I'd like to say yes, but I have no idea when we'll be able to use the truck. Maybe Tyrone has other errands he didn't mention to Clarissa. I can't leave you over there in an empty house."

"Trust me, I *prefer* to be there," she said, and stalked to the car.

"I'm afraid that by encouraging you to come back, I've dragged you into the same quicksand that's pulling me under," he said. "I'm not sure I can take it."

"Everything will be fine," she said, tapping the roof of the car for emphasis.

"That's what you think," he muttered as he got in the other side.

It wasn't until they were backing out of the drive that Maisey saw the curtain in the drawing room move and knew her mother had been looking out at them.

5

Maisey had returned to Smuggler's Cove only an hour and a half after she'd left it, so it wasn't any surprise that the key to Unit 9 wasn't under the mat. Keith drove her around the bungalows, looking for Rafe. Although they didn't have a truck yet, they thought they could move a few smaller items in the car. But Rafe wasn't around. They could see where he'd been cutting up a tree limb that'd crashed through the roof of Unit 4, so he hadn't been gone long. She figured he must've run to town for a new saw blade or something.

Without any way to get into the unit that contained the furniture, there wasn't a lot they could do. So they sat on the porch steps and talked for forty-five minutes. Keith said she should leave the island, get out while she could. But she said she wouldn't abandon him, that she wouldn't be defeated so easily.

Slowly his mood seemed to improve. He might still have been brooding when he went to get the truck, but he was no longer ranting about Josephine.

As relieved as Maisey was that they'd be together more and she'd be able to offer advice and support, she was also relieved to be alone for a while. Not having to put any further energy into smiling or listening or saying the right things allowed her to relax for the first time since she'd set foot on the island. That also gave her ample opportunity to mull over the meeting with her mother, which still made her angry. But she told herself to take her own advice and quit letting Josephine upset her. "You can't give her that much power," she'd told Keith.

Easier said than done, but they both had to try . . .

Maisey had no idea when her brother would be back—if the truck was even available—so she changed into shorts, a T-shirt and sandals and went down to the beach. She'd seen the seaward bungalows briefly when they'd gone looking for Rafe; she knew that Unit 1 sat crooked on its pilings, Units 2 and 3 had lost their porches and Unit 4 had that hole in the roof from the tree limb Rafe was removing. But the damage seemed even worse now that she was examining it up close.

Rafe had plenty of work ahead of him. Would he be able to finish before the next major storm? She wondered about that as she went to the water's edge, took off her sandals and waded in the surf.

The rhythmic slap of the waves proved calming. She imagined her father standing at her elbow, gazing out across the water, and wished he was really with her.

Although Maisey would've liked to stay at the beach all afternoon, she didn't dare linger. Because of her long day of travel, the battery in her cell phone was dead. She'd plugged in her phone before leaving the bungalow, but she didn't have it with her and didn't want to make Keith come searching for her once he returned with the truck. So, after about thirty minutes, she went back.

When she caught glimpses of a black vehicle through the trees, she hurried out of the woods. She had no idea what color truck her mother had purchased to help maintain the estate. But she didn't see any sign of her brother. It was Rafe Romero with his Ford F-250. He was up on her porch, putting the key under the mat as promised.

She wished she could duck back into the shelter of the trees until he was gone, so she wouldn't have to confront him again. But her movement had drawn his attention.

"Back already?" he asked.

She walked toward him, carrying her sandals in one hand. "It was a short visit."

He glanced up and down the road. "Where's Keith?"

"He must still be at Coldiron House, trying to get the truck."

"But he'll be coming?"

"Any minute." She spoke with enough confidence that he nodded, told her the key was under the mat and left.

Maisey was sure Keith wouldn't be much longer. But when another hour passed, and she still hadn't heard from him, she began to worry.

Where could he be?

Her cell was now charged, so she tried to reach him.

The call went straight to voice mail. She texted him afterward but didn't get a response that way, either.

Had he and Josephine had another of their famous screaming matches—about her, or what

Josephine had said about Ellie, or even that comment about Keith's work at the flower shop?

Anything was possible. When it came to Keith and Josephine, it didn't take much to cause a fight, especially on a day like today when one or both were on edge. And if they *had* argued, Keith might've left the island instead of coming to her aid. It didn't matter that she'd moved here to help him, or that she needed *his* help to get settled. If he was upset, he wouldn't think twice about taking off on another bender until he'd exhausted what little money he'd been able to earn or pilfer from the house and flower shop.

Keeping an eye on the road beyond her windows, Maisey paced for several more minutes. Then she went out to sit on the front steps and stare down the drive. "Please come," she whispered, but he didn't. Another hour passed and still . . . nothing.

At that point, she broke down and called the house.

Fortunately, Josephine didn't answer.

"Coldiron House. This is Clarissa speaking."

"Clarissa, it's Maisey. I was there for . . . for tea earlier."

"Of course. I remember."

"Is Keith around?"

This question was met with an uncomfortable pause. Then Clarissa said, "Not at the moment."

Maisey was beginning to feel ill. Surely, if he'd

run off, he wouldn't do what he'd done before, with those sleeping pills . . . "Do you know where he is?"

"No, ma'am."

"He didn't mention where he was going?"

"Not to me."

"Did he take the truck?" He might be on foot. The ferry wasn't more than three miles from the house—a walkable distance. Or if he'd *really* wanted to piss Josephine off, he could've taken the Mercedes and left it at the wharf for her to collect later.

"I'm afraid I don't know that, either, Miss Lazarow."

"You can call me Maisey. Would you mind checking?"

"On the truck?"

"Yes. I need to use it."

"Um, okay." She seemed surprised by the request but reluctant to say no. "If you'll hang on a moment . . ."

Maisey was massaging her temples, cursing herself for being so misguided as to think she could help someone as volatile as her brother, when Clarissa came back on the line.

"Tyrone said your brother *did* take the truck."

Was there any chance he could be on his way over?

If so, he'd answer his phone, wouldn't he?

Unless he'd lost it or forgotten it somewhere . . .

"Do you know when he left?" she asked.

This time there was no hesitation before Clarissa answered. "It's been nearly two hours."

Then he wasn't coming to Smuggler's Cove. He could've driven around the entire island at least twice in two hours. She wanted to find out whether he'd left in a rage, but she doubted Clarissa would know—or confirm it if she did. Josephine trained her staff well. They would protect the family's privacy, or they'd be sued for breach of contract and no longer have a job. Clarissa knew the time of Keith's departure, which suggested he'd given her reason to notice it. That was about the only indication Maisey felt she was going to get.

Poor Clarissa. If there'd been a scene like one of the many Maisey had witnessed in her lifetime, the girl had probably felt like cowering in a corner.

"Do you have any idea when he might return?" By this point, Maisey thought the question was futile, but had to ask.

"We aren't expecting him anytime soon," she replied.

"Is he safe?" she asked in a small voice.

"Excuse me, miss?"

"Never mind. Thank you." After she disconnected, she slid her phone halfway across the porch; she could no longer bear to look at it, after that news. "What the hell am I going to do now?"

she asked aloud. The possibility that Keith might try to harm himself terrified her. But she couldn't help him if she didn't know where he was. At the moment, she wasn't in a good situation herself. She didn't have so much as a blanket or a pillow.

And it was growing dark.

The beach was cold and damp, but there was nowhere soft enough to lie down in the bungalow, and nothing to cover up with. Hugging herself, Maisey tried to go back to sleep. She wasn't ready to wake up, was exhausted in a bone-deep way. With dawn breaking, she hoped it would get warm quickly and she'd be able to nap for a couple of hours before she had to face the day.

"Maisey? Is that you?"

Startled to realize she had company, she came more fully awake and squinted at the man standing over her. He looked like a giant amorphous shape surrounded by a halo of bright sunlight. At first she had no idea who he was. But after she blinked the sleep from her eyes, she saw that it was only Rafe, wearing jogging clothes and a pack-like contraption strapped to his back that made him appear larger than he was.

Maisey's face grew instantly hot. She was wearing several layers of clothes—almost everything in her suitcase. She must look like some kind of homeless person. Which, in fact, she was . . .

Scrambling to her feet despite the restriction caused by all those layers, she started brushing away the sand clinging to her cheek, hair and clothes. "Sorry. I—I didn't mean to alarm you. I didn't expect anyone to be on the beach this early."

"I'm just glad you're *breathing*," he said. "I had a terrible feeling I'd discovered your . . . never mind."

The glare of the sun made it hard to interpret Rafe's expression. She couldn't see his face clearly, but his tone conveyed surprise.

Once she shaded her eyes, she was surprised herself. The contraption on his back was a child carrier, and there was a child in it—a girl, who had to be five or six, with blond pigtails and sunglasses.

Why was he carrying such a large child? And *on a run?* Most people found it challenging to exercise without the extra weight. But . . . he looked stronger than a lot of men. Maybe that was how he'd gotten to be so muscular. Maybe he liked to push himself.

"Why are you down here?" he asked. He didn't add, "Looking like *that,*" but she heard it in his voice. "Did you lose your key? If you couldn't get in, you should've come to my place. I would've helped you."

She cleared her throat. "No, I've got the key."

He gestured at the indentation her body had

made in the sand. "Then what's this about?"

Maisey was relieved when the child spoke, because it saved her from having to come up with an answer. She wasn't sure what to say. Her mother was *so* private, and Rafe worked for her mother . . .

"Who is it, Daddy?"

Daddy? Yesterday, when she first saw Rafe, Maisey hadn't even considered the possibility that he might have children. Had he ever been married?

"It's our new neighbor, sweetheart," Rafe replied.

"Our *neighbor?*" the child echoed. "We have a *neighbor?*"

"We do now. Her name is Maisey Lazarow."

Wrinkling her nose, the girl rolled her head back; she seemed to be looking at the sky instead of at Maisey. "She doesn't *sound* like Mrs. Lazarow."

"Because she's not," he said. "This is her daughter."

"Silly!" she said with a laugh. "She doesn't have a daughter."

He adjusted the pack. "Maisey moved away a while ago. And now she's back."

Curiosity lit her face as she sobered. "How old is she?"

The way they were talking—as if Maisey wasn't right in front of them—seemed odd. If those sunglasses made it difficult for the child to see, why didn't she remove them?

"Thirty-four," Maisey volunteered, but that was an unexpected question. Generally, to a child of that age, an adult was an adult. But this girl acted as though she had *no* frame of reference. "How old are *you?*" Maisey asked.

"Five and three-quarters."

Almost six. Maisey had guessed correctly; this wasn't a toddler. "Nice to meet you. What's your name?"

"Laney," she announced, and wrapped her arms around her father's neck in an impulsive and exuberant hug.

Maisey shifted her eyes to Rafe.

"I would've told you," he said. "You didn't let me get that far."

"I see. Well, you certainly don't owe *me* any explanations. Congratulations on having such a beautiful daughter." That wasn't an empty compliment. Although the girl acted a little . . . different from other kids her age, she was exceptionally pretty. Maisey could see a lot of her father in her. Her hair was lighter than Rafe's, but she had his smile and bone structure.

It wasn't until Maisey noticed the collapsible cane dangling from the child carrier that she realized the sunglasses weren't the reason Laney couldn't see. The girl was blind, which explained why Rafe was carrying her, even on a run. He probably couldn't leave her alone when he worked out.

"Are you exercising, too?" Laney asked.

Out of habit, Maisey shook her head. Then, feeling silly since the child wouldn't be able to tell she'd responded, she followed up with, "No. I—I was sleeping."

"On the beach?" She giggled. "Daddy, *I* want to sleep on the beach!"

Rafe's gaze swept over Maisey. "I'm pretty sure it's too cold this time of year."

"It wouldn't be if you had some blankets," Maisey said.

Laney swung her legs to show her enthusiasm for the idea. "We have blankets. We could take them from our beds!"

Feeling awkward and self-conscious, Maisey rubbed her arms, even though the adrenaline that had shot through her at being startled awake had done a great deal to ward off the chill. "How long will you be visiting, Laney?"

Laney rolled her head back again. "Visiting who?"

"How long will you be staying with your—"

Rafe broke in. "She lives with me."

"Oh." Maisey combed her fingers through her hair and encountered several tangles that told her she must look as unkempt as she feared. "Then you should have plenty of chances to camp on the beach."

"With our blankets," Laney added.

"You wouldn't want to go without them unless you had to," Maisey said.

"Why did *you* have to?" Rafe asked.

"I ran into a little . . . trouble last night, but I'll get everything worked out today." She started to back away, toward the road that led around to their units. "See you later. Have fun, Laney."

Raphael's daughter waved. "I like your voice. You seem nice. She's a nice lady, isn't she, Daddy? Do you like our new neighbor?"

Maisey spoke before he could respond. "There's no question that *you're* nice," she said, then turned and ran.

6

Maisey tried calling Keith as soon as she got back to the house. He didn't answer, so she left another voice mail and sent another text.

Seriously? You won't answer my calls? Are you okay? I'm not mad. I swear it. I just want to know that you're safe.

She stared at her phone for several seconds. Then she called Coldiron House.

Clarissa answered again.

"Is Keith there?"

This time she didn't need to identify herself.

Clarissa recognized her voice. "No, Miss Lazarow. We haven't seen him since yesterday."

"Really, you can call me Maisey," she said.

"Yes, Miss . . . Maisey."

"There you go. No formality required when dealing with me." She left all that to her mother, who loved her lofty station in life. "Keith hasn't called?"

"Not that I know of. Maybe Mrs. Lazarow has heard from him. Would you like to speak to her?"

Maisey considered that, but decided against it. If Keith and Josephine had argued, Josephine would be the last person to know where he was. And Maisey didn't want to hear their mother blame this latest setback on her. Josephine would undoubtedly claim it happened because she'd walked out on their tea yesterday and "upset" everyone. "No, thanks," she said, and disconnected.

After that, she wandered from empty room to empty room, trying to figure out if she'd be smarter to grab her suitcase and ask Rafe to drive her to the ferry so she could return to New York. Maybe yesterday when Keith had suggested she go back, he'd done it because he knew he wouldn't be capable of maintaining the relationship she expected them to have . . .

In light of his recent actions, that made sense. But it was too late to bail. She'd seen it that way on the ferry, and she saw it that way now. Coming to Fairham had been a last-ditch effort to save herself as well as Keith.

Besides, it wasn't possible—financially or emotionally—to undo everything she'd done to get here. And there were so many memories in Manhattan, memories she'd rather forget. She didn't have work to go back to, anyway, not if she couldn't write *or* illustrate. Even if she was capable of creating more children's books, she could do that here, as her mother had pointed out. There was nothing to bring her back to New York. The life she'd lived there felt as if it had burned to the ground. Only ashes remained.

Closing her eyes, she forced herself to stop her frenzied pacing and thought of her father. His kindness. His smile. His comfort. She liked it on this side of Fairham, where she felt close to him. She should stay here.

But what about her mother and brother? Could she handle living so close to them? They were *both* difficult, for different reasons. Jack used to say her brother was worse than her mother. At least her mother was strong, determined, driven. In Maisey's mind, though, "strong, determined and driven" couldn't make up for being narcissistic and insufferable.

That was what she normally thought, anyway. Right now "weak" and "unable to cope" frustrated and disappointed her just as much.

Opening her eyes, she kicked her suitcase. She

must've been remembering Keith in a far more favorable light when she'd raced back to Fairham.

But that didn't mean she could bear to see him hurt . . .

With a sigh, she checked her phone again. Still nothing. Which meant she couldn't save her brother if he was in trouble again; she had no way to track him down. With the friends he found online, playing interactive video games and gambling, he could be anywhere. No one had guessed he'd wind up in New Orleans the last time. She could only pray he wouldn't do anything like what he'd tried there . . .

She could also get herself situated, so she wouldn't end up sleeping on the beach again. Last night, after she'd realized she was stranded, she'd gone over to Unit 9 to see what, exactly, was there and found only large furniture, all of it stacked up and too heavy to move alone. That included the mattresses propped up on their sides, squeezed in behind all the furniture.

But she had more time, energy and sunlight today. She could pick out exactly what she wanted and then see if Rafe would help her move it, even though she'd told him she didn't need his assistance.

She planned to use the internet on her cell phone to look up the number for Smitty's in Keys Crossing. The store sold groceries, fishing paraphernalia and sundries, and the goods they carried were eclectic enough that she'd probably find bedding, towels and washcloths. Maybe she could order what she needed and pay one of Smitty's baggers to deliver it—if they still had baggers and those baggers had vehicles. Not everyone on the island drove cars. Most preferred scooters.

One way or the other, there were solutions. She just had to be determined and creative.

But . . . first things first. After sleeping on the beach, she desperately wanted a shower.

She was standing under the spray, reveling in the simple luxury of hot water, when she heard someone banging on the front door. Hoping it was her brother, she rinsed the soap from her hair and jumped out.

She had to use one of her skirts to dry off. She didn't have any towels, which gave her a new appreciation for terry cloth. Her skin was still damp, making it a challenge to pull on a pair of cutoffs and the tank top she normally reserved for yoga class. But if Keith had come back, she didn't want to miss him.

"Let it be him," she mumbled, and hurried to the door.

It wasn't Keith; it was Rafe. He kept turning up—but then that was to be expected. They were living next door to each other and were currently the only occupants of Smuggler's Cove. There was bound to be some interaction. Besides, she couldn't consider his appearance a *bad* thing. Since she'd have to humble herself and ask for a hand with the furniture, this would give her the perfect opportunity. She just wished he'd come fifteen or twenty minutes later. She'd scrambled out of the shower so fast she hadn't put on a bra *or* combed her hair, which was sopping wet.

Cracking open the door, she stood in the gap. "Hello."

He was freshly showered, too—but further along in the process. Although his hair was still wet, it was combed, he was fully dressed in a pair of faded jeans, a T-shirt and work boots and, once again, he smelled as good as he looked.

"You never returned my key last night," he said.

"Oh, my gosh! I'm sorry!" Because she'd been afraid he'd catch her on his porch and come out, she'd decided to wait until he was more likely to be asleep. She hadn't wanted to talk to him for fear he'd ask how the move went, didn't want him to know that Keith had left her in such an impossible situation. Then she'd become so absorbed in her own misery she'd forgotten. And, as luck would have it, he'd caught her sleeping on the beach, anyway.

"Here, I'll get it." She opened the door wider and started to turn, then hesitated. If she was planning to ask for his help, she had nothing to gain by putting it off. "Actually, if you're on your way there now, would you mind if I tagged along?"

He scowled as he looked past her, into the house. "You don't have any furniture yet?"

"No, not yet."

When she didn't elaborate, he said, "Don't tell me you're planning to get it by yourself . . ." She could hear the skepticism in his voice.

"Maybe, if you have the time, you and I could lift the heavier stuff into your truck?"

A bemused expression appeared on his face. "Didn't I offer to do that yesterday?"

"Yes. And it was very nice of you."

"Even though my offer was rejected, along with my invitation to dinner."

She ignored the dinner part. "Something came up for Keith that . . . unexpectedly took him away."

He scratched his head. "Must've been pretty important, since he left you stranded."

"Oh, it was. He wouldn't have abandoned me unless . . . unless he had to. Anyway, I appreciate you helping me out. I'll try not to hold you up."

"No problem."

"Great." She wished she had time to dry her hair, but she hated to make him wait. He had to be on his way to work, or he wouldn't have needed the key she'd forgotten to return. "I'll just grab my shoes."

He took hold of her wrist and, when she

frowned up at him, lowered his gaze to her chest. "Unless you want me to drive into a tree or something, you might want to change your shirt, too."

She looked down at where her hair had soaked her tank and realized why he'd made that suggestion. "Oh. Of course."

He'd let go almost as soon as he touched her, but he didn't glance away, and he didn't try to hide the fact that he liked what he saw.

A sexy smile curved his lips as Maisey quickly folded her arms to cover herself. Apparently he enjoyed throwing her off balance. "I can't believe you'd point that out and embarrass us both," she said.

He raised his eyes to meet hers. "I'm not sure *embarrassed* would be the right word for me."

She was more flattered than offended, and that took Maisey by surprise. So did the warmth pouring through her. She hadn't been aroused since before Ellie died. Not that she was willing to admit to being aroused. Surely it couldn't happen that fast or that easily with someone she barely knew, not after she'd struggled for months to fulfill her husband's sexual needs without feeling so much as a twinge of desire. "I mean . . . most men would simply pretend they didn't notice."

"Have you ever tested that theory?" he asked dryly. "Because I'm guessing those would be men who've made love to a woman far more recently than I have."

She hadn't managed to shame him, which told her she should drop the subject and go change. But she couldn't resist a comeback. "What's it been—a whole week?"

"You wouldn't believe me if I told you." He reached down and picked up a box of cereal, what was left of a gallon of milk, a bowl and spoon he must've set on her porch before knocking. "Anyway, hate me for having a sex drive if you want, but I brought you breakfast."

She was tempted to refuse the food and figure out some other way to get her furniture. She didn't think it would be wise to continue to associate with Rafe. As nice as he'd been—to carry her luggage, offer to help her move, bring her food—there was something about him she found threatening. And it wasn't hard to guess why. After what had happened before, when they were younger, they were too sexually aware of each other. There was no forgetting the past, regardless of any pact they might have agreed to along those lines—perhaps because that incident had been so unsatisfying. Rafe hadn't been interested enough to make it anything more.

But the last thing she needed was to spoil her fresh start by sleeping with her neighbor, especially if it was only to prove she could finally capture his full attention—or that she *was* attractive and desirable and her husband should never have thrown her over for someone else.

"Really? You have to think about whether you'll accept my food?" He shook the jug to cause the milk to slosh. "That says something, doesn't it? Since you're obviously not in the best of circumstances."

"No, I want it." She *couldn't* refuse. She was too hungry. She hadn't eaten since the oatmeal she'd cooked early yesterday morning before leaving for the airport, and that cup of tea at Coldiron House. She'd been too tense to choke down a sandwich. "I should be more leery of you, though," she added to show that her acceptance was a grudging one.

"Trust me, you're leery enough," he said.

"Merely trying to learn from my past mistakes."

He tucked the cereal box under his arm, as if he might not give it to her, after all. "Did I hear you correctly? You're insulting your only source of help? Is that what happened yesterday with Keith?"

"You're tough. You can take it." She felt a smile tug at her lips as she jerked her head to invite him in. "Any chance you could carry that into the kitchen while I change?"

After putting on a bra and a dry shirt and combing her hair, she found him leaning against the wall. "It'd be nice if there were somewhere to sit in here," he said.

She handed him the key she'd retrieved when she changed. "Yes, it would."

"So . . . why isn't there? What could be more important to your brother than making sure you have a bed to sleep in and the other stuff you need?"

She released an exaggerated sigh. "It's a *long* story."

"Which is the short way of telling me you're not going to explain."

"Wouldn't want to bore you," she said as she opened the Frosted Flakes and poured them into her bowl.

He lowered his voice. "I get that you're a proud person. I'm even beginning to think you might be the kind of proud that drives everyone nuts for no good reason. But . . ."

"*Excuse* me?" A slight quirk to his mouth told her he was teasing, but no one wanted to be thought of as being "the kind of proud" that drove everyone nuts. That made her sound like her mother. "You don't know anything about me!"

"I know you're a Lazarow," he said.

She hesitated before adding milk to her bowl. "What does that mean?"

"Who else would sleep out on the beach rather than go to a neighbor for help? If you weren't so determined to keep up appearances, you could've slept on my couch. Saved yourself a lot of needless misery. We *are* old friends—sort of."

"One sexual encounter—a long time ago—

87

doesn't make us friends," she pointed out. "And you should be thankful I didn't come knocking at your door. You don't want a needy neighbor."

"Is that so?" he said. "Because it looks like I've got one whether I want it or not." He opened several of the cupboards and left them that way. "You have no furniture, no blankets, no food. What's going on? I can see why you might not want to come to me. But what I don't understand is why you didn't stay at the house where you were raised. Where you could eat to your heart's content. You could've slept in a nice, warm, expensive bed, *Princess* Lazarow, instead of huddling alone, out on the beach, where anything could've happened to you."

There was so much of what he'd said that she wanted to address—the comment about her mother and brother and the "princess" reference that suggested she considered herself too good for regular people (like him, no doubt). But all of it was painful and convoluted and something she'd been trained not to discuss with outsiders. She couldn't imagine he'd want to hear the dirty details, anyway. In many respects, she'd been blessed with more than most people. The rest of the islanders certainly viewed her that way. Complaining would only make her look ungrateful and spoiled. So she skipped over everything except the least personal part of what he'd said. "Stop being so dramatic. Except for a few mosquito bites, nothing bad happened while I was on the beach."

"It could have. Fairham doesn't have a lot of crime. But shit happens everywhere. No point in creating the perfect opportunity."

Her spoon clinked against the bowl as she took her first bite. "Where's your daughter?" she asked instead of continuing to argue with him.

"We're not talking about Laney right now," he replied.

"I'm curious."

"Where do you think she is? I work. Someone has to watch her."

She brought another spoonful of Frosted Flakes to her mouth. She would never have chosen a prepared cereal with so much sugar—she wouldn't have chosen a prepared cereal at all— but she had to admit it tasted better than the usual healthier choices. There was something cathartic about drowning her sorrows in what she used to eat with her father on Saturday mornings—while Josephine slept in and wasn't there to voice her disapproval. "You have a sitter at the house or . . ."

"I take her to my mom on weekdays, when my mom's arthritis doesn't make it too hard for her."

"Where's *her* mother? She can't help?"

"No."

He didn't answer her question about Laney's mother, didn't offer anything else. Figuring that might be a sensitive subject and feeling she had no business sticking her nose in his private business, she let it go. "So your mother babysits for you."

"Yes. And I pay her. That way we both benefit."

"She's never remarried?"

"No, after my father died, she might've dated here and there, but not for some years, at least not to my knowledge."

"I don't think I ever learned what happened to your father."

"He was a dietician and personal trainer. He'd just quit his job to open his own gym when he was robbed and stabbed only a few feet from the warehouse space he'd rented for his new business. That's why my mother came here. She wanted to get away from the crime, out of the big city."

"How old were you when he died?"

"Four."

They'd both lost their fathers young. "That's sad."

He lifted his shoulders as if to say it was in the past. "She really should've remarried."

"She still lives on the island, then?"

"Hasn't moved since she brought me and my brother here."

Maisey didn't remember either of the Romero boys from elementary school or Fairham High. They'd both graduated before she entered ninth grade. But she'd heard of them. They'd been popular in high school, especially with the girls. Then there was the trouble they caused—partying, ditching school, getting in minor scrapes with the law. Rafe's reputation was part of the reason she'd been so interested when she finally met him. That he was sinfully good-looking didn't hurt, either. "How long has your mother had arthritis?"

He gave her a look that suggested he was finished answering her questions. "How is this turning into a conversation about me? You're the one who slept out on the beach."

Maisey had no intention of discussing how she'd spent the night. "I'm curious, like I said."

"About *my mother?*"

"More about your daughter. I saw her this morning, and I *still* can't imagine you as a father."

He frowned. "Why would I be any different than other men? Do you think I eat children for dinner?"

It felt odd to smile. Her mouth was so out of practice. And yet, since he'd come this morning, she found herself smiling quite often. "Maybe not *every* night."

"Great," he responded with a grimace. "In your mind, I'm not only a failure in bed, I can't be trusted with a child."

"You told me you've changed, grown up." She slid down the counter to get out of the sunlight streaming through the window. She was also trying to avoid the scent of his cologne. She thought that might be what was wreaking havoc with her mind. She didn't like when a man used too much, but there was just a hint of it on Rafe and, otherwise, he smelled so clean. "I'm willing to take your word for it."

"You wouldn't have to take my word for *all* of it."

She paused with her spoon halfway to her mouth. "And that means . . ."

She saw a devilish expression on his face. "Not if you'll go put that wet T-shirt back on."

She could tell he didn't expect her to take him seriously. He meant to shock her, make her uncomfortable—teach her a lesson for insulting him. But she felt more tingly and breathless than outraged. *That* was the real shock. Forcing her gaze away before he realized she was more susceptible to that suggestion than she cared to admit, she said, "You had your chance eighteen years ago."

"When I was drunk off my ass and wasn't expecting to be propositioned? Especially by an underage virgin who told me she was eighteen?"

"That was a pretty detailed recap," she retorted. "So much for forgetting . . ."

"*You* haven't forgotten," he said. "You're still holding me accountable for that night, assuming I haven't changed or couldn't have changed enough to suit you. I'm trying to tell you it was hardly a fair test of my ability."

"Don't act like I didn't give you another opportunity," she said. "I approached you the following week, remember? And you turned me down."

Hooking his thumbs in the pockets of his jeans, he crossed his ankles. "You were too young."

"*And* you had too many other girls throwing themselves at you."

"Who were older," he said, as if any guy would've made the same choice.

She took another spoonful of cereal. "You didn't want me. Admit it."

He studied her for several seconds. "You expected the world to bow at your feet. That's hardly an aphrodisiac."

"Ah, the Lazarow thing again. You're intimidated by my name."

"I'm not intimidated in the least. Well, maybe a little," he conceded. "You *are* one of the 'untouchables.'"

She chuckled. "Well, for the record, you were right to reject me. I was angry and acting out, had no clue what I was doing."

"You'd never make that mistake now . . ."

"No."

"Because you're the one who isn't interested in me."

Unsure where he was going with this, she stopped eating. "True."

"Bullshit."

She forced down her last swallow. "You don't believe me?"

"I think I can tell when a woman finds me attractive. You look away whenever I catch your eye, which is a pretty reliable sign. You've just changed, lost the moxie you once had, that's all."

She wished she could laugh, scoff at him. This was an outrageous conversation. She wasn't even sure how she'd fallen into it, or how it had progressed so far so fast. She'd seen Rafe for the first time in *years* only yesterday. But he was right: she was as attracted to him as she'd ever been. And she'd felt so little of anything positive in the past two years she didn't know how to handle the sudden influx of hormones.

She did, however, know better than to let on. "Don't tell me you've already been through all the other women on the island."

"A womanizer like *me?*" He scowled facetiously. "I went through them years ago."

"You wouldn't want to quit too soon. You're bound to find a glutton for punishment here and there."

He lifted one eyebrow. *"A glutton for punishment?"*

She should've heeded the warning in his voice. But he'd started this little battle. She felt she should be able to give as good as she got. "Women who don't mind a man who can only last thirty seconds or so."

Assuming she'd landed the coup de grâce, she smiled sweetly. No way could he outdo *that*. But she shouldn't have taunted him, shouldn't have taken it so far. The look that entered his eyes as he stepped forward and boxed her in made her realize she'd thrown out a challenge he was more than willing to meet.

"We've talked about the special circumstances of that night," he murmured, his face just inches from hers.

"That's true. And—" growing a bit nervous, she cleared her throat but would not allow herself to be intimidated into backing down "—and I promise I won't tell anyone how badly it went. Your secret is safe with me."

She stopped laughing when he took her bowl and set it on the counter. "How about you let me make it up to you instead?" he said, and lowered his head to kiss her.

Maisey knew she should push him away. He was being assertive, going after what he wanted. But the way he was pressing his lips to hers so gently, coaxing her to respond with the barest slip of his tongue, gave her plenty of opportunity to refuse.

If only she *wanted* to refuse. Desperate to push the recent past as far away from her conscious mind as possible, if only for a moment, she was suddenly more than eager to let Rafe make her feel something else, something *good*.

Sliding her hands up his arms, she found the soft, curly hair at his nape and closed her eyes as she sank into the kiss.

He seemed surprised when she parted her lips. She realized then that he hadn't taken her capitulation for granted. It had been a risk for him—one he wasn't convinced would work out —and, for the first time, she felt a measure of hesitation. Would he withdraw? Maybe lift his head to ask whether she was really okay with what they were doing?

She hoped not. That would only yank her back into the real world and ruin everything.

To make sure he didn't, she became more aggressive. Instead of just permitting him to kiss her, she clenched her hand in his hair and kissed him back.

"God, I haven't felt anything like this in *so* long," she muttered against his warm, pliant lips.

She wasn't aware that she'd spoken aloud until he caught her face in his large hands and made her look at him. "How long?"

"Years," she admitted.

"That's even longer than me."

She didn't ask how long it had been for him. She didn't want any more conversation, or she'd have to make sense out of what he said and how she replied, what she was doing. She couldn't justify this, which was why she didn't want her conscience to intercede before she could get what she craved. So she moved his hands to her breasts.

He seemed startled, as if he couldn't believe his good fortune. Then he reached around and unsnapped her bra, staring into her eyes the whole time, testing her to see if she'd stop him. When she didn't, when she let him slip his hands up under her shirt and touch her, she heard him suck in his next breath.

"This is going too well. You won't even go out with me," he said as he flicked his thumbs over the tips of her breasts. Obviously, he wanted her to convince him, not change her mind. But she could offer no explanation for her behavior. Where was this sudden recklessness coming from? She'd been so sad for so long, it was almost as if all the needs that had gone unsatisfied during that time were welling up at once.

"Are you going to let that stop you?" she asked, and stood on her toes to reach his lips. When he met her tongue, she groaned and gave everything she had to that kiss, even bit his lip and felt him nip at hers.

"Holy shit," he moaned, closing his eyes as her mouth moved down his neck and her hands traveled up under his shirt.

Feeling strangely gratified that he was already

trembling and breathless, she ran her fingers over his arousal. "Is this for me?"

He turned her face back up to his. "Let's go to my place," he said.

She didn't protest when he scooped her into his arms and carried her there.

7

Maisey knew she was too thin, but Rafe didn't seem to notice or care as he stripped off her clothes. He looked at her as if she was the most beautiful woman in the world and that was all that mattered because it was exactly what she needed.

His bed smelled like he did. Maisey held a pillow next to her face and breathed deeply, thinking how much she liked that scent as he ran his hands over the curve of her hips.

"Wow," he said.

He still had his pants on, but she'd pulled off his T-shirt as soon as he'd deposited her on the bed, which meant she could feel the smooth skin of his chest. Until this moment, she hadn't realized how much she'd missed some of the things she'd taken for granted during her marriage, like the opportunity to curl up beside her husband, warm skin to warm skin.

When Rafe's mouth found her breast, she dragged in a gulp of air and closed her eyes. But as soon as he moved lower, she tried to stop him. She'd always been too self-conscious for that kind of lovemaking. Jack had told her many times that she was hard to reach, hard to connect with, even during sex, because she could never fully let go.

She felt that resistance now, and stopped Rafe as he reached her navel.

She assumed he'd abandon the attempt, move on to something that didn't require so much trust on her part, as Jack had always done. But Rafe seemed more determined. "What's wrong?" he asked.

"That makes me feel too . . . vulnerable. I can't do it."

"Sure you can," he said, but he didn't press her. He watched her intently, reading the expressions on her face while he used his fingers instead.

"That's good," she whispered. *Really* good."

She felt him kiss her thighs, but she was so focused on his fingers that she didn't mind. Then, when she was so lost in the moment she would've let him do almost anything, he pressed her legs apart.

"Relax," he murmured, and when she complied, he settled his mouth on her. The movement of his tongue made her cry out. She couldn't remember ever vocalizing what she was feeling quite like that. But she wasn't herself right now, or she wouldn't be having sex with an acquaintance from her past. She was pretending to be someone who might do something like this, someone who could cast off *all* inhibition without worrying about the consequences. So she dug her fingers into the thick muscles of Rafe's shoulders and arched into him as the pleasure grew into an intense wave that ripped through her.

He must've felt her body jerk, because when he lifted his head, he gave her a grin that said, "Take *that* if you think I'm a bad lover." He'd done what he'd set out to do—vanquished the specter of the last time they'd been together. But he wasn't finished yet.

Caught in the blissful aftermath of that powerful release, Maisey could barely think as he removed his pants—but she forced herself to speak up when he got a condom from the nightstand.

"You don't have to worry about that," she said. "My doctor put me on the pill six months ago to regulate my periods." Her doctor had also said she needed to gain some weight, which she hadn't done.

"That's a relief." Tossing it aside, Rafe kissed her collarbone, her neck, her jawline. "To be honest, those condoms are so old I was almost afraid to rely on them."

She wasn't ready to return to her senses, to Sad Maisey, so she was grateful when he made it clear that he wasn't in any hurry to finish up.

His hands delved into her hair, forcing her to look up at him as if he enjoyed staring down at the love-drunk sight of her. "Those big eyes of yours, so green . . . they take my breath away," he said. "I've never seen a prettier pair."

She didn't get the chance to respond to his compliment. He didn't seem to need any thanks. His own heavy-lidded eyes revealed that he was feeling as swept away as she was. By the time he pushed inside her, she was so sensitive she gasped.

"Oh, boy," he said, and lines of concentration appeared on his forehead, giving her the impression that he wanted to stretch out every sensation for as long as he could.

Rafe was built differently from Jack. Maisey noticed that immediately. She told herself it was tacky of her to compare them, but Jack was the one left wanting, and that somehow seemed deserving, after what he'd done.

"Let's take it slow," Rafe said. Maybe it really had been a long time for him, because he didn't want this to end too soon. But she was feeling the same mounting tension she'd enjoyed a few minutes earlier and craved the same powerful release, which made her urge him on. Gripping his buttocks, she let him know exactly how much she liked having him inside her and, with an exclamation on his part, the rhythm increased.

Every now and then he'd have to pause in order

to regain control. He was trying to hold off so she could get all she wanted. But she had the impression that he was reaching his limit. When her climax hit, his whole body tensed as he struggled to stop his own orgasm.

"You get one more," he said grudgingly enough to let her know he was teasing. But she wasn't convinced he'd be able to fulfill that promise. His breathing was too ragged.

As it turned out, it was only a few seconds later when she heard him groan and felt his body shudder. But she couldn't complain. She felt more satisfied than she'd been since she and Jack were first married and nothing in the world seemed to matter except the two of them.

"You have to admit that was some damn good sex," Rafe said as he dropped, exhausted, beside her.

Reluctant to inflate his ego, she grinned at him. "Except you promised me one more."

He cradled her against his body. "Maybe later."

When Maisey woke up, she was alone. Judging by the sun streaming through the windows, it was midafternoon, suggesting she'd slept for several hours. She was slightly disoriented, which confirmed it had been a while. She blinked sleepily as she looked around, trying to remember why her surroundings were so unfamiliar—and then it all came back to her.

"Oh, jeez," she whispered, and shoved up on her elbows. She'd done exactly what she'd told herself she wouldn't do—and made love with her neighbor.

Was Rafe still around? She couldn't hear anyone in the house . . .

She was about to get up so she could check when she saw a note on the nightstand.

Had to work. Make yourself comfortable and eat whatever you'd like. Be home around six, after I pick up Laney. We'll grab your furniture and get you situated then.
—R

Another day without furniture. They were almost on their way to the unit; instead, she had to reveal how desperate she'd been for a man's touch, so they'd gotten distracted. And now he was at work.

What had she been thinking?

She obviously *hadn't* been thinking. She'd been reacting to the damage the divorce had done to her self-esteem—and, on a more primitive level, she'd been trying to find the same physical satisfaction she'd known when she was married. It was tough to go without the love, pleasure and comfort she'd enjoyed with Jack.

But Smuggler's Cove was her place of last resort! She couldn't make it impossible, or even uncomfortable, to live here. Why create *new* obstacles to make life hard when she was already struggling to overcome old ones?

Going to bed with Rafe was a stupid move. But he'd been telling the truth when he'd said he could do a lot better than he'd done eighteen years ago. She wasn't sure she'd ever experienced *anything* like the hour or so they spent together, starting with that very first kiss. Jack just hadn't approached lovemaking in the same way. He'd been too practical, almost . . . mechanical, at times. But Rafe was all about the moment— *every* moment—and that created such intensity.

Now that he'd satisfied her, however, she was embarrassed to have gone after what she'd wanted so aggressively. She couldn't imagine what he had to be thinking.

Maybe she hadn't changed much since she was sixteen . . .

Or maybe he wasn't thinking anything. Maybe he was just happy that he'd managed to get lucky. For some men, it could be that simple, right? And, over the years, he must've had a lot more sexual experience than she did, at least with different partners. Another one-night stand couldn't mean that much to him.

Feeling slightly better once she'd assured herself of this, she checked the digital alarm clock next to his note. It was three, so she scrambled out of bed. If there was any chance of pretending this had never happened, she couldn't be here when he got home. Besides, she was anxious to check her phone to see if Keith had called, and she'd left it at her place.

The image of Rafe carrying her off, Tarzan-style, entered her mind as she finished dressing. She covered her face in embarrassment, even though there wasn't anyone around to see her. Supporting her weight had seemed natural and easy for him. There'd been something primal in his ability to do that with such ease, and it had made her excitement skyrocket. But Jack would never have attempted it. He wasn't capable of carrying anyone; he put his back out if he lifted a heavy suitcase. So she told herself she didn't care what he'd think of her and Rafe. She had to quit seeing everything that happened in her life through her ex's eyes, quit evaluating her actions and choices as if his opinion still mattered.

Because it shouldn't, even if it did.

Once she was dressed, she decided to leave Rafe a note. It seemed the polite thing to do. She wanted to put some sort of official end to what they'd done, and a hastily written thank-you provided the added benefit of allowing her to escape this uncomfortable situation without having to deal with him directly.

Using the pen she found not far away, she turned over his note and wrote on the other side. "Sorry I made you late for work. I hope you had a great day."

No, that last part sounded odd. He'd probably connect that to what they'd done, so she crossed it out and tried again.

I hope the repairs are coming together for you. Don't worry about the furniture. I'm sure your daughter needs your time more than I do. You work hard enough as it is. I'm going to see if my mother will send her caretaker over with the truck.

She'd had no business asking Rafe to help in the first place. Why should he have to fill in for Keith? She was just being stubborn. Yesterday, even while she shivered on the beach, she'd sworn she'd do *anything* before going to her mother.

But approaching Josephine was suddenly preferable to relying on her new neighbor.

Should she end her note with some reference to the sex? Maybe include a thank-you? Tell him she'd had a nice time?

No. She couldn't do that without sounding dismissive or shallow—or glib. Come to think of it, there wasn't much point in writing what she'd just written, since he had the key to the cottage where the furniture was stored. If she managed to wrangle other help, he'd know about it long before he got home because she'd have to get the key.

"So much for that." Somewhat relieved and yet disappointed at the same time, she wadded up the note and tossed it in the trash can in Rafe's bathroom. While she was there, she was tempted to go through his medicine cabinet to see what he wore that smelled so good. She was ready to blame everything that'd happened today on his cologne. It was certainly easier than blaming herself . . .

Going through his medicine cabinet was intrusive, like searching through his drawers, so she refused to abuse his trust in that way. But she couldn't help glancing around his house as she left. Rafe's bungalow was much neater than she would've expected. The furnishings weren't expensive or particularly tasteful—nothing that would meet with her mother's approval or show up in a decorating magazine—but they weren't tacky, either. For a guy who'd had so little growing up, she thought he'd done quite well for himself. If she had to describe his decorating style, it would be "sensible and comfortable." His bedroom, although slightly more Spartan than the rest of the house, followed this theme. So did his living room, which contained a large flat-screen TV, along with an overstuffed sectional and chaise, a recliner with an accent table nearby and a coffee table in the center.

He hadn't hung much on the walls, though. It wasn't as if improving that space could benefit Laney, since she couldn't see. And Maisey guessed he didn't care enough about art to bother.

Or perhaps he'd get to that with time. She had to remind herself that he hadn't lived in

Smuggler's Cove for very long. Jack would want his space to "show well" should anyone see it. But Jack was a different kind of man—very fastidious and driven.

Maisey was almost at the door when she spotted a pile of children's books on the coffee table and had to stop. She loved books, all books, but especially children's books, even if it was only to look through them to admire other people's work.

Half hoping she'd discover a Molly Brimble story, she sorted through the stack. None of her books was there, but she hadn't seriously expected to find one. If Rafe knew she'd written and illustrated several children's books, he would've mentioned it. He had no reason not to.

Instead of Molly Brimble, she found a lot of Dr. Seuss, *Guess How Much I Love You*—she had to smile at that one—and Shel Silverstein's hugely popular collection of poems, *Where the Sidewalk Ends*. In a second pile was a collection of books on kittens and dogs, and *Chica Chica Boom Boom*, which taught kids the alphabet.

It looked as though he read to Laney quite often. He obviously loved his daughter very much. Maisey was happy for him—happy for them both —but she found it bittersweet that he had his daughter and she didn't have hers. As petty as that flare of jealousy was, her gut twisted as she fingered Laney's books. She knew Rafe and Laney had their challenges, and they'd face more in the future, but Rafe ending up with a child to raise seemed so random and unlikely—not that he'd have a child, necessarily, but that he'd turn out to be such a responsible parent.

How had Laney come to live with him? What'd happened to her mother?

Maisey was curious about those things—curious enough that, after stacking the books in their original piles, she headed back down the hall to Laney's room. When she'd passed it earlier, she hadn't even paused. She'd been too busy telling herself she had no business snooping, that she needed to get out of Rafe's house and forget about anything else.

But knowing she might never have another opportunity, she decided to take a quick peek to see if she'd find a picture of Laney's mother or something else that would reveal some clue as to why Laney was living with her father, whether or not she had any contact with her mother or her mother's family and what had caused her blindness.

Laney had a tall, four-poster bed with lots of frilly pillows and the usual assortment of stuffed animals and toys. Or maybe the assortment *wasn't* so usual. All the toys appealed to the sense of touch, or they made sounds when certain levers or bars were pushed or when various shapes were put into the corresponding holes of a ball. An electric piano stood under the window. The keys were well worn, suggesting that it received considerable attention. But, surprisingly, since the walls in the rest of the house were mostly bare, there were things to see in here—stars on the ceiling, a big mirror over the dresser and a large picture of Laney as an infant being held by her father.

There were no other pictures, no cards propped on the dresser, no letters on the small nightstand next to the Disney princess-themed lamp, no Mommy Hearts Laney T-shirts tossed on the ground—nothing, in other words, to indicate who Laney's mother was or whether she had any involvement in Laney's life.

Maisey moved closer to the photograph of Rafe holding Laney. His hair had been cut differently five years ago, and he looked lighter overall, less muscular. But besides the tenderness on his face, she saw a determined set to his jaw that led her to believe he was thinking some-thing like, "Don't worry. I've got you. I'll be there for you no matter what."

His expression—that smile for the camera—couldn't quite hide the protectiveness he felt, and that made it almost impossible for Maisey to look away. She wished she could have a copy of that photograph. It reminded her of the love she'd felt from her own father, of how powerful a father's love could be.

She thought of the pictures taken of Jack and Ellie. He'd had no reason to assume that Ellie's life would end the way it had, so the look in his eyes was never quite as fierce. But why had that love not been stronger? Once Ellie was gone, Jack had seemed willing to move on, which was partly why Maisey's recovery had been so hard. It was almost as if she'd been left to mourn for both of them. He hadn't even kept any of the pictures of him and Ellie and, much as Maisey was tempted when she got rid of his other stuff, she hadn't been able to make herself throw them out. They were in a box marked Attic, and had been sent, along with Ellie's other pictures, to Coldiron House, where they'd stay until Maisey could bear to reclaim them.

If that day ever came . . .

She chastised herself for being so rude as to poke around. She'd told herself she wouldn't. It felt like an invasion of Rafe's privacy just to *see* this photograph because it laid his heart so bare.

With a final glance, Maisey left Laney's room, locked the house behind her and hurried over to her own bungalow. She was intent on finding her phone.

She could hear it ringing as she came through the door.

Was it Keith? *Finally?* Or Josephine?

Maisey doubted her mother would lower her pride and try to make amends. Still, Maisey ached for that olive branch, for Josephine to show enough love and concern to forget how wronged *she* felt and, just once, let the past go without forcing Maisey to assume all the blame. The little contact they'd had since Maisey left Fairham had been *her* doing. She'd *never* forget how cold and uninterested her mother had acted when she received news of Maisey's pregnancy—and that didn't change when Ellie was born. The morning Ellie died, her mother had been the last person Maisey had wanted to speak to. She'd instinctively worried that Josephine would make her feel as if she deserved what she'd gotten. And yet she'd needed her mother that day. So she'd swallowed her own pride and, out of the depths of her despair, called Coldiron House.

That unforgiving reception had cut the deepest. She couldn't reach out afterward. She didn't have the emotional fortitude it required. But she'd have to now, to ask for a truck so she could move some furniture.

Surely she could approach her mother for something as simple as that. And if it was Josephine on the phone, she'd have her chance.

The call wasn't from anyone she might've expected, though.

Maisey felt her jaw drop as she recognized the number. She'd deleted this person from her contacts list, so there was no name attached. But she recognized those ten digits more quickly than she would've recognized the number attached to her own phone.

It was Jack.

8

Maisey told herself not to answer it. She had nothing to say to her ex, especially after she'd acted so inappropriately with a man who was nearly a stranger to her. Considering how long she'd yearned for Jack to regret tossing her aside, to want her back, it was quite the coincidence that he was calling her *now*. What could he possibly want?

When the call went to voice mail, she waited to see if he'd leave a message. If he had a legitimate reason to get in touch, wouldn't he say so? It could be that some stock or other asset he'd failed to list on their separation agreement had sold and, instead of keeping all the proceeds for himself, he'd decided to do the right thing and pay her half. But considering how hard he'd fought for every dime, including some of the proceeds of her books, it was more likely that he'd heard she'd left Manhattan and wanted to find out what she'd done with his personal belongings. When he moved out, he took only what he could carry that day and had never come back for the rest. Was there something he still wanted?

If so, it was too late to recover anything except the pictures she'd saved in the dark attic of Coldiron House. She'd hawked her wedding ring and donated what he'd left behind to Goodwill. She'd figured the move was the perfect time to get rid of each and every item that reminded her of the man she'd loved so deeply, because they now reminded her of the day she'd gone to Chicago to surprise him on his business trip and encountered him walking off the elevator, holding hands with the woman they'd bumped into on Fifth Avenue.

She saw that she had a voice mail, so she tried to listen. But all she heard was three or four seconds of silence, as if he'd contemplated leaving a message but changed his mind.

"What the heck do you want?" She frowned at her screen. She wasn't calling him back; he could text her if it was important. Maybe she'd reply if he did, since texting didn't require speaking to him directly.

Or she wouldn't. She didn't feel she owed him anything.

Clicking away from her voice mail, she went through her missed calls, hoping to see Keith's name.

It wasn't there.

What was going on with her brother? Her mother hadn't called, either, of course. As usual, Maisey was going to have to be the one to get in touch.

There was one other missed call—from her editor in New York. Beth McKinney checked in on her now and then, hoping to hear that she was back at work. Spotting her editor's name always made Maisey feel a little ill, because she knew she was losing something else that meant a great deal to her. Writing children's books had always been her dream. Other than when Ellie was born, she'd never been happier than when she'd held her first book in her hands. It wasn't easy to get a start in that market; it was even harder to get any kind of foothold. She was foolish for turning her back on everything she'd accomplished since *Molly Brimble Conquers the World* came out seven years ago.

But there was nothing she could do. The more she tried to work, the longer she sat at her desk, feeling inept and overwhelmed and utterly hopeless.

Shoving a hand through her hair, which was wild and tangled, having dried while she was rolling around in Rafe's bed, she was just summoning her nerve for the inevitable call to Coldiron House when Jack tried getting through to her again. Then, contrary to everything she'd told herself to do, she allowed her curiosity to overcome her reluctance and slid the answer button to the right.

"Hello?"

"Maisey?"

His voice nearly made the blood freeze in her veins. How many times had she heard him say her name before? Thousands—under very different circumstances. And yet, after being married for nearly ten years, nurturing each other's careers and having a child together, they were like strangers. That hurt but, somehow, it didn't hurt as much as it used to.

Thank God, she thought when she found she could still breathe. "What can I do for you, Jack?"

"I thought I'd see how you're doing."

"It's been eight months since I heard from you."

"Right." He cleared his throat. "I'm overdue."

She gripped the phone tighter. "Is this a joke?"

"No. Not at all. It's just . . . well, Keith called me last night."

Relief shot through her. Keith was alive—unless he'd done something since then. But Jack was the last person she'd ever dreamed would deliver this news. "He did? Why?"

"You can't guess?" He sounded put out.

"I wouldn't have asked if it was obvious to me."

"It was nearly two in the morning. He was pulling his usual shit."

There was irritation and scorn in that response. Jack had always been disgusted with her ne'er-do-well brother. "What usual shit?" Maisey asked. "I'm confused. Has he been contacting you since the divorce?"

"Of course not. I mean he was ranting and raving and cursing, like he used to when we were married and the slightest thing upset him. He'd call you acting like a maniac. You know how he is."

She knew him a lot better than Jack did, who'd never had enough respect for Keith to invest much emotionally. She'd been dealing with Keith her whole life. At one point, he'd been diagnosed as bipolar, but he wouldn't take his meds. "What I don't understand is why he'd call *you*."

"To cuss me out for what happened between us."

What *happened?* That sounded so passive, as if their marriage had been torn apart by someone else. Jack had cheated! But considering what she'd just done, Maisey felt less indignant than she ever had before. People made mistakes. Who knew what Jack's needs were back then, and whether or not she'd been capable of meeting them. Maybe he'd bumped into Heather Johns at a vulnerable moment, and Heather had managed to make him feel great instead of miserable after the loss of their child. Rafe had made her feel a decade younger and free—for that short time—of all the cares that weighed so heavily on her shoulders, hadn't he?

As easy as it was to villainize her ex, she figured she'd be better off to simply look forward and quit blaming him for her misery. And there was nothing to be gained by taking responsibility for the past herself—since she couldn't identify anything in particular she'd done wrong. Nothing of a serious nature, at any rate. She'd been the best wife she knew how to be; she'd been the best mother she knew how to be. Obviously, none of it had been adequate but, regardless of any regrets, there was no going back. "Was he okay?" she asked.

"Okay enough to tell me what a bastard I am for ruining your life."

She chose to ignore that. "Did he say where he was?"

"I hardly had a chance to ask before he said he'd like to come to New York and blow my head off. I swear, Maisey, there's something really wrong with him. He needs to be locked up."

What would Jack think if he knew about the suicide attempt? She didn't care to find out. "He must've been high when he did that."

"I'm sure he was. But that's no excuse. He can't go around threatening people."

"I'm sorry. He had no business contacting you. If—*when*—I talk to him, I'll ask him to delete your number and never call you again."

He seemed surprised that she was so understanding and apologetic. "I wasn't expecting to hear from him after so long," he said, noticeably less combative.

"He was messed up or he wouldn't have bothered you," she reiterated. It was pretty ironic that Keith had blasted Jack after leaving her with no food or furniture. What about fulfilling his own obligations, for a change? "You don't have anything to worry about. He doesn't know where you live since you moved out."

"You never told him?"

"How could I? I don't have your address."

"You could've gotten it easily enough. It's not like I've kept it a secret."

"Why would I need it?" So she could walk by and ache for what she no longer had? Try to spy on him and his new love interest?

Fortunately, she hadn't stooped that low. But maybe she couldn't take any credit. What dignity was there in being too depressed to even leave the apartment?

"We spent almost ten years of our lives together," he said.

Which he'd thrown away . . .

"You never missed me?" That question, spoken so softly, so fervently, made her stomach tense. What did he want to hear? That he'd nearly destroyed her? That living day to day was still a challenge?

"I can't imagine Keith has the resources to fly to Manhattan," she said. "Even if he somehow got your address, he couldn't come—not unless he's managed to find a new friend who's helping him. As usual, he has almost nothing."

There was a pause, as if he was tempted to pursue the question she'd ignored. But he seemed to think better of it. "I wouldn't underestimate him. Normal rules of society don't apply to him."

"He *might* be dangerous, if he was capable of following through with anything. But he's not. He couldn't even stick around long enough to help me move."

"Stick around where? What do you mean . . . move?"

She eyed a dust bunny in the corner and made a mental note that she'd need a vacuum cleaner, too. The magnitude of the change she was making suddenly felt overwhelming. "I left Manhattan, Jack."

"When?"

"Yesterday. I decided to return to Fairham."

"Why?"

She walked to the window and stared out at the dappled sunshine. "Why not? It's where I'm from."

"Your mother lives there. I never thought you'd go back."

The memory of her father, beckoning her to come see a sand crab, played through her mind. "I'm at Smuggler's Cove, in one of the bungalows, on the other side of the island. That gives me some space."

There was another silence; he seemed taken aback.

"Home is the place that has to take you in, right?" she said with a humorless laugh. "I guess it was inevitable."

"Not really. You love New York. Your friends are here. Your agent and editor are here, too."

Any friends she'd had were *his* friends, business acquaintances, people he'd introduced her to. She hadn't felt comfortable around them after the divorce. Since she'd devoted herself strictly to her husband and her career, she'd been closer to her editor than she'd been to anyone else. But she didn't have another book coming out, so she didn't feel she should continue to waste Beth's time. And she'd let Roger, her agent, go. "Authors live all over. I can fly to New York if I need to."

"Wow," he breathed. "I can't believe you're gone. You're the reason we came to Manhattan."

She pressed her forehead against the glass. "Think of it this way. If I hadn't insisted on going to Manhattan, you might never have gotten hired at Merrill Lynch—and you might never have bumped into Heather again."

When he didn't respond, she drew a deep breath. "Is there anything else? Because I have to go . . ."

"You seem . . . different somehow," he broke in.

She *was* different. Selling their furniture, giving up her apartment and leaving Manhattan had closed the door on the "married" chapter of her life. Maybe he sensed that she'd finally accepted their daughter's death and the subsequent divorce, finally accepted the loss. "I'm sure we've both changed," she said. "I'll let you get back to . . . whatever you were doing."

"Wait . . ."

She hesitated.

"I miss you. Can I come see you sometime?"

She couldn't believe he'd said those words. He *missed* her? After all he'd done to push her away? "I doubt Heather would like that."

"I'm not with Heather anymore, Maisey. We broke up over a month ago. She was just an . . . escape. I've been thinking of giving you a call for . . . a long time. And when I heard from your brother last night, I thought . . . I thought I might as well speak up, say my piece. I let you down in the worst possible way, and . . . I'm sorry about that. I really am. I couldn't face losing Ellie, and I especially couldn't face what it did to you—"

"Jack," she interrupted.

He stopped.

"You don't have to apologize."

"I want to. I owe you that much."

"No. There's no point in rehashing who did what. It's behind us. Feel free to move on without regrets. I hope you find what you're looking for."

"That's it?" he said. "After everything we've been through?"

"Yes, that's it," she echoed. "Could there be anything else?"

"What if I'm looking for what I threw away? What if I realize now how stupid I was to let you go? I'll never find anyone like you, Maisey. I hate myself for what I did."

For a brief moment, she imagined returning to New York. Jack had a place, money. Maybe they could heal together the way she'd always hoped. Maybe she could reclaim her career and they could have another child, and she wouldn't need her mother, her mother's truck or her unreliable brother.

A future with Jack had to beat the one she was looking at here on Fairham. She had *nothing*.

Except the truth. And the truth was . . . that it was too late.

"Maisey? What do you say?" His voice grew plaintive. "Can we at least . . . start talking again? See if there's anything left?"

"I'm sorry, Jack. I'm afraid that's not an option," she said, and disconnected. Her future in South Carolina was formidable, but she couldn't accept the bailout he'd offered her. It was a solution she knew in her gut to be wrong. Whatever she was going to build from here on out, she would have to build without Jack.

"Whew," she murmured as she stared at her phone. She'd dreamed of that call, *prayed* she'd hear from him, for so long. Funny it didn't mean as much now that she'd finally received it.

Sitting cross-legged on the hardwood floor of her empty bungalow, she summoned her courage and called Coldiron House.

• • •

Josephine was carrying her coffee cup back to the kitchen when she heard Pippa on the phone and stopped outside the door to listen. She was pretty sure her housekeeper was talking to Maisey.

"I'm so sorry I wasn't here to welcome you back yesterday . . . Oh, yes, I'm much better, thank you. Your mother told me you're staying at the bungalows? . . . Good for you. I hope you like it there . . . It must've been tough for you to see the damage . . . We've never had a worse one . . . Sure, he'll get them all fixed up . . . That'll give your mother an excuse to do some updating, anyway. She's so good at that . . . Oh, no doubt! It's beautiful."

Living in a damaged bungalow could not be more beautiful, or comfortable, for that matter, than living at Coldiron House. Josephine didn't like the fact that Pippa was encouraging Maisey. There were plenty of rooms here at Coldiron House, and Maisey should be staying in one.

Pippa was too soft—on everyone. Her own children had no discipline. But they loved her. Josephine wasn't sure she could say the same. At times, she wondered why she'd had children at all. If it hadn't been for Malcolm, she wouldn't have. She'd never felt a driving need to procreate, not like most women. As far as she was concerned, kids only got in the way, what with all the unruliness and the mess and the

124

constant demands they made. Then, of course, Malcolm had died and left her to deal with their children, and Keith had been so difficult from birth. Nothing he did could surprise her at this point. But Maisey . . . Maisey had once been a sweet child. She didn't start acting out until she was sixteen. Then even Josephine's "good" child had gone bad.

But she refused to let either of them ruin *her* life.

She heard Pippa say something about Maisey not having any furniture or groceries and turned away. She didn't want to listen to that, didn't want to hear Pippa's shock and outrage. If Maisey didn't have any food, she knew where she could find it. All she had to do was come home and apologize like she should have done yesterday. It might be true that Josephine held Maisey to a higher standard than Keith. But Maisey was capable of bigger and better things.

Josephine had settled at her desk and was looking at various vases and arrangements on the internet—something she often did to explore new ideas for her flower shop—when Pippa knocked softly at the door.

Although Josephine pretended she hadn't heard it, Pippa didn't go away. She knocked again, louder. Then she poked her head into the room. "Sorry to interrupt," she said. "Maisey called a moment ago."

Josephine said nothing, but that didn't discourage Pippa, either.

"She was wondering if Tyrone could bring the truck and help her move a few things. I told her I didn't think you'd mind. I wanted to check with you first, though. Should I send him over?"

Josephine continued to feign total absorption. Pippa should've known Josephine *would* mind. But Pippa saw only the best in everyone.

"Mrs. Lazarow? Can't you hear me?"

"I heard you." She rolled her eyes. "What would you say if I said I didn't care?"

If Pippa was shocked, she didn't show it. "Since you *do* care, I'd say that's no way to improve your relationship with your daughter."

Josephine swiveled to face her. She was ready to challenge that statement, but Pippa didn't retract it. She returned Josephine's pointed stare without flinching.

"After how she's treated me?" Josephine said. "I should welcome her back with open arms?"

"Where will the alternative get you?"

Josephine released a long sigh. Pippa always managed to put things in a certain . . . perspective. "Fine. Send Tyrone over to help her, if you think it's my duty as a mother. Once again, I'll step up—regardless of her ingratitude."

"I'll do that this minute. And . . . ."

"There's more?" Josephine recognized the solicitous tone.

"I thought you might like to invite Maisey over for dinner later, after the move."

"Since yesterday went so well, huh?"

"With Keith who can say where, you only have each other. You wouldn't want to be cut off from the *next* grandchild."

"Surely Maisey won't be having another child for quite some time."

"Resentment can last forever."

Josephine stiffened. "If I didn't know better, I'd think you were blaming *me* for the rift between us."

"I'm not blaming anyone. I'm merely hoping you two can stop hurting each other."

"She's not hurting me." Josephine wouldn't allow that.

Pippa didn't argue. "She needs you."

"So it's up to me to turn the other cheek."

"Maisey has been through a great deal. I doubt she's entirely herself."

Josephine shifted her gaze to the garden beyond her window—a place she loved almost as much as her flower shop.

"Having lost a little girl yourself, I'm sure you can understand," Pippa added sympathetically.

Josephine surged to her feet. She didn't like to be reminded of that child, had no idea how Pippa even knew about Annabelle. *She'd* certainly never mentioned her. Were some of the islanders still whispering about that old scandal? "Don't *ever* bring up that subject again."

The slight flare of Pippa's nostrils suggested she hadn't expected such a harsh rebuke. Normally, they got on quite well. But Josephine had to be firm, had to make sure *everyone* left the past alone.

"Does that mean you'd rather I didn't invite your daughter to supper?" she asked.

Her mind now anchored thirty-two years in the past, Josephine sank into her seat again. "Go ahead and have Tyrone bring Maisey back here, if you want. We'll see if we can get through the evening without her walking out on me."

9

Rafe knew something was up when a blue truck with a Love's in Bloom placard on the door stopped in front of the bungalow where he was working. That was the name of Josephine Lazarow's flower shop in Keys Crossing. Anyone who lived on the island would recognize it. But Josephine wasn't driving—thank God. Maisey's mother often spoke to him with an air of condescension. He told himself it was just her way. She'd been rich and privileged her entire life, had no idea how real people behaved. But it chafed all the same. He preferred to avoid her if he could.

Fortunately, this was Tyrone, the groundskeeper Rafe had met at Coldiron House when he'd gone there to have Mrs. Lazarow sign his construction contract. He'd been back at Coldiron a couple of times since, when he'd negotiated the purchase of his own bungalow, and he'd seen Tyrone then, too.

Wiping the sweat from his forehead, Rafe straightened and squinted against the bright sunlight to see if Maisey might be with him.

Nope. Tyrone seemed to be alone.

"Mr. Romero?"

"You got him." Rafe walked to the edge of the roof so it'd be easier to hear and be heard. "Something I can do for you today, Tyrone?"

"Yes, sir. Miss Maisey sent me to borrow a key to Unit 9. She said I was to tell you we'd bring it right back, so's we don't hold you up none or get in your way."

Rafe had promised Maisey *he'd* help her. He'd been looking forward to it, to taking care of her. But maybe she'd been presented with a more timely opportunity and was anxious to get started. Or maybe Josephine had belatedly realized her daughter was in desperate circumstances and sent over the appropriate help.

"No problem," he called down, and fished the key out of his pocket. "I can give you a hand with anything too awkward or heavy, if you need it."

"Don't trouble yourself. Miss Maisey's convinced we can manage. But I do appreciate the offer—yes, sir."

Miss Maisey was convinced? These days Miss Maisey didn't look strong enough to carry much of anything, which was why he'd insisted on bringing her luggage into the house yesterday. The dark circles under her eyes reminded him of a castaway who'd had to survive for a long period of time without food. And once he'd gotten her clothes off this morning and seen her ribs, that comparison seemed even more apt. She'd appeared fragile to him then, but beautiful. Although she hadn't been all that attractive at sixteen, she'd really come into her own. "You know where to find me if you change your mind." He tossed down the key.

"I do." After catching it, Tyrone held it up, nodded at him, then got back in the truck.

Rafe watched him drive off. He felt he should go over to Unit 9 and help, in spite of having been told it wasn't necessary. He would have, except that he'd started late today, the weather was supposed to turn and he needed to get the hole in the roof repaired before it rained. The bungalows at Smuggler's Cove had sustained enough water damage.

Although he went back to work, his mind remained on Maisey. He could hardly believe she'd let him make love to her earlier. Yesterday, she'd wanted nothing to do with him. Even this morning, she'd acted as if she'd still refuse to go out with him. He'd almost decided she was too much like her mother.

But when he kissed her . . .

He whistled at the memory. A guy didn't stumble into that kind of encounter every day, especially with a woman like Maisey Lazarow. Her cool reserve hid a powder keg of emotion.

Suddenly realizing that he was just standing there, staring off into space, he shook his head. The sooner he finished here, the sooner he'd be able to see her again.

The moment he was certain the roof on Unit 4 wouldn't leak should bad weather set in, he carried his supplies down the ladder, loaded them into the bed of his truck and drove around to check on Tyrone and Maisey.

He found them trying to carry a couch into her bungalow and jumped out to take her end.

"That's okay. I've got it," she said. "You've been working all day. You don't need to do this, too."

Her words were polite, but she wouldn't quite meet his gaze. And when he insisted on taking the couch, she only reluctantly let go.

He stopped her as they were walking out for another load. "You okay?" he murmured, speaking in a low voice so Tyrone wouldn't hear.

Her smile seemed forced. "Of course. Don't

worry about me. Go ahead and pick up Laney. I'm sure she's looking forward to seeing, er, being with her father."

Something felt off, particularly after what had occurred in his bedroom. She was too remote, too anxious to get rid of him. "Should I grab some dinner while I'm in town?" he asked.

"If you want to," she said absently.

"What kind of food do you like?"

She looked startled. "You mean for *me?*"

They'd caught up with Tyrone. "For all of us," Rafe said.

"No, sir." Tyrone shook his head. "My missus'll have somethin' hot and ready for me by the time I get home. She always do. Like clockwork, that woman. And I'm to bring Miss Maisey back to Coldiron House for dinner. Those're the instructions I got before I left."

Rafe nodded. "Got it." As they started down the steps, he put a hand on the small of Maisey's back. He was hoping to get her to turn and smile at him—or do something, anything, to acknowledge the intimacy they'd shared. She could stop by when she got back if she wanted to spend more time with him.

But she moved away as soon as she could and barely glanced up when he said goodbye.

Dinner at Coldiron House was always a formal affair. Although it was just the two of them, they ate in the dining room. So far, Josephine hadn't mentioned what had happened at yesterday's tea. From what Maisey could gather, they were pretending they'd never argued.

Maisey preferred that approach, too. She was beginning to think pretense had its place in the Lazarow household, especially between her and her mother. Acting as if nothing had happened allowed them to go on without apologizing. Pippa had called to invite her to dinner only minutes after Maisey had decided her mother wasn't capable of being magnanimous, which made Maisey feel a little guilty. It wasn't right that she constantly found fault with her own mother. But wrong as she knew it was to feel so bitter, there was no avoiding certain facts. Josephine had always been a harsh disciplinarian, extremely self-centered and absolutely convinced that her opinion was the only one that mattered. She couldn't be questioned without growing indignant. She demanded absolute control of everyone and everything around her. And if anyone ever hurt her, she claimed she didn't care about that person, anyway.

What was a girl supposed to do with a mother like that? Only extremely passive people seemed capable of getting along with Josephine, and Maisey wasn't passive. She *couldn't* be passive, even if she tried. So she told herself to find a way to forgive her mother, to focus on the positive.

But, considering their history, that was a tall order.

"Do you have all the furniture you need?" Josephine asked as she picked at her beet and goat cheese salad.

Maisey had filled her house with more pieces than she'd originally planned. Tyrone had said she wouldn't be comfortable otherwise. He'd also promised to help her move out when the time came. "I have enough to get by," Maisey replied. "I don't want to overdo it, since Rafe hasn't done the repairs yet."

"Rafe?"

Maisey glanced up from her plate. "Mr. Romero."

"I didn't realize he called himself Rafe."

As far as Maisey knew, he'd always been called Rafe. She'd never heard him referred to as Raphael, except by her mother and brother. Perhaps he used his full name for business. Or her mother had read it on his contract.

"Have you had much interaction with him?" Josephine asked.

The image of Rafe, naked above her, flashed through Maisey's mind. Grabbing her wineglass, she drank deeply to cover the blush she felt warming her cheeks. "I had to borrow the key from him to get the furniture," she said when she put her glass down.

"Oh, right. Of course." Josephine lowered her voice. "He's attractive, isn't he?"

Maisey couldn't believe her mother would

want her to admire Rafe. He was a blue-collar worker, no one Josephine would ever approve of. Not for *her* daughter. Not if *Jack* hadn't been good enough. "He seems . . . capable," she said, trying to dodge the question. "I'm guessing he'll do an acceptable job."

"He should." She stirred her salad a bit more. "It's sad someone that handsome doesn't have any real prospects, isn't it?"

Ah, here it was. Acknowledging Rafe's looks was a clever device to make her more credible when she pointed out his drawbacks. Josephine didn't want her getting involved with the wrong guy *again*.

Maisey imagined how shocked Josephine would be if she blurted out that she'd already slept with him.

"Maisey?"

She'd waited too long to answer. "He's got a contractor's license, and a business," she said quickly.

"Which is better than *nothing*," Josephine allowed. "But it'll take constant effort just to cover his monthly expenses. There isn't enough construction on the island for him to do *too* well."

"He seems happy." Surely that had to mean something. "You know he has a daughter, right?"

"I do. He brought her with him once." Apparently finished with her salad, her mother set down her fork. "She's blind, poor thing."

"I figured that out once I saw the cane. What happened?"

"I have no idea."

"I don't get the impression her mother's part of her life. Has he ever been married?"

"I doubt it." Josephine leaned back and folded her hands in her lap. "You know how some people live their lives."

Some people? As if *they* were so much better? As if they hadn't made their own share of mistakes?

That kind of statement drove Maisey crazy, but fortunately Pippa entered the room to collect their plates, creating a distraction. "The salad was delicious," Maisey said with a smile for her mother's housekeeper. "Thank you."

"Tyrone did all the real work when he grew the beets," Pippa responded with a wink.

Maisey waited for Pippa to leave before bringing up the subject she'd been dying to discuss. "Have you heard from Keith?" she asked.

Josephine took a sip of her wine. "Not a word."

"Neither have I. He won't answer my calls, won't respond to my texts. What set him off?"

"What do you think?" She sounded tired and bored, as though it was just more of the same old thing.

"The two of you got into an argument?"

Taking umbrage at that statement, she lifted her chin. "I was merely trying to talk to him."

Maisey had a hard time believing it was that one-sided. More likely, Josephine had berated him for something—maybe she'd mentioned the cucumber-sandwich thing again. Why she cared so much about such small things, Maisey had never been able to understand. Or Josephine had gotten upset that he'd supported Maisey by following her out yesterday and then staying gone for so long.

Still, there was no point in trying to make Josephine acknowledge her part in whatever had taken place. She'd justify it somehow. In her mind, she was never at fault. "And he stormed off?"

"Essentially."

"Do you have any idea where he went?"

"How would I?"

Maisey turned her wineglass around and around. "I was just . . . hoping, I guess."

"He'll call one of us when he hits rock bottom."

If he didn't do something *more* drastic. Her mother didn't address that possibility. Maisey wasn't willing to bring it up, either. Josephine might pretend to be glad whenever Keith was gone, but she missed him. They did so much together when they were getting along.

"Are you going to like being back on the island?" her mother asked. The change in subject indicated that she didn't want to continue talking about Keith.

"I think so. I love Smuggler's Cove."

"You always liked going there when you were little."

That was another sensitive area, since it hinted at Maisey's preference for her father. She suspected her mother had never forgiven her for being such a daddy's girl.

"I heard from Jack today," she said.

When her mother stared at her, Maisey felt a measure of surprise herself. She wasn't sure why she'd shared that. Maybe it kept her from thinking about Keith. Or Rafe. Or she simply needed someone to talk to.

"What did *he* want?" Josephine spat out the pronoun as if she'd eaten something that had left a bad taste in her mouth.

Before Maisey could answer, Pippa came in with their dinner—rack of lamb, mint jelly, scalloped potatoes and asparagus spears. Josephine allowed Pippa to put her plate in front of her but didn't let go of her wineglass.

"He's no longer with the woman he left me for," Maisey said when Pippa had departed.

"You didn't expect *that* to last, did you?"

"I guess I did." She'd assumed he must really love Heather to do what he'd done. That was the only way she'd been able to explain it.

"When did they break up?" Josephine asked.

"Several weeks ago, from the sound of it. But he claims he was having second thoughts for a while."

Her mother cast her a dubious glance. "Don't tell me you'd ever consider taking him back."

Maisey hated the tone of her mother's voice. It called her a fool for even being tempted. But she *was* tempted—in odd moments when she felt weak or lonely or the climb ahead seemed too daunting. She'd been through several moments like that already just since he'd called.

Not that she was willing to admit it. "No. I don't believe it would work out." That was what really stood in her way, wasn't it? Otherwise, the memories of those years right after they were married, when they were so happy, would convince her that they could have the same thing again.

"I wouldn't accept his calls," Josephine said.

For most brokenhearted people facing a call from their beloved ex, that was easier said than done. But with Josephine it was probably true.

Maisey bit off the head of an asparagus spear. "It felt strange to speak to him after so long."

Her mother watched her without eating. "What does he think of you returning to Fairham?"

Where she belonged . . . Her mother didn't add that, but she might as well have. It was there in her voice. She was claiming victory at last.

"Didn't sound as if he liked it."

"Of course not. Now you're beyond his reach."

Not quite. Neither was she beyond the reach

of the despair that had set in after her divorce. That was what frightened Maisey, because it had the potential to drag her back to New York, even though, in her more lucid moments, she knew that wouldn't be wise.

But Maisey doubted her mother would understand how lonely she felt. By Josephine's own admission, she'd never been susceptible to depression or regret. So Maisey let it go. Instead, they talked about Tyrone and how helpful he'd been with moving the furniture, and about Pippa and how glad they were that she was feeling better after her bronchial infection, and the fact that Josephine had expanded the flower shop, where Maisey had spent so much time during her teenage years, arranging flowers, delivering them, taking orders, even stocking the coolers. She said she'd like to see these improvements and then, almost before Maisey knew it, dinner was over. There had been some tense moments when the conversation could have gone sideways, but they'd managed to keep it on track. Her mother even offered to loan Maisey the bedding and towels she needed, and asked Pippa to have them ready. Then she asked what kind of work Maisey was looking for.

"Anything that'll motivate me to get out of bed in the mornings and occupy my mind so I can't dwell on . . . certain things."

"Keith said you haven't been writing, that you

can't write. He said you're more screwed up than he is."

Thank you, Keith. Maisey could envision her brother trying to justify *his* problems by suggesting that she wasn't doing much better. When he blew up, nothing was off-limits—and yet he'd expect all to be forgiven when he returned.

If he returned . . .

"I've been . . . struggling," she admitted.

Josephine pushed out her chair and stood. "Would you be interested in going back to the flower shop to work?"

Leery of this offer, Maisey paused to take the last sip of the coffee Pippa had brought with berries and cream for dessert. For the most part, she'd enjoyed her time at the shop. She'd learned a lot there, and it had given her an outlet for her creativity. But having her mother as her boss? "I wouldn't want to take Keith's place. We have to be careful not to make him feel . . . expendable."

There was a hollow look in her mother's eyes that struck Maisey like it never had before. As prickly as Josephine was, she loved her son. Why else would she continue to take him in? Keep providing for him while trying to convince him to turn his life around? Part of it was her strong sense of obligation, her desire to appear a certain way as mistress of Fairham Island. But vanity and obligation couldn't be all of it . . .

141

"He makes himself expendable," she said flatly. "When have we ever been able to count on him?"

Despite having had the same thought many times—and more often in the past two days—Maisey couldn't agree with that statement. Not without feeling disloyal. It smacked too much of changing sides. But, ironically, it was her mother befriending her now, not Keith.

"Keith and I both have our problems." She would've said, "We *all* have our problems," but her mother didn't believe she had any—or not any that were her fault.

"If it comes to that, he can work there, too," she said. "The way the business is growing, there's room for both of you. And maybe your example will help him, as I said before."

She hadn't said it in those words, but Maisey definitely recalled when Josephine had stated that Keith could use some guidance. "I guess I could try it." She couldn't say no without offending her mother, and it was kind of Josephine to offer. Josephine could always hire someone else; there were plenty of people on Fairham who needed work.

Still, Maisey felt a certain amount of trepidation. She wasn't strong, not these days. Could she get along with her mother well enough to work at the shop again?

Anything that put her in a subservient role

threatened to cause problems. It gave her mother permission to become even more demanding and autocratic.

The question was . . . what else did Maisey have? She received some royalties from her books, but not a great deal and she wouldn't be getting anything for a while. As she'd already said, she needed something to keep herself busy. Besides, she *wanted* to trust her mother.

"You *guess?* Is that a yes or a no?"

"It's a yes, but . . . I'll have to buy a bike first, so that I can get back and forth across the island. Give me a couple of days to see what I can do there."

She was afraid her mother would use that comment to try and persuade her to move back into Coldiron House, which was closer to the flower shop. Maisey couldn't do that, even if it offended Josephine. The one thing she knew for sure was that she preferred to stay in Smuggler's Cove.

Fortunately, her mother didn't press her to change her plans. She said there was a scooter in the garage Maisey could use.

"I bought it for Keith," she explained. "But he doesn't need it now. He didn't drive it much when he was here. He always took my car or the truck, once Tyrone left in the evenings."

Maisey finished her coffee and pushed her cup away. "Thanks. I appreciate you lending it to me. And we'll figure out something else if he does need it."

When her mother had Pippa drive the box of linens and another box of kitchen utensils and dishes over to Smuggler's Cove so that Maisey could follow on the scooter, Maisey felt a surge of gratitude. Maybe Josephine hadn't come through for her at other times, but she'd come through for her tonight.

Maisey put down the kitchen stuff she was carrying as soon as she saw the coffee can sitting on her porch. It was painted a sloppy purple and had some rocks, flowers and even weeds shoved inside. She might've thought anything left on her doorstep had to have come from Rafe, since they lived away from everyone else. Except it had obviously been created by a child. So . . . Laney?

There was a note with it. That *was* from Rafe.

Laney made this for you at her grand-mother's today. I realize it doesn't look like much, but she doesn't know that. She's convinced it's a masterpiece, and I didn't want to disappoint her, so . . . I hope you don't mind.
—R

Mind? He'd clued in to the fact that she'd been a little remote earlier. But she had too much at stake to get seriously involved in the type of relationship they'd started.

Pippa came up the stairs with her box of towels and bedding. "What's that?"

Maisey lifted it carefully so that the flowers wouldn't fall out. "A housewarming gift," she said, and unlocked the bungalow so they could go inside.

"From who?" Pippa asked as she followed Maisey.

"The little girl who lives next door."

"Isn't *that* nice."

It was nice. It was the nicest thing to happen to Maisey in a long time. Maybe that was why it put a lump in her throat. She supposed it had to do with the heartfelt simplicity of what Laney had created, the sweetness of Rafe's daughter and his reluctance to disappoint her, despite the way Maisey had treated him earlier. "Yes."

While she arranged the flowers on the table Tyrone had helped her carry in earlier, Pippa set down her box and began to inspect the property. "This place will be ideal once you get the repairs done."

"I hope so. I love this side of the island."

Pippa smiled, and Maisey realized how gray her hair had gone in the past ten years. She had to be approaching sixty . . .

"I'm sure it holds many fond memories."

"It does," she agreed.

"Will you have everything you need?"

"I think so. I have the basics, at any rate."

"Well, if there's anything else, give me a call. I'll see what I can scrounge up and bring over from Coldiron House—" she winked "—with your mother's permission, of course."

Maisey caught Pippa's arm before she could leave. "Speaking of my mother . . ."

Pippa waited expectantly.

"She was . . . kind tonight."

A shadow passed over Pippa's face. "I know there are times when it might not seem like it, but . . . she loves you—in her own way."

Maisey nodded. She wanted to believe that.

10

Maisey had nothing she could make to give Laney in return. She didn't even have the groceries needed to bake cookies—and yet she wanted to acknowledge Laney's gift in some small way.

She decided she'd have to wait until she could get to a store. But then she remembered the books she'd stuck in her carry-on. She always brought a few when she traveled, in case she ran into a fussy child who might benefit from the distraction. She'd been too focused on her own problems this last trip to notice if there'd been any children on her flight, so she hadn't given any away. One was her first book. The cover featured the illustration she'd done of Molly Brimble, which included two yarn braids, providing a tactile experience for five- to eight-year-olds. Braiding was something Laney could learn to do with her hands, even if she couldn't see.

Suddenly feeling as if Rafe's daughter was the child for whom she'd created this story, Maisey found a pen in the same carry-on and wrote a few words in the front. Then she peered out her window, trying to determine if there were any lights on in Rafe's bungalow.

His place was just far enough away that she couldn't see it through the trees. She'd have to take the chance that he might still be up.

Rubbing her thumb over the book's shiny cover, she walked next door. She missed her work and wished she could get back to it. But she understood why she couldn't. She had nothing to give, was totally depleted.

Sure enough, there was a light on. She didn't want to feel as if she was creeping around in order to avoid Rafe. But she walked more quietly than usual as she went up the steps to his porch and silently propped the book against the lintel.

She was about to leave when she realized she could see him in the living room, sitting in his recliner. Judging by the moving images reflecting off the window, he was watching TV.

Unable to resist, she paused to study him as he drank from a bottle of beer. Then Laney came from somewhere behind him, crawled into her daddy's lap, and Maisey saw him drop a kiss on her forehead.

Feeling oddly nostalgic, she smiled at the sight before hurrying back to her own bungalow.

Rafe wasn't sure what he'd done wrong. He'd thought he'd given Maisey exactly what she wanted. The way she'd snubbed him when he came to help her move confused him. Was it that he'd left after they made love? Did she resent waking up alone in a strange place?

Maybe it was that he didn't tell her he was leaving. But he'd had to work and he hadn't wanted to wake her up. He'd assumed she'd be more comfortable at his place, anyway, where she had a bed and plenty of food.

Laney wriggled in his lap, trying to get comfortable. He knew he should be stricter with her and insist she stay in her room after he put her to bed. More often than not, she fell asleep in his arms while he watched television. But he didn't mind. She was growing up too fast as it was. He feared the day he could no longer protect her like he did now . . .

"Daddy?"

"What?" She'd interrupted an analysis of pre-season football.

"Did the Gators win?"

She heard a lot of the sports talk he listened to before he turned in every night. No doubt the mention of football on TV had reminded her that he'd been watching the Gators last week. But the fact that she'd asked him about it, after all this time, made him chuckle. He'd taught her what the game was, let her hold a ball and tackled her gently to show her what the roar she heard on TV was about—that it showed the approval of the spectators when someone was either tackled or escaped being tackled. It always surprised him how much she retained.

"They did."

She put her arms around his neck and wet his cheek with a sloppy kiss. He sometimes wondered if every child had as much love to give as Laney. "How many touchdowns did they get?"

"Three, and a field goal."

"They kicked the ball?"

"That's right." He smoothed her hair so it wouldn't tickle his chin.

"How many touchdowns did the other team get?"

He doubted this meant anything to her. She just liked being involved, liked his attention. He supposed it was difficult to feel a part of something when she couldn't see what everyone else could see. "Just one."

"Were they sad?"

"I'm sure they were. But someone has to lose. We can't take losses too seriously or there'll always be one side that's sad."

"We want the Gators to win all the time, don't we?"

"We do. But no one wins all the time." He changed the channel. "Don't you think it's a little late for you to be up?"

"*You're* up."

And he wasn't pushing her out of his lap. She knew she wasn't in any real danger of being shooed away. "I'm a lot bigger than you, which means I get certain privileges—like choosing when I go to bed." Lately, his life had become so routine. He had to get to bed at a decent hour so he could take care of Laney and start work as early as he did. Maisey remembered him as a partier, but those days were long gone.

Laney yawned. "I can't go to sleep *yet*."

"Why not?" He yawned himself. "I can tell you're tired."

"I'm waiting to see if our new neighbor likes my present."

"We won't know tonight," he said to buy some time in case Maisey didn't respond at all. With the chilly reception he'd received earlier, he was afraid Laney might be ignored simply because she was *his* child.

"Why not?"

"She told me she'd be getting home late." Maisey hadn't said what her plans were. She hadn't talked to him much at all, not after the sex was over or later, when he stopped by to help her move. But he figured Laney might be able to sleep if he altered her expectations.

"Can we go over and check if it's still there?" she asked a few minutes later.

He picked up the remote on the table next to him to change the channel. "No, we're in for the night, bug."

"Please?" she begged. "I want to know if she got it."

He changed the channel again and was presented with the image of a man being stabbed. Sometimes he was glad his daughter couldn't see what was on TV. "She'll find it when she gets home later. She can't miss it."

He wasn't paying too much attention when Laney slipped off his lap. He'd found an old James Bond movie he liked. But he heard her open the front door, knew she was poking her head out. She listened for cars when she was trying to determine if someone might be coming past.

How she'd discovered what she brought back to him, he had no clue. Maybe she put a foot out and stepped on it, or it had been propped against the door and fallen, but she came hurrying over with a book in her hands.

"Daddy! What's *this?* Did you put it on the porch? Is it one of *my* books?"

Rafe accepted what she was trying to show him—then did a double take. It was a children's book, but it wasn't one of theirs. And Maisey Lazarow's name was on the cover.

He'd had no idea Maisey was a children's author . . .

"It's from our neighbor," he said.

"For *me?*" She clapped her hands at the prospect of a present.

"It's definitely not for me."

"What's it called?"

"*Molly Brimble Conquers the World.* And it's written and illustrated by Maisey Lazarow."

"What does that mean?" Laney asked.

"It means Maisey wrote it herself—and she drew the pictures."

Her face lit up. "She wrote me a book?"

"Looks like she wrote it for all children, but this is your own copy. Would you like me to read it?"

"Yes!" She hopped eagerly back onto his lap. "Wait," she said before he could start. "What's this on the front? I can feel something . . ."

"Those are braids coming from the head of a girl."

"What does the girl look like?"

"Well, she's not pretty like you," he said. "She has big teeth that stick out and lots of freckles. She has a black eye, too. And her hair is bright orange. That's what you're feeling—the hair."

"Oh . . ." She breathed as her fingers slid down the yarn.

He let her explore the barrettes that kept the braids from unraveling. Then he nudged those curious, questing fingers aside. "Shall we see what it says?"

"What does Molly Brimble do to the world?" she asked.

Like most children, Laney had a way of asking questions about things he couldn't possibly know—in this case, not until after they'd read the story. But she didn't seem to think about that. "I'm guessing she conquers it. Isn't that what you're going to do?" he teased.

She didn't seem too sure. "How?"

"Maybe the story will give you some ideas. But first, there's a part Maisey wrote just for you."

Her mouth formed an excited O. "Read it!"

"Dear Laney,
Thank you for the lovely pot and the flowers. It put a smile on my face—especially because you made it. I want all little girls to understand how special they are, so I thought I'd give you a copy of my book. (And if your father doesn't know how to braid, bring this back to me, and I'll teach you myself so you can rebraid Molly Brimble's hair whenever you want.)
Your new neighbor, Maisey"

"She's nice," Laney said with a sigh.

Rafe wasn't feeling quite so generous. He thought Maisey was, for the most part, confusing and standoffish—even if she was beautiful and someone he'd enjoyed in bed.

He couldn't think badly of her *after* he'd read the book, however. It was a sweet story about a tall, gawky girl with uncontrollable hair and a huge heart who sees beauty everywhere except inside herself—and how she comes to accept and even celebrate her own uniqueness.

"Do you like *my* hair, Daddy?" Laney asked, touching her head.

"You have very nice hair," he told her.

"But it's not red, like Molly Brimble's." She sounded disappointed.

"No, it's blond, remember?"

"What does blond mean again?"

"Golden."

"And what does golden mean?"

He wanted to tell her to imagine the prettiest color she could, but how could that help when she had no concept of color? "It means your hair looks the way sunlight feels," he said.

"I like that." Her hands moved back to the braids on the cover of Maisey's book. "Can you teach me to do this?"

" 'Fraid not, bug. Can't say I've ever tried to braid anything." He'd once considered trying

154

with her hair, but he considered ponytails or pigtails difficult enough.

"Can Grandma show me? Because she's my teacher. She taught me all the braille letters."

"She loves to homeschool you, doesn't she? But we don't want to ask her to do this. It'll make her fingers hurt."

She frowned. "Poor Grandma. Does doing braille make her fingers hurt, too?"

"No." He rubbed his nose against hers. "Just touching something, like braille dots on paper, is different."

"Can I ask Maisey to help me, then?"

Since Maisey had extended the invitation, he wasn't sure he could say no. He didn't want to deny Laney something that might be a pleasant experience just because Maisey had kicked *him* to the curb. "I suppose so," he said reluctantly.

She scrambled down as if she expected to march over there immediately. "When?"

"Not tonight. It's time for bed." With another quick peck on her cheek, he got up to carry her to her room.

There was a knock at the door early the next morning. Maisey had stayed up late getting her house organized, so she felt a bit bleary-eyed as she forced her eyelids open. Her first thought was that she had to get some blinds; her next was that Keith might've returned. She hadn't heard from him.

But this knock was far too timid.

"Coming!" she called, and dragged herself out of bed.

After pulling on a pair of cutoffs and the yoga tank that had now dried, she rushed down the hall and past the kitchen to squint through the peephole.

She couldn't see anyone. "Hello?"

"Is it you, Maisey?"

A child's voice . . .

After unlocking the door, she swung it wide to find Rafe's daughter on the porch. *Alone.* The girl had her cane in one hand and her Molly Brimble book in the other. How she'd managed to make her way over and climb the steps to the front door without help, Maisey couldn't even guess. But Rafe wasn't anywhere in sight.

"Laney!"

She put a finger to her lips. "Don't talk too loud," she warned. "I don't want to get in trouble."

"Where's your dad?"

"Making my lunch since Grandma's out of lunch meat."

"Does he know you're here?"

She didn't seem to want to answer.

"Laney?" Maisey prompted.

"Um, he said I had to wait, but it was taking *so*

long. And I just wanted to tell you how much I love my book."

Maisey crouched down so they were on the same level. "I'm happy to hear that."

"I wish *I* had red hair and freckles like Molly Brimble."

"No, you don't," she said with a laugh. "You shouldn't wish to be any different from exactly the way you are, remember? That was the message of the book."

"But Molly's so tall. She can reach things on the tiptop shelf."

"Yes, she came to appreciate what her differences brought to her life. Just like being unable to see probably makes you a much better listener."

She frowned as if she was thinking about that. Then she handed Maisey her cane and her book.

"What . . ." Maisey began but fell silent when Laney's fingers moved unerringly to her face and slid lightly over her forehead, her eyes, her nose, her chin.

"*Laney?* Laney, where are you?"

The panic in Rafe's voice made Laney drop her hands and grope around to reclaim her belongings. "I have to go!"

Afraid she might tumble hurrying down the steps, Maisey took her arm. "Wait a sec. I'd like to walk with you, if that's okay."

"But I don't want my dad to see you! I wasn't supposed to come here."

"You should always obey your father," she said. "But I'll tell him I didn't mind having you visit."

Laney didn't seem too sure that approach would solve the problem, but Maisey didn't give her a chance to protest. "Over here!" she called to Rafe.

He came tearing through the trees as they reached the bottom of the steps, looking immensely relieved once he saw that his daughter was safe. "Laney, you scared the shit out me," he said, obviously upset.

Laney's mouth dropped open. "Daddy, you said a bad word!"

"I don't care!" he nearly shouted. "You didn't do what I told you. What were you thinking?"

She lowered her head.

"I want an answer!"

"I just . . . I just came to see Maisey," she said, her voice small.

"But I told you that you *couldn't* come and see Maisey, remember?"

"It was only for a minute . . ."

Maisey didn't know what to say. She hated to see Laney punished, but Rafe had to teach her that she couldn't go wandering off on her own. The ocean wasn't far, and she could run into any number of dangers. "I didn't mind," she said, trying to keep her promise.

Rafe ignored her. "I guess I'm going to have to take away your new book."

At that, Laney's lip jutted out and began to quiver. "Then I can't learn to braid."

"You'll just have to wait," he said.

"No, Daddy!" She started to cry. "I'm sorry!"

Rafe shoved a hand through his hair and sighed as he lifted his eyes to meet Maisey's. "I can't believe she woke you up. I told her at least five times that she couldn't come over here, that she'd have to thank you tonight."

"I *couldn't* wait," Laney sobbed, her voice plaintive.

Maisey smiled as Rafe, melting at the sight of those tears, bent to pick her up. "I needed to get up, anyway," she said. "Besides, I've invaded her world, and she's curious. I'm sure she wouldn't have disobeyed you otherwise."

"Living next door is hardly invading her world," he said dryly.

"In a way it is. I'm new. It's understandable."

Laney buried her face in his neck. "Don't be mad at me, Daddy."

He pressed her head to his shoulder. "This is the part of being a father I'm not good at," he muttered.

He looked pretty good at it, in Maisey's opinion. She raised her eyebrows in question.

"Discipline," he explained. "Somehow *any* punishment hurts me worse than it does her.

Maybe if she was a boy, or . . . You know, I could be tougher."

Laney had her father's complete devotion, but Maisey could tell she was a good child, so she didn't think he had anything to worry about. "I can't blame you. She's really sweet."

"She's never wandered off before." As he rubbed Laney's back, his eyes flicked over Maisey, making her feel self-conscious about the fact that she was wearing the same tank she'd worn yesterday. Thankfully, this time it was dry. And if Rafe had any interest in what he saw, he didn't reveal it. He merely gave her a polite nod and thanked her for the book before carrying his daughter away.

Maisey knew she'd successfully put him on notice that yesterday was a one-time thing. He was keeping his distance.

She told herself she was relieved. And yet she couldn't forget the vision of Rafe holding his daughter so tenderly as he walked back home. It reminded her of the safety she'd felt in his arms, of how easily he'd carried *her* to his place, and what he'd done to her—and *with* her—after that.

11

Maisey had agreed to meet her mother at the flower shop around three. So she did what she could to arrange her new furniture. Then she ate the leftovers Pippa had brought the night before and jumped into the shower. She wasn't planning on working today. She was just going to get the keys so she could open or close when necessary, meet the manager and then go grocery-shopping.

She left in plenty of time. But she was so busy studying all the changes in Keys Crossing as she puttered through town on her brother's scooter, she arrived ten minutes late, awash with nostalgia. She hadn't realized how much she'd missed Fairham.

"*There* you are," Josephine said as soon as she came through the door. "Where have you been?"

"I'm not *that* late," she replied when she heard the sharp edge in her mother's voice. "I guess it takes longer to get around on a scooter than I expected."

A large woman with shoulders like an NFL lineman stood behind the counter. "Don't worry," she said, her round face wreathed in a smile. "It's not like I'm going anywhere."

"Maybe you're not, but *I* am." Josephine

glanced pointedly at her watch. "I have a hair appointment over on the mainland."

"I'm sorry," Maisey said. "But I'm sure we can manage. Why don't you go now?"

She shook her head, clearly annoyed at Maisey's dismissiveness. "Let me at least introduce you to Nancy before I leave. She's been running the shop for . . . what, two years, Nancy?"

Nancy, who was somewhere in her thirties, tugged on her tight dress. "That's right, Mrs. Lazarow. It'll be two years next month. I started five days before Halloween."

"Nancy's quite talented with the arrangements," Josephine said, but Maisey could easily guess what her mother must think about Nancy's appearance. Josephine set high standards for everyone. She'd once demanded that another employee lose thirty pounds. She'd said she had an image to maintain, and the woman was hurting her "brand."

That employee had subsequently quit, so maybe Josephine had learned her lesson and been kinder to Nancy.

"Pleased to meet you," Maisey said.

"Your mother tells me you'll be taking over your brother's position."

"That's right. Until he gets back."

"Do we know when that might be?" Although Nancy's smile didn't waver, there was something about the hope in her voice that made Maisey wonder if her curiosity about Keith's return was more personal than professional.

Fortunately, Josephine was so rushed she didn't seem to notice. She'd never approve of someone as plain as Nancy for Keith. But, as much as Maisey loved her brother, she felt it was in *Nancy's* best interests that they not get involved. He was too troubled to make anyone a good husband—or even a good boyfriend.

"Not quite yet," Maisey said.

Josephine pulled her keys from her Burberry bag. "As I told you last night at dinner, I've added on to the store and done a few other things, but . . . I'll let Nancy show you all that. I've got to go, or my hair will look like this for another week. Bianca's booked solid."

Maisey gave her mother an air kiss on each cheek before Josephine hurried out the door.

Once she was gone, and her perfume wasn't so overpowering, the scent of the roses and gardenias and calla lilies Maisey remembered so distinctly from her youth became more prevalent. The most fragrant flowers weren't always her favorites, however. She preferred hydrangeas, delphinium, freesia and heliconia to the more traditional long-stemmed roses and carnation-type arrangements. Her mother's creations were high-end, unique, trendy, works of art.

"How long have you been back on the island?" Nancy asked.

"I got in a couple of days ago."

"Your mother must be thrilled."

Maisey decided that comment was better left without a response. "How's business these days?"

"Great. We're getting a lot of orders from the mainland, if you can believe it."

"Do we deliver to the mainland?"

"We do now. Your mother says we shouldn't turn customers away."

"What's putting us on the map?"

"It's not our prices," she said with a laugh. "It has to be the quality. Fortunately, people are willing to pay for superior work."

Maisey took note of the various arrangements waiting in the display coolers for pickup or delivery. "They *are* special."

Nancy showed her the new walk-in cooler. It was twice as big as the one Josephine had before, and it held a more extravagant assortment of flowers. Love's in Bloom also boasted an expanded workroom, a small kitchen area and a tiny, closet-like office to one side, where Nancy could handle the computer work.

"How many delivery people do we employ these days?" Maisey asked.

"Five." Nancy showed her a list of names and numbers pinned to a bulletin board. "Here's a roster," she said.

"Five's a lot for a small island floral company."

"We need them—although we're currently struggling to keep up with the production end, which is why I'm so glad to see you. Your brother was terrific at taking the orders and doing the books. He was good at managing the website, too. But he had no talent for arranging, didn't even want to try. So Suzie Cooper is the only help I've had, and she's been off sick for the past few days. There's some sort of cough going around."

"Pippa at Coldiron House has been down with it, too. But . . . doesn't my mother help out occasionally?"

"Not much anymore. She mostly . . . trouble-shoots."

"Troubleshoots?"

"Figures out ways we can improve the business."

"I see."

"So trying to get by without Suzie has been a real problem."

"Sounds like I got here just in time."

"You did. Suzie might come back for a couple of months, but then she's going on maternity leave."

"Why not hire someone else?"

Nancy picked up where she'd left off, working on an arrangement she'd been constructing when Maisey arrived. "I've tried. Your mother hasn't been happy with their work."

"She's always been particular."

"Which is why business is good. I get that. But . . . we're reaching the breaking point."

No wonder her mother had offered her this job, Maisey thought. And here she'd assumed Josephine had dozens of people to pick from. Apparently she'd already gone through them.

"You're under a lot of pressure. Here, let me see what I can do to help you catch up."

Nancy seemed startled by the offer. "*Today?* But I thought you weren't starting until you got settled."

"If we're behind, we gotta do what we gotta do, right?"

"Thank the Lord you're not a spoiled brat," Nancy joked, and handed her an apron.

It'd been many years since Maisey had worked with flowers. She felt rusty, out of practice, but found herself enjoying the creative aspect. She had less room to use her imagination on internet orders; there, she had to match the picture the purchaser had selected. But Love's in Bloom had plenty of local orders, too, and many people provided only minimal instructions. "Use lots of roses," or "I always like whatever Mrs. Lazarow comes up with." Although Maisey wasn't her mother and didn't have nearly the same talent with flowers, she'd learned from the best, and she wasn't bad. She was proud of what she created.

It was seven before Nancy glanced at the clock

and announced that they should go home. "That's enough for one day. Thank you for pitching in," she said. "You saved my life. Now I'll be able to fall into bed and get some sleep. I can't tell you how much I appreciate everything you've done. You work fast, too."

Maisey liked Nancy, especially when Nancy emphasized her gratitude by giving Maisey a big hug. "God, I feel like I might break you, you're such a stick," she complained. "Why do you have to make me look so bad?"

Although she was obviously teasing, Maisey was as self-conscious about her weight as Nancy was. "I haven't gotten skinny on purpose."

"Some people just have all the luck, huh?"

Maisey grinned at her.

"I'm down about five pounds, but—" Nancy grimaced "—as you can see, it's like taking a cup of water out of the ocean."

As far as Maisey was concerned, Nancy's personality made her attractive despite the extra weight. "Is there a special occasion coming up?"

"Not really." She sucked in her stomach and turned to evaluate herself in the mirror on the far wall. "There *is* someone I'd like to impress, though."

Maisey recalled the way she'd asked about Keith and hoped it wasn't him. "Anyone I know?"

Nancy's smile disappeared. "No. Some guy I met at . . ." She couldn't seem to finish that sentence, so she simply repeated the first part of it. "Some guy I met."

Maybe "some guy" she'd been working with? A guy who was incredibly handsome but just as damaged?

Women typically liked Keith, but no one stuck with him for very long. Maisey wanted to tell Nancy to be careful what she wished for. Instead, she murmured, "I can't imagine that whoever it is won't like you just the way you are."

Impulsively, Nancy gave her another squeeze. "Thanks," she said, and showed Maisey how to close the shop. "In case it's ever necessary," she explained. "So many things have changed while you've been gone."

Maisey was exhausted but oddly happy as she drove her scooter over to Smitty's. This was the first productive day she'd had in a long time. She wasn't writing, which she would've preferred, but at least she was working, creating, helping someone . . .

She was wandering down the aisles, loading up her cart, when she heard someone exclaim, "Oh, my Lord! Look who it is."

A tall, dark-haired woman approached with a chubby baby in her arms and a two- or three-year-old toddler tagging along. Maisey tried to place her—and couldn't.

"Don't tell me you don't remember me!"

Maisey could only give her a blank look.

"It's Dinah! Dinah Swenson! We went to middle school together!"

This was the girl in Maisey's art class who could draw so well? "Of course," Maisey said. "I'm sorry it took me a minute."

"We moved away the summer before high school, so it's been a while. And I've had a bit of plastic surgery," she admitted. "I caught the acting bug while we were living in California, but when I wasn't getting any parts, I had a nose job, cheek implants and then a boob job." Moving the baby to one arm, she held a hand to her left breast. "They look good, don't they? Los Angeles has some talented doctors—the *best*. You can't even tell they're not real. And my face? *So* much better. That's why you didn't recognize me. When I first moved back, no one else did, either."

Maisey nearly laughed but wasn't completely sure Dinah was joking. "You look . . . fabulous," she said. "Not that you weren't pretty before."

Dinah waved her off. "You don't have to be polite. I was ugly as a mud fence. I fixed that, but I can't act worth shit. So I had to give up the dream."

This time Maisey *did* allow herself a small chuckle. "You decided to get married and have a family instead?"

"I did. So much for the glamorous life. Chuckie Ambrose—you remember him? The short, freckled-faced boy who kept getting in trouble in math class for throwing spit wads at me?" She stopped her toddler from pulling the pasta bags off the shelves. "He had a crush on me ever since. And you should see him now. He's six-foot-four, two hundred and fifty pounds! Anyway, he found me on Facebook six years ago, and one thing led to another. Before I knew it, he was buying me a plane ticket so I could fly back and marry him."

"Chuckie, huh?" Maisey grinned. "From what I remember, he wasn't as tall as I was when we were sophomores."

"Like I said, he shot up. Now he's the basketball coach over at the high school. Teaches math, too. Loves it. Would never leave. Which is why *I* had to give up *my* career."

By her own admission, she hadn't actually had much of a career, but Maisey could tell she was merely acting put-upon to show the sacrifice she'd made for love. "Your children are darling."

"Yeah, hopefully they won't have to go under the knife, like I did." She nudged Maisey with her free hand. "I wish I had a picture of the look on your face. I'm joking," she said. "Of course I'm joking."

Maisey didn't remember Dinah being quite so . . . unconventional. "Right."

"What brings you back to town?"

This was the question Maisey had been dreading. She figured she might as well put the word out. Get it over with. The more she acted as if she didn't want people to know, the more curious they'd be. And if Dinah could be so honest . . .

"My husband left me for another woman." Maisey didn't say anything about Ellie; she didn't see why mere acquaintances had to know about her daughter. The divorce provided enough of a distraction. It made her look pathetic, but revealing Jack's abandonment stopped people from probing the deepest source of her pain.

"What a bastard!" Dinah said.

That pretty much obliterated any anxiety Maisey had been feeling, which made it easier to be generous about her ex. "He's not *that* bad," she said. "I guess I just didn't have what he needed."

"Well, if you haven't gotten back at him yet, I'd be happy to help you. I tell Chuckie that he'll be damn sorry if he ever cheats on me." She used her fingers like a pair of scissors.

Maisey laughed and, as she did, she realized how good it felt to laugh—hard and out loud. She was about to tell Dinah as much when she heard her name being called and turned to find Rafe's daughter gripping the handle of a cart guided by an older, pleasant-looking woman with gray hair swept up in a bun. "Laney!"

"I thought that was your voice!" Laney cried. "Grandma, this is her! She's right here!"

Rafe's mother eyed Maisey speculatively. "Hello."

Supremely conscious of what she'd done with this woman's son, but wanting to be polite, Maisey angled her cart so she could talk to both Dinah and Laney's grandmother. "Hi."

"I'm Vera, Raphael's mother."

"It's nice to meet you."

"You, too." She nodded a greeting intended for Dinah, but Dinah was preoccupied, trying to stop her son from taking off his pants.

"No! Mommy said to leave 'em on, Justy," Dinah said. "We'll go change you in a minute."

Vera's attention returned to Maisey. "Laney says you write children's books."

"I've written a few, yes. But right now, I'm working in my mother's flower shop."

Dinah looked up in spite of the fact that her son was now screaming, "Mommy, icky! Poop!"

"You're kidding me!" she said. "You're *famous?*"

Apparently she'd ignored the part about being back at the flower shop. "Not quite," Maisey replied.

"Her book has Molly Brimble in it," Laney announced. "And Molly Brimble has hair that goes all over unless she braids it. So Maisey is going to teach me how to braid so I can keep her hair nice. Aren't you?"

Laney spoke to the ceiling until her grandmother gently turned her head so she was facing Maisey. "When you speak to people, remember to point your nose at them, okay, honey? That helps people know who you're talking to."

"Okay," she said, but she was too absorbed in the excitement of Molly Brimble and those braids to remember her grandmother's advice, because as soon as Rafe's mother let go, her head rocked back again. "Aren't you, Maisey?" she asked. "Aren't you going to teach me how to braid?"

"Sure," Maisey said. "I'd be happy to do that."

"Laney tells me you're Mrs. Lazarow's daughter, and if you're already working at Love's in Bloom, I guess it's true."

"Yes." Did Vera know her mother personally? She didn't indicate one way or the other.

"And you live in one of the bungalows that Rafe will be rehabbing?"

Vera Romero was probably wondering why Maisey wasn't living at Coldiron House. "Yes. My father developed those bungalows when I was a child. I have fond memories of them."

Her expression softened. "I remember your father. He was a kind man."

The familiarity in her voice was so unexpected, Maisey had to wonder how her father and Mrs. Romero's paths had crossed. "Did you know him well?"

Vera hesitated as if she was trying to pick her

words carefully, but Rafe came striding down the aisle before she could say anything. "I'm beat," he said to his mother. "You two about ready to go?"

Maisey hadn't expected him to be there, but it made sense. Due to the difficulty of getting cars on and off the island, it was likely that Vera didn't have a vehicle of her own. Maisey guessed she couldn't drive, anyway, her hands were so gnarled with arthritis.

Vera raised her voice, trying to be heard over the racket Dinah's son was making. "Almost. Laney was just introducing me to your neighbor."

Rafe's eyes passed coolly over Maisey. "Hi," he said, but it was a perfunctory greeting. He didn't sound pleased to see her. She assumed he was angry at the way she'd treated him when he came to help her move last night. She felt bad about it, but he had no idea what she was going through or how carefully she needed to protect herself from getting involved with the wrong man.

"Can I go over to Maisey's house tonight, Daddy?" Laney grabbed his leg. "She's going to teach me how to braid."

Rafe scratched his neck, taking so long to answer that Maisey got the impression he didn't want to say yes. "She's probably too busy tonight."

That was a leading statement. He was obviously hoping Maisey would agree. But when Laney's face fell with disappointment, she didn't have the heart to put the girl off. She figured she might as well fulfill her promise sooner rather than later. "It's fine with me. It won't take long."

"Hi, Rafe." Dinah smiled up from where she was still wrestling—one-handed—with her son, trying to get him to quit peeling off his pants.

"Dinah."

She straightened. "You're looking good."

"So are you," he said absently. Then he told his mother he'd be out in his truck and left.

Dinah gave an exasperated sigh. "I should go, too. I can't stay long with Justin freaking out like this."

"Do you need me to watch the baby while you get what you need?" Maisey held her breath as she awaited the transfer of that small weight. She hadn't had a baby in her arms since Ellie and wasn't sure she could do it without breaking down in tears.

"No, the only thing I really need is some vanilla extract. That's why I didn't grab a cart. But we should get together in the next week or two, catch up."

Relieved to have escaped baby-holding detail, Maisey let out her breath. "I'd like that," she said, and punched Dinah's number into her phone.

As Maisey put her phone back in her purse, Dinah leaned close. "Isn't Rafe about the hottest guy you've ever seen?"

"I heard that," Vera said dryly. "And I'm sure Laney did, too."

"Daddy's too hot?" Laney's face creased with confusion.

Completely unruffled, Dinah fanned herself. "No, he's too *cute!*" she said. Then she rushed off with both kids to get her vanilla.

Vera stared after her. "Don't you think it's strange that a married woman would say that while holding her kids?"

Maisey could hear "Justy" screaming two aisles over. "They weren't old enough to understand what she was saying."

She shook her head, slightly exasperated but not really put off. "I guess I should be used to Dinah by now. You never know what's going to come out of her mouth. At least I should be glad it was PG." Despite her slow and laborious movements, Vera managed to wheel her cart around. "We'd better go. Tell your neighbor goodbye," she instructed Laney.

"Bye," Laney repeated.

Maisey was tempted to stop them. She wanted to get an answer out of Rafe's mother about how she'd known Malcolm. But the two were already trundling away. "See you later," she called out to Laney.

12

Rafe wasn't pleased about seeing Maisey. He'd decided she'd only slept with him to prove she could make him want her. It must've been a game, payback for what had happened before. Why else would she blow hot and then cold?

Or she'd been amusing herself with someone she found attractive enough to have a little fun with but wouldn't consider dating.

He was a father these days. He didn't need that kind of insincere bullshit in his life.

He stood off to one side as Maisey opened her front door.

"Hi, there," she said when she saw Laney.

Laney edged closer to the threshold, hugging Maisey's book to her chest. He'd pulled her back twice, so she wouldn't be hovering too close, but she was so excited she kept inching forward. "Did we wait long enough?" she asked.

That question sounded as if the delay had been pure torture. Rafe hadn't enjoyed it, either. Laney had been at him from the moment they got home, begging him to take her to Maisey's. He'd been holding her off, trying to give Maisey time to have some dinner and unwind. He didn't want his daughter to become a pain in the ass, especially when Maisey had made it so clear that she wasn't interested in being his friend—or anything else. He assumed she thought he was too shallow for a relationship. She'd joked about it when they flirted in the kitchen, but he'd never dreamed he should be taking that shit seriously. He was what, barely twenty, when they ran into each other at that party?

He'd always been told that women have long memories. Now he believed it.

"This is the perfect time." Maisey stepped back. "Come on in."

Rafe guided Laney to the couch, but he had too much energy to sit down himself. He didn't want to be that close to Maisey, anyway, didn't want to pay attention to what she looked like, what she was wearing or what she was doing. So he stood at the window and gazed out while she used the book she'd given Laney to attempt a braiding lesson.

Unfortunately, it didn't go as well as she seemed to expect. It soon became apparent that Laney's little hands weren't quite dexterous enough.

Maisey went over the process several times, step by step, but Laney couldn't follow her instructions. Part of the problem was Laney's inability to complete each step before moving on to the next. Since she couldn't see the end product, she couldn't seem to grasp why it mattered. Forgetting that she had to alternate sides, she'd simply wind the three strands together.

"You'll get it," Maisey said. "Let's try again."

Rafe had to give Maisey credit for patience. The lesson went on for half an hour before she looked up at him. "Maybe I should teach you so the two of you can go over it at home?" she suggested.

"Me?"

"She's so . . . young that it might take some reinforcement."

"Look, Daddy!" Maisey had been so gentle that Laney had no idea she was failing her first class. "I'm doing it! I'm braiding Molly Brimble's hair!"

"You're close, sweetheart," he said.

"It'll just take a minute," Maisey told him, trying to talk him into agreeing.

Swallowing a sigh, he walked over and sat down with them.

"Let me show your dad for a second." Maisey carefully took the book out of Laney's hands.

She separated the yarn into three sections and demonstrated how each side went over the middle. "That's it," she said when he picked up on it after only a couple of tries.

"The things I do for love," he muttered as he clipped a barrette onto the end of Molly's yarn hair.

Maisey shot him a grin. "If only your old friends could see you now."

Ignoring that comment, he stood. "We've got

it, don't we, Laney-bug? Let's go, so Ms. Maisey can . . . do whatever Ms. Maisey wants to do with her evening."

"Can Ms. Maisey come over and have some ice cream with us?" Laney asked.

Earlier, Rafe had bribed his daughter with the promise of ice cream before bed to persuade her to calm down and wait. "She doesn't want any ice cream," he answered before Maisey could respond.

"Thanks," he said, scooping his daughter into his arms. "We'll get out of your way now."

Maisey rested her cheek against the door after she'd closed it. She understood why Rafe was angry with her. He had no clue why she'd turned on him, didn't understand that it'd been a mistake to get involved with him in the first place. He was an innocent bystander who didn't know that her life was like some unfortunate ship that'd been blown onto the rocky coast and smashed to pieces. Everything, even the little she'd had left in her life after Ellie's death and her divorce—namely her career—was sinking to the bottom of the ocean. Someone as beleaguered as she was would be foolish to race into another storm, especially a storm named Rafe Romero.

But that didn't stop certain physical appetites from trying to assert themselves . . .

With a frown at how unsettled she felt after

seeing him, she went to bed. She had to get up early and go back to Love's in Bloom. Nancy was under too much pressure for Maisey to take the time she'd initially planned to set up her house. Until they'd established a manageable routine, Maisey figured she'd have to fit the details of her life around her responsibilities at the shop. Which wasn't a bad thing. The whole point of having a job was to give her some direction, help her battle the gale-force winds she was facing. Maybe, with time, she'd be able to drag herself, battered and waterlogged but glad she was alive, onto solid ground.

Getting some rest sounded great in theory but, hard as she tried, she couldn't sleep. Too many thoughts, worries and conflicting emotions swirled around inside her. There were snippets from that telephone conversation with Jack— *I miss you. Can I come see you sometime?* The hope inspired by any tentative improvement in her relationship with her mother. The concern she felt for Keith, as well as the fear of what he might be doing. The knot that had crept into her throat at the feel of Laney's small hands roving over her face. The memory of how indifferent Rafe had seemed tonight, compared to how focused and engaged he'd been when she was in his bed yesterday. He'd put a lot of effort into pleasing her. She could see why he might be mystified by her retreat. But, as she reminded herself, she should never have gotten involved with him in the first place.

Irritated by her inability to shut off her mind, she climbed out of bed, changed into her swimsuit and pulled a sweatshirt over top, then walked down to the beach.

The moon was so full she didn't need the small flashlight on her key chain, but she'd brought it, just in case. When she found herself as alone as she'd hoped to be, she took off her sweatshirt and dropped it, along with her keys, on the large flat rock that created a little platform—the same rock she'd used when she was younger—and waded into the surf.

The air wasn't nearly as cold as it'd been the night she'd slept outside, because there was no wind. But it was still chilly enough to make the water feel warm by contrast.

Maisey swam hard, trying to exhaust herself, and after an hour or so, she started back to her bungalow. When she passed Rafe's house, she walked partway up the drive to see if he still had a light on.

His place was dark, but picturing him in bed certainly didn't bring her any peace. Her thoughts immediately reverted to how gently and yet confidently he'd touched her, the way he kissed and how comforting it had been to fall asleep with him afterward. That was the first time she hadn't fallen asleep alone since Jack left.

As soon as she got home, she picked up her phone to try calling Keith and saw that she'd received a text.

I've been thinking about you.

It was from Jack.

Josephine froze. It'd been a long time since she thought she could see Annabelle's blond head on the private beach, where whatever nanny they had on staff used to take the children, but she thought she saw it now. Her breath caught and her chest tightened as she stepped onto the patio outside her bedroom for a better glimpse.

There was nothing there. No people. No children. But she could've sworn . . .

No, that was crazy. Impossible. It was just that Pippa had mentioned her the other night. At odd moments, Josephine was tempted to come forward, to tell the whole sordid story. But that was a reckless impulse. One she always managed to quell.

She stood at the railing, watching the sandpipers swoop down on the sand crabs and couldn't look away even when the wind pressed her thin robe to her body, mussing her hair. She half expected to see Malcolm walking around the point where the rocks jutted out into the sea, carrying Annabelle in his arms.

He'd loved Bella so much—which made it such a mystery why Josephine never could.

"Mrs. Lazarow?"

Pippa stood at her bedroom door. Forcing herself to turn away from that lonely stretch of beach, she went back inside to see what her housekeeper wanted.

It was two days later and, except for knowing that he now had Maisey living next door, Rafe's life had returned to normal. Maisey was gone during the days. He was glad of that. He found it was easier to work when she wasn't a few minutes away. He knew she was gone because he passed her on the road every morning on his way back from dropping Laney off. She'd wave when she saw him, but he never bothered to respond. He was trying hard to put her out of his thoughts, to stop reliving that hour in his bed.

There were other women in the world, he told himself. But it wasn't that easy to meet them. He didn't date very often; he didn't like leaving his daughter with a sitter. Most people didn't know what she could and couldn't do, so they weren't comfortable taking care of her. And he was afraid they might not watch her carefully enough, or they wouldn't be as kind as they should be. He had his mother, but he didn't want to take advantage of her.

He was tearing out a wall Josephine Lazarow

had decided she wanted moved—to open up the kitchen area of Unit 1—when he came across something wedged between the studs.

A metal box. As he pulled it out, his first thought was that Maisey's father might've stashed some money in his precious Smuggler's Cove development. Rafe couldn't think of a more likely explanation. Someone wouldn't go to so much effort to hide something unless it had great value. But it wasn't cash. Once he opened it, he found . . . pictures.

Maisey never answered Jack's text. She did, however, take her phone out every once in a while to reread what he'd sent her. Considering how easily he'd moved on, his entreaties were sort of . . . gratifying. No woman wanted to be so forgettable.

Or was he regretting what he'd done simply because he didn't have anyone else at the moment? He hadn't expressed any second thoughts when he was with Heather . . .

Nancy came up behind her while she was staring down at her screen, wondering if she should text something back to her ex.

"Any word from Keith?"

Maisey slipped her phone into her pocket. "No. 'Fraid not."

"He really should call you," Nancy said.

Maisey might've let that comment go. It was

true. Keith *should* call her. But Nancy seemed to have more of a personal stake in the situation than Maisey would've expected. She also seemed to know Keith well enough to be assertive in her disapproval, which seemed . . . odd.

After adding the cardholder to the flower arrangement she'd just finished, Maisey confronted her new boss. "Has my brother called *you?*"

Nancy's face flushed beet-red. She began to deny that she'd had any contact with Keith, but then sighed. "Shoot. I can't lie. I'm terrible at it. And it's harder with you. Here you've been going the extra mile to help me every day, and . . ."

"And?" Maisey wasn't pleased that Nancy seemed to know more about Keith's well-being than she did. Why would he let his own sister worry? He was an adult; he had the right to live as he chose, even if it wasn't good for him. But to take off with no word after a fairly recent attempt at suicide? To make her fear for his well-being day and night, on top of everything else she was dealing with?

"He's okay," Nancy admitted. "That's what I felt I should tell you. I—I heard from him a couple of days ago. He's fine."

Maisey was too angry to be relieved. Wasn't this just like her brother? How could she have trusted him enough to move home? "Where is he?"

"Not on the island."

That was cryptic. Nancy's loyalty was coming into play—fueled by her infatuation. Maisey had sensed her interest the day she started at Love's in Bloom. "It's not like I'm going to chase him down, Nancy."

"I *can't* be any more specific than that. I don't know exactly where he is. All I know is that he asked me to wire him some money not too long after he left, and then again yesterday, on my lunch hour."

"And you did it?"

Nancy spread out her hands. "I had to. I couldn't say no. I was afraid of what might happen to him. He didn't have five bucks to his name, couldn't even grab a bite to eat."

Or line up his next fix. How many times had he led others down the same road? Why did Nancy think all his friends eventually abandoned him?

Dropping her head in her hand, Maisey kneaded her forehead. "Have you been sleeping with him?"

Dead silence. Obviously, Nancy hadn't expected her to be so forthright.

Maisey didn't insist on a reply. "I'm not going to mention a word of this to my mother," she went on. "I just . . . I feel I should warn you. You're aware that my brother has serious problems, right? That he's a drug addict?"

Nancy twisted the charm bracelet she was

wearing. "He says he's been clean since he got out of rehab."

Maisey hated that she had to have this conversation, but she didn't think it was fair for someone as innocent as Nancy to become mixed up in his problems. "I hope that's true. I don't actually know. But I do know that he'll say whatever he needs to in order to get what he wants."

And someone like Nancy would be particularly susceptible to his charm. That was why Maisey had to speak up. Nancy didn't have a fighting chance against someone so charismatic, not without some sort of guidance. "You seem like a nice person. I really don't want to see you hurt."

Nancy was blinking rapidly, fighting tears. "It'll be okay. He'll repay me when he's back on his feet."

Which would be when? At the rate he'd been going, it would be never . . .

"He cares about me." She threw that out as a final defense, but Maisey could tell she was trying to convince herself more than anyone else. Keith took advantage of people and then moved on. It wasn't intentional as much as it was a matter of convenience. He'd never had to try very hard to get what he wanted, so it never meant a lot to him. He took the generosity of others for granted—and expected anyone he tossed aside to still be there if he decided to return.

"I'm sure he does," Maisey said. "You're a very

kind person. Just . . . do me one favor, okay? Don't send him any more money. You shouldn't have to do that."

"How can I say no?"

"He has other options."

"Like . . ."

"If he gets desperate, he can always come home."

"And deal with your mother? I don't mean to speak ill of my employer. I'm grateful for my job. But he told me . . ."

The bell rang over the door. Raising one hand to indicate that she'd be right back, Maisey arranged a cheerful expression on her face, and walked out front.

It wasn't a customer. At least, it wasn't an ordinary customer. Vera Romero was there, with Laney.

"Surprise!" Laney cried as soon as Maisey said hello. Maisey had been relieved that she hadn't seen Laney since trying to teach her to braid. Laney was easy to love—but that was the problem. Maisey didn't want to fall in love with her or anyone else right now. And having a relationship with Laney would throw her into frequent contact with Rafe. "Hello."

"I've been practicing." She held up Maisey's book. "Doesn't Molly Brimble's hair look nice?"

Laney's braiding skills had improved. Rafe must've been working with her. Or Vera, if her poor fingers could manage it. "Definitely. You're doing a superb job."

"She's spent *hours* on it," Vera confided.

"She's getting good." Maisey clasped her hands together. "So . . . what can I do for you? Do you need flowers? Is there a special occasion coming up?"

"The way I feel some days, I think my funeral will be the next special occasion I attend," Vera joked, rubbing her gnarled hands.

Fortunately, Laney didn't seem to understand what her grandmother was talking about. "Ohh . . . it smells nice in here," she said, preoccupied by her new surroundings.

"It's all the flowers," Maisey told her. "Wait right there." She went into the back and got several different kinds. "This is a rose." She held it under Laney's nose. "You've smelled a rose before, haven't you?"

"Yes." Her confident expression confirmed that she recognized it. "It has soft petals but sharp points!"

"Those are the thorns on the stem. You have to be careful of them, for sure. But this other flower doesn't grow thorns. It's called a gardenia."

Wrinkling her nose, Laney pulled back.

"*Too* strong?" Maisey asked.

"I don't like it," she replied.

"What about this one?" Maisey held out some wisteria.

"Nice," Laney breathed. "It's . . . hardly there."

Maisey guided her fingers to the small petals. "Feel how fragile these are."

"Do you *make* flowers?" Laney asked.

"No. We buy them from the farmers who grow them on the mainland. Then I put them in pretty arrangements."

"Why?" she asked.

"Because flowers brighten a room. And they make people feel good."

"Oh! That's what I want to do when I'm big," she said solemnly.

Knowing there was little chance of that, Maisey felt a weight on her heart. And then she heard herself say, "We can make one together sometime."

Cursing herself for that stupid offer, she exchanged a smile with Mrs. Romero. "So what brings you in today?" she asked, letting Laney keep the wisteria.

"Laney and I were wondering if you might be free for dinner at my place this Sunday."

"Me?" Maisey brought a hand to her chest. Why on earth would Rafe's mom be asking *her* to dinner? He'd be there if Laney was, especially on the weekend. But Maisey was positive he hadn't put Vera up to this. He wouldn't even wave at her in the mornings.

"Sure. You've been gone for a long time and, the way folks come and go around here, I'm guessing a lot of your friends have moved on. We thought we'd welcome you back with a nice homemade meal. Of course, I can't compete with the kind of fancy meals your mother serves at Coldiron House," she added with a self-deprecating gesture, "but . . . I'm not a *bad* cook. With these hands, it just takes me a bit longer than it used to, that's all."

"I don't want you to go to any trouble," Maisey hedged, but Laney interrupted before she could firm up her refusal.

"Please?" She folded her hands under her chin in a prayer-like pose. "I'm going to set the table. And we're going to have blackberry pie and ice cream at the end."

Now Maisey wanted to say no more than ever. That sounded entirely too homey. She couldn't let herself be drawn into Rafe's life—not if she wanted to resist the sexual temptation he presented.

Problem was, she couldn't bring herself to disappoint his sweet, beautiful child.

"Sure," she said. "What time?"

Vera handed her a piece of paper with an address on it. "Three?"

"Fine." She wasn't scheduled to work on Sunday. The shop closed at noon, anyway. So even if Nancy got behind again and called Maisey in, she should be able to make three o'clock. "What can I bring?"

Rafe's mother glanced around. "How about some flowers?"

13

Rafe had gone out on a date. He'd taken a woman who worked at the building supply place where he shopped on the mainland out for dinner. What had happened with Maisey had sort of kicked him in the ass, reminded him that if he wanted to find a companion, he needed to keep looking. It'd been a long time since he'd made the effort; he'd been too complacent if not too busy.

He'd chosen a nice restaurant, where the food was good, but he hadn't enjoyed himself. He'd known even before he went to dinner with Gina Cook that she didn't really appeal to him. He'd only invited her because she'd hinted that she wanted him to when he was checking out yesterday—and his mother had been nagging him so much lately. Vera felt he'd be happier if he had a wife. And she was afraid that when she died, he'd have no one to help him with Laney.

"You need to get married," she kept saying.

He agreed. He wanted to give Laney everything a child should have. Laney had it hard enough, being blind. But he couldn't change the kind of person her real mother was, and he couldn't marry solely for practical reasons. He hadn't met the right woman yet, hadn't fallen in love.

Gina Cook *definitely* wasn't the one. He hadn't found her remotely interesting. He'd realized almost immediately that he wasn't physically attracted to her, either. When she'd taken his hand or snuggled up under his arm as they walked, he'd been irritated instead of excited.

He considered going back to his mother's place in Keys Crossing to pick up Laney, figured he should've done that on his drive home. It was no fun spending Friday night alone. But when he'd left the island earlier, she'd said she'd be keeping his daughter overnight.

Rafe wasn't stupid; he knew Vera was trying to give him some privacy in case he did experience a romantic spark. He could tell Gina was hoping things would go that way, too. She'd invited him in, hinting that he could stay the night—and yet he'd declined. Since he wasn't truly interested in her, he didn't want to start anything. Having a daughter, and knowing he'd one day be at the mercy of the men in that daughter's life, had changed his perspective.

Besides, Rafe preferred not to create an awkward situation, since he knew that even if he did get naked with Gina, he'd be thinking of Maisey. He hadn't been able to get her off his mind after that first day, when he'd encountered her peering into the windows of the bungalow next door. Why he felt a certain . . . affinity for her, he couldn't say. And why he had to be perverse enough to want to see her again when she wanted nothing to do with him was even more baffling.

Maybe it was karma, revenge for his wild youth. Or she was getting back at him for the fact that *he'd* once brushed *her* off.

Hoping a swim in the ocean might siphon off some of the excess energy that kept him pacing, he pulled on his swim trunks and went down to the beach. But he discovered almost as soon as he got there that he wasn't alone. A sweatshirt and a set of keys sat on the big rock where he always put his own stuff.

Maisey had gotten there first.

He squinted, trying to distinguish her head in the roiling waves. The moon was full, but it still wasn't easy to see her among all those white-caps . . .

Eventually, he spotted her. She seemed to be intent on her swim and completely oblivious to everything else.

He ordered himself to go home and leave her to her exercise. She'd made it clear that she didn't like his company. But swimming alone wasn't safe, especially so far out, beyond the breakers. The ocean could be changeable this time of year, when the colder weather was setting in. As frail as she looked these days, he wasn't convinced she was capable of fighting the currents.

Did she know what she was doing? She'd

grown up on the island, was most likely a seasoned swimmer. She had to be aware of the risks. And yet . . . he couldn't walk away. He was too afraid she'd drown if he did.

He stood in the shadows, out of sight, and watched until she came out of the sea. She wasn't anything like the curvy women he'd always preferred, he thought distantly. She was too thin. But that didn't stop him from admiring her swan-like beauty. Seeing her put every nerve on alert; there was just . . . something about her.

She hadn't brought a towel. She merely yanked on a sweatshirt.

Afraid she might hear him if he tried to hurry back ahead of her, he remained hidden by the shrubbery, didn't move when she walked past.

She came so close he could've touched her. He was tempted to do that, to give her a good scare and teach her that danger lurked everywhere, even here—especially since she'd scoffed at him when he'd told her she shouldn't sleep out on the beach. But he refrained, and he was glad he had when, instead of going straight to her own bungalow, he saw her hesitate, then turn toward *his* house.

Curious to see if she'd knock, he followed as quietly as he could.

She got as far as the bend in the drive, until she could see the light in his house. Then she stopped, shifted from foot to foot, muttered something—a curse?—and pivoted so fast she would've seen him standing off to one side if she hadn't been so preoccupied with whatever was on her mind.

Had she been working up the nerve to offer him an apology?

He felt he deserved one . . .

Sighing at her inexplicable nature, he returned to the beach. But while he swam, he kept thinking about that box he'd found. It had been buried in that wall as if it contained some great treasure—or some great secret—no one was meant to see. But he'd looked through the contents and couldn't imagine why anyone would want to hide those pictures.

He'd been planning to deliver them to Coldiron House. It was obvious that they belonged to the Lazarows. But he hadn't done that yet. He'd been in too much of a hurry when he dropped Laney off at his mom's before his date.

And now he was glad—because it gave him the perfect excuse to visit Maisey.

Having just dried her hair, Maisey was sitting on the couch in a pair of pajama shorts and the only clean, dry sweatshirt she had left. Jack had sent her another text: **You can't tell me you don't feel anything**. She was thinking about whether to respond, and what she might say, when she heard the knock at her door. According to her phone it was 10:40 p.m.—too late for Laney to be out. And Rafe had spent the past few days ignoring her.

Had her mother driven over?

Josephine wouldn't come *this* late . . .

Maybe Nancy had spoken to Keith and he'd returned in a huff, eager to yell at her for warning off the woman who'd been helping him.

Leaving her phone on the coffee table, Maisey braced for a confrontation. She didn't want to deal with one of her brother's infamous rages. But at least then she'd know he was okay. And there was no way to avoid his mood swings; that was simply part of being related to him.

"Who is it?" she called.

"Me," came the response.

Rafe.

She opened the door to see him holding something—a rusty iron box. "Hello." She looked around but Laney didn't seem to be with him. "Where's your daughter?"

"At her grandmother's."

"Does she stay over often?"

"Not usually. I had a date tonight."

Maisey refused to believe the twinge of emotion she felt could be jealousy. She had no claim on Rafe. "How'd that go?"

His expression revealed nothing. "Fine." He lifted up the box. "I came across something today that might belong to you."

"What is it?"

"Baby pictures. *Your* baby pictures, from what I can tell."

"Seriously? Where'd you find that?"

"Surprisingly enough, it was buried in a wall in Unit 1."

"Buried?"

"Pretty much. There wasn't any indication this box was there. It was behind the Sheetrock, wedged between two studs."

"That's so . . . odd." Stepping back, she motioned him inside. "What would my baby pictures be doing *in a wall?*"

"I have no clue. I was going to take them to Coldiron House. But I figured you might like to go through them first."

"Are you *sure* they're mine?"

"They have to be. I recognize your mother. She's in some of them, holding your hand. Keith is with you in others. And there's a man who looks like he might be your dad."

"Oh." Trying not to think about the fact that she and Rafe were alone for the first time since they'd been in his bed, she took the box over to the coffee table. "I was, um, having a little wine." She gestured at her glass. "Can I get you some?"

He hesitated as if he'd refuse.

"Come on. You can't stay mad at me forever. At least, I hope you can't. And I owe you for the Frosted Flakes." She offered him a grin, hoping she could convince him to stay. Maybe if they had a talk, they could get past the other morning. She didn't want living next door to each other to be uncomfortable—not to mention that she'd be having dinner on Sunday at his mother's.

He gave a curt nod. He didn't seem sure he was making the right decision, but happy that she'd received the answer she was hoping for, she hurried to the kitchen and poured him a glass.

She pointed to the chair beside the couch as she brought it out. "Please. Have a seat."

"Aren't you being a bit formal?" he asked.

She glanced at the box he'd brought. She was eager to look through it. Finding photographs of her in a wall seemed rather mysterious, but she could see her brother pulling a prank like that. Maybe Keith had felt their parents favored her or had taken too many pictures of her, so he'd decided to punish Josephine by hiding them.

She couldn't imagine why they'd been in the wall, but whatever the reason, she'd have time to sort through them after Rafe left. Right now, she wanted to deal with the problem she'd created by sleeping with him.

Swallowing because her throat was so dry, she said, "I'm sorry about the other day."

He held his glass loosely. "We're going to talk about that?"

"I think we should. If you don't mind."

"Actually, I'd *like* to understand. So why don't

you start by explaining what you're apologizing for?"

"All of it," she said. "I had no business . . . being as aggressive as I was and—and getting physical with you."

He chuckled humorlessly. "In case you couldn't tell, I was fine with the physical part. But acting like you hated me after? That was a little . . . unexpected."

"I understand. It would be confusing to have a woman seem so . . . interested and then—"

"Cold as ice?" he finished when she paused to search for the right words.

She took a sip of her wine. "If that's how you'd like to phrase it."

"How would *you* phrase it?" He sounded genuinely perplexed. "I mean . . . what'd I do?"

She shook her head. "Nothing. It—it wasn't you."

"Who was it, then? From what I remember, there were only the two of us, doing a whole lot of panting and moaning. I was pretty sure you enjoyed yourself."

"Of course I enjoyed myself," she said with an embarrassed grimace. "I'm not pretending I didn't."

"Then what?" he asked.

Her phone buzzed, signaling another incoming text, and they both looked down. Rafe was a few feet away and probably couldn't read what Jack had sent, since Maisey grabbed the phone right away and cleared the screen. But the speed of her reaction had tipped him off.

"You're already seeing someone," he guessed.

"Not exactly. But I am, um, considering getting back with my ex-husband." She wasn't considering that at all—not in her saner moments —but she thought it might give her the battle shield she needed against this new threat.

"I see." He rubbed a hand over his mouth and chin. "That explains a lot. How long have you been divorced?"

"Not quite a year."

"Where is he now?"

"In New York."

"That's where you used to live? I think I heard Keith mention New York when you first arrived."

She nodded, and silence fell while he stared into his drink. Then he said, "How long were you married?"

"Almost a decade."

"That's more than a minute or two."

"A third of my life."

He drained his glass. "You're still in love with him, then?"

She wanted to say that she wasn't sure how she felt, that she was trying to figure it all out. But those words wouldn't be decisive enough. In spite of everything, she could feel the attraction whenever Rafe was near. "Yes."

Leaning forward, he set his empty glass on the table. "Does he know you had sex with me?"

"No. And I doubt I'll tell him. It's not necessary."

"Since you split up."

"He left me for another woman, after he'd been having an affair with her for several months. I hardly think he can expect *me* to remain faithful."

Rafe clasped his hands, which had hung loosely between his knees. "He cheated on you?"

"Yes."

"So I was . . . what? Revenge sex?"

She felt her face heat. "No. Not revenge. I don't . . . I don't have a way to . . . classify it."

He said nothing. He just rubbed his palms on his thighs. Then he pushed to his feet. "Thanks for telling me."

"I'm sorry."

"Don't worry about it. I guess I deserved it, huh?"

She followed him to the door. "No, I . . . What we did had nothing to do with before."

He didn't respond.

"Rafe, listen. I just want to put my life back together. As you probably guessed when you found me sleeping on the beach my first night here, I'm not in the best shape. I'm not ready to get involved with *any* man. What happened near the end of my marriage was—" she didn't even want to remember the past two years in order to explain it "—a challenge for me."

He rammed his hands into his pockets as he turned. "So why move here, on this side of Fairham, to live in a hurricane-damaged bungalow? Why not return to Coldiron House, where you'd have your mother and her servants to look after you?"

"Whatever preconceived ideas you may have about what it means to be a Coldiron-Lazarow, growing up in that house wasn't as easy as it appeared, okay? We had what we needed in material terms, yes. There was always plenty of money. But there were . . . other problems. Serious problems. And not the kind that disappeared just because Keith and I have grown up."

This seemed to take him off guard. "You're not talking about abuse . . ."

That was an ugly word. One she generally reserved for physical attacks, and only Keith could accuse their mother of that. "I'd rather not go into detail. Surely you know my mother well enough to tell that she's . . . a difficult personality. She . . . Never mind. Forget it." She was talking too much. "I don't want to make excuses. I just want you to know that I wasn't in the best frame of mind when you kissed me, and I acted as if . . . as if I couldn't wait to get your clothes off."

He sighed, and when he spoke again it sounded

as though he was talking to himself. "You weren't responding to me, then. You were missing your husband and working off steam."

He'd had a lot more to do with her eagerness to feel him against her than she'd made it sound. Even Jack had never turned her on to that degree, not in quite some time. He'd been too lazy in the bedroom to try, especially after their first few years of marriage. Until he'd left her for someone else, she'd decided that was normal. Married couples often fell into a routine where work and other responsibilities took precedence. Then, when he'd gotten involved with someone else, she'd decided it must've been *her* fault their love life had grown so . . . stale. She hadn't been alluring or sexually desirable enough to maintain his interest.

But she wasn't about to go into all of *that* when simply agreeing with Rafe gave her the out she'd been searching for. "Since we barely know each other, I guess so."

"Got it. I appreciate the clarification."

"Of course." She held the door with one hand while leaning outside. "It was probably just a . . . a welcome release for you, too, right?"

He shrugged. "Sure. Whatever."

That didn't tell her much. In an effort to waylay him for another moment or so, she called after him. "Rafe?"

He turned to face her.

"I hope, despite everything, we can still be friends."

"I'm always up for a new friend," he said, but it was a throwaway statement, a polite way to wrap up this visit.

"I mean it," she insisted.

Her phone, which she'd left on the coffee table, pinged with another text message.

He nodded toward it. "I'll let you get back to your ex," he said, and headed down the steps.

As Maisey watched him go, she told herself she felt better. They'd come to an understanding. He wouldn't expect anything from her in the future; she was safe. That had to make it easier when she bumped into him here and there—and when she saw him at dinner this coming Sunday.

But she didn't hurry back inside to respond to Jack. She remained where she was, feeling an unexpected impulse to go after Rafe. Only her curiosity about the box he'd brought over kept her from chasing after him.

Drawing a deep breath, she told herself she'd done the right thing—*of course* she'd done the right thing—and returned to her couch to go through those pictures.

14

The lid was dented and hard to get off. Maisey almost wished she'd asked Rafe to remove it before he left. She broke a fingernail before she managed to pry the two pieces apart. Then she found exactly what Rafe had said she'd find—photographs. But these photographs weren't of her. At least, she didn't think so. The subject, a young girl, had the same color eyes and hair, since Maisey's hair had been much lighter when she was that age. Although the resemblance was uncanny, there were distinct differences, too. The girl's forehead was a bit higher, her mouth not quite as wide, her eyes closer together.

Puzzled, Maisey took out picture after picture and studied each one. Despite the similarity of the subject's features, she might've concluded that this girl had no connection to her. That some renter had left the photos in the bungalow years ago and, mysterious though it seemed, they'd wound up in one of the walls—as a subcontractor's joke or an act of spite by a stranger.

Except that her parents were in a few of them, as Rafe had said. That tied her family to the pictures. Seeing her father's likeness made Maisey yearn for him. Malcolm had been patient, kind. She'd been too afraid of her mother to go to Josephine for any type of nurturing. It was her father who'd provided the love she needed, and she missed his calm, unwavering support. He was the one who'd let her know, with his tacit disapproval, that her mother's and brother's behavior was not acceptable or even usual for most people. Without that, she might've thought *she* was the abnormal one.

She paused to stare at a photo in which the same girl—at about two years old—was puckering up to give Malcolm a kiss.

He was obviously close to this child. So *could* it be her? Maybe she wasn't remembering her own baby pictures clearly. Maisey couldn't see Malcolm being quite so loving with anyone else.

Unless it was a member of his extended family. That would account for the likeness—but didn't make much sense. Josephine had never cared for the Lazarows. As a result, they rarely associated with them. And there was another thing. Her father was the youngest of his family, and had married later in life, so his siblings wouldn't have had little kids by the time he met Josephine.

This girl had to be someone on the Coldiron side. Maisey had a lot of cousins, some she knew and some she didn't. Was it possible that her father had once been close to one of those children, someone he hadn't maintained a relationship with?

He could've been different back then, more carefree and demonstrative. There was no doubt that living with Josephine had changed him. Toward the end of his life, he'd seemed downright miserable. Even at seven or eight, Maisey had understood—instinctively, since it was never expressed—that her father was only enduring his marriage for the sake of his children. Secretly, she'd believed he was doing it more for her than Keith. Keith was almost as temperamental as Josephine. Malcolm couldn't relate to him, which was also part of Keith's problems. Unlike her, he hadn't shared a special bond with their father, had never had that anchor to temper the emotional ups and downs he suffered.

Instantly feeling guilty for acknowledging her father's favoritism, Maisey told herself he'd stayed for both of them. He could've stayed for financial reasons, too. Although she hated to believe her father would let money trap him like that, after having been through a divorce herself, she understood how hard any kind of separation would've been. The Coldirons had the wealth and power to strip him of everything, including his children. And back then, when her grandfather was alive, they'd have been ruthless enough to do it.

Despite the oddness of that photo, it wasn't until she came across another picture, one including Keith, that her heart started to jackhammer in her chest. She hadn't completely discarded the possibility that this child might be her. It remained the most likely explanation. But in this particular photograph, her brother seemed to be about four, and the girl in question stood taller.

Since Maisey was two years younger, and he'd been big for his age, there'd never been a time when she was taller than Keith. She'd never even come close.

That eliminated any lingering doubts Maisey had. She *couldn't* be this child. It was impossible. She could only be the newborn who showed up in a few of the older pictures at the bottom of the stack.

So . . . who was this girl? And why were they grouped together, posing as if they were siblings?

This *couldn't* be an older sister. She and Keith didn't have a sister. It was always just the two of them.

Or had there once been three?

Rafe went straight to his room and tore the sheets from his bed. He didn't want to climb back under them, didn't want to lie there before falling asleep thinking he could smell Maisey Lazarow's scent. For whatever reason, being with her the other day had been more significant, more memorable, than it should've been.

But that didn't mean he *couldn't* forget her. No way would he *finally* lose his heart to someone who didn't want it. A knock sounded as he stuffed his sheets in the washer. Since it was nearly midnight, and he'd just left Maisey's a few minutes ago, he figured it had to be her. His mother could no longer drive. Generally, she didn't need to. She lived close enough to the grocery store and other businesses that, if he couldn't take her, she could walk from her small rental house or have her purchases delivered. If there'd been any problem with Laney, she would've called.

At least, he hoped this wasn't about Laney. But he supposed it was a possibility and couldn't help feeling uneasy—until he opened the door and found Maisey standing on his porch. Then he let his breath go.

"What can I do for you?" He regretted his slightly irritated tone when she flinched.

"Never mind. I'm sorry I bothered you." She turned to leave but by then he'd noticed how pale she was, a detail he hadn't spotted immediately in the dim glow of his porch light.

Suddenly concerned that something terrible had happened, he hurried out and caught her by the arm. "What's wrong?"

"Nothing, I just . . . Forget it. It's late. We can talk about this tomorrow or . . . or some other time."

She was upset. Deeply. "Maisey," he said, "is it your ex? What happened?"

Surely she wouldn't come to *him* for help with another man. Unless . . . Had her ex made a physical threat? Frightened her so much she didn't dare remain at her house?

"No. It—it has nothing to do with Jack. I'm sure I'm overreacting, that it can't be what I'm thinking. I'll let you get to bed."

She started down the steps but, once again, he stopped her. "Overreacting to *what?* You're not making any sense."

"That box you brought over," she said.

"What about it?"

"Where *exactly* did you find it?"

"Inside a wall I was tearing down in Unit 1, like I said."

"Which wall? Why was it there?"

"I can show you where the wall was. But I'm afraid I can't answer your other question. I have no idea why it was there. I've found unexpected things inside walls before—a dead rodent, a wasp's nest, drugs, even some hidden money once. But never a collection of pictures."

The wind had come up. She hadn't put on a sweatshirt or a jacket and hugged herself to ward off the cold. "Can we go down there together tomorrow, so . . . so you can show me?"

"We can go now if you want." He could tell she was anxious about it; he was just having trouble understanding why.

"Are you sure? I hate that I'm keeping you up."

"I can wait a few more minutes. Hang on, while I grab a flashlight."

He pulled a sweatshirt from his drawer when he got the flashlight, and insisted she wear it. Then they walked down to the beach.

She followed as he climbed the porch steps to Unit 1 and stood behind him as he unlocked the door.

"Here we go," he said when they reached the kitchen. "There was a wall right here, behind the stove."

The sleeves of his sweatshirt were too long, but she didn't take the time to roll them up. "How could someone have gotten it in there?"

"Easy. They removed the stove and pushed the box through the hole where the vent had already compromised the Sheetrock."

"But most stoves don't last more than a decade or two, do they? All the appliances would have to be updated regularly. So wouldn't someone see it when the stove was replaced?"

"Whoever it was probably did a rudimentary patch, which wouldn't have taken too much effort. The guy who was doing the replacement might've assumed someone screwed up when they installed the vent. It's not like you'd wonder if something was back there."

"So it could've been anyone who had access to this unit in the past . . . thirty years."

He was puzzled by her defeated tone. "What do

you mean? It had to be your mother or father. Who else would've had access to those pictures *and* this bungalow?"

"My mother never came over here. She had no interest in the bungalows. They were my father's project."

She said that as if they'd been more than his project—as if they'd also been his refuge. "Then it was your father."

"Not necessarily. It could've been Keith. Or someone who worked for us. We had house-keepers—quite a few while I was growing up. Back then, they never stuck around for long."

"Why not?"

She bit her lip and glanced over. She was tempted to confide in him; he could tell. But he could also tell when she decided against it, answering with a cryptic, "A lot of reasons."

Although she didn't like to talk about her family, the subject aroused plenty of emotion. "Why would Keith hide your baby pictures?" he asked.

The way she stared off into space, her mind a million miles away, only made Rafe more curious. Thanks to Josephine Lazarow's father—Henry Coldiron—and the money and property he'd passed on, the Lazarows always seemed to have it all. Especially their spoiled daughter who'd acted, eighteen years ago, as if merely telling him who she was would get her anything she wanted.

If things *weren't* as he'd assumed, what had her childhood really been like? She'd acted hesitant when he'd mentioned abuse. He hoped nothing like that had ever happened. If it had, he doubted he'd ever find out. She was too private; she hadn't even answered his question about why Keith would hide the photographs.

"How long ago do you think they were put there?" she asked instead.

He studied her carefully. Something wasn't right, but Rafe couldn't put his finger on it. Sure, it was strange to have found a box of old photographs in a wall, but at least he'd recovered them. They hadn't been lost forever. She should feel relief or gratitude that he'd saved them.

Instead, she was spooked, agitated, uneasy.

Was there something in those pictures he'd overlooked? He'd only glanced through enough of them to determine who they belonged to. He'd been too busy to do any more.

"Hard to say," he said. "From what I can tell, there've been no major renovations since the bungalows were built, which means it could've happened any time since the early eighties."

"I see. Of course." Her smile looked forced. "Thank you. I—I appreciate you bringing me down here. I owe you one."

"You don't owe me anything," he said. Even if she did, he didn't plan on collecting. Now that he knew she was still in love with her ex, he was going to keep his distance. He didn't need to get involved in a romance triangle—or be the man who warmed her bed while she repaired her marriage to someone else.

She went out ahead of him and he locked up. He expected to find her waiting at the bottom of the steps so they could walk back together. He had the flashlight, which made the going easier. But she wasn't there when he descended. She wasn't farther ahead of him, either.

He assumed she'd hurried off—had already rounded the corner—until he cast the beam toward the beach and happened to catch sight of her sitting on the sand, facing the ocean.

Swallowing a curse, he walked over to her. "Maisey? It's getting late. Aren't you going back with me?"

She didn't turn around as he approached. She hugged her legs to her chest and rested her chin on her knees. "No. I think I'll sit here for a while. You go ahead."

But he couldn't leave her. Not if she was thinking about getting in the water, like she had the other night. "You're not planning on going for a swim, are you?"

"Possibly," she replied with a shrug that said it was none of his business.

"I'd rather you didn't."

She finally looked up at him. "Why?"

"It isn't safe," he explained. "The currents can get tricky at this time of year."

"Thanks for your concern. I don't mean to be rude, but I grew up on this island—using *this* beach." She went back to staring at the frothy waves. "I know Fairham at least as well as you do."

Placing his hands on his hips, he followed her gaze and saw the moon sitting there, almost on top of the water. It was a beautiful sight. Maybe she was just enjoying the view . . .

Part of him thought he should shut up and back off. He had no say in what she did.

But the other part . . . "I don't doubt that," he said. "Problem is, you might not know the limits of your own strength. It's possible that the currents have grown stronger in the past decade. I've felt them. They've tested *my* strength. So I'd rather not worry about you putting yourself in danger. You should avoid swimming until next spring."

"Worry?" she echoed as if she couldn't believe he'd chosen that word. "You don't have to worry about me."

Purposely misinterpreting that, he gestured for her to get up. "Great. Let's go."

No response.

"Maisey?"

She didn't answer him. She just stood and started peeling off her clothes, which gave him the feeling he'd all but dared her to do it.

"Come on," he said. "You don't have to prove anything to me. I'm not *trying* to stick my nose in where it doesn't belong. Can't you feel the wind? The change in the weather? The water won't be the same as it was the other night."

"You know I went swimming the other night?"

"I was going to hit the water myself, when I saw you."

Nothing.

"Think about it," he said. "Why get wet? You're already cold."

He thought he'd spoken rationally, but she didn't listen. As soon as she'd stripped down to her bra and a tiny pair of white bikini underwear, she marched to the shore.

Frustrated, he went after her. "You're not going in there."

"It's got nothing to do with you!" she retorted, obviously shocked that he'd try to interfere.

"You wanted to be friends, right? A friend wouldn't let you do this. Neither would a neighbor."

"Go to bed, Rafe. I'm not your concern." She sounded tired, far too tired to even be considering a dip. He got the impression she almost hoped she *would* drown—or at least didn't care much if she did—which was what really made him nervous.

"Sorry, but you're not swimming tonight," he said.

"Get out of my way!"

When she tried to circumvent him, he picked her up and heaved her over his shoulder.

"Put me down!" she screamed.

"Will you stay away from the ocean if I do?" He carried her up the beach without even bothering to bring his sweatshirt or the other clothes she'd removed. He figured they could get that stuff in the morning.

"I'll do what I want!"

"Then I'm not letting you go."

"This is ridiculous." She began to fight him in earnest—to the point that he was afraid he might drop her. So he set her down but used the weight of his body to pin her against one of the pilings for the first bungalow.

"Maisey, listen to me," he said. "What you're doing isn't fair. I don't want to lie awake fearing that I'll find your body washed up on shore come morning. The fact that you insisted on going in the water over my objections won't be any consolation to me or anyone else. And I sure as hell don't feel you should make me stand out here so I can watch over you. You're my neighbor, not my daughter."

She still fought to free herself. When she couldn't manage it, she stopped resisting and glared up at him. But he didn't get the tongue-lashing he expected. Tears filled her eyes and began rolling down her cheeks.

"Whoa, it's okay," he murmured, easing the pressure. "Why don't you tell me what's wrong instead of doing something reckless?"

He could sense that she was horrified by her own display of emotion. She was fighting those tears for all she was worth. Keeping herself rigid, she clenched her jaw. But the harder she tried to regain control, the more overwhelmed she became. It was like seeing a trickle of water break through a dam before the entire thing burst. A second later, she was sobbing and shivering and holding him tightly, as if he was all she had to cling to.

"Hey." He shifted so she could fit more comfortably against him. "Whatever's going on, it can't be that bad. Why don't you tell me about it? I'll help if I can."

He wasn't sure why he'd made that offer. If this had to do with her ex-husband or her divorce or even her family, there was probably nothing he could do. But he *wanted* to protect her.

Determined to carry her own burden, she didn't open up, didn't tell him a thing. She just laid her face on his chest. At least, that was how it started. A second later, she was sucking and nipping at his neck, and the memory of what it had been like to bury himself inside her immediately made him hard.

He unfastened her bra. As his hands came around and cupped the soft flesh of her breasts,

Rafe told himself he was a fool. Maisey was running from whatever she felt, trying to combat negative emotions with physical pleasure. It wasn't *him* she wanted.

The truth was so obvious that, after grappling with his own desire for several seconds, he moved his hands up to her shoulders. "Maisey, stop."

He pressed her against the piling again and lifted her chin, hoping he could finally get her to talk to him. But she rose up on her toes to reach his mouth, to kiss him with one of those hot, wet kisses that had nearly driven him out of his mind the last time, and he let her do it.

Their tongues met, and fresh intensity gripped them both. She was squirming against him, making it plain that she wanted to be even closer.

He considered getting rid of her panties. They were the only scrap of fabric still on her body. He wanted to take her right here, on the beach with that moonlight bouncing off the sea. He knew where this was leading, just as he knew he wouldn't have the strength to refuse that impulse if he let her kiss him much longer.

"No!" he said against her lips, and this time he forced himself to put some conviction behind it when he pulled away.

Unrepentant, she narrowed her eyes. She seemed to be asking him why he'd reject something he'd so obviously enjoyed before, especially when she was making it free and easy.

But it wasn't free *or* easy. Given how complicated she was, he doubted she'd even speak to him after.

Still, he wanted to rise to the challenge in those stormy eyes, to pretend he'd be able to walk away afterward. But he knew it would be a mistake. He wasn't the reckless, take-what-you-can-get young man he'd once been. These days, he was a father, and he was looking for more than a quick lay.

They stood, their eyes locked, both of them breathing hard. Then she shoved at his chest, as if she intended to go around him. But he didn't trust her not to head right back to the ocean, just to show him that she could. So he threw her over his shoulder again and carried her to her bungalow, where he deposited her on the doorstep before returning to his own place.

If she went for a swim after that, he couldn't stop her, he told himself. Because if he had any more contact with her, he'd rip off what little was left of her clothes and give her exactly what she'd been asking him for.

15

Maisey sat in the middle of the cold floor, hugging herself and rocking back and forth in her underwear, too upset to get dressed or even go into her bedroom and crawl beneath the covers. The discomfort she was inflicting on herself somehow seemed . . . not deserved exactly, but appropriate to her sense of tragedy and loss.

She glanced at her phone, which was lying on the coffee table. Maybe she should call Jack. He knew her better than anyone, knew her family, too. Despite what had happened between them in recent years, he'd been her mainstay for almost a decade. He was the person who'd rescued her from Fairham the first time. Until Ellie's death, she'd been more or less happy with him.

But she didn't want talking to him to weaken her resolve. Reconciling to escape what she might have discovered about her family would not create a firm foundation for getting back together. Their marriage had fallen to shreds, and she wasn't any more capable of weaving it together now than when it had first started unraveling. The last thing she could endure was another painful breakup.

If she told Jack about those pictures, what good would it do, anyway?

I wouldn't put it past your mother to have buried a child and never said a word about it, he'd say. But even he probably wouldn't guess her deepest fear, what made her sick inside. He'd call her morbid for considering the possibility that . . . maybe . . . if the child was dead . . .

No! Surely her mother would not have murdered her own daughter. But . . . say she'd flown into a rage and started beating the girl in those photographs. Malcolm, their father, would never have allowed her to go that far, would he? He wouldn't have helped cover up the death of one of his children, either—even if it was an accidental death.

Or could she really trust that? There were instances when Malcolm *had* allowed Josephine to go too far with Keith, weren't there? She'd never forget Keith's cries and the screaming. Besides, the last time she'd seen her father, she was ten. What did she know about his life and the secrets he might have kept?

You must remember something . . .

Jack would say that, too. And right there was the worst of the problem. Since Maisey had begun asking herself if there was *any* possible way she could've had an older sister, several hazy images had emerged—images of the child she'd seen in those pictures standing in the yard, her blond hair shining in the sun. Or banging on the kitchen table in some kind of patty-cake game. Or trying to pick Maisey up . . .

That was the memory that upset Maisey the most because the more she thought about it, the more convinced she was that Keith hadn't always been the oldest in their family, despite the fact that her parents had never referred to another child. Which raised the ugly question: What had happened to their firstborn? And why didn't anyone acknowledge that there'd been *three* Lazarow children?

She had to be wrong, she told herself, regardless of what those pictures suggested and what she seemed to be remembering. It was fear that had caused her brain to conjure up those "memories." Keith was older than she was by two years. If there'd been someone else in the family, he would've mentioned it at some point. Wouldn't he?

That was who she'd call—and, damn him, he'd better pick up . . .

Brushing her hair out of her eyes, she got up and crossed to her phone.

Keith didn't answer. That came as a disappointment but no surprise. She left him another message.

"Listen, it's important that I talk to you. Please . . . Call me as soon as you can. Tonight, okay?"

Dropping her phone back on the table before

she could break down and call Jack next, she sank onto the couch. Who else could convince her that what she saw in those pictures wasn't what she feared?

Josephine was the obvious answer. But Maisey couldn't go to her. She wasn't sure she could believe what her mother might tell her. She didn't even want her to know she had these pictures. Not yet. Not until she had some idea of what they meant.

A parade of housekeepers marched through her mind. As a younger woman, Josephine had been even more demanding than she was now; she'd gone through quite a few household employees. Although no one had dared to call child services, some disagreed with the way she treated her children and left because of that. Some disagreed with the way she treated her employees and left because of *that*. And some tried to become the mother Josephine wasn't. Those were the ones who were fired even though they were good employees. They made Josephine feel diminished, and feeling diminished was one thing she'd *never* tolerate.

If their mother had had two daughters, some of those housekeepers would have known the eldest, or known about her. Would they speak up if Maisey contacted them? Where should she start? Was that child gone before her parents moved to Fairham? There'd been a few years when

Grandpa Coldiron was still alive, still living on the island, and Josephine had lived on the mainland. Like Keith, Maisey had been born in Charleston.

Had Josephine had another child in Charleston? One before Keith?

Her phone rang, causing Maisey to jump. She was almost afraid to pick it up in case it was Jack. She knew all the anger and doubt she felt toward her mother would come pouring out the second she heard his voice.

The number shown on call display had a local area code. It wasn't Keith's. But she'd left him a desperate message, so she thought—hoped—it was him. He could be using someone else's phone, perhaps Nancy's. It was even possible that he'd returned and hadn't let her know. At least he was getting back to her.

"Hello?"

No response.

"Keith?" She gripped her phone that much tighter.

"It's me. I've been worried about you. Are you okay?"

Rafe. "How—how'd you get my number?"

"Nancy from the flower shop gave it to me."

"You know Nancy?"

"She's in the phone book."

"She was still awake?"

"Said she was."

"I see. I—I'm fine. Thank you for checking on me. I'm sorry about how I behaved . . ."

"Don't apologize. I just wanted to tell you that I put your clothes on the porch."

"Okay. But . . . can I just say I'm not as crazy as I must seem? My life's out of control right now, that's all."

"I'm getting a hint of that. So . . . why don't you tell me what's going on?"

How could she tell anyone the dark suspicions that were creeping to the forefront of her brain? Or that she couldn't shake various memories of the terrible beatings her brother had received at the hands of her mother? Those beatings had taken on added significance the moment she realized the girl in those pictures must have been part of her immediate family.

She couldn't say any of that. What she feared was too vile. She'd been shaking inside since she'd pried the lid off that metal box.

And what if she raised the question in someone else's mind, and she was wrong? How could she do that to her own mother?

She squeezed her eyes shut. "It's . . . nothing."

"It's not nothing," he said, his voice a deep rumble. "It has to do with those pictures or you wouldn't have come over here, asking about them. Why have they upset you so much?"

Her heart started to pound. She could hear each thud in her ears. She could hear her own breathing, too. *Tell him. And let him tell you that what you're afraid of could never have occurred. Nightmares like that only happen to other people.*

Except she wasn't exempt from anything. Expecting him to convince her would be futile. He would have no way of really knowing. He didn't understand what her mother was truly like. Few people did. They saw the physical perfection of Josephine's face and figure, and the "I've got it all" front she put on and assumed it was real. Even most extended family members would be shocked to learn how Keith had been treated.

"They haven't. I—I was trying to figure out how my—" she swallowed, trying to get enough moisture in her mouth to say the only thing she could to suggest nothing had happened tonight "—my baby pictures ended up in that wall."

She covered her eyes with her free hand, hoping he hadn't looked through them *too* carefully . . .

"I've been thinking about that," he said. "Maybe your father left them in his truck and whatever contractor he was working with stole them to . . . who can say? Get back at him for something. It could be a matter of simple jealousy. Someone who had to work hard for a living resenting someone who didn't—that sort of thing."

She relaxed a little; Rafe didn't doubt that those

229

pictures were of her. "Yeah, that must be it. I—I can't come up with a better explanation."

"So . . . you're okay?"

"Yes, of course." It was kind of him to call, to offer her some solace. After the way she'd treated him, it would've been perfectly understandable if he'd left her to deal with her own problems. She'd been so inconsistent.

She thought of how gently he'd touched her breasts, her face, other places, when they were naked together. That experience had been nothing like the encounter she'd had with him eighteen years ago.

She wasn't interested in sex now that she'd calmed down. She just wished she could curl up beside him, if only to feel someone close, someone as self-assured as Rafe. She wanted to listen to him breathe.

That was a strange thought, considering that she still had feelings for Jack. But there it was. Yes, she was sexually aroused by her neighbor. She was also drawn to Rafe's strength—and the deep affection he felt for his little girl. He treated Laney like Maisey's father had treated her. That kind of love seemed to be the only safe haven life had to offer. No wonder she was attracted to it.

"I didn't mean to strong-arm you at the beach," he said. "But swimming alone at night—it's dangerous. You understand, right?"

Her phone beeped, signaling another call. She was surprised to see that it was Keith, calling from his usual number.

"I understand," she said quickly. "I'll let you get some sleep now."

There was a slight pause. Then he said goodnight and she switched over.

"Maisey, what's up?" Keith asked. "Are you hurt? Your message sounded distraught."

So many responses went through her mind. If he could call her so easily now, why hadn't he done it before, to assure her of his safety at least? And how dare he strand her without furniture or a vehicle or anything else? She understood that he wasn't quite stable. But she wasn't in a great position herself. Couldn't he think of someone else, for a change?

No. He couldn't. Whether she had nature or nurture to blame, he'd never been as well-equipped to deal with life as she had. Trying to hold him to the same standards would only disappoint her and make him feel even less capable, driving a wedge between them.

She'd made this decision before, and she made it again now. She had to forgive Keith and work with whatever he was able to put into their relationship. "I'm . . . okay, I think. How are you?"

"I could be better. But then, that's usually the case."

She'd always felt a little guilty for being

happier than he was. She'd never fully grasped the kind of depression her brother faced—not until Ellie died and her marriage crumbled. *Then* she'd understood how hard life could be. "Where are you?"

"In Charleston."

That close? It made sense, since he probably didn't have the money for a plane ticket. She was glad he hadn't gotten *that* much out of Nancy. "At a motel or . . ."

"Staying with a friend."

Was that true? Most of the friends he'd had growing up had gotten married. Those who lived in or near Charleston led productive lives. They wouldn't want to hang out with a guy who was using, wouldn't want to become enablers by allowing him to stay with them for indefinite periods of time. Keith had complained about them turning their backs on him in the past.

Briefly, she wondered if Nancy was paying for his room. Maybe he was even on Fairham, living at Nancy's.

Maisey wanted to press him for the truth, find out if what he'd told her *was* the truth. She didn't think it was fair of him to take advantage of Nancy's infatuation. But Maisey knew bringing up that subject would only make him angry and probably wouldn't change his behavior, anyway.

"Are you planning on coming back anytime soon?" she asked.

"To Coldiron House? Not if I can avoid it."

"Are you still . . . clean?" She knew better than to ask that, too, but it just slipped out.

"This is why I haven't called," he snapped. "I don't want to hear about all the ways I'm letting you down."

So he *was* using. She was tempted to point out that he was letting himself down more than anyone else. But that argument had proven futile in the past. He didn't seem to care what he did to himself.

Afraid the conversation would end in a fight, or that he'd simply hang up, she dropped it. "Keith, did we grow up with . . . someone else?"

"What are you talking about?"

The irritation she'd heard in his voice was gone; she'd captured his attention. "An older sister, maybe?"

There was a long silence.

"Keith? I realize it's an odd question. We couldn't have lost a sibling without knowing it, but . . ."

"This is about the blonde girl with the dimples."

Maisey's stomach plummeted to her knees. "Yes! She was with us in the beginning, wasn't she?"

"God, how can *you* remember her? You were so young! I wasn't even sure *my* memories are right."

Knocking the lid on that metal box, she withdrew the picture that had convinced her this girl could not be her. Keith was there as the smaller and younger of the two. "I'm not sure, to be honest. I seem to recall . . . brief glimpses of *someone*—a sister—if I can trust my own mind." She wasn't ready to tell him about the pictures; she wanted to see what he remembered first.

When he cursed, the panic she'd been feeling rose in her throat like bile. "Why are you bringing this up now, Maisey?" he asked.

He sounded impatient, as if he didn't want to deal with the subject—didn't even want to be reminded of it.

"Because I know she existed."

There was another protracted silence. Then he said, "How?"

"I have pictures." She hated to think what offering him actual proof might do. Her brother didn't need another stumbling block. She'd come here to help him, protect him, encourage him. She doubted that drawing him into her confusion and fears would fall in line with those goals. But maybe whatever had happened to the girl in those photos was part of the reason her brother couldn't function normally in life. Maybe validating his thoughts, feelings and memories would give him a chance to work through the past and provide him with some peace of mind. Besides, only Keith could confirm or alleviate Maisey's fears.

"Where'd you get pictures?"

When she explained, he said nothing.

"You still there?" she asked.

She heard him take a deep breath. "Yeah, I'm here."

"After seeing these photographs, it's like . . . I remember her," she added.

"I remember her, too," he admitted.

Maisey felt her mouth drop open. "Why haven't you ever said anything before?"

"My memories aren't clear, and you're younger than me. I thought maybe I was crazy, imagining things. Or that it was a cousin or a friend."

"You could've at least *asked*."

"Why? Something about the possibility made me uneasy. Things were hard enough. I didn't want to examine it too closely. Besides, you've always been happy. I didn't want to mess you up if it turned out I was right. I just kept telling myself those memories couldn't be real. I still want to believe that."

So did she. But they *had* to be real if she and Keith shared them, didn't they? "Where'd she go, Keith?"

"Who knows?"

"Who knows?" Maisey repeated. *"Someone* must know. Children don't just . . . disappear!"

"She did," he said. "She was with us one day and gone the next, and I never heard Mom or Dad speak of her after that. No one else, either."

"Have you ever *asked* Mom about her?"

"I tried. Once. I told her I remembered playing with someone."

"And how'd she respond?"

"She beat me for even mentioning it. Then she said I had no idea what I was talking about and that I just wanted to start trouble. I never dared to bring it up again."

Maisey picked up the photograph that featured Josephine holding the hand of this mystery child. Their mother wouldn't be able to deny the girl's existence if Maisey presented proof. But if this was something their mother had reason to hide, Josephine could go to great lengths to do so, which would only make it harder to reach the truth.

The truth . . . Did Maisey even want to go after it? Was she prepared to handle what she might find? "Do you remember which housekeeper we had at the time?" she asked Keith.

"No," he replied. "And once more . . ."

When he stopped talking, she dropped the pictures she'd been holding into the box and got up to pace. "Are you going to finish that statement?"

"Once more, I think it would be better, for everyone concerned, if you . . . if you forgot about whoever she was."

A blast of anger shot through Maisey. "You're most likely talking about our sister—one of us! Don't you think we owe her a little more than to ignore she ever existed?"

"My life is screwed up enough as it is," he said.

"At least you've had a life for thirty-some years. That may be more than she got."

"If she's gone, nothing we do is going to bring her back, Maisey."

Had he really just said that? "You're assuming she's dead, then."

There was no response. He'd already disconnected.

16

The next morning, Saturday, wasn't a good one for Maisey. After spending so many hours worrying about the pictures Rafe had brought her, she'd gotten very little sleep. And Josephine stopped by Love's in Bloom shortly after they opened. Maisey wasn't prepared to withstand her mother's critical eye, so she watched with a touch of anxiety as Josephine moved briskly through the shop, checking this, telling Nancy to order that, frowning when she found the slightest detail not to her liking.

Nancy followed her, smoothing a shirt and slacks that were as tight as all her other clothes. Given the criticism she was hearing at every turn, she had to be feeling inadequate, even though she was doing a superb job of running the business.

Maisey smiled as Nancy approached—to let her

know not to worry too much—but she couldn't actually say that. Her mother was right behind Nancy and looked up a second later.

Maisey directed her smile at Josephine next, and received a curt nod but no greeting.

"I'll clean the glass out front again," Nancy told Josephine, "and make sure we don't stack the arrangements too close together."

"That front area should be an arrangement in itself," Josephine said, continuing her lecture. "Those display cases are important. They give us the opportunity to instill confidence in anyone who walks through the door, to assure them they've come to the right place if they want flowers."

"That is *such* a good point," Nancy murmured. "I can see it now."

Josephine paused next to Maisey and plucked out all the silver brunia she'd added to the wedding bouquet she was building. "Get rid of those. They look tacky," she said with a grimace. "Simple is always more elegant, and elegant is the name of the game for a wedding. How many times do I have to tell you that?"

Maisey wished she could launch an argument for keeping the silver brunia, but she could see the improvement almost immediately. No one had an eye for beauty quite like her mother.

Josephine moved on. Not until she was satisfied that she'd discovered and discussed every imperfection did she return to Maisey's work-table. "Are you settling in okay?"

Her mother's rejection of the silver brunia, and her irritation over it, had stung. Maisey was out of practice; she could've used a few words of encouragement. But her mother had always set her expectations high.

Maisey wondered if she'd *ever* be able to reach them. "I am."

"Any word from Keith?"

Maisey kept her eyes on what she was doing. "No, I haven't heard from him. You?" She wasn't sure why she lied—partly to stay out of their power struggle and partly because of the loyalty she felt toward her brother, she supposed. In order to survive their childhood, they'd had to stick together.

Josephine frowned. "He won't contact me, not until he's destitute. But you know I'll hear from him then."

The longer Nancy helped him, the longer he could go on . . .

"Are you coming to dinner tonight?" Her mother's expression lightened as she changed the subject.

"I wasn't aware I'd been invited."

When Josephine focused, once again, on Maisey's bouquet, Maisey was tempted to hide it. But this time Josephine merely gathered up the cast-off leaves and stems. "Pippa will be in touch," she said as she dropped the rubbish into the trash can nearby. "She probably doesn't want to call you first thing in the morning. But she's making pasta, and it's always spectacular. I wouldn't miss it, if I were you."

Telling her what she'd be missing if she didn't accept the invitation was as close as her mother ever came to saying, "I'd like you to be there."

Maisey was already exhausted. But they were nearly caught up on their orders, so she was only planning to stay until two. That meant she should have time to take a nap before dinner, if only she could get her mind to shut down instead of circling repeatedly back to those damn pictures. Even while she worked, she'd been arguing with herself. She kept insisting that she must be mistaken in thinking she'd had a sister. Or, if a sister had once existed, there must be a logical reason for that sister to be gone. A terrible accident had taken her life. Something like that. And her parents had been too heartbroken to ever speak of it.

Maisey knew how that felt, didn't she?

But her mother was too practical for that sort of emotion. And it wasn't just that her parents had never mentioned a sibling. *No one* had. Not a servant or an aunt or a cousin. Surely their father would've eventually said something, no matter how sad he was. Maisey didn't plan on pretending Ellie had never existed. In her mind, that dishonored the memory of the little girl she'd cherished.

"Well?" her mother prodded.

Maisey managed a smile. "What time?"

"Six. I don't like to eat too late."

"Can I bring anything?"

Josephine seemed surprised. "Like *what?*"

"It's the polite thing to ask when someone invites you to dinner, Mother," she said. "I could get the wine or bring dessert, so Pippa won't have quite as much work."

"Pippa's well-paid to do her work. Besides, polite or not, since when have *you* ever brought anything to my house?"

Maisey bit her tongue. She'd been twenty-four and just out of college when she left the island. Had her mother expected her to bring something to dinner back then? Not only had she been young, they'd been so at odds they could hardly have a civil conversation.

Maisey was aiming for a fresh start, hoping that if she treated her mother with more respect, she'd get a little respect in return. But Josephine had to get that jab in. "Never mind," she said. "Sounds like you have everything you need."

Her mother didn't seem to care that Maisey had withdrawn her offer. "Pippa will make sure of it." She opened her umbrella, since it was beginning to drizzle outside. "Remember, don't be late."

If she *was* late, her mother would start without her, then give her the silent treatment. Josephine punished anyone who didn't put her wishes and plans above their own.

Maisey shook her head as Josephine hurried off.

Nancy came up behind her. "Your mother's an interesting person, isn't she?"

Maisey gave her a rueful smile. "Yes, I'd have to say she is."

"She means well."

Maisey was trying to believe that after a decade of believing otherwise. Josephine did have many impressive qualities. Not only was she beautiful, she was smart, strong-willed and extremely self-disciplined. And, in most instances, she'd been justified in meting out *some* kind of punishment when she'd spanked Keith. Keith had given her parents *so* much trouble, trouble he could easily have avoided. Having witnessed what had happened on both sides, Maisey could sympathize —to some extent—with all parties, except that Josephine never expressed any regret when she hurt him too badly, never showed any doubt that such a harsh spanking had been just the thing for such a wayward, headstrong boy.

"I'm sure she does," Maisey said.

"She helps a lot of people."

Her mother did contribute quite a bit to charity. "She has her moments."

"She offered to pay for me to join Weight Watchers."

Nancy's take on that was so generous—to assume Josephine cared about her health and well-being when she made that offer—that Maisey liked Nancy even more. "Did you take her up on it?"

"No. I was afraid it would cause a problem between us. She's so . . . particular. I didn't want her judging everything I put in my mouth, thinking if I went off track that I was wasting her money."

"Sounds like a wise decision."

Nancy toyed with the ribbon on the counter. "Your brother has some serious issues with her, but I keep telling him that she loves him, in her own way."

If Nancy was looking for confirmation, Maisey wasn't the one to ask. She believed Keith and Josephine loved each other, on some level, but she thought the opposite was also true. "Speaking of my brother . . . I heard from him last night."

Nancy averted her gaze. "That's a relief. He's okay, then?"

Maisey placed the last lady's mantle spray in her arrangement and turned so she could give Nancy her full attention. "You know he's okay. Don't you?"

Her mouth opened and closed as if she was searching for an answer. Then her shoulders drooped, and she sent Maisey a sheepish look. "Yes, yes, I do."

"Is he staying with you?"

She seemed reluctant to answer this question, too, but finally she nodded. "I'm sorry." She sounded genuinely distraught. "I would've told you, but he . . . he asked me not to. And it's not like he's been with me the whole time," she added. "He wasn't on the island for the first few nights."

"You really did give him money so he could get a room?"

"Not a lot. Only enough to . . . to go somewhere and calm down."

Nancy had no idea how long "helping Keith" could stretch on. He always had a great excuse when he needed to borrow money, and he could be very convincing with all his promises to get clean and pay it back. When he was in a good mood, he had so much charisma that it was only after frequent bad behavior on his part that his friends cut him off or started to avoid him.

But Maisey didn't want to undermine Nancy's belief in him. Maybe Keith cared more about Nancy than Maisey had cynically assumed. Maybe, for her, he really would change.

"Nancy, you are *such* a nice person. Please . . . be careful to . . . to look out for yourself."

That was about all Maisey could allow herself to say. Fortunately, Nancy seemed to understand that the sentiment behind those words went a bit deeper.

"*No* is a hard word when you're in love with someone, isn't it?" she murmured.

Maisey slipped her arm around the other woman's shoulders. "He needs to overcome his addiction before he gets serious with anyone."

With a nod, Nancy went into the office.

From then on, except for when they had a customer, they worked in silence. At two, when she was ready to go home, Maisey felt as though they were finally on top of the business that had come in but she was even more exhausted than she'd expected to be.

And it was still raining.

The air was brisk as she scootered home. Soon it would be downright cold and the roads would be slick. Driving a scooter didn't seem so practical with winter coming on, but Maisey wasn't about to spend what funds she had left on a car. She figured she'd bundle up, if she had to, get by somehow.

By the time she reached her bungalow, she was so chilled she could hardly feel her hands.

Waterproof gloves would be one of her first purchases, she decided.

"Maisey? Is it you?"

The sound of that small voice had Maisey searching the shadows. A moment later, she saw Rafe's daughter. She was under Maisey's bungalow in a harness tied to one of the pilings, and she had two little chairs, a small table and a pile of toys beside her. It looked strange to see a child of five restrained like this, but Maisey knew Rafe had to make sure his daughter didn't hurt herself. What else was he going to do when he couldn't watch her every minute?

But why was she *here?* Where was *he?*

She was about to ask when Rafe strode to the front of her porch and peered down. Because of the overhang, she hadn't noticed him there when she pulled in.

"You're soaked," he said.

"I never thought the drive from town could seem so long." She shielded her eyes from the drops that were still falling. "What's going on here?"

He gestured toward her house. "Laney and I thought you might like to have your shutters fixed."

"Are they done, Daddy?" Laney asked.

"Not quite, bug. We just got here, remember? It takes a bit longer than that. But I'm working on it."

Maisey slipped the strap of her purse over her head. She had to wear it across her body while riding the scooter. "You don't have to spend your Saturday working on my account."

"We haven't been working," Laney said. "We went running on the beach. And then we played on the sand. And then we had lunch. And then we cleaned our house. And then Daddy said it would be nice if we fixed your place up so you'd be surprised when you got home. *Are* you surprised?"

Her excitement was endearing. "Most definitely," Maisey admitted, starting toward her. "I feel guilty for taking up your father's time, though, especially if it leaves you stuck under my house."

"I like playing here."

Rafe probably thought it was a good place, too. She was safe, out of the rain, she had space to do what she wanted with her toys and she wasn't underfoot.

"I'm going to be fixing this place up, anyway," Rafe called down. "Might as well do it sooner rather than later so you can enjoy it."

It was difficult not to think of how she'd broken down in front of him last night. Was he feeling sorry for her? Was this a result of her tears?

She couldn't forget how she'd behaved afterward, and how firmly he'd pushed her away. She'd been stupid to go over to his place when she was so upset. "That's nice of you, considering . . ."

He leaned on the railing as he gazed down at her. "Considering?"

She glanced at Laney. "Considering it's an imposition," she finished instead of mentioning her erratic behavior.

"What are neighbors for?" he said.

Maisey wiped the rain from her face. "Can Laney come in with me?" No way could she leave the child tied to the pilings under her house now that she was home. Since this was hurricane country, the houses were built high and people used that space almost like a second porch—or at least a storage area—and Rafe had set her up comfortably. But there was no longer any need to keep her restrained.

"If you don't mind, I'm sure she'd love that," he said.

"Are you coming for me, Maisey?" Laney called. "Did you say I get to go inside with you?"

"Yes, I'm coming for you." She spoke loudly so Laney could place her by her voice.

As soon as Maisey unhooked the harness, Laney lifted her arms so Maisey would pick her up. Maisey was glad to do that, but the child was so big it wasn't easy. Maisey didn't have the strength Laney's father did. It also took her by surprise when Laney gave her a big hug, as if they'd known each other forever.

At first, Maisey resisted hugging her back. It might not have been a rational impulse, but this wasn't *her* child. It felt . . . disloyal somehow, like accepting a replacement.

But having such a sweet girl cling to her was too inviting. After a few seconds, Maisey closed her eyes and pressed her cheek against Laney's.

Rafe couldn't see them; he was on the porch, above them. Why shouldn't she soak up this drop of innocent love?

"Thank you," she murmured to Laney. "This is a very nice welcome."

"Should we practice braiding?" Laney's small hands cupped Maisey's face. "Or wait! I could play my recorder for you!"

"Your recorder?" She pointed to the ground. "It's right there."

Maisey put her down and somehow Laney found it without too much searching. Obviously, she'd learned to remember where she put things. Someone with a visual handicap would have to do that, she supposed, in order to function in a completely dark world.

"Here it is." She held up a plastic flutelike instrument.

They left the rest of her toys with her little table and chairs and Maisey led her up the steps. Rafe was hanging the new shutters, but he paused to glance over at them. "You sure it's okay for her to come in?" he asked.

Laney's hug—how solid and fulfilling it had been—was still vivid in Maisey's mind. "Of course," she said. "She's going to play her recorder for me."

"She loves that thing."

Maisey liked the way his tool belt hung low on his narrow hips. She also liked his faded jeans and how his T-shirt stretched across his chest.

She realized she was just standing there, smiling at him, when he gave her a hesitant smile in return. "What?"

She shook her head. "Nothing. I skipped lunch today so I'm about to grab a bite now. You hungry?"

"Just ate. So did Laney."

"*I'm* hungry!" Laney said.

"Laney-bug, I fed you less than an hour ago."

"But I still have room for ice cream," she argued.

Maisey laughed. "Fortunately, I happen to have some."

Rafe scowled at his daughter. Laney couldn't see that, of course, but Maisey was willing to bet she could hear it in his voice. "You're not supposed to hint for treats, remember?"

Her bottom lip jutted out. "She *asked* if we wanted to eat."

"Nice try," he said. "You know she didn't mean ice cream."

"Don't *you* have room for dessert?" Maisey asked.

He moved some of the extra shutters he'd carried up so she and Laney could get to the door. "I guess I always have room for ice cream," he said and when he looked up, Maisey saw a boyish smile curving his lips.

"I'll bring it out in a few minutes."

Maisey made a sandwich while she listened to Laney play her recorder. She was surprised that she could actually recognize some of the tunes— "Mary Had a Little Lamb," "Hot Cross Buns," "Jingle Bells." "You're good!" she told Rafe's daughter. "Who bought that for you?"

"My dad found it on the computer for me."

When Maisey had finished her sandwich, she dished up some chocolate ice cream for Rafe and Laney.

"Aren't *you* going to have any?" Laney asked.

Astonished that Laney had been able to tell, Maisey hesitated. "How'd you know I'm not?"

"I heard you put out two bowls. Not three."

Maisey hadn't been conscious of making enough noise to provide that information. "I have to go to my mother's for dinner this evening. If I have dessert, too, I won't be hungry."

"Oh."

After guiding Laney to the table, Maisey put a spoon in her hand and showed her where the bowl was. "You won't move until I get back, will you?"

Laney was already digging into her ice cream. "Hmm?"

Most children would've looked up to answer a question posed directly to them, but Rafe's daughter didn't. Laney couldn't see Maisey's expression, so Maisey understood why that kind of reflexive movement would be superfluous to a blind child. But it made her believe Laney had been blind since birth. Otherwise, she figured that reflex would still cause her to look up. "Will you stay put until I get back?"

"I don't know my way around your house," she said, as if staying put would therefore be a given.

"Right." Maisey carried Rafe's bowl out to him. "Ready for a break?"

"In a sec." He was up on a ladder he must've gotten from his truck because it hadn't been on her porch when she'd first returned. His hair was wet and so was his T-shirt—more proof he'd been out from under the porch roof since she'd gone inside.

As she waited for him to finish inserting a screw before he came down, Maisey peered out at the rain. She liked the soft patter hitting her roof, liked how it dripped off the eaves and made the leaves so shiny and green. Rain in New York City was a completely different experience, with masses of people carrying umbrellas and staring down at the wet sidewalk as they hurried along.

She wasn't looking forward to driving back to town on her scooter, however. She hoped the rain would stop by the time she had to go.

"Thanks," Rafe said when he eventually descended and took his bowl.

"Why don't you come inside so you can sit down?" she asked.

"Sounds good." He held the door and indicated that she should go in ahead of him.

"It's yummy, isn't it, Daddy?" Laney had recognized his step when he entered the house.

"I haven't tasted it yet," he said. "But I have no doubt it will be."

Laney dropped her spoon in her bowl. Her mouth was smeared with chocolate. She attempted to lick her lips, but missed most of it. "Do you want me to help you eat yours?"

He laughed. "I think you've had enough for one day. And I'm sure I can handle this all on my own."

"You're supposed to share," she said.

He chuckled. "Maisey did share, and you're done with yours."

When Laney started to get down from her chair, he stopped her. "Let me wipe your face before you go anywhere."

"I've got it," Maisey said. "Relax and enjoy your ice cream."

Laney waited patiently while Maisey retrieved a washcloth and cleaned her up. "Want me to play my recorder again?"

"I think the noise might be getting on Maisey's nerves," Rafe said, and winked at Maisey as if *he* was the one who didn't want the racket.

Maisey shot him a wicked grin. "I'd *love* for you to do that. And when your daddy's finished, we'll follow him outside so he can hear you better."

"I've already spent two hours being serenaded, thanks." He gave Maisey a comically disgruntled look and, for no apparent reason, she remembered the intensity on his face when he'd pinned her against the counter and kissed her that first time.

Suddenly self-conscious, she went to the sink to rinse off her plate. "I guess your daddy's right. It's time for a break from the recorder," she told Laney. "But if you want, we could go lie on my bed, and I'll read you the next Molly Brimble book."

"There's *more?*" Laney asked.

Gratified by the excitement in her voice, Maisey turned off the water. "Several. I have two of them here. I can get the rest from my mother's house when I go over for dinner tonight." She frowned at the sight beyond her window. "If it ever stops raining. It probably won't be smart to bring them back if it doesn't. They'll just get wet."

Laney clapped her hands. "Oh, I hope it stops. I *love* Molly Brimble. I want to hear them all."

Finished with his ice cream, Rafe came over to rinse out his bowl and brought Laney's, too. Maisey could feel the heat of his body as he stood next to her. She told herself she'd only noticed such a minute detail because she was still wearing the damp clothes she'd had on when she got home.

But being cold had nothing to do with admiring

the way his jeans fit him as he walked across the room.

"You ready?" Laney asked, reaching Maisey without any help.

"I'm ready." She led Rafe's daughter into the bedroom. There, she changed into a pair of dry sweats and they read the Molly Brimble books she had—twice. No doubt Laney would've asked her to read them a third time, since she couldn't seem to get enough, but she fell asleep midway through *Molly Brimble's Spidery Adventure*.

Maisey set the books aside and pulled Laney close. She told herself she'd rest for a few minutes. It wasn't polite to fall asleep while Rafe was there, fixing her house. But she must've nodded off because the next thing she knew, Rafe was lifting his daughter out of her arms.

"You done for the day?" Maisey murmured.

"Yeah. Shutters are up. They look great."

"You can leave her here with me until she wakes up, if you want. I'll make sure she gets home safely."

"That's okay. If she sleeps too long, she won't want to go to bed tonight."

"I should walk you out . . ."

"No," he said when she started to get up. "You need the rest."

"I can't be late for dinner," she mumbled.

"What time do you need to be there?"

Maisey was *so* tired. She tried to drag that

detail from her brain to her mouth, but she wasn't sure if she ever did. Laney roused and said something about Molly Brimble to her daddy. When he put her down, she didn't get back in bed. At least, Maisey didn't think so. Everything was a blur. She felt Rafe pull up the covers. Then she succumbed to the exhaustion that had been tugging at her for what seemed like forever.

17

The sound of her phone, ringing on the nightstand, broke into the quiet darkness. Maisey wanted to ignore it, to stay blissfully submerged beneath the chaotic thoughts of her conscious mind. But whoever wanted her to answer was persistent. The ringing would stop, only to start again.

Finally, she opened her eyes, saw how the day's light was waning and bolted up into a sitting position. Dinner with her mother! Had she missed it? Was Josephine or Pippa trying to call?

She grabbed her cell just as it rang again.

This call wasn't from either; it was Rafe.

"You still asleep?" he asked when she managed to answer.

"I was." She shook her hair out of her face. "What time is it?" She should've set the alarm on her phone.

"Five-thirty. You couldn't seem to come up with the time you needed to be at your mother's, so I decided I'd better wake you early."

She scrambled out of bed so fast she got tangled up in the blankets and nearly tripped. "I appreciate that."

"So you're okay?"

"It's at six. I won't have time to get cleaned up, which won't go unnoticed, but I can make it if I hurry."

"There's just one problem," he said.

She straightened. "Besides dressing and getting over there in half an hour? What's that?"

"It's still raining outside."

"Then I guess it won't matter that I don't have time to shower and change." At least she'd have a good excuse for her appearance.

"Go ahead and get ready," he said. "I'll drive you over."

Maisey covered a yawn. "You're going to give me a ride?"

"I have to go to town, anyway. Laney and I are out of milk."

"But . . . it won't take that long to pick up some milk. How will I get back? Or I could ask Pippa to drive me . . ."

"No need. My mother has a lengthy to-do list for me. I'll go over and cross a few things off while I wait. You can call me whenever you're ready."

Driving with Rafe would be faster, safer and far

more comfortable than freezing on her scooter. It wasn't as if she had any rain gear, other than the umbrella she'd brought from New York, which would be useless. But she could easily guess what conclusions her mother would draw if she found out that Rafe had been kind enough to provide her with transportation. She didn't want to spend the entire evening listening to Josephine point out the many reasons he wouldn't be right for her. Maisey knew she was in no shape for another relationship; she didn't need to hear what her mother had to say about Rafe's occupation and social status. That was just so offensive.

"I . . . I hate to put you out. You already spent your afternoon fixing up my house. You can't be thrilled about doing more repairs, even for your mother."

"They've got to get done. Might as well be tonight."

Time was ticking away, and she couldn't come up with a good excuse to decline his offer. "Thanks," she said. "I'll be ready in fifteen minutes."

"I'll be there."

As she took off her clothes and jumped in the shower, Maisey caught sight of herself in the mirror and couldn't help pausing to touch the single stretch mark she'd gotten when she was pregnant with Ellie. This was all that was left of her daughter, all she could touch . . .

Briefly, she wondered if Rafe had noticed it when he'd seen her. Only about four inches long, it wasn't too obvious since it was off to one side.

He hadn't said anything, so she assumed he hadn't.

Rafe's truck smelled like he did, but since Maisey associated that smell with their time in his bed, she tried not to notice.

Laney reached out to her from the child's seat in the back as soon as Maisey got in, and Maisey twisted around to squeeze her hands. "Looks like you're all buckled up," she said.

Delighted with the attention, Laney beamed, and Maisey smiled at how incongruous it seemed for Rafe to have a child's seat in his big work truck.

"You're smiling." Rafe sent her a curious glance as she put on her seat belt and he backed down her drive.

"I never could've pictured you as the man you are today," she said. "Not when we met eighteen years ago."

"You need to forget about eighteen years ago."

"Why? It's funny that you've been domesticated. Are you going to tell me how it happened?" She still knew next to nothing about Laney's mother.

He steered around a pothole. "What do you want to know?"

Conscious of the fact that Laney could hear them, Maisey chose her words carefully. "I'd like to hear how you came to be in this, uh, situation."

"Sure," he said. "I'll be happy to tell you about it—as soon as you tell me how you came to be in the situation *you* are."

"We went over that when you brought me the . . . box from Unit 1. What's left to tell?"

"What box?" Laney asked.

"Just an old box I found," Rafe replied before speaking to Maisey again. "I know you're divorced, and I know about . . . the reason. But I don't know how you met him."

"After I graduated from college, I came home for the summer to run my mother's flower shop, where I'd worked quite a bit over the years. As spoiled as you seem to think I was, my mother's always been determined to teach Keith and me about the value of work. I started at the shop the summer before ninth grade and worked there until I left for college."

It was beginning to rain harder, which made her even more grateful for the ride.

He adjusted his windshield wipers as he turned onto the paved road. "So that's where you met? Did he come in to buy flowers for someone else? Was he already engaged or married at the time?"

"Ouch! No, of course not," she said, but being able to laugh at her situation helped. She could hardly get mad at him for being insensitive. A cheating husband was almost a cliché. "I told you there were . . . extenuating circumstances. Regarding what he did to cause the divorce . . ."

"I didn't realize there were any extenuating circumstances a woman would accept for that kind of behavior, unless—don't tell me *you* were seeing someone else first."

"I was never unfaithful! It's . . . a long story."

Rafe shrugged. "Yeah, well, so's mine."

"And you're not going to tell me."

"As soon as you're finished, I will."

She rolled her eyes in exasperation. "Fine. So, back to when we met. He'd just graduated from the University of South Carolina but wasn't quite sure where he wanted to live and start his career. So he came here to stay with his grandparents for a few months while he made those decisions."

"Who are his grandparents?"

"The Hendersons."

"Never heard of them."

"They didn't stay long. They'd only lived in Keys Crossing for a year when he came out to visit, and right after we got married, they went back to Philadelphia to help his aunt, who'd been diagnosed with a brain tumor. That's where he was raised."

"Did she make it? The aunt?"

"She was alive when we got divorced. I have no idea what's happened to her since. I haven't stayed in contact with his family. I cared about his parents a great deal, but . . . they reacted strangely to the divorce, as if I was more to blame than their beloved son. It became awkward." Fortunately Laney hadn't been able to understand enough of the conversation to even try to keep up. She was humming to herself, seemingly oblivious to what they were saying.

"What'd he do for a living?"

"While he was here, he worked at the public beach as a lifeguard."

"A lifeguard? Somehow I can't imagine Josephine Lazarow approving of a man who's making barely more than minimum wage."

"She didn't approve of him. They hated each other."

"I see." Rafe adjusted his rearview mirror, and Maisey saw his eyes flick toward it every once in a while so he could check on his daughter. "And you resisted that for love? Impressive. Too bad it didn't work out—at least so far. We could've chalked one up for the common man."

"No one's perfect."

He seemed surprised by her comment. "Why'd you go to the public beach when you have a private one? The public beach is for the rest of us lowlifes."

"Don't say stuff like that," she said. "I actually met him at the grocery store. One of the bungalows was empty, which didn't happen all that often during peak rental season, so Keith and

I were going to have a barbecue there with our friends. Jack saw me deliberating over the different cuts of meat and offered his expertise."

"Right before he asked for your number."

"He asked, but I wouldn't give it to him."

Rafe slung one arm over the steering wheel and slowed to navigate a tight bend in the road. "Then how'd you start dating?"

"You won't believe this, but . . . he followed me home."

"To Coldiron House? He didn't turn back when he saw those big gates and realized who you were?"

"He didn't care. That's one of the things that drew me to him. Some of the other guys I'd dated were so . . . intimidated by my mother. But Jack . . . he was willing to stand up to her."

"You're saying that following you home actually worked? That makes Jack sound more like a stalker to me."

"It wasn't like that. He was romantic. Told me what I needed to hear."

"Which was . . ."

She couldn't hold back a wistful smile. "It wasn't five minutes after he pulled through the gate behind me that he said he'd never seen a more . . ."

"Beautiful woman," Rafe filled in when, embarrassed, she let her words fall off.

"Yeah."

"I can't believe that worked, either."

"You know how gorgeous my mother is. I've always lived in her shadow, and I wasn't a very pretty child. For most of my life, I thought I was ugly."

One eyebrow went up. *"Ugly?"*

She shifted in the seat. "You didn't think I was very hot when you first met me. Admit it."

"I don't remember that."

"Oh, come on!"

"You weren't as pretty as you are now," he admitted.

"At least you're honest," she said dryly.

"I'm not finished yet. Maybe you weren't a *stunning* beauty, but you weren't anywhere close to ugly, which makes it hard for me to think you'd fall for that line."

"Yeah, well, someone who's always been beautiful wouldn't understand."

"Beautiful?" he repeated.

"Don't pretend you don't know what I mean."

He ignored that. "So you gave him your number."

"I did, and he called me the next day." She chuckled as she remembered Jack's eagerness.

"To ask you out?"

"To tell me he was already in love with me. It was a bit . . . over the top, especially when I hear myself tell the story. But it was flattering, all the same."

When Rafe said nothing, Maisey assumed she was going into more detail than he cared to hear, so she summed it up. "Anyway, long story short, we got engaged by the end of summer."

"I don't remember anyone mentioning that you were getting married. A Lazarow wedding would be a big deal around here. Was it at Coldiron House?"

She shook her head. "My mother refused to pay for the wedding, or even attend it, so we eloped. We were so poor in those early years . . ." And yet those had been the happiest she'd ever known, before Jack had really grabbed hold of his career and let it consume the bulk of his time. Back then, she'd been the most important thing to him.

"I'm not entirely clear on why your mother didn't like him. Was it the bad start? That he was working as a lifeguard when you met and she decided he wasn't worthy of you?"

"She tried to blame it on that. I remember her coming into my room to have a talk with me. She sat on my bed and told me he'd never be able to keep me in the kind of comfort I was accustomed to. I swear, it sounded like something a soap opera villain would say."

"You weren't buying it."

"Not for a minute. Jack was smart, driven, ambitious. I was convinced even she could see that."

"What was the real story?"

"Honestly? I believe it was the fact that he didn't like her. He didn't approve of how she tries to control everyone and everything, and she could feel it. She's used to being revered and demands a certain . . . deference, if you will."

"He refused to pay her homage."

"Yes. And he can be as stubborn as she is."

"It doesn't sound like he made much of an effort to get along with your family. But . . . I wasn't there. It could be that leaving the island was the best thing for you."

"Trust me, I was more than eager to leave."

"So you married and moved to New York to make your fortunes."

She was glad when he turned up the heater. "Pretty much. I'd always wanted to write children's books. He had a degree in finance and planned to go into investment banking. Manhattan seemed like a perfect fit for both of us."

Rafe looked over at her. "Are you going to tell me what went wrong? I mean . . . before the extramarital stuff? You've alluded to . . . other challenges."

She stared out at the rain. "Things happened—some that were beyond our control. I'm sure he wasn't the only one to blame, even though he . . . did what he did."

"Is that why you're considering taking him back? Because you feel partly responsible, like you owe it to him or yourself to try again?"

"It's possible, I suppose." They'd reached Coldiron House. As he pulled up to the gate, she gave him the code that would allow him to get through. "I haven't decided what I'm going to do," she added.

"What happened to the other woman?" Rafe asked. "Did he leave her, too?"

"That's what he claims. He says he never really loved her. And now . . . you get off the hook once again."

"Off the hook?"

She indicated the house. "We're here and I have to go in, but you still haven't told me anything about yourself."

"There's always the ride home."

"I'm going to hold you to that."

He parked behind her mother's Mercedes. "I have to admit you seem sort of . . . philosophical about Jack."

She grabbed her purse, prepared to get out. "And what conclusions are you drawing from that?"

"It's easier to be philosophical once you get past something."

Did the change in the way she was looking at Jack and her divorce—the softening, the forgiving —really signify what Rafe was suggesting? She certainly hadn't been so emotionally detached in New York. "You don't think I'm still in love with him."

"No. But that doesn't mean you won't go back to him." He reached across her lap to unlatch the door. "Have fun at your mom's."

"You're leaving already?" Laney said, her voice filled with disappointment.

She'd been so quiet since the beginning of the drive that Maisey had almost forgotten she was there. "Yes. I'm having dinner with my mom, remember?"

"Can I come with you?" she asked.

"Laney, you're going to Grandma's with me." Rafe spoke quickly, before Maisey could respond.

Maisey hesitated. "You have a really good dad," she told Laney. "That makes you a lucky girl." She threw Rafe a parting glance. "Thanks for the ride."

"No problem. Call me when you're ready to go home."

During dinner, Maisey had gotten her mother's permission to sort through the boxes she'd sent to Coldiron House so she could bring home a few things she needed—like the Molly Brimble books she'd promised Laney. She also planned to search for any sign of another Lazarow sibling, which, of course, she hadn't mentioned. But that wasn't the reason it required all her nerve to enter the attic. She'd never liked it here, not since the day she'd gotten locked in as a child. She was only about six—close to Laney's age—when Keith lured her up there to play. They'd immediately gotten lost in their explorations. But then, just as they were really having fun, he'd hurried her back downstairs because he had to leave for baseball practice. He'd told her to stay out of the attic while he was gone, and if she hadn't been so excited about what they were finding—old clothes, including a wedding dress, and old toys—she probably would've listened.

Instead, she went back and continued to play with a trunk full of fancy clothes and costume jewelry until she heard a creak in the hall. Afraid she'd be caught and punished, she hid, which was why, to this day, she wasn't sure if it was her mother or someone else who'd come and locked the door. She sat there alone, shivering in the dark since the light switch was on the *outside* of the room. Surrounded by terrifying shapes and sounds, she was too scared to call out in case she got her brother in trouble. She had no doubt Keith would get most of the blame; he was older and generally the instigator. So she huddled there, trembling and crying for a very long time.

It was her father who finally came for her. Maisey still had no idea how he'd figured out where she was. He hadn't been calling for her. He'd simply opened the door and said her name —and she'd run to him.

"You need to stay out of here," he'd murmured

as he'd gathered her to him and carried her out.

Maisey had learned her lesson. But she remembered being surprised that it wasn't Keith who, once he got back from practice, had noticed that she was missing. Not until after her father brought her down to dinner had she understood. Her brother was in yet another state of emotional upheaval, having learned that his baseball coach wouldn't be putting him on the starting roster.

When her father had let her stay in his lap instead of making her take her own seat, her mother had stared daggers at them across the dining table. Josephine had always accused Malcolm of spoiling her. But the memory of that cold look gave Maisey chills, even now. Since then, she'd decided that Josephine had known where she was all along and had been trying to put the fear of God into her—if not by locking her in, then by warning her with that malevolent expression to stay out of where she didn't belong.

Propping something against the door so it couldn't swing shut on its own—and couldn't be shut without some noise to serve as warning—she tried to shake off that unsettling incident. The knowledge that someone, either a member of her own family or one of the household staff, had locked her in the attic on purpose wasn't something she'd ever forget. She glanced over every time she heard the slightest sound . . .

"Stop it," she mumbled as she turned her back

on the door. Not only did she have a good excuse to be in here, her mother had no idea she intended to do anything more than what she'd indicated.

Her eyes skimmed the covered furniture, old lamps, dusty heavy-framed pictures stacked along the wall and the bevy of boxes and old steamer trunks that crowded the confined space. If she and Keith had once had an older sister, there'd have to be some evidence of it. She figured she'd check with the state's vital records department. Maybe she could discover a birth or death certificate. According to the internet, which she'd checked on her phone, there were states that allowed access to *un*certified records—South Carolina being one—which would work for her purposes. She didn't need a certified record to learn what she wanted to know. She would, however, need a name and a birth date to get even that far, and she had neither.

Hopefully, she'd be able to find something here. The problem was figuring out where to look. The attic contained castoffs from three-quarters of a century, going clear back to when her young, widowed grandfather lost his wife to a congenital heart defect and immigrated to America. That made her task a daunting one, and she didn't have a lot of time. Her mother would probably wonder what she was doing if she spent the next three hours digging around. She didn't want to make Rafe wait too long, either.

She'd focus on her father's stuff first. The day after Malcolm's funeral, Josephine had said she couldn't remain in the house and jetted off to France to visit her aunt, where she stayed for a month. And when she returned? Except for the urn on the mantel, that single token, she'd demanded the household help get every reminder of her late husband out of her sight, as if he'd abandoned her on purpose and she was angry instead of sad.

Maisey remembered being baffled by her reaction. She'd been devastated by her father's death and yet her beautiful mother had simply picked up and moved on as if she'd never been married. Even after she returned from France, she'd left again almost immediately, this time to California for a shopping expedition on Rodeo Drive. And she'd brought home a lot more than clothes. That was when Maisey had met the first of her three stepfathers, although the last one had come into Josephine's life while Maisey was in New York, so she'd had little or no contact with him. She was glad of that. Vince, the first one, had been much younger than Josephine and was far more interested in money and cars than in being a parent. The second had tried to touch Maisey in an inappropriate way one night while he was drunk. She'd never dared to say anything about that incident, but her mother must've suspected because he was gone within three months and they never saw him again. The last one, a retired tennis pro, had been Josephine's "traveling companion." According to Keith, they'd gone everywhere together—Africa, New Zealand, Europe, Japan. Until her mother had kicked him out.

Considering the circumstances right after Malcolm's death, one of the servants could easily have shoved some small proof of a third Lazarow child into a box without realizing what it signified. Maybe a picture that had a name or a date written on the back, since none of the ones recovered by Rafe had that information. Josephine hadn't been paying attention when Malcolm's things were being stored; she'd been too busy ignoring the whole process.

It took Maisey several minutes to find her father's belongings, but she was relieved to discover that they were all organized in one corner. That seemed respectful. She figured it would also be helpful from a practical standpoint.

After pulling over an old piano bench that was stored in the attic, along with the baby grand that went with it, she opened the flaps of the first box.

The sight of her father's sweater, folded neatly on top, made Maisey's stomach tense. She wasn't sure she was in any condition for the emotional journey this search would require. Malcolm had been gone a long time, but somehow that loss tied into more recent losses. It was only the pictures of that mysterious sibling (if it was a sibling) that kept her going.

She sorted through what had been saved of her father's clothes, his model airplanes, which he'd loved to build, his flag for having served in the Vietnam War and the jewelry and trinkets he'd kept in a small leather box. She found no pictures —but she did come across a packet of letters, all addressed to her father at his office. She'd just noticed that they had no return address, but were all postmarked here on the island, when she heard her mother at the door.

"Are you finding everything?"

Maisey jerked her head up, probably a little too fast to look as innocent as she wanted. She tried to cover that with a smile. "Not yet. I thought I'd go through a few of Dad's things first. I miss him so much."

Her mother's eyes narrowed. "How did you even know where his stuff was?"

"I didn't. I—I stumbled across it." Not sure what else to say, she added, "Want to go through it with me?" She couldn't think of anything that would disarm her mother more quickly than thinking this was a sentimental project.

"God, no. Why would I want to do that? He loved you more than he did me, anyway," she said, and left.

Maisey let her breath go. She was convinced

that her mother believed her about the trip down memory lane. But Josephine was now on alert and would probably be listening for her until she came down. Maisey couldn't stay up here much longer.

She could take a closer look at what she'd found later.

She called Rafe to say she was ready to go home, then repackaged her father's possessions and went through her own storage to reclaim the books for Laney, along with some warmer clothing.

After hiding the letters at the bottom of the box she was taking with her, she hurried out of the attic.

Her mother was in the drawing room, watching television while petting her little Yorkie, who was far more indulged than they'd ever been.

"I'm taking off," Maisey said, stopping at the entrance to say goodbye.

The front door was only about ten feet away. She wished she was already through it when her mother gestured toward the window at the storm outside.

"The weather hasn't cleared. How are you getting home? Do you need Pippa to give you a ride?"

Lightning flashed as if to punctuate that question. "No, not tonight. Rafe's coming back to get me."

"*Rafe?*"

"Raphael." Her mother knew his nickname. Most recently, Maisey had used it when she explained how she'd arrived at Coldiron House. Almost as soon as she'd walked through the door, Josephine had commented on the fact that she wasn't wet, despite the rain, and she'd been forced to tell her she'd had a ride.

"You mean he's been waiting for you this whole time? When you told me he had to come to town, anyway, I assumed it was just to run some errand."

"He had to fix a few things for his mother."

"And now he's done?"

"I guess so. When I called him, he said he'd be right over."

"That's convenient," she said.

"He's a good neighbor," Maisey said. A much better neighbor than she'd been to him . . .

"Is that *all* he is?" Her mother's eyes narrowed. "You're not getting mixed up with him, are you?"

"Mixed up?" Maisey knew what Josephine meant. But she thought forcing her to be specific might show her how ridiculous she was being.

"He'd love to marry you. Then he'd own all of Smuggler's Cove."

"*I* don't own Smuggler's Cove. You do."

"You will one day. I'm sure he's aware of what you stand to inherit."

"He's not a treasure-hunter, Mother."

"You don't know that. Don't be fooled by his handsome face. I've been with plenty of men who are attractive. Trust me, they need to bring more to the table than that. Good looks alone don't make a marriage work."

Maisey didn't think her mother had the first clue about how to make a marriage work. Josephine had been through four husbands—not to mention the other men—and she probably wasn't finished yet. Only her marriage to Malcolm hadn't ended in divorce. Even then, Maisey was positive it would have, if Malcolm hadn't been determined to hang on for the sake of her and Keith. "Rafe's a nice guy, that's all. I'm impressed with the way he cares for his daughter."

"His *blind* daughter. *That* wouldn't be an easy job," her mother said.

Her emphasis on certain words told Maisey what she really meant. She wasn't sympathizing with Rafe or praising him. She was pointing out how difficult it would be to take on the responsibility of a special-needs child—if Maisey were to become his love interest. "I'm sure that's true," she said. "Fortunately, he seems to understand that there couldn't be anything better to devote his life to."

Recognizing the small rebellion in her reply, Josephine pursed her lips and shook her head. "You're bound and determined to learn the hard way, aren't you? When you could just as easily find someone who doesn't have children and who has plenty of money?"

"I don't need anyone else's money," Maisey said. "I'll make my own."

Her mother arched her eyebrows. "Working at the flower shop?"

She wanted to say, "You need me there as much as I need to be there," but she knew her mother would fire her simply to prove her wrong. So Maisey hefted the box higher, as if it was getting too heavy, and said, "I'll be on my feet again soon. Thanks for dinner."

18

His mother was planning to go to the farmers' market in the morning, so Laney had begged to stay over again. They had some elaborate plan to make dinner for Maisey. News of that had come as a surprise to Rafe, but he'd guessed instantly what his mother was up to. So he'd taken her aside and told her to stop with the matchmaking, that he knew Maisey wasn't interested.

His words hadn't done much to dent her enthusiasm, however. Somehow she'd been able to ascertain *his* interest, which was all she needed to get excited. She and Laney had continued to plan their special meal the whole time he was fixing the icemaker in her fridge. His mother whispered in his ear when she hugged him before he left that any woman would love him if she'd just give him a chance.

By the time he walked out, he had no doubt that it was going to be one awkward dinner . . .

He figured he'd talk to Maisey about it, make sure she understood it wasn't his idea. But he didn't know how to bring it up. She seemed so distracted when she climbed into his truck. After a rather subdued greeting, she slid a box between them, put on her seat belt and stared at Coldiron House until he'd turned around and she couldn't see it anymore. Even as he pulled out of the drive, she didn't speak. She seemed . . . pensive.

"How was it?" he asked.

She roused herself from whatever she was thinking about. "Same as always."

He took that to mean it wasn't great. "What's in the box? If it's leftovers, that was some meal."

He'd been hoping to get a smile out of her, but it didn't work. "Just a few things I might need. When I moved, I shipped most everything I didn't sell." Belatedly, she twisted around in her seat. "Where's Laney?"

"She's spending another night with her grandma." He thought he might as well move right into the issue of tomorrow's ambush. He wasn't likely to get a better opportunity. "I guess she and my mother are having you to dinner?"

"She and your mother? You won't be there?"

"It might be easier on both of us if I stayed away. My mother can be a little too blatant about trying to find me a wife," he said with an apologetic glance. "And I think she currently has her sights on you."

Even that didn't get much of a reaction. "I wondered if that was the reason she wanted me to come, but . . . I'd hate for you to miss it because of me. I can cancel . . ."

"No, don't do that," he broke in. "You're Laney's new favorite person. She'd be disappointed. I'll be fine on my own. There's a football game I'm going to watch."

"If it's on TV, you can watch it at your mother's. You should go. We can outmaneuver one little old lady."

He wasn't as optimistic. "You have no idea how obvious she can be."

"I do. Trust me, my mother can be obvious about certain things, too—mostly when she doesn't approve," she added drolly.

"Am I supposed to connect those two statements? Are you saying she wouldn't approve of me—because that's what you were thinking, right?"

She blushed. "She doesn't approve of anyone she hasn't recommended."

Maisey had dodged his question, but her body language had given her away so he let it go. He knew what Josephine was like. Maisey's mother didn't view him as an equal, so of course she wouldn't deem him good enough for her daughter, who would one day inherit half of what she owned. Josephine wouldn't want to see her empire fall into the hands of a simple contractor.

"Who would she recommend?" he asked.

"Someone who worshipped her instead of me."

The fact that they were alone provided Maisey with the perfect opportunity to drill him about how he'd become a single parent. She'd admitted she was curious. But she seemed to have forgotten the discussion they'd had before. She didn't speak the whole way home, not until he pulled into her drive. And then it was only to thank him for the ride.

He almost offered to carry that box in for her. Judging by how heavy it had looked when she brought it out of Coldiron House, it wouldn't be easy to haul up so many steps. But before he could open his mouth to suggest it, he saw Keith sitting on her porch.

She noticed her brother at virtually the same instant. "Look who's back," she muttered.

Maisey supported the box with one knee so she could wave as Rafe shifted into Reverse and backed down her drive.

"So you've been staying with Nancy?" she asked Keith when he came down to take the box and follow her up the stairs.

"Did you get that information from her?"

Apparently Nancy had been too afraid to let him know about their conversation at the flower shop. "I guessed," Maisey said to protect her. "Is she the one who brought you here?"

"I borrowed her car."

"I didn't see . . ."

"It's out on the street."

She unlocked the door. "Nancy's a nice person."

"No doubt about it," Keith said, but it was a throwaway statement and that bothered Maisey.

"*Too* nice."

"What do you mean?" He'd picked up on the censure in her tone—and responded with some belligerence.

She stepped out of the way so he could deposit the box on the floor. "She's in love with you. You understand that, don't you?"

He yawned and stretched as if he hadn't been getting enough sleep. "I care about her, too."

Care. That wasn't the same thing. Not by a long shot. "It wouldn't be right to break her heart," she said.

"Don't start on me. Nancy and I are friends. I've never promised her any more."

"That doesn't mean she won't hope for it."

He shrugged. "You can't stop someone from hoping."

Maisey scowled at him. "Come on, I work with her."

"Because I walked out and left you a job."

"What? Mom was going to give me one, anyway. You can't be mad about that. Nancy's the issue here. I don't want to see this end up where I think it's going."

"What happens between Nancy and me is none of your business," he growled.

Clenching her jaw, Maisey bit back the rest of what she'd been about to say. She didn't want to get into an argument with her brother. Maybe she *was* sticking her nose in where it didn't belong . . .

"You hungry?" she asked as she tossed her house key on the counter.

"No, Nancy and I had dinner earlier."

Yeah, and *she'd* probably done the cooking. Nancy would do anything to make him happy and comfortable. Maisey's irritation rose up again, but she stifled it. "Are you going to let Mom know you're back on Fairham?"

"When I'm ready."

When Nancy was tired of giving him money, in other words. Maisey didn't like how cynical she was becoming in regard to her brother, but she couldn't seem to avoid it. She found it much harder to feel the sympathy she'd felt for him when she was living in New York.

"Where'd you go with Raphael?" he asked. "Don't tell me you're dating him. Mom'll shit a brick if she thinks you're with some blue collar guy now."

"I'm not dating him." She opened the flaps of the box she'd brought home from Coldiron House. "Mom had me over for dinner, and he gave me a ride since he was going to town, anyway."

"Did Mom say anything about me?"

"No, not really. I asked her if she'd heard from you, and she said she hadn't." Maisey left out the other part, the part about how he'd come back when he had no other option. That would only make him angry, even though it was true.

He used one foot to nudge the box he'd hauled in. "So what's this?"

"Some extra clothes and books I had shipped to Coldiron House." She dug deep, down to the bottom, and pulled out the stack of envelopes she'd hidden there. "And some letters I found in Dad's stuff."

Keith slumped onto the couch. "Why were you going through Dad's stuff?"

"I was looking for answers."

"To what question?"

She blinked at him. "The obvious question. Who's the girl in the photographs I told you about?"

"That's why I came," he said, sounding disgruntled again. "I want to see those pictures."

She went to get the metal container, which she'd slid under her bed. "Here you go."

Putting it on the coffee table, she sat down to await his reaction.

He stared at her apprehensively before taking off the lid. Then his face went stone-cold—no expression whatsoever.

"Do you remember her?" Maisey prompted.

He gazed at the picture, which showed a girl who looked a lot like her but was older than he was. "Keith?"

After dropping that picture in the box, he put the lid back on and shoved it away. "We don't want to deal with this," he said. "This is a nightmare waiting to happen. We need to leave it alone. Burn these. Or bury them."

She studied him. What did he know? More than she did; that was clear. "Why?"

He sprang to his feet and began to pace. "Why do you think? Do you want to destroy our family? The Coldiron name? See Mom go to *prison?*"

Maisey's fingernails curled into her palms. "Don't tell me she had something to do with this child's disappearance."

"Oh, don't be naive! Whatever happened couldn't have been aboveboard. We'd know a hell of a lot more about our sister—and that's who I'm *sure* she was—if that was the case. It wouldn't be like this. She wouldn't have been . . . cut out of our lives as if she never existed."

"Do you realize what you're saying?" Maisey asked. "Because it sounds to me like you believe Mom might've killed her. And that's crazy!" She *hoped.*

He whirled around to confront her. "You know what Mom was like. How . . . vicious she could get whenever she felt there was discipline to be meted out. What else might've happened?"

"Maybe she was . . . taken. Rich people can be a target for that sort of thing, a—a ransom situation. Or she could've run away or been accidentally left behind or lost. She could even have been put up for adoption. You've heard Mom say she never wanted kids to begin with."

"And no one ever said a word to us about any of that?"

"Grief—or shame—could've prevented Mom and Dad from talking about it."

"Shame is what I'm afraid of! Or self-preservation. In any of those scenarios, there would've been people who remembered her, people who would've mentioned her to us."

"The same holds true for *any* scenario," Maisey argued. "A child doesn't disappear without anyone noticing."

"Mom could make it happen. Pay for . . . for whatever cover-up she needed. She'd have *no* compunction about doing everything possible to save her own skin."

"But surely Mom's not a *killer!*"

When he said nothing, just stared at her, she could tell he wasn't going to refute that.

"Don't you think?" she prompted.

He pinched the bridge of his nose. "She was so

big on discipline. She believed children should be seen and not heard, didn't want any of us to slow her down or get in her way. If we did, we'd be punished. She probably hit Annabelle too hard. Maybe Annabelle couldn't take it like I could."

Annabelle. Although there was a lot to respond to in what he'd said, chills rolled down Maisey's spine at the mention of this name. "You remember what she was called."

He grimaced. "It just popped into my head. Annabelle. I called her Bella. It was easier."

"You said Mom probably hit . . . Bella." She fumbled, could hardly get her mind around having another sibling, let alone referring to that sibling directly. "Then what? What else do you recall?"

"I said 'probably.' If you think I can tell you what happened, I can't. I remember playing with her, okay? I remember her trying to protect me when Mom got mad. I remember—" he scrunched up his face as if he couldn't bear to see what his memory was showing him and grabbed his hair with a fist "—I remember her being locked in her room, crying. She peed on the floor because she couldn't get to the bathroom and Mom spanked her."

Maisey felt sick to her stomach. "How old was she the last time you saw her?"

"I can't even tell you when the 'last' time was! I had to be three or four years old. The memories are convoluted, blurry. I've dreamed about this so much that I can't say what's real anymore. I know she was our sister. For a while. She must have been. And then . . . she was gone."

Maisey shook her head, rejecting the scenario he'd put forward, even though she'd considered it herself. "If Mom hit her too hard and ended up . . . ended up hurting her that badly, Dad would've gone for help. He wouldn't have covered up a murder."

"Dad did anything for Mom. He had to. He had no choice. Not if he wanted to live any kind of normal life and be with us."

"He did let her get away with a lot," Maisey conceded, "but he also did what he could to protect us."

"To protect *you*. Somehow you brought out the best in him. He never did much for me."

Because he couldn't. Keith was every bit as quarrelsome, stubborn and difficult as Josephine. But Maisey had to acknowledge the severe beatings Keith had received. She'd been a witness to many of them. "If that's true—and I'm not saying I believe it—what did they do with her body? How would they answer to everyone who inquired after their oldest daughter?"

"I'm guessing there was no body. A body would trigger an investigation, and there was no investigation or we would've heard about it. I think she just . . . disappeared. Anyway, I can't answer those questions. I can't even ask them," he replied. "I don't want to discover the truth."

"That's why you think I should let this go. You're afraid of what we'll find."

"You should be, too! We need to destroy these pictures right away. No one puts a child's photographs in a wall and then plasters over them without good reason. I'm guessing Dad was supposed to get rid of them and couldn't bear to do it. So he hid them instead, saved them for the sake of his own memories and the love he felt for her. Maybe he even took them out occasionally and looked through them."

That image—of her father secretly coming to the bungalow and getting out the box of photographs—nearly broke Maisey's heart. "He would've gone to the police," she insisted.

Jaw hard, hands curled into fists, Keith stepped up to her. The anger that flared from somewhere inside him could come at unexpected moments, or with little provocation, but he'd never frightened her—until now. "Damn it, you've gotta listen to me!"

"You're high," she said as the truth dawned on her. "You never act so . . . aggressive unless you're on something."

"Oh, screw off." An irritated grimace punctuated those words. "I don't have to answer to you." Whirling around he went to the fireplace, shoved in one of the Pres-to-Logs she'd purchased at the store and pulled a lighter from his pocket.

She grabbed the stack of pictures. "What are you doing?"

"What do you think? I'm going to burn them."

"No!" Maybe he was right. Maybe they *should* be destroyed. But she wasn't prepared to do it tonight. First, she needed to determine whether or not she could live with herself if she made that choice. "I—I'll do it later. If I decide to."

"This isn't entirely up to you," he cried. "I have a say, too!"

She wished she hadn't told him about the pictures. She'd never dreamed he'd be so difficult. She'd just needed to know if he remembered anything. And he had . . . It was *his* memories that gave meaning to the photographs.

The log crackled as it began to burn, and she backed away, putting the couch between them. "We should agree before we do anything . . . drastic."

"Don't be stupid! We have to!"

"No, we don't!"

He circled the couch, coming after her, and she slid around the other way to avoid him. "Keith, stop! You're scaring me. I don't like it when you're high. You're not yourself. And this is . . . this is something that's going to require more thought."

"Sending our mother to prison won't bring Annabelle back, Maisey. If she's dead, it was an accident."

"Child abuse is an accident?"

He continued to advance on her. "It is if Mom didn't mean to kill her."

She hurried around the chair as he drew closer. "Do you know more than you're saying, Keith? Do you know what really happened?"

"No! How many times are you going to ask me that?"

"Then why are you suddenly so ready to protect Mom?"

"You'd rather ruin her?"

"Of course not! But what about Annabelle? Don't we have some obligation to our sister?"

"You didn't even know her. You were just a baby."

"*You* knew her. Maybe it's time we figured out exactly what happened. Then we could make an informed decision. There could be something in those letters I brought home. We haven't even looked through them."

"We shouldn't look through them. We should give our poor father some privacy." He knocked over the chair and ran into the table trying to reach her, but she darted back behind the couch.

"No. I'm not ready for this, not yet. I might never be."

"You don't get it," he said.

She wanted to cover her ears, run out of the house, maybe even go back to New York. "Get *what?*"

"Nothing you dig up will be good. It can only hurt us—all of us. We're Coldirons. We have a reputation to protect."

"Being Coldirons doesn't put us above the law, Keith. This is getting out of control. Calm down."

"*Calm down?* I'll calm down after you give me that damn box!" He shoved one side of the couch at Maisey, pinning her against the wall. "And I'll take the letters, too."

Rafe heard breaking glass. At first he thought someone was busting into his house. Then he realized the sound wasn't close enough. And someone was screaming.

No, he could hear two people—a man, cursing like crazy, and a woman, pleading with him to stop.

Maisey! Had she gotten into an argument with her brother? Or had her ex shown up?

Grateful that Laney was in town with his mother, Rafe got out of bed, yanked on a pair of jeans and shoes without bothering to fasten either and charged out of the house. "What's going on?" he yelled, catching a glimpse of white clothing as someone ran past the bushes in front of his house.

Rafe took off after whoever it was—and nearly collided with Keith.

"Bitch!" Keith yelled at the person he'd been chasing—Rafe could only assume it was

Maisey—and wiped at a trickle of blood running from his left temple.

"What's wrong?" Rafe asked.

Keith had no patience with being stopped. He tried to go around, but Rafe cut him off.

"I said, what's wrong?"

"Get out of my way!" Keith shouted. "She hit me with a damn box, that's what's wrong. But this is between me and my sister. It's none of your business."

When Rafe heard movement behind him, he glanced back to see Maisey clutching what looked like a handful of letters. "What's the problem?"

"Call the police," she said, breathing hard. "We have to call the police."

Rafe didn't want to go that far, but he wasn't about to let Keith harm her. He held out one hand in a placating manner, making an effort to get Keith to settle down. "Let's just . . . take a deep breath," he said. "You don't want to hurt anyone, Keith. Especially your sister."

Keith's eyes took on a glittery quality that made Rafe fear he *did* want to hurt somebody. Rafe had seen that look before; it almost always coincided with violence. He raised his fists in case he had to protect himself, watching warily to see whether Keith would throw a punch.

Keith didn't take the swing promised by that fierce look. He gritted his teeth as he spoke to

Maisey, said she didn't "understand" what she was doing and stalked off, back in the direction of her bungalow.

A minute later, he came tearing down the road in the car that had been parked a few yards beyond the entrance to Maisey's drive.

"He—he's messed up. He shouldn't be driving." She made an attempt to get in front of him—hoping to stop him—but Rafe jerked her out of the way.

"Watch it," he said.

Keith paid no attention to them. Rafe got the impression that he would've hit Maisey had she still been standing in the road. While they both watched, he bounced over the potholes, taking them far too fast as he tore out of the development.

Once he was gone, Maisey seemed stunned. Then she began to tremble—a reaction to the adrenaline.

"Do you want to tell me what's going on?" Rafe asked.

She lifted her hands as if she was shocked to see she still had the letters. "No. I—I'm sorry for disturbing you," she started. "I . . ."

Stepping closer, he clasped her by the shoulders and made her look at him. "Maisey, stop. Quit trying to face whatever it is alone. Tell me. Trust me."

He could see the pain in her eyes despite the

darkness. Something terrible was going on—something that ran deep.

"I can't trust anybody," she said. "Not with this."

19

Rafe insisted she come inside his bungalow. Maisey could hear him in the kitchen about ten steps away. She wanted to confide in him, tell him what his find in the wall of Unit 1 could mean, if only to have him convince her she was wrong. He seemed steady these days, the voice of reason. She felt she needed that perspective.

But what if he wasn't as trustable and dependable as she wanted to believe? What if, like Jack, he'd ultimately let her down? At least with her husband, when he was her husband, she'd had plenty of reason to expect him to stand by her. Rafe owed her nothing. It wasn't as if they'd built a relationship over years or even months. They were just getting to know each other—now that her confidence in others, and herself, was at an all-time low. She couldn't assume he'd act in her best interest, not when it really mattered. Besides, what kind of daughter would cast suspicion on her own mother? Especially for something as heinous as the death or disappearance of a sibling?

Maisey could easily imagine how fast word of a missing Coldiron-Lazarow would spread here on the island. Once *that* ugly specter had been raised, there'd be no burying it again. The mere suggestion would do irreparable harm. That was why Keith had reacted the way he had. He was high, which shattered his self-control and amplified his negative emotions or he wouldn't have gotten so mean. But beneath the effect of the drugs, he was acting out of the loyalty he felt to Josephine, despite his ongoing battles with her. The fact that Maisey wanted to keep digging, to reach the truth, could ruin Josephine's good name—maybe a lot more—and he wasn't willing to take that risk.

Maisey didn't want to hurt their family any more than he did. She wasn't out to destroy anyone. But she'd meant what she'd said when she asked her brother that question about their older sister. Didn't Annabelle deserve a champion? A voice? When they were children, she and Keith had stuck together. They'd sympathized with each other and done whatever they could to protect each other. Although their father had tried to stay neutral, even he had attempted to run interference for them. What if Keith had been the one to go missing? Wouldn't he want her to stand up and fight for him? For the life he could've had but didn't?

"Maisey?"

She hadn't realized Rafe had come back in the room. She'd been too deeply mired in her own thoughts.

"Here you go." He tried to hand her a cup of tea, but she was too jittery to accept it. When she hesitated, he set it on the side table and came to sit down beside her.

"Take a few sips whenever you're ready. It might help you feel better."

The warmth of his thigh pressed against hers was far more soothing than anything else could be. "Thank you."

He watched her from beneath those thick eyelashes of his. "So . . . out with it. What happened tonight?"

Maisey tried to avoid his gaze, which demanded that she level with him. She couldn't—although she found it next to impossible not to respond to his earnestness. "We got into an argument, and Keith threw a—a paperweight that was a gift from my editor through the front window. That's all." She was still sort of surprised he hadn't thrown it at her, since she'd just broken his grip and started to escape the cabin with her father's letters.

"That's *all?* He said you hit him with something."

The metal box. It was the only way she'd been able to break away from him once he'd pinned her behind the couch. "We had a little scuffle."

"Over what? What were you arguing about?"

"Nothing."

He seemed disappointed that she wouldn't open up. "Why are you being so secretive?"

"It's . . . family business."

He frowned as she leaned over and managed to swallow a mouthful of the tea he'd prepared. She didn't really want it, but she didn't want him to feel he'd gone to the effort of making it for nothing—her mother's training kicking in despite her distress.

"I should go," she said. "I'm . . . keeping you up. I'm embarrassed that Keith and I . . . that we dragged you out of bed. You must be furious that I moved in. I told you I wouldn't be any trouble, and here . . ."

He caught her hand as she stood and pulled her back down, almost into his lap. "Tell me," he insisted. "Something must've set Keith off to make him bust that window—and to make you feel desperate enough to hit him. What was it?"

She could use a friend more than ever now, and it felt as though Rafe was offering her that kind of support. But . . .

"Not really," she said sadly. "He's bipolar and has a drug problem and . . . struggles from day to day." She hoped he wouldn't go back to Nancy's and take his rage out on her, but she didn't think he would. This was about Annabelle, and Nancy had nothing to do with that.

He eyed the letters she'd put on his coffee table, the ones she'd kept Keith from burning when he'd destroyed most of the pictures. "Why was he trying to catch you?" He pointed. "He wanted those?"

The letters. She nodded.

"Why?"

"I don't know. I haven't read them." She'd barely gotten them home before finding—and arguing with—her brother. Now she needed to decide if she should open them or destroy them as Keith had said. Maybe her brother was right and examining the past would only blow up in her face. Lord knew she wasn't in the best situation to tackle any more problems.

Chances were there was nothing in those letters, anyway. When she'd taken them, she'd thought her father must've kept them for a reason. It seemed odd that they were all written in the same shaky handwriting and had no return address. But that didn't mean they had any connection to Annabelle.

She pressed three fingers to her forehead. She'd come home to heal, not turn her life upside down all over again . . .

"Hey, I can't stand watching you suffer." When Rafe slipped his arm around her, she couldn't help leaning into him. She wished she could absorb his strength, his warmth—let him yank her away from the emotional precipice she was teetering on.

"It—it's nothing," she stammered, but she couldn't seem to get over that scene with Keith. He'd never turned on *her* before. He'd always acted as if he'd protect her.

But it was Rafe who'd come to her rescue, Rafe who was sitting with her now, offering comfort. "Are you sure?" he asked.

He ran his hand up and down her arm. She could have let him caress her all night. She allowed herself to lean a little closer, hoping he wouldn't notice or, if he did, that he wouldn't mind. "Yeah."

"You don't think he'll come back?"

Did they have to talk? She just wanted him to hold her.

"Maisey? Are you going to answer me?"

She was clinging to him too tightly. She forced herself to sit up straight. "No, he won't come back."

"I'm not convinced. Why does he want the letters?"

"He doesn't want me to read what could be in them."

"And that is . . ."

She said nothing.

"Okay, you don't want to tell me. That's fine. But Keith *could* return, so you should think of that."

"Even if he does, it's not like he'd ever hurt me."

He must've heard the uncertainty in her voice, or he was going by what he'd observed earlier, because he gave her a funny look.

"He's my brother," she said with more conviction, and tried to get up again, but Rafe tightened his grip.

"Whoa. Hang on. I'm not saying he *would* hurt you. I'm just saying people who are on drugs can be unpredictable."

"I'll lock my doors."

"That might not be enough. Not when we know he's high and still upset. Why don't you stay here for the night?"

She couldn't think when she was so close to Rafe. In some ways, he made her confusion greater; in others, he did the exact opposite. "But I—I can't! I need to let you get back to your life."

"There's plenty of time for that. You can have my bed. I'll take Laney's."

"No."

He squeezed her shoulder. "I'd rather you stayed. So I know you're safe."

What about the pictures? "Keith started a fire. It's in the grate, so it's not going to burn down the bungalow. But . . . I should put it out. And there's really no need to bother you when I have a place of my own."

"Having you stay here won't be a problem. I'll go over, douse the fire and lock up."

She imagined what he might see. Whatever was left of those photographs would be on the floor—the ones she'd managed to knock away from the flames. Would that give anything away?

Probably not. Her brother had destroyed the picture that revealed Annabelle's age in relation to his. That had been the first one to go. So even if Rafe looked more closely at the remaining photographs, he wasn't likely to see anything that would make him think they were more than he'd first assumed. Finding them scattered around wouldn't tell him anything—other than that she'd gotten in a fight with her brother, and her brother had tried to burn her baby pictures.

As conscious as she was of imposing on Rafe, she didn't have the energy to fight him. She was too tired. And what if Keith did come back? It'd been ten years since she'd had to cope with his emotional outbursts in person. They'd been daunting enough over the phone and when they were directed at someone else.

"Thanks." She let Rafe persuade her to lie down so he could put a blanket over her before he left. "Will you bring back my pictures?" she asked.

"What pictures?"

"You'll see. They're on the floor."

"Sure," he said, and the next thing she knew he was back and carrying her down the hall.

20

When Rafe woke up, Maisey was sprawled all over him. They still had some clothes on—what little remained after taking off, at some point during the night, anything that had been too restrictive to sleep in. She was still wearing what she'd been wearing when he found her running from Keith—a thin button-up sweater with panties, although she was now minus her jeans and bra. He was in boxers and a T-shirt. But he had his hand up under her sweater before he was even completely aware of what he was doing.

He came more fully awake when the feel of her made him hard. Then he froze. He'd told himself he wouldn't be stupid enough to get involved with a woman who'd never take him seriously. But his body didn't seem to care about anything except the next few minutes . . . Rafe had been with quite a few women over the years. Not very many since Laney was born but enough to know that Maisey excited him more than anyone he'd touched in a long time.

She opened her eyes. She looked groggy at first, but quickly grew more alert. No doubt having his hand on her breast had something to do with that.

Again, he ordered himself to stop—and, again,

he ignored that command. He craved the same fulfillment she'd given him once before, and he had plenty of ways to justify going after it. Maybe she wasn't interested in a relationship with him, but she didn't seem opposed to getting physical. They wouldn't even be in the same bed if it weren't for her. Last night, when he'd returned from her place, she'd been asleep. She'd awakened briefly as he lifted her from the couch, but when he'd put her in his bed, she'd made it clear that she didn't want to be alone, so he'd lain down with her and she'd cuddled up against him. There'd been no sexual overtones in her actions. But her desire to be close to him had been so simple and shameless it reminded him of Laney, crawling into his lap when she needed love or reassurance.

Rafe had been happy to comfort Maisey. He didn't want to make her feel as if his support came with a price tag that included sex. But he couldn't pretend he didn't want her. He experienced such a strong physical reaction whenever she was around.

She didn't speak. She seemed to be holding her breath, waiting to see what he'd do next.

He almost wished she'd refuse his advances. Then the decision would be taken away from him.

When she didn't, when he was fairly confident he could have what he wanted, his desire grew until he could feel tension in every muscle. Still, he would've gotten out of bed if not for the way she was looking at him. Something had changed, and the promise of what that change could mean held him in place.

He had a chance. She was doubtful, skeptical and resistant, but she wasn't *indifferent*. Because of that, he became transfixed, especially when she reached up and touched his face.

That caress demolished his defenses. He didn't know where she stood with her ex, whether she'd be willing to take on her disapproving mother in order to go out with him, or how long she'd be staying on the island. But this moment felt like the first truly honest moment they'd shared. She was interested in him, even if she didn't want to be.

As their eyes met, he decided he'd take it a step further, see how she reacted.

He kept his gaze on her face while he undid her buttons. But once he pushed her sweater open and looked down, he could barely breathe. "God, you're beautiful," he told her. "The prettiest woman I've ever seen."

She grimaced. "You made fun of Jack for saying that."

"Because he was using it as a pickup line. I've already got you in my bed. I'm just telling you the truth."

"That's the truth? With all the women you must've known?"

Why was she always throwing his past at him? If he'd had a serious interest in any of those women, he wouldn't be living alone. But she used his reputation like a shield—something she could wedge between them to keep him from getting too close. "I was young and a bit wild," he said. "But I've never preyed on women, never purposely broken anyone's heart."

"I didn't mean you went around *trying* to hurt people . . ."

"So what *did* you mean? Are you going to hold my past against me forever?"

"I'm not holding anything against you," she said. "I'm just . . . trying to keep things in perspective."

"You're trying to distance yourself, to make sure I don't sneak up on you in a weak moment and somehow get you to care about me."

Her gaze remained steady. "Maybe."

"The question is why?" he said. "Why are you fighting the attraction? It was your ex who cheated on you, not me. I've never been a cheater."

"Have you ever made a commitment?" she asked. "What's the longest relationship you've had?"

He didn't want to answer, knew it wouldn't reflect well on him. He hadn't had a relationship that'd lasted more than a few months. But until Laney came along and changed his priorities, he hadn't been ready to get serious. "Some people take more time to grow up than others."

"I can only offer friendship, Rafe."

He shook his head. "No. That's not enough."

"No?" she echoed in surprise.

"People don't want to sleep with their friends, Maisey—most people, anyway."

He could see her chest rising and falling.

"But . . . I'm not in a good situation."

"How will pushing me out of your life make it any better?" he asked. "You can't stop living, can't isolate yourself just because you've been hurt."

"*Just?* I need some time!"

"Fine. Give me a reason to wait."

Obviously tempted to succumb to that plea, she watched him warily. "How?"

"You can start by telling me what you're feeling right now."

Goose bumps broke out on her skin as he ran his fingers lightly over her right breast. "I'm sure you can guess what I'm feeling," she said.

He *could* guess, but getting her to acknowledge it seemed important. "Do you want me inside you?" he whispered, sliding his lips over her breastbone, her clavicle, her neck and then up to her ear. "If so, you're going to have to say it."

She hesitated so long he raised his head. She was torn; he could tell by the concern on her face. "Rafe . . ."

"Say it."

She quivered when he trailed his fingertips between her breasts and lower, over her stomach.

"I should go," she murmured, but she didn't get up. Her eyes closed in a sign of surrender as his hand slid inside the tiny scrap of fabric that constituted her underwear.

"Come on, Maisey . . . ?"

"I want you," she admitted, and the desperation in those three words was enough. Their tongues met the moment his mouth touched hers, and the tension built almost as quickly. Despite his efforts to take their lovemaking slow, to savor every sensation, he could feel the urgency rising up inside them both. She seemed so much more invested this time; that excited him more than anything else.

He was trembling as he removed the rest of their clothing and tossed her panties on the floor. He told himself to calm down and let the pleasure creep over them both. Illogical though it was, part of him believed that if only he could make this spectacular enough, she wouldn't be able to shut him out later, like she had before. But the wonder on her face when he settled himself between her thighs nearly got the better of him. This wasn't just about the pleasure. This was a real connection. That was why she was fighting what she felt; it frightened her.

He couldn't allow himself to thrust or it would

all end too soon. She didn't speak while he grappled for control, but when he started to move, she gripped his buttocks and pulled him deeper. And the fact that she never broke eye contact when she did that turned his blood to fire . . .

Rafe had never achieved climax with so little friction. But as soon as Maisey gasped his name, he had to accept that he'd lost the battle to make it last. He could feel her watching him as he came inside her.

"You're not too freaked out, are you?" he asked, dropping back on the mattress. He knew he'd pushed her into something she didn't feel ready for.

"No, but . . . you're crazy to want anything to do with me. My life is out of control."

"You think I don't know that?"

He coaxed half a smile out of her with a grin.

"What happened with your brother last night?" he asked.

She glanced away. "I can't talk about that."

"There has to be a reason Keith was burning those pictures."

"He was angry, high—didn't know what he was doing."

"And the letters? Why would he want to burn those, too?"

When she pulled the sheet up to cover herself, he sensed that she was already retreating. This wasn't a subject she wanted him to pursue, and yet whatever was going on in her life had to do with what had happened last night. "I haven't read them, like I said."

"You must have some idea."

She shook her head. "Stop pressuring me. It's too personal."

He leaned up on one elbow. "I can't be there for you if you won't let me."

She seemed about to break down and tell him. But then her eyebrows drew together and her chin came up. "See? This is what I was worried about." She started to get out of bed, but he caught her hand.

"Don't run away."

"I told you I need time."

"And I'll give it to you."

With a sigh, she fell back onto the bed. "Okay, then why do we always have to talk about me? What about *you?*"

"What about me?" he asked mildly.

"Where's *your* brother? I remember you have one."

"Sam lives in Virginia with his wife and kids."

"Does he visit very often?"

"Hardly ever."

"Not even to see your mother?"

"He likes to pretend Mom's fine. He sends her a few hundred bucks for Christmas. But that's about it."

"Does that upset her?"

"If it does, she hasn't said anything. I keep her pretty busy. Watching Laney gives her a purpose, a way to make a living."

"So you're the only one taking care of her."

"In case you haven't noticed, I need her as much as she needs me," he said wryly.

"You could always hire someone else to watch Laney."

"I guess I could, but I'm more comfortable having Laney spend her days with someone who cares about her as deeply as I do. Makes it easier for me to work."

She bit her lip. "I love the way you are with her."

"Aren't I like most fathers?"

"Some, maybe. The good ones."

He smiled. "See?"

"See what?"

"I have a heart."

She laughed. "How old was Laney when she came to live with you?"

He reached over to move a strand of hair out of her face. "Three months."

"*Three months?* That's young! Was she with her mother before that?"

"No. She was in the NICU. She was born at twenty-five weeks, weighed less than two pounds."

Maisey sat up against the headboard. "Is that why she's blind?"

He nodded.

"I didn't realize a newborn could survive at twenty-five weeks."

"She almost didn't," he said. "I've never seen a baby so small. I could hold her in the palm of my hand."

"Did you know when she was born that . . . that she wouldn't be able to see?"

"Yes. The doctor told me almost immediately."

There was a troubled expression on her face. "It's odd, you know? How some babies, born with so many problems, not only live but flourish. And others, born at the usual forty weeks— perfect in every way—can't."

He found that to be a strange comment. "I guess. But what makes you think of that?"

Her face grew shuttered. "Nothing. Just that she must be a fighter to have overcome so much."

"She *is* a fighter."

"What happened to her mother?" She held up a hand. "Don't tell me she died during childbirth or something equally horrific."

"No. Natalie couldn't deal with the whole thing, I guess."

Her eyes widened. "You *guess?* You don't *know?*"

"It's not like she explained it to me. Once they released her from the hospital, she took off and never looked back."

"She wasn't worried? Wasn't interested in sticking around to help her baby?"

"She must not have been too concerned, because I haven't heard from her since."

She gaped at him. "I can't even imagine that. Have you ever tried to reach *her?*"

"Not recently. I'd rather not hear from her now. It's been too long, and we're comfortable with our lives. I'm afraid she'd just get in the way or make things even harder. But I tried at first. She didn't answer any of my calls, and less than a day later, her phone was disconnected."

"That was it?"

He punched up his pillow. They weren't touching, but they were only a few inches apart. "Pretty much. I went by her place, but her roommates said she'd packed up and left, and they didn't know where."

"And her family?"

"She once told me they lived in Utah, but that was all I had to go on—that and the fact they were upset she was pregnant and not married."

"Do you think they might be part of the reason she ran away?"

"Could be. Or maybe, when Laney was born with so many problems, she just decided to pretend she'd never had a baby."

Maisey didn't say anything for several seconds. Resting her cheek on her hands, she stared back at him.

"What's going through your mind?" he asked.

"I'm wondering if you were ever a couple."

"Only for a few weeks. Natalie was an exotic dancer. That's not how we met—we met at a nightclub when we were both out with friends—but when I learned what she did for a living, I wasn't too excited about it. I didn't want her to continue, knew it would be a problem between us if she did. Then her profession became a moot point because, as I got to know her better, I realized we weren't well-suited at all."

"So did you break up before or after you learned about the baby?"

"Before. But I remained in contact with her. She talked about giving the baby up for adoption. I told her I was willing to coparent, but I never dreamed I'd take over completely."

"Why didn't *you* put Laney up for adoption?"

"I considered it. I even called an attorney. I told myself it would be better for her. I just . . . couldn't go through with it."

"So you decided to be a single parent . . ."

"Yes." Those had been difficult times, but he didn't regret having a child. He loved his daughter far too much for that. "I can't really explain why I couldn't give her up. It didn't make sense to take on a baby alone, especially because Natalie and I were together for such a short time, but . . ."

"Taking care of her had to be hard for you at first," she said.

"It was." He chuckled without mirth as he

remembered how terrified he'd been when they put her in his arms that day. He'd never been around a baby before, had no clue how to care for one—especially a blind baby who weighed barely six pounds when they released her.

"Did you have a girlfriend at the time?" she asked.

"No."

"So, no help."

"My mom's been there for us, as you know."

"Still. It must've required a huge lifestyle change."

"It did."

"How were you making a living?"

"I was working construction for a guy in Charleston." That was before he'd had his own license, so he hadn't been earning a lot. "Our first night together was dicey. I must've called the hospital every time she cried."

He loved the smile that curved Maisey's lips.

"Anyone would've been frightened. To be honest, I think most guys would've put her up for adoption."

"But she was *my* kid. And she was blind. I felt she really needed me and that . . . maybe giving her up wasn't best. Maybe no one else would be able to protect her like I could."

"When did you move back to the island?"

"Almost as soon as Laney got out of the hospital. My mom was having trouble making ends meet, so I figured, if she'd watch Laney, I could work for all of us."

"What about your job in Charleston?"

"I commuted that first year, until I got my own license."

"So once you made the decision to keep Laney, you never had second thoughts?"

He took a deep breath. He wasn't sure how honest he wanted to be. He felt guilty for ever having the doubts he'd had, but he'd be lying if he said he'd never had them. "I can't claim *that,*" he admitted. "At first, I told myself I'd try it for a week. Then the next week would come, and I'd tell myself I'd try it for another week."

"And then?"

He grinned as he remembered how quickly he'd fallen in love with his child. "Pretty soon I couldn't possibly consider giving her up."

When Maisey winced instead of smiling, he was again confused by her reaction. "Is something wrong?" he asked.

"No. Of course not." Her smile came back, but he felt it was simply to mask that odd expression. "Does Laney go to school? Because if we've had a school for the blind built since I lived on the island, I haven't heard about it."

"No. There's nothing specifically for disabled people here. But Laney's getting plenty of love, and she's happy and secure. Those are the things that matter most to me. We can think about school next year or the year after. When she's a bit older."

"She'll need to be independent one day. You won't always be around to take care of her."

"That's a scary thought. But she'll be ready. My mom homeschools her, so it's not as if she isn't being taught. And I do what I can. Laney knows her braille letters and numbers and a few words. She's learning more every day. But we're not pushing too hard. There's no hurry."

As she stared off into space, he got the impression she was remembering . . . something. "Maisey?"

When he said her name, she blinked. "Yes?"

"What have I said that's made you sad?"

"Nothing, but . . . I need to get back to my place and . . . do a few things." She slid out of bed without touching him.

"You've had a little too much intimacy for one day?" He was teasing her about her skittishness, but a knock sounded before she could respond.

"Oh, God," she said. "Who could that be?"

"I have no idea," he replied. "Unless it's your brother. Stay here." He pulled on a pair of sweats and a T-shirt and hurried out, expecting to see Keith. Who else could it be? It was Sunday morning, and he wasn't expecting anyone.

But a stranger stood on his porch—a man about five-foot-eleven with his dark hair cut neatly and his hazel eyes rimmed by a pair of glasses. He

317

was well put-together in chinos and a button-up shirt with expensive-looking loafers. Rafe thought he had to be selling insurance or something, despite the weekend—until he opened his mouth.

"I'm looking for Maisey Henderson. I was wondering if you know her or could tell me where she lives."

Rafe stiffened. "Henderson? You mean *Lazarow?*"

He frowned. "Is she using her maiden name for more than just her books these days?"

"I guess so. That's the name I know her by."

Although it was obvious he didn't like the sound of that, he didn't comment on it further. "She told me she lives here in Smuggler's Cove, but . . . I drove around a bit. None of the other units seem particularly livable."

"She's in the bungalow next door," he said. "I haven't had a chance to rehab it yet."

Rafe could only assume this was Maisey's ex, straight from New York City. He was going to let the encounter end right there, but Maisey must've overheard, because she came out of the bedroom, looking stunned. *"Jack?"*

Jack's eyes darted between them. Although she was fully dressed, the state of her hair made it apparent she'd been in bed. And that, coupled with his own dishevelment, suggested they'd been in bed together.

"Don't tell me you . . . that you're with . . ."

She cleared her throat. "Let's go to my place."

Rafe watched as she hurried over to gather up the pictures and letters on the coffee table. He thought she was going to walk out and join her ex-husband without even acknowledging him. He couldn't help flinching as she brushed past. He'd been a fool to set himself up for this, he thought.

But just after she'd stepped outside, she turned back, pulled him to her by grabbing his shirtfront and, although her gaze was troubled when she briefly lifted her eyes to his, kissed him like she meant it. "I'll call you later."

21

Rafe had covered her broken window with cardboard. He hadn't mentioned it, but Maisey knew it could only have been him. He was the type to fix it for her—as best he could until he could fix it right. He'd also swept up the glass last night when he'd come over to douse the fire . . .

"Keith did this?" Jack said, whistling to show his shock as he went to inspect the damage.

Her brother had done a lot more than break her window. He'd burned most of the photographs Rafe had found, too. There were a few pictures of Annabelle, which Rafe had picked up and brought back to his bungalow. She had those with her. But, like the picture that established Annabelle's age, all the photos including Josephine and Malcolm were gone. Other than the picture of Annabelle standing taller than Keith, those were the most telling. Not only did they establish a tie between the subject and that subject's probable parents, they proved that Josephine had once had contact with a child who looked very similar to Maisey but was older than Keith.

"That's the least of my problems," Maisey said. "The window can be fixed. But the pictures . . . there's no way to replace them."

Jack sank into the nearby chair and rubbed his face. He hadn't liked finding her with Rafe and was still a little pale under his fake tan. But after what he'd done while they were married, he was being tolerant. As they'd walked over, he'd said he understood that she was on the rebound; he also said she needed to be careful about walking into the arms of the wrong kind of guy. He'd even tried to talk to her about how much he missed her, and the difference between love and lust, saying it was crazy to throw away ten good years of marriage—as if *he* hadn't already done that.

Maisey had cut him off by thrusting the pictures into his hands. She didn't want to deal with the divorce or what she might or might not be feeling for Rafe. She was too concerned about having had an unknown sister.

"Are you sure they establish that there was an older sibling?" he asked.

She wouldn't have told him what the pictures signified, but Jack wasn't from the island, would most likely never live on Fairham and he knew all the rest of the dirt on her family. Because he was familiar and yet removed, he seemed like the only person she could safely use as a sounding board, now that Keith had reacted so negatively.

"That girl you're looking at? It isn't me."

"How can you be so confident of that?"

"I told you, Keith destroyed the most important pictures. He wouldn't have bothered if they weren't damaging."

He frowned. "I wouldn't put anything past Keith."

Maisey reached for one of the letters she'd brought home from Rafe's and opened it carefully. It was from someone named Gretchen Phillips. As she looked through a few more, she proved her initial suspicion that they were all from the same person—this Gretchen, who hadn't provided a name or return address on any of the envelopes.

Putting the pictures down, Jack shifted his focus to the letter in her hand. "Is there any way Gretchen Phillips could be a man?" he asked half-humorously.

"I doubt it. Why?"

"It might be that you've only uncovered proof of an affair."

The fact that he could say this so nonchalantly after she'd uncovered *his* affair only a year and a half ago surprised her, but she ignored that. "Could be something like *The Bridges of Madison County*, I suppose."

"Is that what you're hoping?"

"No." She could understand if her father had been tempted to stray. It wasn't as if Josephine had given him much love or attention. She always had to be the one in the spotlight. But Maisey didn't want to discover something that would destroy the tremendous respect she had for Malcolm. Bad enough that he'd never mentioned her sister.

"It's better than the alternative, isn't it? Maybe the girl in those pictures belongs to another woman—a woman who took her and moved elsewhere."

Having a half sister would be far easier to accept than the more macabre scenarios Maisey had conjured up. "I guess that's possible. We look alike, but having the same father could explain that."

"There you go. Even though it would be a shock, you could learn to live with it."

Heartened by his words, Maisey began to read. She understood that she might be severely disappointed. Nothing was certain. But if there was any chance of solving the gut-wrenching mystery, she had to pursue it . . .

She skimmed over the words. Then she read them more slowly.

"What is it?" Jack asked.

"There are no protestations of love here, no bedroom talk."

"Then what?"

"I can't say for sure." At first, the contents seemed completely unrelated to the pictures. She couldn't even figure out why her father would hang on to these letters. "It's some woman rambling on about how she has bills to pay, and her car's broken down, and if she could just get another car everything would be better. Then he'll never hear from her again . . . blah, blah, blah."

Jack sifted through the other letters. "Going by the date stamps on the envelopes, that letter was early in their correspondence. So he did hear from her again. A number of times."

Setting the first letter aside, Maisey moved on to the next. "He bought her the vehicle she was asking for."

"That's an expensive gift."

She shook her head in confusion. "A lot of people have asked my parents for help, but I'm betting this is the only car they ever gave away."

"I get the feeling your mother wasn't aware of it."

She looked up. "So why would he do it?"

"He was in love with Gretchen?"

Maisey didn't believe it. "I don't think so. But—" she scanned two more letters "—the car he bought was a nice one. A Lexus. Even secondhand, it'd be pricey. She thanks him for it, then goes on to say that it needs new tires and brakes since she has to drive it across the country to look after her poor, ailing parents." She read aloud: " 'I got no income. Getting too old to be much good to anyone. If you could help me out again, I'd be greatful'—spelled g-r-e-a-t-f-u-l," she interjected. "Doesn't seem like the type of person my father would be having an affair with. Sounds too uneducated—and quite a bit older."

He handed her the others. "Maybe these will tell us more."

She read them the rest, then passed them back to him. "They're all in the same vein."

"With poor spelling and terrible grammar," he agreed when he finished reading them for himself. "She keeps complaining about the trials in her life and then she asks for more money."

"Did you see the one where she said her oldest daughter was sick and needed dialysis? Where she asks for forty thousand dollars?"

"I did. That's a lot of money. But equally surprising is the sense of entitlement that runs through them." Paper rattled as he skimmed the letters again. " 'It's such a small amount to ask from someone who has everything,' " he read aloud. "What's small about a *car?*"

"In comparison to what he stands to lose, it may not be much," Maisey said. "What you call a sense of entitlement could be a veiled threat. Did you see this P.S.?" She held up the letter that troubled her the most. " 'You wouldn't want to lose what you stand to lose.' "

"You're thinking *blackmail?*"

"Doesn't it sound like that to you? As if this Gretchen Phillips has something potentially damaging on my father—or my mother?"

"Yes, but it might not have anything to do with the girl in these pictures," he said.

"What else could it be?"

"Anything. Maybe *she* was never your father's mistress, but she knows of an infidelity. Or she's aware of a business indiscretion that could get him in trouble. She never mentions an Annabelle, never even alludes to a child."

"You mean there could be *two* secrets?"

"It's not *im*possible, but I guess it's not as likely as what you're thinking. Question is, who was this Gretchen?" he asked. "Do you remember a housekeeper or a nanny by that name?"

"No, but she was familiar with our family and our family's routine, so she had to be fairly close. That's clear when she suggests various places my father could leave the money—'so my friend can pick it up and you won't have to go out of your way none,' " she quoted.

Jack scratched his head. "Are these *all* the letters?"

"All the letters I found."

"I'd hate to think there were more. Your father gave her quite a sum of money over this three-year period."

"I wonder what finally made it stop?" she asked. "Where'd she go?"

"Maybe your father hired a hit man."

Maisey scowled at him. "I hope you're joking."

"That's what they do in the movies."

"I don't care. It isn't funny."

"I didn't mean it." He pursed his lips. "She talks about getting old. And these letters are from twenty-eight years ago. She's probably no longer alive."

"*Something* must've happened to interrupt the flow of money. She was milking the situation for all it was worth."

"So it's logical to assume she'd continue—until she couldn't," he said, finishing her sentence.

Fresh concern made the hair on the back of Maisey's neck stand on end. She needed to learn more about this woman.

"I wish I could call Keith and ask him if he remembers Gretchen Phillips. Not only is he older than I am, he's spent a lot more time on Fairham."

"Keith's too unpredictable," Jack said. "He hates your mother, and yet he comes over here and gets into a big fight with you over protecting her."

That might seem illogical to her very practical ex, but Maisey understood that Keith and Josephine's relationship could never be classified in such a cut-and-dried way. "He doesn't hate her. His emotions are like mine—confused. We want to *finally* get along with her, to be at peace, to feel accepted and loved—the usual things kids want."

"She's not capable of giving you any of those things. I've said it for years."

"Perhaps."

He grimaced. "Especially if she's anything close to what you're thinking here, with all these pictures and letters."

"She can't be *that* bad, can she?"

Jack clasped his hands between his knees. "To be honest, Maise, if your mother gets angry enough . . ."

Wasn't that what had Maisey so worried?

He moved over to the couch, where she was sitting, and took her hand. She allowed it, since she knew he was trying to be supportive, but his touch felt strange, uncomfortable. "You don't need this on top of everything you've been through."

A large part of which *he'd* caused.

Briefly, her mind flashed back to the day before Ellie's funeral, only a week after her death, when he'd hit her up for sex and she'd forced herself to comply. She'd been so broken, so hurt and yet she felt obligated to perform the way he seemed to think a wife should. She'd never forget how shocked she'd been that he didn't seem to care whether she felt *any* desire.

"It's . . . upsetting," she admitted.

"Rest assured that I'm here for you. I'll stay as long as you need me."

Did she need him? Or would she be better off if he left? "What brought you here?" she asked.

"I felt we should sit down and talk, face-to-face. See if there isn't some way we can work through what happened and put all the tragedy behind us."

Maisey had no idea how to respond. She wasn't ready to take him back. But, despite some memories she wished she could repress, she couldn't say she wasn't grateful to see him at this particular point. He was someone to confide in— someone who knew the intricacies and diffi-culties of her messed-up family. "I appreciate that. But . . ."

"But . . ." He frowned when she pulled her hand away.

"I'm seeing Rafe right now."

"The guy next door? You've only been here a week! You said you stayed over at his place because he stepped in when Keith was chasing you."

She'd told him the whole story. *He* was the one who'd isolated that as the reason.

He did have a point, however. She couldn't be

too enamored of someone she didn't really know. "There's a strong attraction," she said. "I can't deny that."

He ran a finger down the inside of her arm. "And what do you feel toward me? Could you ever forgive me, Maisey?"

She glanced at the clock. It was getting late. Soon she had to be at Rafe's mother's. She didn't have time to go into this now, couldn't decipher her feelings, anyway. "I know Ellie's death was hard on you, too."

"That's it," he said fervently. "If we hadn't lost Ellie, our marriage would never have fallen apart."

Maisey wanted to believe that, but was it true? It seemed to her that something must've been missing in recent years, or they could've survived their daughter's death. He'd shut her out when Ellie died. But, if she was being strictly honest, he'd done that before, when he got so involved in his work.

She remembered how it felt to be with Rafe. The excitement she'd experienced when he touched her had been missing from her marriage to Jack, especially during the last few years. Could she point to apathy in the bedroom, and elsewhere, as a sign that they *wouldn't* have made it? That they were slowly drifting apart even before Ellie died?

Or did she have unrealistic expectations of

marriage? Would *any* marriage eventually travel down the same path? Where one spouse constantly expected the other to tolerate and understand and not complain?

"I can forgive you," she said. "But that doesn't mean I want to get back together."

He scooted forward. "I'll prove myself to you. Give me the chance."

She glanced at her phone again. If she didn't shower right away, she wouldn't have time to get ready. "How? We live in separate states."

"I've taken two weeks off. I'll stay someplace in town and we'll see how it goes." He slid one arm around her shoulders. "You know I'll always love you."

Was that even true? Or was he simply reeling from his latest split?

Her phone buzzed. Grateful for the distraction, she used the excuse of picking it up to break free. It was Rafe, with a text. **You still going?**

"Is that him?" Jack asked.

She heard the displeasure in his voice but nodded.

"What does he want?"

"I agreed to have dinner at his mother's place today."

Despite the muscle that moved in his cheek, Jack managed a pleasant smile. "No problem. I brought this on myself, and I'm willing to do whatever I have to in order to fix it. I'll go back to Keys Crossing, find a room and . . . and you can call me after dinner."

"Okay," she said, and sent Rafe a reply. **Yes. Can I catch a ride?**

Rafe wasn't sure what to expect when Maisey left her bungalow and climbed into the passenger seat of his truck. He'd felt as if he'd finally broken through her defenses, finally convinced her to give him an honest chance—and then her ex had appeared.

"Where's Jack?" he asked as she put on her seat belt. He hadn't spotted a car in Maisey's drive.

"He went into town."

"To catch the ferry?"

"No, he's planning to get a motel."

"For how long?"

"He took two weeks off work."

"And he plans to stay here the whole time?" As far as Rafe was concerned, that couldn't be good.

"Sounds like it."

He put the transmission in Reverse. "Are you glad to see him?"

"Not especially."

After backing out of her drive, he paused before going any farther. "It's okay, Maisey. I'm not going to put any pressure on you. As a matter of fact, I want you to spend as much time with him as possible. If you still love him, maybe you should go back to him. I'd rather have that happen now than later."

She nodded. "I got it. And I appreciate your patience."

He didn't see that he had much choice. He had to think about Laney, couldn't take the sort of risks he might've been willing to take if it was only *his* heart on the line. If Maisey wanted to be with her ex, if she was just going to leave Fairham again, he and Laney would both be better off if she did it before they could get too fond of her.

Maisey manufactured some small talk as he drove, acting as if everything was fine. He had to give her credit for putting forth the effort. But he could tell she was as uncertain where they stood with each other as he was, and that made him nervous. Even though he'd resisted, he'd gotten excited about her. Why he'd let that happen, he couldn't say. He'd known from the beginning that she was out of his reach.

She had him stop at Love's In Bloom, so she could get the flowers she planned to bring. Then she held the flowers on her lap to keep them from tipping over.

When he pulled into his mother's drive and waited for Maisey to get out instead of killing the engine, she glanced over at him. "You're not coming in with me?"

"No. Tell Laney I went to watch football with an old friend, and I'll be back to pick her up later. I'll take you home, too, of course."

"But . . . isn't your mother expecting you?"

"She won't mind."

She set the flowers on the floorboard. "You don't want to be around me."

He stared across his mother's small yard before focusing on her again. "I've decided to give you some space as well as time."

Her throat had gone so dry she could barely swallow. "How much space?"

He didn't answer, making it apparent that he was backing off completely.

She frowned. "And if *I* want to see *you?*"

"You know where I live, but . . ."

She waited.

"Make sure you're done with Jack first."

She rubbed her forehead. "Rafe . . ."

"Don't feel you have to apologize or explain anything. I think it'll be smarter just to wait and see what happens. Maybe what you want—your feelings—will become clearer with time. Go on in. Have a nice dinner."

"In a minute." Leaving the flowers where they were, she clung to the door. "First, tell me this. What is it you see in me? Why are you even interested in getting to know me?"

He felt his eyebrows go up. "Are you kidding?"

"Not at all. You say you—you think I'm beautiful, but that's not enough to build a relationship on."

"I like the way you are with Laney, how you treat her with such inherent kindness. I like the soul of the person who wrote *Molly Brimble Conquers the World*. I enjoyed seeing the world through that author's eyes. I like how brave you are, how determined to handle your own problems, even though I wish you'd confide in me. I like that you're willing to stand up to your mother, when so many people aren't. You could've gone home to her, but you didn't. I like how, when we're in bed together, you look at me as if I'm all that matters. Do you need me to go on? Maybe some of these things are subtle, and I admit there's a lot more I need to know, but a relationship has to start somewhere, and I consider this a pretty good foundation."

"But I've been a wreck since I got home! What about that part? I nearly attacked you on the beach!"

"And I wanted you even then."

"You pushed me away."

"Because I understood why you were doing it. That it wouldn't fix what was wrong. And I'm not going to settle for a hookup every once in a while. Your husband cheated on you. You've been through a painful divorce and now you're trying to start over. A relationship with you will take time, and what you've been through means there'll be a few bumps along the way."

"It's not just that, Rafe. If you want the truth, if

you *really* want to hear what's wrong with me, I'll tell you. I haven't been myself since Ellie died. No matter what I do, I can't get over losing her. I watch you and Laney, and I'm *so* envious!"

He almost broke in to ask who Ellie was, but the words pouring out of Maisey were anguished and coming fast. He was afraid that if he interrupted, she'd only try to dam them up again.

"So envious that sometimes I feel guilty about it." She dashed a hand over her cheeks to wipe the tears that were beginning to stream down her face. "I ache to hold her in my arms the way you hold Laney. I want to be with her more than anything in the world. But that's impossible."

"Because . . ." he said softly.

"She's dead. She died two years ago from SIDS. Which is like saying the bogeyman came to get her, you know? It's impossible to accept, because she was fine when she went to bed. Then, sometime during the night, she just stopped breathing—for no apparent reason. I keep asking myself what I could've done to save her. But I didn't get the chance." She sniffed and wiped her face again. "So I don't blame Jack for finding someone else. I wasn't the same after that—I was a hollow, empty shell."

He started to say that she was also his *wife*. That "for better or worse" meant just that. But she raised a hand as though she had to get it all out at once.

"And maybe it wouldn't be so bad, maybe I could've recovered by now, if I could work. But I can't write a word. Now I'm arranging flowers at my mother's shop for not much more than minimum wage and who can guess how long I'll be there." She hiccupped as she gasped for more breath. "So are you *sure?* Are you positive you really want to be with *me?*"

He'd thought she considered herself too good for him. He was shocked to find that wasn't the case at all. She hadn't mentioned her mother's approval, or lack of it, once.

She glared at him, as if after hearing the ugly truth he couldn't possibly say yes.

He put the truck in Park and turned off the engine. "How old was Ellie?"

More tears fell as she closed her eyes. "Six weeks."

No wonder Maisey had lost so much weight and looked so fragile. "I can't believe Jack didn't take better care of you."

"No one would want to deal with such a sad, miserable wife."

He took her hand and waited for her to open her eyes. "Don't make excuses for him. We all have choices, even when times are tough. Those are the defining moments of our lives."

She made an effort to overcome her emotions. "So what's *your* choice? Now that you know what you'd be getting into? Don't you agree that you'd be happier going after someone else?"

Giving her hand a slight tug to pull her toward him, he leaned over and kissed her. "I haven't changed my mind about you."

That look she'd given him when they were in bed together, the one that had created such hope, appeared on her face again. "You can't mean it."

"We all have rough patches. You'll get through it."

His confidence in her seemed to help. She even smiled. "Does that mean you'll come in and have dinner?"

When he hesitated, she touched his cheek. "I want you there."

"Sure," he said, and released his seat belt.

22

Maisey couldn't keep her eyes off Rafe. She listened for his voice, blushed when she caught him looking at her and couldn't stop herself from gravitating to whatever part of the kitchen or living room he was in. It was all rather terrifying. So was the thrill that went through her whenever he touched her, even accidentally. She was on the rebound—not a good time to become infatuated. That warning voice hadn't fallen silent. And yet . . . she felt alive again.

Maybe she was finally beginning to get over

Ellie's death. Just telling Rafe about the loss she'd suffered had somehow lightened that load. And when she felt his hand linger on the small of her back as he pulled out her chair for dinner, or saw him grin at her across the table while they were eating, she felt he was encouraging her to let go of the pain and embrace something new and hopeful.

"You look so happy. What are you thinking about?"

Maisey blinked. Vera was watching her with a quizzical expression.

"Um . . ." Maisey felt heat rise to her cheeks because it definitely wasn't something she could share. "I was thinking about how delicious dinner was."

They'd been busy cleaning up, which was probably why Vera found that silly grin of hers so unusual. "You enjoyed it?"

"Immensely."

"I'm pleased to hear it." She patted Maisey's hand. "I might've poured it on a bit thick, but my son's a wonderful man. I stand by every compliment."

Maisey almost laughed. Rafe had been right. His mother *was* very obvious when it came to her matchmaking. Vera had seated Maisey next to Rafe, then proceeded to extoll his many virtues throughout the meal—what a caring son he was, what a wonderful father, what a hard worker.

Once, when he could do it without Vera's noticing, Rafe had rolled his eyes at Maisey to acknowledge what was going on, but for the most part he took it in stride. There was only one point when he said, "Mom, enough. Maisey doesn't want to hear one more feat of strength, or clever thing I've said, or unlikely repair I've made that no one else on earth could possibly have figured out. But thanks for the sales job."

His mother had blustered that she wasn't giving anyone any sales job. "I'm just telling the truth!"

"Maisey knew me when I was in my early twenties, okay?" he'd said dryly.

"You got the bad behavior out of your system early," she'd responded. "That's what counts."

"You didn't approach it that philosophically back then," he'd teased.

That had shut her up, for a while. But it didn't take long for her to try again, although more subtly.

"These are the last ones," Rafe said as he carried in their dessert plates.

Laney was up on a chair, her hands in the soapy water. Vera was letting her wash some plastic cups they hadn't used, because she was so intent on being part of the cleanup.

"Thanks, Rafe," Vera said. "Isn't he helpful?" she added as an aside to Maisey.

This time, Rafe waggled his eyebrows behind his mother's back as if to say, "Could you ever find anyone better?" and Maisey almost burst out laughing.

"That's very nice of him," she concurred, biting the insides of her cheeks.

"Laney and I can take over now," Vera announced, shooing them back into the living room. "You two go in and see what's on television. We'll be out in a little while."

When they sat down on the couch, Rafe put his arm around her, and Maisey snuggled against him.

"What would you like to watch?" he asked as he surfed through the channels.

"Football."

He gave her a disbelieving look. "Really?"

She grinned back at him. "Absolutely."

He drew her closer as he put on the game, and not long after that, Laney came out. She could make her way around her grandmother's house with remarkable ease. Vera had explained that they just had to be careful not to leave anything out that she might trip on.

Maisey expected Laney to cross over to her father and climb in his lap, as she'd watched her do through the window a few days earlier. But Laney surprised her by coming, unerringly, to her.

"Maisey, can I sit by you?" she asked.

"Of course," Maisey said, and helped her get settled.

Soon Maisey was so relaxed and comfortable with Rafe on one side and Laney on the other, and the TV droning on, that she felt herself begin to drift off.

"Are you tired, Maisey?"

Maisey lifted her heavy eyelids to smile at Laney. "Yes. Are you?"

"No."

"I guess I'm more relaxed than tired." Maisey ran her fingers through Laney's hair.

"That feels good," Laney murmured, wriggling closer to her.

"*You* feel good," Maisey said, and meant it. She was so content she hadn't even approached the questions she'd been planning to ask Vera about how she might've come to know Malcolm—or if Vera had ever met someone by the name of Gretchen Phillips. As a longtime island resident, Vera could easily have heard of her, if Gretchen had ever lived on Fairham. But tonight, Maisey hadn't allowed herself to dwell on the things that had taken over her thoughts most recently.

She knew she'd have to try to unravel her mother's dark secret before she left Vera's, though. It was too good an opportunity to pass up.

It wasn't until the football game ended that Maisey got up and went into the kitchen where Vera had disappeared about an hour earlier. She figured she wouldn't be missed; Rafe was tickling Laney, to gales of laughter.

She found his mother sitting in the dining area, knitting.

"You didn't want to do that in the living room with us?" she asked.

Vera turned down the music on a small radio at her elbow. "No, I like to listen to my music while I knit, and this chair gives me the best back support. Can I get you anything? Would you like another piece of pie?"

Maisey patted her stomach. "I've had plenty for one day. That's more than I've eaten in quite a while."

"Looks to me like you could use several weeks of big meals," Vera joked.

"I am a little too thin," Maisey admitted. "Do you mind if I sit down with you?"

"Tired of football?"

"Just want to talk to you for a few minutes."

Although she seemed taken aback, Vera motioned to the opposite chair. "No problem. Have a seat."

"The other day, when we were in Smitty's, you mentioned that you were acquainted with my dad."

"I was. I liked him a great deal."

"How'd you meet him?"

"When my boys were in middle school, I was working as a maid at the Drift Inn but couldn't quite cover all my bills. So I took on a second job, waiting tables in the evenings. Your father came in alone one night, just before closing. He seemed upset."

"Do you have any idea what might've been bothering him?"

"No. He said some vague stuff about having a tough week. But I knew who he was and where he lived, and I wanted a job that paid more than I was making so I could spend more time with my boys. I'm afraid that's why they got so wild in their teens," she confided. "They didn't have enough adult supervision. It would've been different if Clifton had lived." She sighed with a hint of nostalgia. "Anyway, I gathered up my nerve and asked your father if he needed any help."

"Did he hire you?" If so, Maisey didn't remember.

Her expression grew even more reflective. "No. He said there weren't any openings at Coldiron House. But he started to come into the diner regularly, and tipped me well."

Maisey watched as Vera's hands went back to manipulating her knitting needles with that same regular motion. "Did you know my mother?"

Her needles stilled. "Not as well, no."

"You and my father must've been about the same age."

"We were. But there was no funny business going on, if that's what you're worried about. He was just generous with me. Far as I can say, your father was always true to your mother."

Maisey could hear that Laney was giggling even more loudly. "How familiar are you with my mother?" she asked Vera.

"I see her around town occasionally. But I wouldn't say we're friends. We're not even acquaintances. We don't have any reason to go to the same places. For one thing, flowers have never been a luxury I could afford. Unless they're from the supermarket . . . Not that I didn't enjoy the gorgeous arrangement you brought. I swear I've never seen anything like it."

"Thank you."

"Did you arrange it yourself?"

"I did."

"It's spectacular."

If only *her* mother could say that once . . . "Have you ever heard the name Gretchen Phillips?"

Vera gave her a bemused look. "I have, but . . . Why would you ask about her?"

Maisey hadn't decided how much to divulge, but figured she'd have to divulge *something* to keep Vera talking. "I found some letters from her, addressed to my father."

"Where?"

"In the attic at my mother's house."

"You don't say! I didn't realize she knew your father. But maybe she did some work at Coldiron House. Most everyone around here's applied there at one time or another."

"What type of work would she have done?"

"Well . . . let me see. When I first came to the island, Gretchen managed the motel where I worked. But she had a bad back, had trouble being on her feet all day. So she quit when Rafe was maybe . . . six? Did some child care in her home after that. She occasionally watched my boys when their regular sitter wasn't available. So maybe she watched you now and then, too."

"I don't remember her," Maisey said.

"You wouldn't. She left when you were quite young."

"How young?"

"I'm guessing you couldn't have been more than two."

"Have you seen her since?"

"No. Haven't heard from her, either."

It seemed odd that Gretchen had moved on so long ago. Maisey would've been six to nine through the years Gretchen was sending those letters to Malcolm and, according to the postmarks, they'd been mailed here on Fairham. "Do you know where she went?"

"I'm afraid not."

"Can you think of anyone who might've kept in touch with her?

"Lord, that was a long time ago, nearly thirty years. Let me see . . ." She set her knitting to one side.

"She'd still have some family or friends on the island, wouldn't she?"

Rafe came into the kitchen, carrying Laney. "What's going on in here?"

"Maisey was asking about an old acquaintance of mine—Gretchen Phillips. You don't know anyone by the last name of Phillips who still lives here on Fairham, do you?"

"There's Ranger Phillips, that old fisherman who used to run the charter business."

"That's right!" Vera exclaimed. "He was connected to Gretchen in some way."

Maisey straightened the salt and pepper shakers that sat next to the napkin holder. "He couldn't have been her husband?"

"No, her husband died in a car accident before she ever started at the motel," Vera replied. "Like me, she was a widow with two little kids to raise."

"Could Ranger have been her brother-in-law?" Maisey asked.

"That'd be my guess," Vera replied.

Rafe shifted Laney to his other arm. "Why are you so interested in this Gretchen woman?"

"She might know something about an incident that happened a long time ago."

"An incident?" he repeated.

Taking a deep breath, Maisey rubbed her hands on her thighs and stood up. "My mother once mentioned that Gretchen had some old documents about the history of Fairham Island. I'd like to get a copy of them." She'd learned from Jack, when he was seeing Heather, that a lie was most believable when it was close to the truth. But this was the best she could come up with.

"I didn't realize she had any interest in the history of the island," Vera said. "But if you get those documents, I'd love to see them, too."

"I'll definitely share them. Maybe I should check with this . . . Ranger, you said his name was?"

"Yeah. He lives out beyond Smuggler's Cove on that remote finger of the island that juts into the sea," Rafe said.

"I've been out that way several times, mostly when I was in high school. We used to have parties there. But I don't remember anyone living in the area."

"He's lived there for as long as I've been on the island," Rafe said. "You probably just didn't notice. He's not one to show himself if he can help it. He's sort of a hermit."

"Does he still run the charter service?"

"I'm sure he goes out now and then, but he's gotten too old to do much of that," Rafe said. "You ready to go?"

"Yeah. I guess it's about that time." Time to go back to those pictures and letters so she could try to figure out if her mother had done something as terrible and unforgivable as she feared.

"Grab your bag, Laney-bug," Rafe said.

Vera managed to clamber to her feet, which took considerable effort. "Why don't you leave our little girl here with me? It's getting late already, and you'll just have to bring her back tomorrow morning. If she stays, we can both sleep in a bit."

"But you've had her every night this weekend," he said.

She waved his words away. "Doesn't matter. You spent some great time with her today, and you've got to work at first light."

Rafe tilted Laney's face up so he could look into it. "You want to stay another night, bug?"

She put her head on his shoulder as if she'd rather go home, but her grandmother knew just how to counteract her reluctance.

"You have yet to take a bath and play with that shark toy I bought you, remember?"

Immediately, her head popped up. "I forgot!" she said, squirming to get down. "Can I take a bath right now?"

Rafe arched an eyebrow at his mother as he set her on the floor. "You bought her *another* toy?"

"We were learning about sharks last week. This will let her feel the shape of the body and understand that they move underwater."

He shook his head. "You spend almost every dime you have on her."

She shrugged. "Oh, well. My money goes where my heart is, I guess. And it's not like I'm going hungry. Look at me, I could stand to lose a good fifty pounds."

Laney had already hurried down the hall to the bathroom, where they could hear her turning on the water. "I need to get in there before she burns herself or something." Vera started after her granddaughter but turned back to Maisey at the last second. "Thank you for coming. You remind me a great deal of your father."

Maisey followed Rafe to the door, where they called out a goodbye to Laney that made her come racing out of the bathroom in nothing but her underwear.

"Bye, Maisey!" She must've tracked Maisey by her voice because she found her easily and threw both arms around her legs.

Maisey struggled to hoist her up. Rafe lent a hand and she was able to give her a proper hug. "Goodbye, Laney. Thank you for helping with dinner. It was delicious."

Laney reached for her father, who took her from Maisey. "You be good for Grandma," he said.

"And you be good, too," she added in a loud whisper. "Don't tickle Maisey tonight."

"I thought girls liked to be tickled," Rafe said, playing along.

"Not *all* girls," she told him soberly. "And I want Maisey to come back."

"You're afraid I might chase her away?"

"Just don't tickle her," she said again.

"Thanks for the tip." Laughing, Rafe kissed his daughter on the top of her head before putting her down.

"She's something special," Maisey said as they walked to his truck.

He opened the door for her. Then he kissed her on the head, too. "So are you."

Jack was waiting for Maisey when Rafe pulled into the drive. They'd had such a great time at his mother's that he'd almost forgotten her ex-husband was in town—and that Jack was trying to win her back. "Looks like you have company," he said.

A shadow passed over her face. "I don't know what he's doing here. I told him I'd call him later."

"I don't think finding him here is too much of a mystery. You were gone for five hours. He's probably eager for his turn with you."

"Apparently," she muttered.

But was *she* eager to be with *him?* That was what Rafe wanted to know . . .

She began to climb out, then hesitated. "I'm going to ask him to leave the island."

Rafe turned off the radio. "Are you sure that's what you want?"

She studied him for several seconds before nodding.

This was welcome news, but . . . "How is he

likely to respond? I don't have to worry about him mistreating you, do I?"

"No. He's not temperamental, not like my brother, if that's what you mean. He's the type to sulk or . . . or get back at me in more subtle ways. And if I'm not going to be around him, that won't matter."

"Still, you've got to get through 'no' all the way to goodbye, and you've had a rough week. Maybe I should come in with you . . ."

"That's not necessary. He'll leave if I tell him to. I just need some time alone with him to explain how I feel."

Rafe wanted to ask her to explain her feelings to *him,* too, but he didn't push. In the course of this one afternoon, things between them had changed. He had to let it go, let whatever they were feeling develop slowly. Even though he couldn't help feeling threatened by the man who'd captured her heart so completely once before, being too insistent would only wreck the magic. "Okay. I'll be next door if you need me."

"Today was fun," she said.

"It *was* fun," he agreed. "You fit right in."

She opened her mouth as if she was going to say something else. But then she glanced over at the house and saw that Jack had come forward. He was standing at the porch railing, looking out at them. "I'd better go."

"Good night," Rafe said, and watched her walk

up the steps before he backed down the drive. In his view, if Jack truly cared about Maisey, he wouldn't have cheated on her, especially after an experience as painful as the loss of a child. Although she'd been surprisingly understanding about the infidelity—saying the death of their baby had been hard on both of them—Rafe couldn't forgive Jack quite so easily.

And he certainly didn't feel bad about trying to take Jack's place.

As it turned out, Jack didn't accept the news as well as Maisey had expected. She'd never really denied him before—not from that first day when he'd followed her home until the day before Ellie's funeral, when he'd demanded sex. As soon as she told him she'd rather he didn't stay on Fairham, that she didn't want to resurrect their marriage, the humility he'd demonstrated earlier disappeared.

"You won't even give me a chance? I flew all the way down here! I've barely arrived, and you're sending me back?" he cried.

"Jack, you had your chance," she said. "We both did."

"We were going through hell! Weren't ourselves! What kind of chance was that?"

Once again, he didn't seem to take any responsibility for even the things he could've changed. She began to suspect his apology had been mere words, and that he felt mere words should be enough. He'd come to Fairham believing he could get her back, regardless of what he'd done. And why not? The direct approach had always worked with her before.

Because he'd played on her insecurities and she'd allowed it.

"It doesn't matter," she said. "I'm done."

"So what are you going to do?" he shouted. "Continue screwing your neighbor? You think getting together with some small-time contractor is going to help you win your mother's approval?"

At no point had Jack ever cared about her relationship with Josephine. If anything, he'd exploited the rift, since isolating her had given him more power in her life. "*Now* you're worried about how I'll get along with my mother?" she asked.

"Well, that's why you came back here, isn't it? To take your place as princess of Coldiron Kingdom?"

How could he accuse her of arrogance, when he knew that her mother had always made her feel flawed and inferior—not like a princess at all. "I returned to help Keith, Jack."

"Nobody can help Keith, Maisey. He's a mess, and he'll be a mess for the rest of his life. It's time you quit kidding yourself about that."

"So I shouldn't try? I should give up on him? He's my brother!"

"Some people just can't be saved. Even if you don't come back to New York, you should get the hell out of here."

Feeling a renewed sense of determination, since he was being so dismissive about Keith, she clenched her jaw. "I don't know how long I'll stay, but . . . for now, this is where I'm going to start rebuilding my life."

"And how are you going to do that?" He jerked a thumb in the direction of Rafe's cottage. "By lying on your back for that gym rat next door—who probably didn't even graduate from high school?"

"How dare you say that! Rafe's not a gym rat. His work is physically demanding. And he's a lot smarter than you think!" Jack had hidden his jealousy when he found her at Rafe's this morning, but there it was, plainly evident—and the judgment inherent in those words stole her breath away. Who was *he* to decide how she should cope? He'd walked out on her, chosen someone else. "Anyway, what I do is no longer your concern. I'll decide how to live from here on out."

"No, you won't! You'll let your mother manipulate you like she does everyone else. Pretty soon you'll be at her beck and call. Never mind that she probably killed your older sister!"

"You need to stop! We have no idea what happened."

"You showed me those pictures, read me those letters. I know what you believe."

"What I *fear!*" They were both screaming now. "There's a difference."

"But it all adds up, doesn't it?" he said. "If you really want to find out what happened to your missing sister, try looking for a small coffin in that monstrosity of a house! Or maybe not. Knowing Josephine, she would've had the nerve to bury her in the family graveyard in the middle of the night. Or she ordered your father to do it, and he sucked up to her like he always did."

Maisey gasped. "Get out. And don't ever contact me again. I never would've trusted you enough to show you those pictures if I thought you'd turn on me like this."

"Who's turning on whom?" He stalked to the door, but the second he threw it open, he stopped abruptly. Dinah Swenson, the friend she'd met with her children in Smitty's, was standing there, holding a small loaf of bread with a bow on it—and she'd obviously heard everything they'd been yelling because her jaw was practically on the floor.

23

"Is it true?" Dinah asked, sitting down across from Maisey.

Maisey had let her in as soon as Jack tore off in his rental car. She didn't know what else to do. She had to talk to her, had to address what had just come out. Hopefully, she'd be able to do enough damage control . . .

"I don't know." Feeling her heartbeat flutter in her throat, she toyed with the curly ribbon on the banana nut bread Dinah had shoved into her hands. "I found some . . . some old pictures that have raised very disturbing questions. But I honestly can't point a finger at my mother—no more than at my father or anyone else. I'm not even sure I had an older sister. So I hope . . . I hope I can depend on your discretion." She braved a glance at Dinah's face and was startled to see a bemused look.

"I meant about Rafe," Dinah clarified. "Are you really sleeping with him?"

Maisey sat up taller. Of all the shocking things Dinah had overheard, she was focusing on *that?*

When she didn't speak right away, Dinah peered at her more closely. "It's true, isn't it! You lucky bitch! I mean . . . I'm happily married and all that. Chuckie's *great* in bed. But I'd be lying if I said I've never dreamed about getting it on with Rafe."

Maisey's shock must've shown on her face because Dinah rocked back, hooting with laughter. "I'm joking, all right? I also heard that business about your mother, which is what got you so freaked out, but you can trust me."

Maisey's stomach tightened painfully. Despite

what Dinah had said about trust, she didn't strike Maisey as the most discreet person in the world. "I can?"

"Of course. But you should know the rumor's already out there," she said.

"What rumor?"

"That there used to be another child living at Coldiron House. That she went missing shortly after you guys moved here. That no one knows where she went and no one dares to ask. I've heard it all before."

"How? You're *my* age, and . . . and whatever happened, if anything did, happened a long time ago. *I've* never heard anything about it—at least not until now."

"It's not something anyone would say to you. People around here, they don't want to bring down the wrath of Josephine. But my mother referred to it on the phone just the other day, when I called to tell her I'd run into you."

Maisey fidgeted with her phone. "Your mother's still in California, isn't she?"

"Yep. Loves it there. Would never leave."

"What'd she say?"

Dinah sent her a look that said she should prepare herself. "She told me it was reassuring to hear you'd shown up, since your sister never has."

Maisey felt sick. *"Really?"*

Sympathy showed on Dinah's face as she raked her fingers through her long hair. " 'Fraid so."

"Did you ask her what she meant?"

"Why would I? I knew what she meant."

"That's what I don't understand. *How?*"

"I've heard it various places—most recently at the bingo parlor."

"You're kidding!"

"No. I go there every once in a while to get out of the house after taking care of the kids all day."

"I meant you're kidding that people are still talking about it."

"They'll always talk about a good mystery."

"Who mentioned it at the bingo parlor?"

"Ozzie Mullins."

Maisey remembered Ozzie Mullins. Ozzie had been her English teacher. "What'd Ms. Mullins say?"

"She said your parents had three children when they came here, but no one knows exactly what happened to the oldest."

"Did she . . . have any theories?"

"Most people believe your sister fell to her death."

"From . . ."

"The cliff right there at the Point, the one overlooking the beach."

Maisey winced. "She fell onto the rocks below?"

"Presumably, but . . . it was high tide."

"So her body was never found."

"Exactly. The way I heard it, the police came

out but found no trace of her. They did find her favorite doll, however, which she always carried with her."

"Then why are you acting skeptical? As if you don't believe that's what really happened?"

"Because it was a bit strange," Dinah said. "The newspaper never ran the story, and your mother let her entire staff go immediately afterward."

"Maybe she was grieving. Maybe she didn't want the entire island talking about her loss, so she asked the newspaper not to print it, and they decided to respect her wishes. And maybe she let the staff go because she needed to be alone." Maisey understood what it was like to lose a child. When Ellie died, she'd felt like crawling into a hole and never coming out—and at least she'd been able to give her daughter a proper burial.

"There were three people working at the house at the time—a cook, a maid and a housekeeper. All three took their 'severance' package and moved off the island and they did it within weeks. Not one of them would address the questions they were asked about your mother."

"By the police?"

"No, the police seemed satisfied that it was just an unfortunate accident. It was everyone else on the island who had questions. All the secrecy—that's the strange part."

"You're suggesting . . ."

"I'm just letting you know how it looked—

why people have been whispering about it for so long."

"Because the newspaper didn't print the story? And three people were let go and moved away?"

"Because it looked like the paper had been paid off, and the servants, too—that they were supposed to keep their mouths shut and disappear."

"So why hasn't anyone challenged the story? One of these . . . doubters who keep gossiping about it?"

"My guess? No one's sure enough about their suspicions to make an actual accusation. The possibility that something else might have occurred has been floating around for years, but there've been no family members banging on the doors of the police department, demanding they take another look. No evidence of foul play. Who wants to accuse a wealthy and powerful resident of murder without any more to go on than some household staff who were suddenly dismissed? Especially if none of them talk?"

"But it's been years! Surely one of them would've broken his or her silence by now, if . . . if something sinister had happened. Don't you think that an attack of conscience would've driven someone forward in more than thirty years?"

"Not necessarily. Not if all they have are suspicions, like the rest of us."

"But if they never really knew anything, why would my mother fire them?"

"Maybe she was afraid they knew more than they did. Maybe she was just being cautious—putting a stop to something before it could even start. No one has the real story. That's what Ozzie believes. She heard from someone who heard it from Lois Jenkins, who worked as a maid for your mother, that *she* thinks your mother pushed your sister to her death."

Maisey's blood ran cold. "What would make her think that?"

"She claimed your mother hated the child. That she was more than cold and unfeeling. That she was actually cruel."

Despite Maisey's own doubts and insecurities, loyalty came rising up like a tidal wave. "That's a steep cliff. A child of five or six could easily have fallen, could easily have hurt herself on the rocks and then been pulled under by the tide."

The question was . . . had she? Maisey wanted to believe the answer to that was yes. But she had her doubts, too. Certain elements of the story made her uncomfortable—like how strange it was that her mother had never said anything about losing a child. Josephine had never so much as spoken Annabelle's name, not in Maisey's recollection. Neither had her father. There'd been no pictures in the house, no room that used to belong to Annabelle, *no trace*. And what about the letters to her father from that Gretchen woman? The intimation that there *had* been something in the past capable of ruining them?

"It *could've* been an accident," Dinah agreed. "That's exactly the reason no one has ever challenged the story directly. So cut yourself a slice of my fabulous banana bread and enjoy it. You know how everyone's always loved whispering about your family. It's the gossip that turned a tragic fall into more of a mystery than it ever really was."

Maisey hoped so. But after the way she'd seen Josephine punish Keith, she could all too easily imagine her mother doing the same, or worse, to Annabelle. She felt a chill at the very mention of the servants describing her mother as "cruel."

And the fact that Malcolm might have been complicit in some way was even more upsetting.

"Who can I ask if I want to learn more?" Although Maisey had Gretchen Phillips's name, she didn't want to bring that up, didn't want to say anything about her father or the letters. Jack had referred to them when they were shouting at each other, but Dinah didn't seem to recall that. Maisey could easily picture her coming to the door and being shocked by what she was hearing, shocked enough not to catch every word.

Still, Dinah knew more than Maisey wanted anyone to.

"You could ask your mother," Dinah replied,

as if it was as simple as that. "I'm guessing she's the only one who really knows."

Maisey hoped not, because Josephine would *never* tell. Not the truth. Not if it didn't reflect well on her. Maisey would have to rely on Gretchen Phillips, or someone else, to fill in the blanks. There had to be a reason Malcolm had bought that woman a car and given her so much money . . .

After thanking Dinah for the bread and chatting with her about various other things, Maisey explained that she probably wouldn't go to bingo but would be happy to go out for a drink sometime. Then she followed Dinah to the door.

"Chuckie wants to see you," Dinah said. "I made him stay home with the kids tonight, but would you mind if he came along when we go out for that drink?"

"Of course not," Maisey said.

"You can bring Rafe, too." She tossed Maisey a grin. "I promise not to drool."

"I'm not sure . . . I mean, Rafe and I aren't technically together, so . . . I doubt he'll be coming with me."

"Well, just in case you'd *like* to bring him."

"Thanks. See you soon," Maisey said and closed the door. But she didn't settle in for the night. She grabbed her purse and found the key to the scooter.

It was eight-thirty. She wanted to visit Ranger Phillips before it got any later.

● ● ●

Ranger Phillips lived in a shack. Although she didn't remember him, Maisey had expected someone with a charter business to have a more . . . traditional home. This place was even more remote than Smuggler's Cove. If not for the "Charter Service" signs—handmade and tacked to a tree here, a fence there—leading her on like a series of garage sale signs, she never would've found it.

As she pulled up, she could see the flicker of a lantern through the window, could smell chimney smoke and guessed that Ranger didn't have utilities.

Parking her scooter well down the rutted drive—she was hesitant to leave her getaway vehicle where she might have trouble making an escape, if necessary—she cautiously approached the door. A muddy truck sat beneath a makeshift carport and, as she got closer, she could hear the hum of a generator as well as the babble of a TV.

She considered going home and coming back when it was daylight. But she had to work in the morning and didn't want to put this off. The question of what had happened to Annabelle was eating at her and would continue to eat at her until she confirmed that it was the accident the police had determined it was.

As soon as she knocked, the volume of the television dropped. A second later, she sensed that someone was peering out at her. The curtains moved and there was a shape to one side. But she doubted Ranger Phillips could see her, since she was standing in the dark. The tall trees surrounding his property blocked even the moon's light.

"Who is it?" came a gruff voice.

"My name is . . ." She drew a deep breath. "My name is Maisey Lazarow."

"What do you want?"

She bit her lip when he didn't open the door or act the least bit friendly. She was feeling more and more uncomfortable about showing up here. Would it bring the old gossip raging back to the forefront? Was she stirring up something that should be left as it was?

She didn't have those answers.

"Hello?" She cleared her throat. She had to ask, didn't she? "I'm looking for Gretchen Phillips."

"Who?"

"Gretchen. I believe she might be related to you—through marriage."

"She's dead," was his response. "Died of lung cancer nine years ago."

Maisey's heart sank. Had she gathered up her courage and come here for nothing? "So you . . . you kept in contact with her?"

"Why do you want to know?"

"It's sort of hard to explain through a door. Is

there any chance you could speak to me face-to-face?"

Silence. At first Maisey thought he'd ignore her request. But then she heard shuffling and the door opened a few inches. Once she saw that he lived with at least five cats, some of them trying to poke their curious noses into the evening air, she understood why he'd been so cautious. He didn't want to worry about his pets getting out.

"Thank you for . . . for speaking to me."

"Why are you looking for Gretchen? You wouldn't even have known her."

She was beginning to sweat under her jacket. "No, no, I didn't. But . . . my father did, and he . . . he left me a note that I should reach out to her one day."

Every bit the seasoned fisherman, with a weathered face, hawkish nose and thick, coarse hair that didn't appear to have been brushed today—or recently cut—he squinted at her. "And what would your mother have to say about that?"

Maisey almost stumbled back. "I—I don't know. I haven't discussed it with her."

"You'd better leave well enough alone, girl," he said, and closed the door.

Shocked that he'd presume to tell her what to do, Maisey knocked again. "Mr. Phillips?"

"Go away!" he yelled. "I have nothing more to say to you."

Maisey was breathing hard as she trudged over

to her scooter, but it was from emotion, not exertion. Ranger Phillips knew something, something he wasn't saying.

You'd better leave well enough alone, girl . . . Hadn't Keith told her essentially the same thing?

Almost as if the thought of Keith had triggered a phone call from him, her phone buzzed. She glanced down at it, nearly answered, but decided not to. She'd deal with her brother later. She couldn't go yet; she had to try one more time to get Mr. Phillips to talk.

Rafe couldn't help watching the clock. He'd dropped Maisey off a couple of hours ago. He thought he'd hear from her tonight, once she got rid of her ex. But . . . nothing so far.

He went to the window and peered out, even though he knew he wouldn't be able to see her cottage. With Keith acting so crazy last night and this guy from New York waiting at Maisey's house earlier, Rafe couldn't relax.

Should he check on her?

No. She'd think he was crowding her. He'd promised to give her time and space, and he needed to keep his word. He was fairly certain he'd heard a car earlier, which meant Jack was gone. Considering everything she'd been going through, she was probably exhausted and confused. Maybe her ex had rekindled bad memories.

How could he not, given the loss they'd suffered and what he'd done afterward?

She was asleep, Rafe told himself. That was why she hadn't called him. With Laney at her grandmother's, he'd hoped they'd spend the night together. But . . . she must want to be alone.

He should follow her lead and go to bed. Work would come awfully early in the morning if he didn't get some rest . . .

But he knew he wouldn't be able to sleep and didn't see any point in lying there only to stare at the ceiling. So he went into the kitchen to crack open a beer, and that was when his phone finally rang. He hoped it was Maisey, but it wasn't. The number wasn't one he recognized.

"Hello?"

"Where's my sister?"

Keith.

"You're asking *me?*"

"She's not answering, and I want to talk to her."

"Maybe she doesn't want to talk to you."

There was a brief pause. Then he said, "Listen, I was an asshole last night. I admit it, and I'm sorry. That's what I have to tell her. And we have . . . other things to discuss. She's not with you?"

"No. But I can walk over and see if she's home, tell her to give you a call, if that would help."

"I'd appreciate it," Keith said.

Rafe didn't feel like doing Keith any favors. He wasn't ready to forgive him for nearly running

Maisey down. But Rafe was eager to stop by and see why she wasn't answering her phone, and this provided him with an excuse.

Once he got over there, however, no one came to the door. He would've checked the beach next; he'd found her there before, had seen her seek the calming influence of the ocean when she was upset. But he looked for her scooter first and discovered that it wasn't where she usually parked it.

He stood in her driveway and turned in a slow circle, wondering where she might've gone. The lights were on in her house, as if she didn't plan on being away long. Had she driven to town for some reason?

"She's not here," he said when he called Keith back.

"Where could she be?" Keith sounded irritated, impatient.

Rafe didn't know whether to mention Jack. "What about your mother's place?"

"Maisey's not at Coldiron House," he said. "*I'm* at Coldiron House."

Of course. That must be how he'd gotten Rafe's number. Josephine had it. "Your mother hasn't heard from her, either?"

"Not today."

Rafe frowned as he searched for possible answers. The store was closed this late on a Sunday night, so she couldn't have gone there . . . "Then I don't know what to tell you."

"If you see her, can you have her give me a call?" Keith asked.

"Sure." As Rafe walked back to his house, he reached into his pocket to see if he had his truck keys. Part of him was tempted to go looking for her. The other part insisted that he'd seen too many movies. Her scooter was gone. That suggested she'd left of her own free will.

Unless Keith had shown up to finish their argument from last night—or had her meet him somewhere—and his call had been some kind of cover-up.

No, that was crazy, Rafe told himself. Despite the anger he'd witnessed last night and that unnerving, cold look on Keith's face as he tore past them, surely he wouldn't harm his own sister . . .

24

After much coaxing and one plea—"I can't leave until I know what you're keeping from me"—Ranger Phillips had let Maisey into his house. If it hadn't started to rain while she was pounding on his door, she was convinced she'd still be out there. He'd quit ignoring her only after she'd said, "It's cold, and it's wet. *Please?* I'm not leaving, no matter how long this takes."

Regardless of *why* he'd let her in, she wasn't

feeling a whole lot more comfortable. Ranger was old and stooped and lived simply—all positive associations that reminded her of her grandfather on Malcolm's side. But the comparison ended there. This place wasn't particularly sanitary. His living room was so cluttered with garbage there was barely room to move. He'd had to clear a spot for her on the couch. Although it would be difficult for him to haul away his own trash, she had no idea how he lived as he did. The stench was almost overpowering.

Not only that, but Maisey thought Ranger himself seemed strange, remote, even antisocial.

"I realize we're talking about something that happened a long time ago," Maisey said, trying to keep from shooing away the cats that were creeping closer. Between the smelly fishing nets he had piled everywhere, and the litter boxes that needed to be cleaned, she could hardly breathe.

He continued to eye her dubiously.

"And I understand that you probably don't want to get involved," she went on. "You've never met me before and you don't owe me anything. But like I said, I hope you'll help me, anyway."

Obviously agitated, he scratched his head. "I've been trying to tell you, I *can't* help."

"I don't believe that. You know something about the summer my sister died."

She'd been afraid that saying those words out loud—"the summer my sister died"—might be the key to Pandora's box. She hadn't even known she had a sister until a few days ago. But she'd seen and heard enough since then to be convinced of it, and she was so compelled to learn the truth that she couldn't stop herself. All the distrust, anger and resentment she felt toward her mother made her defensive of this child whose existence had been erased.

Besides, Maisey had to start the unraveling process somewhere. People weren't going to volunteer information—not to her. She was excluded from the gossip circles that had kept the rumors alive for so long.

"She fell," he said. "Ask anyone. You don't need me to tell you that."

"The interesting thing is . . . no one wants to talk about it. Not to me." And not *everyone* knew. Rafe and his mother hadn't acted as if they'd heard anything.

"That surprises you?"

"No, but it means I have to ask." Well aware that she was taking one more step toward her own sort of cliff, she gently set aside a cat that had climbed into her lap. She loved animals, but enjoying Ranger's pets was the last thing on her mind. If her mother ever heard that she was asking these questions, Josephine would cut her off for good. There would be no more *home*. She probably wouldn't even be allowed to stay in Smuggler's Cove. And she had so few assets left . . .

Was she really willing to go *that* far, especially after everything she'd endured in the past two years? Could she handle uprooting herself again and going somewhere else?

She wasn't sure she could, and yet she didn't feel she had any choice. If Josephine had used her name, money and power to avoid justice, *someone* had to take a stand against her.

"You might not like the answers you get," he warned.

"Why?" she asked. "Was it not an accident?"

He dropped his head to stare at the worn rug.

"I just want the truth," she said. "If you know it, why not tell me? What do you have to lose?"

He looked up and his eyebrows—severely in need of a good trim—rose high. "What do I have to lose?" he echoed. "Only my house. And where will I go if I get kicked out of here?"

"What do you mean?" she asked.

"It's your mother who lets me live here."

"*Lets* you?"

"It's her property, ain't it? She owns most all the land on the island, except once you get over to Keys Crossing. She could turn me out anytime."

"You're not paying rent?"

He motioned around them. "Does it look like I can afford to pay rent? Would I be living like this if I could?"

"But does she even know you're here?"

"I'm sure she does."

"And she's letting you stay out of the goodness of her heart?"

"I wouldn't say that."

"Then what?"

"She's not going to kick me out if she thinks I know something she doesn't want me to talk about."

A second cat approached Maisey, a black one that stared up at her with wide, unblinking eyes. "What if I was careful not to tell her, or anyone else, where I received my information?"

"I'm afraid she'd come right to me, anyway. Who told you about Gretchen?"

"My father . . ."

"No. He didn't leave you a note to look her up. I don't believe he'd do that."

Did she dare reveal what she'd discovered? She didn't know whom she could trust, but . . . she had to trust someone. "It wasn't as direct as I made it sound, but . . . he saved her letters for a reason."

"He saved them?"

"Yes. Over a three-year period, she wrote him many times, asking for money."

His lips pursed.

"Was she blackmailing him?"

"I don't like getting involved in other people's lives," he replied.

"The little girl who died that day deserves a voice!"

He got up and began to pace.

"Please, Mr. Phillips."

"Your father was protecting someone."

"Who? My mother?" she asked.

With an uneasy glance over one bony shoulder, he said, "No, your brother."

The cats scattered as Maisey jumped to her feet. "What do you mean?"

He swung around to face her. "Annabelle didn't just fall off that cliff. Someone pushed her."

"But it couldn't have been my brother! He was only about four at the time!"

"That's all I'm going to say." He raised his hands, which trembled slightly from nerve damage or age or anxiety. "Now you'll have to leave."

Maisey didn't budge. "You honestly think Keith pushed Annabelle."

"Everyone who's ever had anything to do with him knows he's not like other people."

"That doesn't make him a murderer!"

He grimaced. "Forget I said anything. Please. I have my own troubles."

"How can you accuse a four-year-old of such a heinous act?" she asked.

"I can only tell you what my sister-in-law saw that day. I don't like the idea that a four-year-old could do something that bad, either. No one does. That's why everyone prefers to think it was an accident."

Maisey shivered in spite of the woodstove that

was doing a very efficient job of heating Ranger's humble abode. "Keith could never have done that! Even if he did push Annabelle, he wouldn't have realized how badly he'd hurt her. He must've shoved her out of anger or frustration."

"That's a possibility. I'm not saying it ain't. Now you need to leave. I wasn't there that day, and I don't like spreading gossip."

He was afraid of what might happen to him as a result of what he'd disclosed, but Maisey didn't think he had any reason to worry. She wasn't going to tell anyone this . . . this craziness. She couldn't accept such a preposterous explanation!

But then that memory of someone locking her in the attic rose, unbidden, in her mind. She'd been playing for quite a while before the light went off and the door closed. Had it been long enough for Keith to get home from practice and find that she hadn't listened to him about waiting until he returned? Had he decided to punish her? He'd already been upset about being left out of the starting lineup . . .

On some level, she believed it *was* something he'd do. She could see him as a boy, taking his anger and frustration out on her and feeling she deserved it for displeasing him. She'd seen him do similar things most of his life.

How many times had her mother stepped in to rescue him from one mess or another? Josephine had taken him out of public school and put him in private school because he was skipping too many classes and getting into so much trouble he wasn't going to graduate. Then she'd paid to have him go to three different colleges. She'd even had to intervene at the final school, when the administration accused him of cheating on his exams, to make sure he received his diploma.

He claimed he hadn't cheated, but Maisey had always wondered, even if she'd never wanted to admit it.

"How did Gretchen see what happened?" she asked dully. "That cliff overlooks a private beach."

"What do you mean?" he asked. "She'd just bent down to tie your shoe, so she was right there. When she glanced up . . ." His words fell off.

"She was with *us?*"

"Of course. You don't know? She was the first person your mother hired as a nanny when your family moved to the island."

Maisey's blood ran cold. She'd been standing there, as a two-year-old, when it happened? Had watched her sister fall to her death? Get swept out to sea?

She didn't remember a thing about it. Thank God . . .

"Did anyone else see?"

"No. Like you said, that cliff overlooks your family's private beach. There was no one below. And when Gretchen told your mother the story,

Josephine paid Gretchen to keep her mouth shut and move off-island."

Maybe Gretchen had moved, but she hadn't settled for that initial payment. She kept coming back for more . . .

"So she was blackmailing two grieving parents who were trying to protect their young son from being blamed for such a tragedy."

"It wasn't like that."

"How do you know?"

"Gretchen told me! I was putting in a swamp cooler at her house when she got home that day . . ."

"*You* were at her place?"

"Yes. My brother had passed away. I was doing what I could to help out."

"And . . ."

"And when she showed up, she was a wreck. Shaking and crying. Said your brother was the devil himself."

How many times had Maisey heard that? No one trusted Keith. He'd behaved too badly. But she couldn't believe he'd killed his own sister. Not knowingly. Not on purpose. "Yet Gretchen had no compunction about turning the situation to her advantage and blackmailing my parents. My father sent her thousands of dollars, even bought her a Lexus!"

"It's easy to judge when you've always had everything you need," he said. "She had her own kids to raise. One of 'em—Sarah—had a rare kidney disease and died before she turned twenty."

Sickened by the whole sordid story, Maisey shook her head. Her father had been protecting Josephine, as she'd thought. Just not in the way she'd first imagined. "That's no excuse."

The lantern cast odd, moving shadows across Ranger Phillips's seamed face. "Would you rather she'd come forward with the truth? Rather have had your brother taken away? Put in an institution? That was what he needed. If you ask me, it's *still* what he needs."

Maisey didn't want to hear that, but despite all her love for Keith, all her loyalty to him, she wasn't entirely sure she could refute it. He'd always had severe emotional problems. Did he even remember the incident at the cliff? If he'd meant to push Annabelle that day, did he feel any remorse?

She recalled the conversation when she'd told him about the pictures, and he'd said he vaguely remembered a sister, too. Had he just been playing along? Because right after he admitted to having memories of Annabelle, he'd pointed a finger at *Josephine*.

Maisey didn't know what to think, what to believe. And the more she went over that conversation, the more frightened and confused she became. He'd come over the very next day, demanded those pictures and burned the most meaningful ones. He'd wanted the letters, too. If it wasn't for Rafe, he would've gotten them.

Had he done all that to protect their mother, as he claimed?

Or had he done it to protect himself?

As soon as he returned to his own house, Rafe texted Maisey. **Keith's looking for you. He's at Coldiron House. Where'd you go? Are you okay?**

He didn't get a response, so he tried calling her, but she didn't pick up.

He waited another thirty minutes and dialed her number again—with the same result. Then he called Keith, but Keith didn't answer, either.

Could they both have gone to bed? Although he'd been listening for the scooter, he could've missed the whine of that small engine.

He sent another text to Maisey. **Hello? Can I get an answer?**

Nothing.

Frustrated and growing concerned in spite of all the reasons he shouldn't overreact, he walked back to her place. The lights were still on, the scooter was still gone and Maisey still wasn't answering her door. He did see something he hadn't noticed before, however. There was a slip of paper half-under the doormat. He pulled it out and found a short note. "I just learned something else. Call me. —Dinah."

"I can't believe it," Maisey said. "That's what I've decided. I can't believe it."

Rafe shoved his hands in his pockets. It was past midnight and he had to work at dawn, but when he'd called Maisey one final time, she'd answered. She'd said she was just getting home, hadn't checked her phone since before she left and hadn't been able to hear it while driving the scooter. It wasn't until she'd reached his place, and he'd shown her the note from Dinah, that she'd finally explained where she'd been—and why. At last he understood the reason she'd been so torn up about those pictures, and what had started that fight between her and her brother.

"The sad thing is . . . most people who know Keith probably *could* believe it," he said. Rafe sympathized with her, but he had to be honest.

"I'm his sister," she said as she prowled restlessly around his living room. "I know him better than anyone."

He was on his feet, too, but he wasn't moving. He had his hands shoved in his pockets as he leaned against the wall, watching her. "And yet you think he might've locked you in an attic once without ever coming back to let you out."

"I can't be sure it was him." Picking up Dinah's note, she waved it at him. "But that's what I'm afraid *she's* going to tell me."

"You think Dinah will back up Ranger?"

"What else could this mean? What more could she have found out?"

"You'd rather believe it was your mother who pushed your sister."

"I'd rather it was an accident, that Annabelle just . . . fell. That's not a pleasant thought, either, but it's not as awful as the alternatives. And if . . . if Keith *did* push her, I hope he did it without intending any real harm. He's always had a temper, often acted out. But he couldn't *purposely* have wanted to kill our older sister. You should've heard him talk about her. He has fond memories of her trying to stand up for him."

"Maybe he was jealous of her, resented the attention she received. Or it could've been momentary. What if she grabbed a toy he was holding and he lashed out? At four years old, he wouldn't have realized how permanent the consequences of his actions would be."

"Exactly my point. But say he did push her. Is he hiding the truth from me now? Shifting the blame to my mother when he knows *he's* the one at fault?"

"Only he can answer that. It could be that he doesn't remember, that he's blocked it from his mind. Or . . ."

"Or?" she prompted.

"Maybe that's why he struggles with substance abuse. He's having a hard time living with himself." As she approached him, Rafe caught hold of her arm and led her to the couch, where they both sat down. "When he called earlier, he told me he wants to apologize. He's been trying to reach you."

"I saw that. I haven't responded because I haven't decided what to do. Keith's always had his problems, but I thought I could trust him. We've looked out for each other our whole lives. It breaks my heart to think my brother—who sometimes seemed like my only friend—isn't the person I thought he was."

"And his apology?"

She sighed. "Is it sincere or more smoke and mirrors?"

He took her hand. "I'm sorry. None of this is easy."

"Thanks. I appreciate that you're trying to help, trying to be there for me. But I feel guilty for sharing information that's so potentially damaging about my family. It's because I was stupid enough to tell Jack that Dinah overheard."

"You told me Dinah knew."

"She did, but this note means she's talking about it again. What if word gets back to my mother?"

"What if it's time for the secrets to come out? Maybe facing reality is the only way for Keith to heal." Maybe it was the only way the family could heal . . .

She bit her lip. "Do you think so?"

"If it's been bothering him enough."

"But what then?" she asked. "Does he deserve to be punished? He was four—hardly an age where you'd expect him to be capable of murder. And yet his actions during the years since won't speak in his favor."

That was what really frightened her. She *could* believe he'd done it, even if she didn't want to.

"You need to talk to him about it. You should talk to your mother, too, get it all out in the open."

That would be difficult, and he knew it.

"This could destroy what's left of my family," she said. "My mother and I are only now starting to get along—to a point. I was hoping our relationship would improve, not be torn to pieces again."

"Sometimes things have to get worse before they get better."

She slumped back on the sofa. "I should never have come home."

"Do you really mean that?" He bent his head to catch her eye. "There's nothing here you like?"

"Even you scare me," she said.

He sat up straighter. "*Me?* Why?"

"Because I like you too much."

She held herself so rigidly, as if she was braced for the worst, which told him she thought her admission would scare him away. And he couldn't blame her. She'd been able to rely on so little in her life.

He lifted her chin with one finger. "That's not a problem," he said, and kissed her.

That kiss had to be the longest, most sensual kiss he'd ever given a woman. He loved the taste of Maisey, the way she parted her lips at just the right moment and leaned into him to accept his tongue. She was trying to patch up her battered heart enough to trust him. That was a start.

But he knew this situation with her family could blow up in her face—and if that happened, he wouldn't be enough to keep her on Fairham. Then all the things he was beginning to imagine—coming home to her at the end of the day, giving Laney the mother she needed and Maisey a child to love, perhaps even getting her pregnant with a second child—would disappear, too.

25

Maisey woke up to the feel of Rafe's hands sliding possessively over her body. They hadn't made love when they went to bed. Maisey's thoughts had been so deeply mired in what she'd learned about her brother and Annabelle, she'd been grateful when he hadn't made any advances. But she was feeling far more receptive now.

Almost everything about Rafe was intoxicating to her—the way he smelled, the way he touched her, the way he moved with so much coordination and confidence.

"I wonder if I was ever really in love with

Jack," she murmured. "At least . . . by the end."

He lifted his head to look down at her. The sun was just beginning to pierce through the blinds, but she knew there was enough light for him to see her expression. "What do you mean by that?"

"What I feel when you touch me is so . . . potent."

A flash of white suggested a smile as he said, "I'm glad you want me."

"I'm sure a lot of girls want you. Not every guy looks like you do in a pair of jeans."

She was teasing him. She expected him to make some sort of funny retort. But he remained serious. "The physical side of what we have is undeniably great, but . . . I'm worried about other things."

"Like . . ." He seemed genuinely troubled.

"Even if I work hard, I may never match Jack's income, Maisey. And I'll certainly never be able to give you the kind of life you knew growing up."

"The funny thing is . . . Jack and I were happier *before* we had money," she said. "So that's all I want, Rafe. I just want to be happy again."

He nuzzled her neck. "Then I'll see what I can arrange," he said, and as he made love to her, Maisey experienced the most liberating sense of letting go. It felt as if she was soaring effortlessly through the air, confident that, when the time came to land, he'd catch her.

"A girl could get addicted to you," she said when he rolled off.

He took her hand to kiss her fingers. "Just any girl?"

She grinned at him, and he grinned back before getting up to go to work.

Maisey wasn't feeling quite so content *after* Rafe left, not when everything she'd learned last night pushed its way to the forefront of her mind. She had to get up, too, had to go to work. But she wasn't looking forward to seeing Nancy. At this point, Nancy would probably be feeling more sympathetic to Keith than she was.

Or maybe not. Rafe had told her Keith had called from Coldiron House. Something must've happened between him and Nancy, or he wouldn't be at home.

Unless he'd gone back to tell their mother about those pictures . . . God, Maisey hoped not. His texts said he wanted to apologize. But the timing made her uncomfortable.

She thought of how he'd torn out of Smuggler's Cove, how he might've hit her if not for Rafe, and wished she could obliterate that memory. Not only did it fill her with renewed shock and outrage, it made the idea that he'd pushed Annabelle to her death more believable, and the possibility that he was marshaling his forces against her more frightening.

Except for the other night, she'd never been afraid of her own brother. But he seemed even more unpredictable as he got older.

Or had she never really known him? Would he go to Josephine and make her aware of the threat Maisey posed now that she was learning the truth?

Concerned that he'd do exactly that, she crawled out of bed, threw on the T-shirt Rafe had discarded when they'd gone to bed and hurried to the living room to find her phone. She'd gotten Dinah's number when they'd bumped into each other at the grocery store. Maybe what Dinah had learned would help Maisey navigate this dark labyrinth. Maisey didn't want her mother and brother teaming up against her. They were formidable enough on their own . . .

Dinah didn't answer but called back almost immediately. "Sorry about that," she said. "I was potty-training Justy."

"How's it going?"

"I'm not sure it's wise to bribe kids, especially with M&Ms first thing in the morning, but I'm desperate."

"He's only two, isn't he? A lot of kids are older than that by the time they're fully potty-trained." Maisey had read so many books on parenting when she was expecting Ellie that she could've cited chapter and verse.

"Believe me, he's ready. He knows what he's doing when he goes in his pants. He *should* be potty-trained by now, but he's making me work for it."

"Good luck."

"The joys of motherhood, right?"

Maisey flinched and quickly changed the subject. "I got your note last night."

"Yeah, I was hoping to catch you at home, but you were gone by the time I returned. Where were you?"

She didn't want to tell anyone more than she absolutely had to. "Rafe's."

"I thought so. I would've walked over, but I wasn't sure you'd want me barging in. Or if you'd want him to know what's going on."

"Thanks for being careful about that," she said without admitting she'd already told Rafe. She'd probably still be keeping it from him if he hadn't been the one to find Dinah's note.

"Okay, good. Because leaving that note was a little awkward."

"Awkward?"

"I promised I wouldn't say anything to anyone about your sister, but . . . I called Chuckie after I left your place, and he said something I thought I should pass along."

Maisey sank into Rafe's easy chair. Expecting someone to keep something like that from her own husband would probably be asking too much, so the inclusion of Chuckie didn't upset her. "And that is?"

"Before I tell you, are you sure you want to take this further? I can only imagine how upsetting it must be to . . . to learn what you're learning."

"My relationship with my mother has always been complicated, Dinah."

"This can't be making it any easier. I feel bad for you. But what I have to say isn't about your mother. That's the reason I thought I should speak up. It's not fair that she's getting the blame when . . . when I'm no longer convinced she deserves it."

Because it was Keith . . . "What is it? What do you have to tell me?"

"There *is* someone who saw part of what happened."

Maisey had started to recline in Rafe's chair. At this, she raised it again. Ranger Phillips had said there was no one else. "Who? And how, considering where it happened?"

"Lindsay Greenberg is Chuckie's mother's friend. She claims she was searching for seashells for a picture-frame project when she heard Gretchen cry out . . ."

"Lindsay Greenberg?" Maisey broke in.

"You don't remember her? She's taught voice lessons on the island for years."

An image appeared in Maisey's mind—of a woman who had flyaway hair and a twinkle in her hazel eyes. No one loved music or crafts more than Lindsay Greenberg. "I *do* remember her. I took a few lessons from her when I was twelve—before I faced the harsh reality that I'd never learn to sing."

"I'm sure Lindsay didn't tell you that you couldn't sing. She encourages everyone."

"No, I came to that conclusion myself." And Josephine had agreed with her. Maisey remembered her mother saying something like, "You'll find what you're good at eventually."

Once Maisey had begun writing children's books, she thought she'd found her niche. But . . .

"So what happened with Lindsay?" she asked.

"She heard a hysterical scream—a call for help—and climbed around that next rocky outcropping to find Gretchen Phillips standing at the top of the cliff with you and your brother. Your mother wasn't even there."

Maisey rubbed her face. So far, this was exactly what Ranger Phillips had told her.

"Maisey?" Dinah prompted when she didn't respond.

"I'm here."

"I felt you should know, even though . . . even though the rest of what I have to say might not be any better."

"Go on . . ."

"She recanted it later, and said it was just an accident, but Gretchen first claimed it was your brother."

Maisey let her breath seep out. Sure enough,

exactly what she'd expected. "He was only four, Dinah."

"Just because she said it doesn't make it true, Maisey."

This brought Maisey's head up. "What do you mean?"

"You'd think Gretchen would be beside herself after witnessing something so horrific, wouldn't you?"

"Wasn't she?"

"Not really. Lindsay told my mother-in-law that her response seemed sort of . . . choreographed. She was *acting* upset, but when Lindsay looked closer, there were no tears. And when Gretchen didn't think anyone was paying attention, she seemed more agitated than heartbroken."

"How was Lindsay able to see clearly enough to make all these observations?"

"She was the one trying to comfort Gretchen while the police searched for your sister."

Maisey couldn't stay seated any longer. She got up and began to circle Rafe's living room. "Gretchen could've been in shock. That'd make anyone act strange."

"That's what Lindsay assumed. She even understood why Gretchen might want to move away from Fairham after that. But she told my mother-in-law that the more she thinks about that day, the more suspect Gretchen's behavior seems. She said Gretchen kept asking her, 'You weren't there when she fell, were you?' Lindsay assured her time and again that she hadn't been able to see what happened, but she thought it was a weird thing to ask."

What could this mean? Surely, Gretchen would have no reason to *lie*. No one with any conscience would implicate a child if that child was innocent.

"I'm not saying Gretchen pushed her," Dinah said. "But what if it *was* an accident? What if she was afraid she'd get blamed, since she was supposed to be watching you three? So she made that up about Keith? That's plausible, isn't it? No one would want to be blamed for that kind of negligence, especially when the child who died was a Lazarow."

"And Keith was a difficult child—always throwing tantrums and acting out—so he was a handy scapegoat," Maisey said.

"She didn't like him. She admitted it several times, in private, to various people before she moved. Said Annabelle was the sweetest thing in the world, but he was a little monster."

Chilled, Maisey perched on the couch and slipped her bare legs up under Rafe's T-shirt. "It doesn't sound to me as if *she* was much of a gem."

"I never met her myself, so I can't say. But . . . I felt you should hear what Chuckie told me before you assumed the worst about your mother."

The fact that Gretchen had blamed Keith so that people wouldn't believe she'd allowed such a terrible accident was one thing. But black-mailing Malcolm afterward? That took her deception, if it was a deception, to a whole new level.

She couldn't be *that* bad, could she?

Maisey grimaced at her own thoughts. What was she thinking? There were people who'd do whatever they could get away with. The true-crime shows Jack loved to watch proved that, didn't they?

"Would Lindsay ever talk to *me?*"

"I don't know her that well personally," Dinah replied. "But I've seen her at my in-laws a few times, and I can tell she's a good person. I'm sure she wouldn't mind if you approached her."

A buzz alerted Maisey to an incoming call. She didn't want to be interrupted right now, but she couldn't ignore it. The new call came from her mother's cell.

"Dinah?" Maisey said.

"Yeah?"

"I've got to go. But thank you. I appreciate everything."

"You're welcome. And if you'd like me to go to Lindsay's with you, I will."

"No, I'd rather not overwhelm her. I'll call you once we've talked, though."

After they'd said goodbye and Maisey switched over, she held her breath. What had Keith told their mother? Was Josephine about to disinherit her and order her out of Smuggler's Cove?

Josephine was tough enough to do it.

Closing her eyes, Maisey released her breath. "Hello?"

"Where are you?"

Her mother was upset. It was apparent in the terseness of those three words. "What—what do you mean?"

"I'm at your door. The scooter's here, but you're not answering."

26

Maisey cursed under her breath as she disconnected. What was her mother doing in Smuggler's Cove?

Keith must've told her about the pictures. What else would bring Josephine to this side of the island? If she wanted to see Maisey, she'd simply have Pippa call and invite her to dinner. Or she'd show up at the flower shop.

"Shit. Shit, shit, shit," she muttered as she pulled off Rafe's shirt and scrambled to collect her clothes. She had to decide what she would and wouldn't reveal should Josephine question her about Annabelle.

If Keith had told Josephine about the pictures, had he also mentioned the letters Maisey had found in the attic? The pictures had been discovered by someone else and brought to her. That was innocent enough. But her mother would feel they should've been brought to her. And the letters wouldn't be viewed in the same light. She'd secretly taken them from Coldiron House, and she'd refused to let Keith destroy them. Josephine would feel betrayed that she hadn't acted to protect the family name . . .

Dropping onto the floor, Maisey searched for her bra and one missing boot, which had been kicked under the bed. What was she going to do? What was she going to say? Should she be ready to launch her own offensive? Take a stand and demand some answers?

That would start World War III . . .

She was in such a frantic hurry she *couldn't* decide how far she'd go—not until she knew why her mother had come. That meant she had to walk into her bungalow feeling unprepared and defenseless.

She raked her fingers through her hair as she jogged next door. She preferred to present a dignified appearance. That kind of thing mattered to her mother; in her view, it showed self-respect. But, in this situation, dignified was pretty much impossible. It would be obvious that she'd spent the night with Rafe the second she walked in with her makeup smudged and her hair tangled. She could say she'd been out for a walk, but it wouldn't be very credible, especially since she had to be at work soon and hadn't even showered.

Bottom line, her mother would definitely suspect and lying might make matters worse.

Josephine wasn't waiting in the car or on the porch, but the Mercedes was there, parked in the drive. It wasn't until Maisey entered the house that she realized her mother had let herself in. How, Maisey didn't know. Either she'd inadvertently left the door unlocked, or her mother had a master key to the whole development. Or maybe Keith had reached through the cardboard covering the window they'd broken when they were fighting—because he was there, too. The second she spotted him, Maisey knew dating the "wrong" man would be minor in relation to everything else. Her brother had texted her an apology and left her several voice mails last night, pleading with her to understand why he'd behaved so terribly, but she hadn't responded. She'd been reeling, needed some time. And then she'd been so focused on Rafe . . . He was the only person who made her feel safe and whole. She almost wished he was here at this moment; he wouldn't allow the encounter to get out of hand.

But she couldn't rely on him to fight her battles. She didn't want him to witness what was about to happen, anyway. She was fairly certain Keith had reversed his apology and stabbed her in the back.

"What's going on?" Her whole body tingled with anxiety as they both scrutinized her.

"We need to have a talk, Maisey."

It was Keith who'd spoken. The animosity between him and Josephine seemed to have disappeared. They were united now that they felt the family was in peril.

"Sit down." Josephine gestured to the chair beside her. She had the pictures of Annabelle in her lap, as well as the letters. Keith must've gotten them from her bedroom, which meant he—and probably Josephine, too—had seen that her bed was perfectly made. Entering her house and bedroom without an invitation felt like an invasion of privacy, but she couldn't complain, not when she'd stolen the letters from Coldiron House in the first place.

Maisey perched on the edge of the chair her mother had indicated. "Did you know?" she asked as she watched Josephine look through the photographs.

Her mother lifted the top one. "About Annabelle? How could I not know?"

"About the blackmail," she clarified.

"No. Your father kept that from me, which is a surprise. I never would've guessed he had it in him to be so deceptive. But then . . . he knew this woman probably wouldn't survive another day if she tried to blackmail *me*."

Maisey clasped her hands in her lap. "It's

comments like those that frighten me, Mother."

"Because I won't allow someone to take advantage of me?"

"Because you seem willing to go to such lengths to stop it."

"No one's ever going to get the best of me. That's all there is to it." She paused as she studied another picture of Annabelle. Maisey wanted to know what she was feeling, if she was feeling anything for her missing daughter, but her face remained an emotionless mask.

"Would you rather Father let her tell the truth?" Maisey asked. "If he hadn't paid her, she might have, you know."

"I'd rather she'd respected our agreement when I paid her to keep her mouth shut and leave. If she wasn't going to abide by those terms—if she was going to turn around and break the law—she deserves whatever she gets."

"So it's true." Maisey looked at Keith. Was he accepting responsibility for Annabelle's death?

"I don't remember it," he said, his voice deadpan. "If I'd done something that terrible, you'd think I'd remember."

"It was an accident, like I told you," Josephine said, her voice matter-of-fact.

"So then . . . why the payoff?" Maisey understood she was pushing the line with her mother, but she had to ask.

Josephine's eyebrows slid up. "If you must

know, your father and I didn't see any point in making Keith's life more difficult by having him grow up with that stigma. We didn't want you to grow up under the shadow of a tragedy like that, either. Didn't consider it wise to invite that kind of inspection of our lives. That's why we paid the staff to leave. Why should we all suffer the rest of our lives over an accident?"

Keith grimaced as he rubbed his temples. "What if it wasn't an accident? What if there's something fundamentally wrong with me? I mean, we've always known there *is* something wrong."

"It *wasn't* intentional," Josephine insisted.

As Maisey watched Keith pace in front of her empty fireplace, she couldn't help remembering how he'd behaved when he'd tried to burn the pictures. "Did you lock me in the attic?" she asked.

He stopped. "What?"

"Did you lock me in the attic that day when we were playing in there and you had to go to baseball practice?"

He seemed perplexed. "I don't recall the day you're talking about. When did we play in the attic?"

Maisey opened her mouth to explain, to remind him of that old trunk filled with clothes, but Josephine cut her off. "*I* locked the door." Josephine piled the pictures and letters off to one side. "You'd been told not to go in there, and you disobeyed. You needed to learn a lesson."

A flash of anger flared up. Was it necessary to go that far? She'd been so young and frightened . . . "You left me there for hours!"

"Maybe it seemed like hours to you, but it wasn't that long. I sent your father to get you before dinner."

Maisey thought about what Dinah had told her. Her own mother obviously believed Gretchen Phillips's version of the story, except that Josephine was convinced Keith hadn't pushed Annabelle intentionally. She must be glad Annabelle's body was never discovered. It meant there was no burial, no headstone. And ridding the house of every reminder had made it easier for the living to forget and move on.

But was it the truth that Keith's hand was the one that pushed her? How would they ever know? He claimed he didn't remember the incident, and although Maisey was skeptical—he'd lied in the past to cover his drug use, to get money, whatever—he seemed genuinely bewildered and upset to think he might've been responsible for such a tragedy.

And Maisey had one other question. Why had Josephine come here, now, to address this? Was she hoping to disarm Maisey? To get her to back away for fear she might find it *was* intentional?

Maisey stared at the stack of pictures. "Why didn't you ever talk about her?"

Josephine's chin came up the way it always did when she felt as if she was being criticized. "Why would I?"

"Because you miss her as much as I miss Ellie?"

"You're too sentimental. Being that sensitive will only get you hurt. Missing Annabelle won't bring her back." She stood. "I'm taking these letters and photos. They don't belong to you, anyway. And I don't ever want to speak of this again. Understood?"

Obviously, Josephine considered the situation handled. Her explanation made sense, tied it all up neatly. But what about Lindsay Greenberg's comments on Gretchen Phillips's behavior? Was there something more they didn't know?

"You're telling me to leave it alone."

"There's no reason to pursue it."

Keith was the reason. What Lindsay had noticed could mean he wasn't the one who'd pushed Annabelle. Dinah had raised at least a small amount of suspicion that Gretchen might have used him—a little boy with a difficult temperament—to hide her own negligence. Maisey wanted to look into that. But with Gretchen dead, how would she figure out what had really happened?

Maisey checked the time on her phone. "I'd better get ready for work," she said. "Nancy's expecting me."

Josephine, regal as ever, bowed her head. "Then we'll get out of your way."

Her mother gestured for Keith to precede her, but he didn't. He walked over to Maisey. "I'm sorry about how I behaved the other night. I . . . I wasn't myself."

"I got your messages. Thank you."

His frown suggested he could tell she wasn't ready to forgive him. He'd rushed right back to Coldiron House, and he'd drawn Josephine into this, even though they'd both believed, at the time, that their mother might've been responsible for Annabelle's death. Had that been the case . . .

Maisey refused to follow that thought to its conclusion. Now she knew it couldn't have been Josephine, it didn't matter. It was probably punishment enough for him to learn that *he* was responsible. That revelation couldn't have been easy to hear, and wouldn't be easy to live with.

Swallowing her indignation, Maisey forced herself to hug him. "We'll be able to put it behind us."

"There is one more thing," Josephine said, her hand on the door.

Maisey looked past her brother. "What's that?"

"It's time you took your life a little more seriously."

A chill ran down Maisey's spine; she'd seen that determined glint in her mother's eyes before. "And what does that mean?"

"I presume you were next door?"

Despite all the reasons she probably wouldn't

be believed, Maisey was tempted to lie. She didn't want to stand against the gale-force wind that was her mother's disapproval, especially when she'd just been found out—and chastised—for removing those letters from the attic of Coldiron House. But she didn't think that would be fair to Rafe. If she was going to continue to see him, she had to acknowledge the relationship, even if it meant defying her mother once again. "Yes."

"As I thought. Then, let this serve as a warning. If you continue to see Raphael, you won't inherit Smuggler's Cove. You won't inherit anything," she said, and walked out.

Nancy was quiet at the flower shop. Maisey considered asking her what had happened with Keith, but decided against it. She could tell Nancy was upset, and she wanted to give the poor woman some solitude, if that was what Nancy needed. Besides, Maisey could guess where things stood. Nancy had probably pushed him for some kind of commitment, or told him she loved him, and he'd backed off.

"I was wondering if you could make a delivery on your way home tonight," Nancy said as Maisey was getting ready to leave.

"A delivery?" She'd never been asked to handle that side of the business before.

The first smile of the day appeared on Nancy's face. "Sort of."

"I'm on a scooter, so a delivery might be hard—unless the flowers are going somewhere close and I drive *really* slow. Is it an emergency?"

"No, never mind." She pretended to hit herself in the head in disgust. "I forgot about the moped. I'll call one of our delivery people."

"Where do they need to go?"

Nancy's smile broadened. "To your place."

"*My* place?"

Her thighs rubbed together—she was wearing her usual too-tight pants—as she walked over and brought Maisey a card. "This goes with it."

I can't quit thinking about you. —Rafe.

"He called in an order?"

"An hour ago," Nancy said. "See that big arrangement of hydrangeas over there?"

"The one you spent the last hour on?"

"I wanted it to be perfect, because it's for you."

"That's so nice! Of both of you. But . . . how'd he know hydrangeas are my favorite?"

"He asked me what you'd like best. It was so sweet. I got the feeling it was the first time he'd ever sent flowers."

"I didn't realize you knew which flowers I liked."

She winked. "I've seen the way you favor them."

Because she paid attention, noticed those subtleties about other people . . .

Maisey waited as Nancy carried the arrangement over to her. She'd done a fantastic job; it was gorgeous. But there was no way she'd be able to carry something of that size home on her scooter, not without ruining it. She wasn't even sure she dared to accept it. Was she willing to gamble her inheritance—Smuggler's Cove, the only connection she had left to her father—on what she was feeling for Rafe? Was it even possible to fall in love in her current situation? What if their fling—or relationship or whatever it was—didn't last? She couldn't support herself on what she was making at the flower shop, especially if her mother threw her out of the bungalow . . . And, at the moment, she couldn't count on reviving her writing career.

"What's wrong?" Nancy asked.

"Nothing," she said. "You're very talented. You know that?"

Tears filled Nancy's eyes. She muttered a quick thanks and turned away so Maisey wouldn't see them, but Maisey stopped her. "Are you going to tell me what happened with Keith?"

"He doesn't love me," she said. "You knew it all along—and you tried to warn me, but I . . . I didn't want to listen."

Maisey pulled her close for a hug. "Some of the hardest things are for the best," she told Nancy, and she had to wonder if that same advice applied to her.

27

Keith was waiting for her when she got home. But Maisey wasn't happy to see him. He was the reason Josephine had shown up out of the blue this morning—when Maisey was the least prepared to deal with her—and made that nasty ultimatum regarding Rafe. He'd also hurt Nancy, as Maisey had feared. It'd taken some prying, but before she left the flower shop, Maisey had managed to get out of Nancy that Keith owed her close to two thousand dollars, most of which he'd borrowed in the past ten days. So not only was Nancy grappling with the harsh reality that he didn't care about her the way she'd hoped, she was out a lot of cash.

Reluctantly, Maisey got off the scooter. Then she paused to stare up at him. How was she going to handle this meeting? She didn't want another argument, but she couldn't see how she'd avoid that—until he came toward her and she saw the slump of his shoulders and the sheepish expression on his face. For the time being, he was contrite.

"I'm sorry about this morning," he said.

He had more to be sorry for than that. But he seemed to forget his own mistakes almost as soon as he made them, seemed to expect everyone else to disregard the damage he caused. Because of that, and all his other problems, it was impossible to know how to be a good sister to him. Maisey didn't want to discourage him; she wanted to help him gain control of his life. But was she helping him? Or enabling him? Did her love and support just allow him to continue acting like a human wrecking ball?

"You're not going to say anything?" he asked as he met her on the steps.

"I don't know what to say," she replied. "You complain to me about Mom almost nonstop, but then you turn on me and run right to her . . ."

"I didn't turn on you," he broke in. "I was trying to protect our family. I told you I felt we had to destroy those pictures and letters—even tried to do it myself. I knew one of us would be hurt if we didn't." He shrugged. "But I thought it would be Mom. That's ironic, don't you think?"

Ironic, yes. But did he feel any remorse for what he'd done to Annabelle? *Should* he?

"And now?" she said. "Do you still want to wipe out all trace of our sister?"

"I don't want anyone talking about what happened, that's for sure."

She sent him a sharp look as she let them in the house.

"What?" he said. "Would *you?* Why do you think Mom and Dad went to so much trouble to keep this quiet? It's not an easy thing to live with! For me—or for any of us . . ."

"So you honestly weren't aware that—that it wasn't Mom."

He grabbed her arm. "Of course not!"

She wished she could accept that as the truth. But her trust was so battered . . . "Keith . . ."

"Maisey, listen to me," he said. "I have my problems. I can't argue with that. No one knows how messed up I am more than you do. But you have to believe me when I say I don't remember seeing Annabelle fall, let alone pushing her. I would *never* purposely hurt her—or you."

"How do you explain almost running me down the other night?" she asked.

"I didn't almost run you down. If I'd meant to hurt you, I would have. You don't think I could've stopped you if I'd been willing to go that far?"

"No, because Rafe was there to prevent it."

"I mean before he came out! I wanted those pictures, but it wasn't as if I was beating you up to get them. I could've knocked you out with one punch if I didn't care about hurting you. And I never locked you in the attic. I didn't even know that Mom did until she admitted it today."

His grip on her had loosened as he spoke. Maisey pulled away to put her purse on the counter. "What about Nancy?"

"What about her? She has nothing to do with this."

"I just saw her at the shop. She's heartbroken—not to mention you borrowed money from her you can't repay."

"I'll pay her back. She's not the right person for me. You've known that all along. And now she does, too. That's what you wanted, isn't it? For me to break it off?"

"Preferably *before* you took her money, but . . . yeah, leading her on would be wrong."

"See? I'm not leading her on. It's over."

Exhausted from being on her feet at work all day, Maisey dropped onto the couch. "Coming home to Fairham has been nothing like I expected."

"You're blaming me for that, but it's not my fault. I'm fighting an addiction that has such a hold on me I can't shake it. The other stuff I do . . . that's our childhood and all the crap we went through."

"Which you had no control over. I get that. But how long are we supposed to hang on to the possibility that you'll get on top of your addiction? How long are we supposed to hope you'll get over the past?"

"I'd do it *now* if I could! You have to believe that. Or are you giving up on me?"

Was she? And would that be fair, when she knew so many of his problems were due to his emotional makeup—and his childhood—as he'd just said?

"No. Of course I'm not giving up on you."

He lowered his voice. "You believe I pushed Annabelle on purpose, don't you!"

She couldn't quite meet his eyes. It would be a lie to claim she hadn't wondered. But now that he was putting a voice to her doubts, they sounded outlandish again. She felt terrible for allowing her mind to go in that direction. Her return to Fairham hadn't gone as smoothly as she'd hoped. She hadn't been able to rely on Keith for anything. But she'd known he wasn't emotionally stable, which was why she'd come back to help him in the first place. And he was right—he could've hurt her when he burned the pictures. He could've hurt her countless times over the years, and he'd never done so. Did she really have reason to doubt him *that* much?

"I'm in a difficult transition, and having all of this come up in the middle of it . . . I admit I'm confused."

"Dad believed it," he said flatly.

"Did he ever say that?"

"Of course not. Mom and Dad didn't talk about Annabelle, to either of us. But he wouldn't have paid that woman, that Gretchen Phillips, so much money if he didn't believe in his heart that Annabelle's death wasn't an accident."

"That's not necessarily true. There's a stigma either way. He obviously didn't see any point in putting you through the wringer of public opinion when he had the money to make the whole thing go away."

"But secrets don't remain secrets forever."

"This one might have, if Mom hadn't decided to remodel the bungalows."

He thrust his hands in his pockets. "I can't get my shit together, Maisey. I've tried. I have. There's something wrong with me, something I can't overcome. I make life worse for everyone around me."

"Don't talk like that," she said.

"It's true! Even you've lost faith in me. And if I don't have you, I don't have anyone."

She stopped him before he could leave. "I haven't lost faith, Keith. I've just been . . . dealing with my own problems."

"I wish I could remember what happened that day on the cliff," he said. "I wish I knew *why* I did it." He paused for a few seconds. "Why that should matter, I don't know. In fact, I don't know why I do half the shit I do."

What Dinah had told Maisey popped into her mind. Had everyone blindly accepted as truth something that might have been a calculated misdirection? She hesitated to tell Keith what Lindsay Greenberg had to say about that day. She didn't want to hold out false hope. But her brother looked so depressed, she felt he needed *some* encouragement. "Maybe you didn't do it."

He lifted his troubled gaze. "What are you talking about? You heard Mom."

"I heard her. But she wasn't there."

"Which means . . ."

"Annabelle could've fallen on her own."

"If she did, why would Gretchen Phillips point a finger at me?"

"Maybe she didn't like you." He hadn't been popular with many of his caregivers, teachers or other authority figures, so that wouldn't be unusual. "Or she wasn't paying enough attention to where Annabelle was walking or playing and was afraid she'd get blamed for being negligent."

"Would she blackmail Dad if she was really the one to blame?"

"Why not? It was a way to get money, to survive. And we know she was struggling financially."

He looked hopeful, but then he shook his head. "You'd be better off without me," he said. "Everyone would."

Again, he moved to go, and again, she stopped him. "Don't overreact. That's all I'm saying," she told him. "Let me see what I can find out before you decide you're some kind of deranged psychopath."

"Both Gretchen and Annabelle are dead, Maise. And you and I don't remember. There was no one else there. So how are you going to find out anything?"

If he had any recollection of that day, he'd also remember that Lindsay Greenberg had come upon the scene . . .

Gaining renewed conviction from that detail, Maisey drew a deep breath. "Gretchen had kids, family and friends she interacted with. She must've said *something* to *someone* through the years. Perhaps she confessed on her deathbed."

He stared at her for several seconds, as if he wanted to hope she was right. But then he said, "And what if all your research convinces you it *was* me?"

"I'll stand by you even then. I believe you're trying to be a good person. You were only four when this happened. If you were responsible in some way, it could've been a simple misjudgment. But let's not accept anything blindly. Let's get to the bottom of it, find out everything we can and then figure out what to do."

"Go for it," he muttered, "but I'm sure you won't be happy with the results. Considering all the shit I've done wrong in my life, I'm probably guilty as sin."

"You deserve the benefit of the doubt."

"I lost the benefit of the doubt a long time ago," he said.

Maisey stood at the railing and watched as he left. He was so down on himself that she worried he might give up on getting that fresh start and do something drastic again.

If she could prove he hadn't killed Annabelle, it would boost his morale and might help him get past the assumption that he was so deeply flawed nothing he did would make any difference.

She just hoped that what she learned would help instead of hurt.

The flowers arrived at ten to five, as Maisey was heading out. She was going to town to see if she could track down Lindsay Greenberg. But she took the gorgeous bouquet Rafe had bought for her, and Nancy had so carefully arranged, and put it on the coffee table first. Then she sat down to read and reread the card. *I can't quit thinking about you. —Rafe.*

She couldn't quit thinking about him, either. That was the problem. She wished this could be easy. That she could pull away for a while until she felt stronger. Maybe she'd be able to build a relationship with her mother so Josephine wouldn't be opposed to seeing her with a man like Rafe, as long as he made her happy. But what she and Rafe felt was so urgent and immediate and . . . there didn't seem to be any toning it down.

Before lunch, he'd texted her to see what she was doing for dinner and invited her out. She'd told him she had plans. But she knew that as soon as she got home tonight she'd go over to his house. Already, she couldn't wait to see him. So what good would it do to pretend otherwise?

With a sigh, she picked up her phone. She had a weakness for Rafe; that was all there was to it. Even if it cost her entire inheritance, she couldn't seem to stay away from him—and these gorgeous flowers and his thoughtful note only made her more aware of the power he held over her. "Why can't you ever play it safe?" she asked herself as she texted him. **What time are you getting Laney?**

Going over there in a few. Why?

Can I catch a ride into town?

Will you let me take you to dinner if I say yes?

She chuckled as she shook her head. He was obsessed with getting her to go out with him. In his mind, that would legitimize the relationship, assure him she was interested in more than what went on between them at night.

But what if they ran into her mother?

Where do you want to go?

The Grotto?

The Grotto was expensive. Given the flowers and that elegant a dinner, she guessed he was also trying to prove that he could manage a few of the finer things in life.

It wouldn't be fair to turn him down, then hurry over to his bed after dark. Maybe *she* felt more comfortable keeping their relationship out of the public eye, but he was equating her willingness to be seen together with her level of interest.

How about something simpler? A salad? What does Laney like?

I wasn't planning to bring Laney.

Why? I'm sure she'd love to go with us. Let's take her to that pizza place with all the games. We can help her play Skee-Ball and she can go in that pit with all those plastic balls the kids jump in.

He didn't text back; he called instead. "Your plan doesn't sound too romantic," he said, but she could tell he was happy that she'd included his daughter.

"The flowers are romantic enough," she said.

"They arrived?"

"A few minutes ago."

"Nancy said that kind was your favorite. I'm not even sure I've seen them before."

"I can almost guarantee you have. You just never paid attention to what they're called."

"How was your day?" he asked.

"It got a little complicated when my mother

showed up this morning and found out I was at your house."

There was a long silence. "What'd she have to say about that?"

"I'd rather not discuss it."

"Didn't go well."

"Not particularly."

"She doesn't want you to see me."

"No."

The silence stretched out again. Then he said, "I can't say I'm surprised, but . . . I have to admit that sounds pretty unfair. I've never done anything to make her dislike me. I've worked hard, been reasonable with my prices and I'm doing a good job. She doesn't know how we met, does she?"

"I haven't told anyone how we met."

"So it's just that I don't wear a suit to work."

And the fact that he had a special-needs daughter, which her mother viewed as an unnecessary burden . . . "She doesn't want me to make another mistake."

"How does she know I'd be a mistake?"

"She thinks she knows everything."

"Are you going to listen to her?"

"To be honest? I probably would if I could. I'm in no condition to get involved in another relationship."

"But . . ."

"None of that seems to matter. I want you, anyway."

"Careful," he said, his voice sexy and low. "I'm just around the corner. If you get me too worked up, we'll be late for dinner."

She imagined his bare skin against hers, his hands touching her . . . "There are worse things than putting dinner off for twenty or thirty minutes, right?"

"I expect you to be naked by the time I get there," he said, and hung up.

28

So much for slowing things down and using caution. Maisey couldn't get Rafe's clothes off fast enough. Almost as soon as he walked through the door, she pushed him up against the wall and unbuttoned his pants. Fewer than three minutes later, they were on the floor, in too much of a hurry to even make it to the bedroom.

Maisey had never experienced such overwhelming desire. That was part of what scared her. If she was going to enter a new relationship at such an ill-advised time, and against the wishes of her opinionated and powerful mother, she didn't want to be doing it for the wrong reasons.

Lust is different from love, Maisey.

Jack had told her that . . .

Or did she just want to believe this was lust

so she didn't have to face the frightening possibility that it could be much more?

"I'm sorry your mother doesn't like me," Rafe said when he'd had a few minutes to catch his breath. "I hate that her dislike of me separates you from your family. That it puts you right back in the terrible position you've been in for the past decade."

His arms tightened around her as she shifted closer. "Fortunately, I like you enough for both of us," she said.

"But will there ever come a time when you'll resent me for it?"

"Of course not. It's not *your* fault."

He pushed her gently onto her back and leaned up on one elbow to look down at her. "What do you have to do in town? I assumed you were visiting your family, but now . . . I'm guessing that's not the plan."

She ran a finger over the contours of his face. "I need to talk to someone, a woman by the name of Lindsay Greenberg."

When she got close to his mouth, he bit her finger playfully. "I know Lindsay Greenberg."

Maisey wasn't surprised. Fairham wasn't that big, and Rafe had been back long enough that he'd probably bumped into most of the residents. She was curious to hear the context, however. "How?"

"Fixed her roof last winter. But . . . why do you want to talk to her?"

"She might know something about the day my sister fell from that cliff."

"Really? Why her?"

"According to Dinah, she was there." She told him about her phone conversation with Dinah and what had happened when her mother and Keith arrived afterward.

He groaned. "You're going to continue to chase this thing?"

"I have to." She dropped her hand. "I came here to help my brother, but since I've been home, things have only gotten worse for him."

"Through no fault of yours."

"True. He's his own worst enemy. But what Dinah told me has created some questions in my mind, and I won't be able to rest easy until I've done everything I can to find the answers."

He tapped the end of her nose. "Even though you might uncover information that would be more damaging to your brother?"

"I don't think he pushed her, Rafe."

"Because . . ."

"Because he didn't lock me in the attic."

"That's not an entirely logical conclusion."

"Love is never logical," she said. "But knowing he's not the one who locked me in enables me to trust him—a little. That's all. And since I'm probably the one person in his life who *can* muster any trust, I have to defend him, and the only way I can do that is to follow any lead that might bring in new information. Lindsay doesn't seem like the kind of person who'd make things up. I guess I'm hanging my hopes on that."

"I'd have to agree with you there. She's a sweet person—a real Pollyanna."

"Maybe learning he didn't do it will encourage him to keep fighting, to make the changes he needs to make in his life."

"I get how much this means to you. And I agree it might help if you could free him from the belief that he's a born psychopath. But you do realize that for your father to have paid Gretchen Phillips that much . . ."

"He must've believed her story," she finished. "Yes, and Keith realizes that, too. That's what hurts him the most. No decent person wants to see himself as capable of murder, even at such a young age—*especially* at such a young age," she said, correcting herself. "That implies he was predestined to be bad, as if he's never had any choice in the matter. Not only that, we tend to believe what our parents think of us, right? So knowing Dad bought into that story makes Keith think he *must* be to blame, even though he doesn't remember it. I hope to convince him otherwise."

Rafe said nothing, but she could tell from his expression that he wasn't completely sold on what she planned to do.

"You don't think I should pursue it," she said.

"It could go very wrong," he responded. "I can't imagine that your mother will be happy to have you poking around in the past. Why would she want that old scandal back in the light when she paid so many people to let it fade away in the first place?"

"I'm sure she won't like it, since she believes he did it, too."

"Exactly. She'll see no point in stirring the pot."

"Still, I have to do it."

He sat up. "You're prepared to piss her off?"

She sat up, too, and leaned over to peck his lips. "It won't be the first time." She was feeling less confident than she sounded. Taking on her mother was a scary proposition, but she had to live according to what her heart dictated. And right now her heart told her she had to investigate the details surrounding that terrible day. She was also fairly certain she was falling in love with Rafe. But she wasn't going to say that. She wasn't ready to admit it.

As he stood, he extended his hand and drew her to her feet. "Let's get dressed and go see what Lindsay has to say, then."

"You know where she lives?"

"I know where almost everyone lives. I've worked all over this island."

She bent to grab her clothes, then he pulled her up against him for one last kiss.

Lindsay was every bit as sweet as Rafe had said. In her late fifties or early sixties, she was tall, willowy, attractive. She had a ready smile to go with her gently lined face, and she immediately welcomed them into her small house.

"Sit down. Can I get you cup of tea or something else to drink?" she asked as she gestured toward the sofa.

"No, we're sorry to barge in on you like this . . ." Maisey started, but Lindsay, who obviously didn't remember her, interrupted.

"Oh, it's no bother. Any friend of Rafe's is a friend of mine. With what I owe him, he can barge in on me anytime."

When Maisey shot Rafe a questioning look, he shrugged. "It was nothing," he said.

"It was definitely something!" Lindsay argued. "I doubt I could've survived last winter without him. I had a serious leak in my roof, one that was causing a lot of damage. So I hired him to fix it—and asked if I could pay for the repairs in installments, since . . . well, since so many of my students had moved away. Winters can get lean, what with everyone hunkering down to avoid the cold. Many of my students head off to college as they get older, so business ebbs and flows like the tides around here. Anyway, he came over immediately and spent one whole day patching the hole. But when I tried to give him my initial payment, he wouldn't accept it. And he hasn't accepted any of the others I've tried to make since. He says he likes having me in his debt— as if he'd ever ask for anything in return."

"You can give Laney a few voices lessons when she gets older," he said. "I'll consider that a fair trade."

A warm sensation washed over Maisey. Rafe hadn't mentioned that Lindsay owed him money, hadn't said a single word about his good deed. "He makes people feel important, doesn't he?" Lindsay murmured.

Rafe looked startled, even embarrassed, by the compliment. He didn't like them making a fuss over him, but what she'd said was true. Maisey felt like an entirely different person when she was with him, as if all the terrible things in her life didn't matter as much as all the wonderful things she had to look forward to.

"You might not be so happy we stopped by for a visit when you hear why," he told Lindsay.

Lindsay sobered instantly. "What is it?"

Rafe touched Maisey's arm. "Do you know who this is?"

"I'm assuming it's your girlfriend. I've been waiting for you to introduce her."

"It's Maisey Lazarow, Josephine's daughter."

Her eyes flew wide. "Oh! Of course. I recognize the family resemblance now, but . . . I—I didn't see it at first."

And she'd probably never expected Maisey to be with Rafe.

"I'd like to talk about that day you were on the beach below Coldiron House," Maisey said, but she was pretty sure Lindsay had guessed that the minute Rafe identified her.

"I don't think it would be wise to go into it," she said, "not after all these years."

"It's important we revisit it, Ms. Greenberg. I'm worried about my brother. He's heard he's responsible, and if he *didn't* do it, he needs to know."

Lindsay took several seconds to respond; Maisey could tell she was reluctant to help despite her plea—until Rafe leaned forward to lend his support. "We're only looking for the truth, Lindsay," he said. "If Keith is guilty, he'll have to accept that. We all will. But if he's not . . ."

"I understand—but what if I'm wrong?" she asked. "That's why I've mostly kept my mouth shut. Every once in a while, I'd try to speak up. My conscience demanded it. But then this other side of me would override that impulse, just in case I was wrong and would be getting an innocent person in trouble."

"Gretchen's dead," Rafe said. "You can't hurt her. But you might be able to help a very conflicted man sort out something that's incredibly painful to him."

Her chest rose and fell as she took a deep breath. Then she nodded.

"Can you tell us how you came to be where you were that day?" Maisey asked.

"The shells at the public beach were all broken. So I parked at the bottom of the Point, hiked around the mountain and over those big rocks so I could search your beach. I'd just realized the tide was in, that I wouldn't be able to get down there, when . . . when I heard a scream."

"Then you turned and looked up, or . . . How close were you?"

"I couldn't see the Point from where I was. I was afraid someone from the house would spot me poaching on your beach. I didn't feel I was doing anything wrong, but I was still trying to stay out of sight. Once I heard that panicked scream, I scrambled higher to get around to where I could see. When I did, I saw Gretchen Phillips standing at the top of the cliff with you and your brother."

"Where was my mother?"

"In the house, I guess. A maid came out to search before she showed up."

"But no one recovered my sister's body."

"No. Before too long, the police arrived, and they looked, too. But the only thing they found was your sister's doll, bobbing in the surf."

"What was Gretchen doing while everyone else was searching? Was she looking, too?"

"Not with any real intensity. She was just sort of . . . watching. Someone else had taken you and Keith by then. I went up to console her and when we could safely do it, we both went down to the water's edge."

"I've heard that . . . that you found her response to the situation strange. In what way?"

"Besides the fact that she wasn't really searching the waves for any sign of Annabelle? That she didn't seem intent on finding her?"

"Yes."

"Well, for one thing, what was she doing with three small children at the top of that cliff? There were far easier ways to get down to the beach, including the stairs leading from the house. She couldn't have taken you to the beach, anyway, since the tide was in. I thought *that* was strange —that a caregiver would take small kids to such a dangerous spot. And then, when Annabelle fell into the ocean, Gretchen started screaming, but she didn't move. Didn't grab you two and run to the house to get help. Maybe they would've been able to find Annabelle if—if Gretchen had acted with more sense."

"Did anyone ever ask her why she just stood there?"

"Of course. She claimed she was too shocked by what had happened. That she was immobilized by the horror of it all."

"Which could be the truth," Rafe pointed out.

"Yes," she allowed. "See why I'm so confused? And yet the one thing that made me the most uncomfortable isn't anything I can even explain.

It was just a feeling that she was hiding something. What, I couldn't begin to guess. Who'd hide anything about the death of a child? I went to visit her right after the incident, to see if I could get rid of my misgivings. But she said she didn't want to talk about it. Then she up and moved away, and within weeks it was as if Annabelle had never existed."

"Do you have any idea where Gretchen went? If she stayed in contact with anyone?"

"No," she said. "We didn't have any friends in common . . ." Suddenly, she stopped. "Wait a second. She used to babysit one of my current voice students. I wonder if they kept in touch."

"Would you mind giving us her name and address? Or a phone number?"

"Her name's Heidi Hildebrandt. I wouldn't feel comfortable giving out her address without permission, even to you, Rafe—because she's my client. But I'll bet you can ask around to find out where she lives. She owns the bakery in town."

"I know her place," Rafe said, then focused on Maisey. "I'll take you over there."

"Right now?" Maisey asked. "Shouldn't we get Laney first?"

"Going to Pizza Planet will make up for us being a little late. She isn't used to having me come at a set time, anyway, since my work doesn't always end at five."

Maisey waited until they were out of Ms.

Greenberg's house to ask Rafe how he was familiar with Heidi.

"I replaced her water heater a few months ago," he said.

"Did you do it for free?" she asked.

He gave her a crooked smile. "Smart ass."

Rafe knew he was finally gaining Maisey's trust when she slipped her fingers through his as they approached Heidi Hildebrandt's house. "Are you making a statement here?" he asked, raising their joined hands.

She scowled. "I'm cold," she replied, as if that was the only reason she'd taken his hand, but a smile appeared a second later.

She held on to him the whole time they were talking to Heidi, who gave them the name of a town in Louisiana where she said Gretchen had spent the last thirty years of her life.

"That was easy," Maisey murmured once they'd left.

"Gretchen's been dead for nine years. I'm sure Heidi couldn't see any harm in revealing where she used to live, especially when you told her we just want to confirm that Annabelle's death was an accident. That was brilliant, by the way. Enough information but not too much."

"What I told her was essentially the truth. I'm glad she responded to it—not that I have high hopes we'll be able to find out anything after so long."

"At least you're exploring all avenues. That shows your love for Keith right there."

When they climbed back into his truck and she slid over next to him, he glanced at her as he started the engine. "You keep acting as if you like me this much, you're going to get my mother all excited. You understand that, don't you?"

She tilted her chin defiantly. "If you're going to call me out on everything I do, I guess I'll keep my distance."

She started to slide over again, but he knew she was teasing. Hooking her around the shoulders with one arm, he brought her back against him. "I'll pretend not to notice."

Laney loved going to Pizza Planet as much as Maisey had expected. Some of the other kids looked at her oddly when they realized she was different. That made a fierce protectiveness take hold of Maisey, and she watched Laney extra closely as a result. But Laney couldn't see the reaction that was making Maisey so defensive. And her natural exuberance won over two little girls almost right away. The three of them played in the sea of multicolored plastic balls while Maisey and Rafe stood nearby, holding their pizza plates and smiling at the parents of the other children, while keeping an eye on the action.

"Are you worried about when she goes to school?" Maisey asked Rafe.

"I've been trying not to think about that. I want her childhood to be as normal as possible, and yet . . . she's going to need special care."

"That's something you may not be able to get here on the island."

"True. At some point, I'll probably have to move to Charleston."

Maisey hated the thought of that. She couldn't picture him anywhere except in his bungalow next door. Of course, depending on how everything played out, she might not be living there, either . . .

"When?"

"Not for a couple of years."

Laney fell over and couldn't get up, so Rafe stepped in to help.

One of the girls Laney had been playing with watched with avid curiosity. "What's wrong with her eyes?" she asked, crinkling her nose as she looked up at him.

"She can't see," Rafe said mildly.

"Why not?"

"She was born very early, and her eyes didn't have the chance to develop properly."

"Oh."

That seemed to handle it. They went right back to playing as if Laney's blindness didn't make any difference. That meant Maisey could relax, but she suddenly remembered her mother's assertion that taking on the care of a blind child would be an unnecessary burden. How could she even think that?

Her cell rang and a sense of foreboding made her hesitate.

"Who is it?" Rafe asked when she didn't answer it right away.

"It's either Pippa—or my mother."

"Are you going to take the call?" He didn't sound as if he wanted her to. No doubt he was worried that Josephine would continue to do whatever she could to sabotage their relationship.

"I have to," she said. "If I don't, it'll only make matters worse."

They didn't have time to discuss it. Stepping off to one side so she wouldn't have to handle this conversation within hearing distance of Rafe or Laney, Maisey slid over the answer button on her smartphone. But she knew she was in trouble when the first words out of her mother's mouth were, *"What the hell do you think you're doing?"*

29

By the time she ended the call, Maisey was visibly upset. Rafe hadn't been able to hear what was said, but he'd been watching her out of the corner of his eye, and he knew from the way she'd ducked her head while talking that she was arguing with her mother.

"What's going on?" he murmured when Laney, who'd asked him to fix her ponytail, was once again distracted by her new friends.

"My mother fired me from the flower shop and kicked me out of the bungalow," Maisey said.

He felt as if someone had just slapped him. "Because you're dating *me?*"

"Because she can't control me. I won't allow her to."

"So it *is* because you're dating me."

"Not only that." Maisey was so angry she seemed to be pushing each word through her teeth. "Heidi called and told her about our visit."

"Why would she do that?"

"Who knows? To curry favor?"

"Oh, shit." He stabbed a hand through his hair. "Your mother doesn't want you digging up the past."

"No surprise there." Maisey set her jaw. "So nothing to be upset about."

There was a lot to be upset about. The fact that Josephine would go so far shocked him. He knew that Maisey's relationship with her mother was a rocky one, but he'd never expected the matriarch of Fairham to be quite *this* unreasonable. Wasn't she glad to finally have her daughter back in her life? Why would she cut her off again?

"What are you going to do?" he asked.

"What can I do? I'll have to move."

"Off the island?"

"If I can't find another job, I'll have no choice."

"You could always stay with me . . ."

"No. We're not ready for that yet."

It would serve her mother right if they moved in together. But he was sort of relieved by Maisey's response. Because of Laney, he wasn't sure making that kind of arrangement—so soon—would be a good idea. This was the first serious relationship he'd had. He needed to protect it—protect them all—by letting it develop naturally. He'd only offered because he felt partially responsible for Maisey's sudden homelessness.

"If money's an issue, I can help you for a while."

"I'll be okay," she said. "I have some savings. After that's gone . . . I'll figure something out."

He wished there was a way he could make things better. "Maybe *I* should talk to her."

"Don't. It would be a waste of breath."

"You don't think she'd listen to me."

"No. And I'm afraid it would only cause her to fire *you*."

That would be a mess . . . "How long do you have?"

"She wants me out tonight, I guess. She didn't give me a specific date. But next week will have to be soon enough."

"She'll let you stay that long?"

"What's she going to do? She'd have to get the police to enforce her demands, and I doubt she'll make that call right away. Appearances are too important to her. If I know my mother, part of the reason she hid Gretchen Phillips's claim that Keith pushed Annabelle was to save herself the shame of having a son who could do such a thing."

"So you don't think she did it for him."

"Not entirely. There had to be something in it for her. That's what it always comes down to."

He put his arm around her. She was so disillusioned about her mother, and he couldn't blame her. "I'm sorry, Maisey."

"It's okay. Since I don't have a job, I can fly to Louisiana first thing tomorrow."

"I wish I could go with you."

"You have responsibilities here. I'll be fine."

He frowned as he turned to face her. "Are you sure Keith and I are worth it?"

The determination on her face when she met his gaze told him she was every bit as strong as she needed to be. "I'm obviously betting you are. But that doesn't even matter. The right to make my own decisions and live my own life—that's worth anything."

He agreed. But he didn't want to become a casualty of her mother's cruelty, didn't want her mother to split them up, after all.

Although Rafe had wanted her to stay the night, Maisey had refused. He'd said she could slip in after Laney was asleep, but she was too consumed with what she was feeling after that conversation with her mother to be able to sleep. She was sure she'd just keep him up.

There went her dreams of finding common ground with the queen of Fairham. She'd been foolish to hope. It was impossible, since *Josephine* was impossible. Their phone call had made that completely clear.

"You think you're helping Keith?" her mother had snapped. *"He wouldn't even know he'd pushed Annabelle if not for you! Do you have any idea how that's affecting him?"*

"How is it my fault that he found out? I didn't go searching for those pictures. It was fate that they wound up in my hands."

"It's thanks to your low-class lover, not fate."

"Don't say that about Rafe! He's a very nice man."

"You don't know what kind of man he is. You've barely met him. He has a body any woman would lust over—that's all."

"Give me some credit, please."

"You mean I should trust your opinion? The same person who chose Jack?"

"That's hitting below the belt, Mother."

"I don't care. You always seem to feel free to do whatever you want. Once you got those pictures, you went searching for everything else you could find."

"It was the logical thing. What should I have done?"

"You should've come to me."

"So you could take the pictures away and destroy them? Tell me it was none of my business?"

"It is none of your business."

"Annabelle was my sister!"

"That doesn't change anything. She's gone. I did what I had to in order to protect your brother. But you were so sure you'd caught me doing something terrible, you set out to destroy me. That's the type of love you've always had for me."

"Destroy you? That's not true! I was rocked by what I found. You'd never even mentioned that I had a sister. That would freak anyone out. I just wanted the truth. That's all I want now."

"You have all the truth you need, but you don't have the sense to leave well enough alone. Don't you dare go traipsing off to Louisiana. There's no point in making this worse."

"There are questions that aren't answered yet."

"Leave it alone, Maisey."

"No. I'm sorry, but I can't. I have to do what I believe is right."

"Fine. Forget it. Forget everything. Just go. Get off Fairham and don't ever come back."

"Get off Fairham and don't ever come back,"

Maisey murmured as she shuffled down the hall. She'd been in bed for two hours—to no avail. Those angry words kept running through her brain, and as much as she tried to convince herself that she didn't care if her mother loved her, it still felt as if Josephine had lodged a knife in her chest.

She sighed as she turned on the light. Then she screamed. Keith was slumped on a chair at her kitchen table, looking as though he hadn't eaten or slept in several days.

"What are you doing?" she cried when she recovered enough to speak.

"Nothing."

As far as she could tell, he'd just been sitting there in the dark, staring out the window.

"How long have you been here?"

"Maybe half an hour. I'm not sure. I didn't check."

Why hadn't she heard him come in? Had she been *that* preoccupied and upset?

Apparently.

"Do you have the master key?" she asked.

He jerked his head toward the bent cardboard Rafe had used to cover up the window he'd broken. "No. I don't need a key."

If she wasn't staying here, that was one thing she wouldn't have to bother fixing. "Why didn't you call me? Tell me you were coming?"

"Because I didn't know. When I left Coldiron

House, I was planning to head to Charleston. Find some way to get high and escape all this . . . shit going on in my life."

"And?"

He shrugged. "I can't keep running from it, can't keep turning to the wrong things to dull the pain. What I'm doing . . . it's killing me. Something's gotta give. So I came here instead. I couldn't think of anywhere else to go."

Maisey got two cups from the cupboard. "You okay?"

"Hell, no. But you can't be doing too well yourself. I heard Mom talking to you on the phone earlier."

"That was a fun conversation, right?"

He frowned at her sarcasm. "She doesn't treat me any better. She says she loves us. And, in some ways, maybe she does. If only she could get over herself long enough to show it. Or maybe she doesn't know what love is."

Maisey put the teakettle on. "You're getting warmer."

"I owe you an apology," he said. "I made a mistake asking you to come back to Fairham. I thought it would be good—for all of us. But, as usual, I couldn't have been more off target. And that became obvious to me the very first day."

"It's not over yet."

He folded his arms and leaned back to study her. "What could change?"

"Anything could change. There's always tomorrow, Keith. Make it count this time. Move away from here. Stay clean. Get a job that allows you to be independent from Mom. Build a life. That's what you were going to do when I came back to help you, wasn't it?"

"I'd get away if I could, but I have nothing, nowhere to go."

"You don't need Mom. You're an adult, a full-grown man! Take yourself out of this bad situation and put yourself in a healthier one."

"How? I'm not capable of it. I was born this way. I'm *defective*."

"I don't believe that."

He rubbed his forehead as if he had a terrible headache. "If what I did to Annabelle can't convince you, I don't know what will."

She pulled out a chair so she could sit down while waiting for the water to boil. "I'm going to Louisiana tomorrow to find Gretchen Phillips's son. Why don't you come with me?"

"Why would I want to travel so far just to hear what I've already heard? Besides, I don't have any money. Who'd pay for my ticket?"

Maisey didn't have much money herself. She had to be careful, especially now that she'd be paying rent somewhere. But she felt this Louisiana trip might be important enough to warrant the expense. "*I'll* pay for it," she said. "We'll fly to New Orleans and rent a car."

"You don't need me tagging along. Besides, what's this trip going to change?"

"Who knows? Gretchen Phillips was acting strange. There must've been a reason."

"There could be a lot of them . . ."

"She was lying about what happened on that cliff. I told you that's what Lindsay Greenberg thinks. I'd like to find out why. Did Gretchen confide in her children and her new friends about her past? Maybe she got married again, and said something about Annabelle to her new husband. We won't know unless we ask."

He glared at her until the teakettle began to whistle.

"What do you say?" she asked, reluctant to break eye contact.

"Grab the kettle," he said, finally glancing away. "I'll go. What the hell do I have to lose?"

30

It was a perfect eighty degrees in Lafitte, Louisiana, less than an hour's drive from the airport in New Orleans. Keith had slept on her couch before getting up early and showering so they could leave at first light. Then he dozed through the whole plane ride and he'd been subdued since she'd rented the car. Maisey assumed he was fighting off one of his dramatic mood swings, or craving another fix.

Rafe had followed them to Coldiron House, where they'd dropped off their mother's truck without speaking to anyone. After that, he'd driven them to the airport in Charleston, even though it meant waiting for the car ferry. He'd claimed he could make up for missing a few hours of work, which was nice of him, because her mother would be looking for any excuse to fire him. That worried Maisey—but it had been convenient not to have to hire a taxi to pick them up where the ferry docked in Charleston.

Rafe had been so good to her. It was going to be hard to leave him. She hoped they'd be able to continue getting to know each other, but she understood how difficult a long-distance relationship would be.

"What are you expecting to find here?" Keith asked, breaking into her thoughts as Maisey drove slowly through the center of town. According to the Google search she'd performed before leaving Fairham, Lafitte was named after the notorious pirate Jean Lafitte, who'd once owned the port. The place Gretchen had chosen for her new home was located in the heart of the Baratarian Basin, with its dark bayou waters and moss-covered trees. There'd been plenty to read about the town on Google—but nothing showed up when she put in the name Paul Phillips.

"I told you," she said to Keith. "I want to talk to Gretchen's son."

"What if he won't talk to us? I can't imagine he'll be eager to implicate his own mother."

"I'm not suggesting Gretchen *pushed* Annabelle —just that she wasn't watching her closely enough. Guilt over something like that might've made her tell the truth to the people who were closest to her. Anyway, that incident happened so long ago, when Paul Phillips was only a child of ten. Since his mother's gone and can't be harmed no matter what he reveals, he shouldn't be *too* guarded. Maybe we'll get lucky."

"He could still be protective of her memory. Or . . . what if he doesn't see any point in even wasting his time with us?"

"Then we'll talk to the people around him. He might have a wife who's heard about it."

Wearing a dark scowl, he peered out at the businesses slipping slowly past his window. "How do you plan to find this man and his wife—if he has one?"

"I told you."

"Ask around."

"That's it."

"Isn't that like looking for a needle in a haystack?"

"Not at all. Do you see this place? It has less than a thousand residents. There's got to be *someone* who knows him."

"That sounded more plausible when we were on the plane. Now I'm realizing how unlikely it is that he even lives here anymore."

Maisey hoped Keith was wrong about the likelihood of tracking down what was left of Gretchen's family. She didn't have the resources necessary to turn this into an extensive search.

Still, she was her mother's daughter in one respect—she didn't give up easily. "If he doesn't, we'll figure out where he went and go there."

"You're *that* determined?"

"If we don't ask now, more time will go by, and that'll diminish our chances even further."

"If we have any chances to begin with."

"I'll hire a private detective, if I have to. I might have to wait until I'm earning regular money again, but . . ."

"All this to learn that I'm not worth the time and expense?"

She sent him a sharp glance. "Stop it. You didn't mean to hurt Annabelle—if that's what actually happened. You're not that kind of person."

She pulled into a gas station with a small convenience store.

"Wait a sec." He stopped her when she unfastened her seat belt. "You can't just waltz in and ask for Paul Phillips. You need a pretext."

"Pretext?" she repeated.

"An excuse they'll believe, so they don't feel

you pose some kind of threat to one of their fellow townsmen."

"I'm familiar with the definition. I was just surprised to hear you say that. You're taking this more seriously than I thought, Mr. Skeptic."

"I want what you want, but I'm not as optimistic about finding it. So what are you going to say?"

She collected her purse so she could buy something as an excuse to approach the register. "How about I tell them that I knew Paul growing up? That I was one of the children his mother once cared for and I'd like to reconnect with him. That makes it sound as if we were friends, even though I don't remember him, but it's basically the truth."

"Sounds harmless," he said.

She opened her door. "Aren't you coming?"

"No."

He was afraid of being disappointed. And, as it turned out, he would've been.

"Any luck?" Keith asked when she returned.

She tossed her purse and the local paper she'd bought in the backseat before climbing in. "No."

"So we're going to keep looking."

"Of course. Everyone in that store was a teenager, way younger than Paul would be. Even the cashier didn't look to be more than twenty. Why would they have any reason to know him? It's not like he would've been in school with them."

Next, she stopped at a swamp tour place. The only employee in the building shook her head when Maisey asked about Paul. So Maisey moved on to a small café that was quite busy, since it was close to dinnertime.

Maisey waited at the hostess station until a server—or maybe it was the owner since she looked to be sixty or older—hurried over to address her while carrying a coffeepot. "One for dinner?"

"Actually, I'm hoping to find an old friend who grew up here."

"Who are you looking for?"

"Paul Phillips."

She frowned. "Sorry, he doesn't live here anymore."

That was a letdown. But at least she'd found someone who recognized the name. "Can you tell me where he might've gone?"

"No clue. But you could ask his sister."

His *sister?* Maisey had been told she'd died of kidney disease. "Sarah's here?"

The woman gave her a sad smile. "No, I'm afraid Sarah passed away a long time ago. Poor thing. She was a sweetheart. I'm talking about the youngest in the family, Roxanne."

Maisey supposed Gretchen could've added to her family after she left. But she'd already been forty-five or so when she moved . . . "Can you tell me where I might find Roxanne, then?"

"Sure." She gestured with the coffeepot. "She owns the video store around the corner. Go down one block and make a right."

Maisey thanked her and hurried out.

"You found him," Keith guessed when she reached the car.

"It's that obvious?"

"You were almost sprinting to the car."

And her excitement was contagious. He was perking up, too. "I didn't find *him,* but I found his younger sister."

"I thought Gretchen only had two kids."

"Apparently she had at least one more. A girl named Roxanne, who's supposed to be nearby, so we should be able to talk to her."

That hit him hard. "Holy shit. Do you think she might know something?"

"It's possible."

"Wouldn't it be great if we learned for sure that I *didn't* push Annabelle?"

She reached over to squeeze his hand. "Why don't you come in this time?"

He said no, but once she located the store and parked in the gravel lot, he seemed less certain.

"You might want to hear this," she coaxed.

"That depends, doesn't it?"

"One way or the other. Even if you pushed Annabelle, that doesn't mean you knew what you were doing."

He unbuckled his seat belt and unfolded his

tall frame as he stepped out. "Fine. Let's go."

There was a mother with four little kids in the store, picking out children's movies. Maisey and Keith waited for her to leave before approaching the woman behind the cash register. She appeared to be in her late thirties, a bit older than Maisey had expected, but even with minimal makeup and her blond hair piled on top of her head as if she hadn't bothered to go to any trouble this morning, she was beautiful.

"Are you looking for something in particular?" she asked.

Maisey couldn't help noticing the unusual color of her eyes. They were that particular shade of blue—which gave her a strange feeling, a sense of déjà vu that she told herself couldn't really mean anything. "Actually, we didn't want to get in the way while you were taking care of business. We're not here to rent a movie. We were hoping you might be able to answer a few questions for us."

She seemed uncertain. "About . . ."

"Your mother."

"Who are you? Why would you want to know anything about my mother?"

"I'm Maisey Lazarow, and this is my brother, Keith—"

"What'd you say?" She glanced at one of them, then the other, her smile long gone. "Is this some kind of cruel joke?"

Maisey blinked in surprise. "I don't understand."

"You must know that I once had a brother and sister with those names. They were killed, along with my parents, in a car crash when I was six. So . . . maybe now you can see why this isn't funny."

The sound Keith made revealed his shock. Maisey understood what he was feeling. She had to steady herself by putting one hand on the counter. "We're not trying to be funny. We're . . ." Maisey peered more closely at Roxanne's eyes, so close to the color of hers and Keith's—a distinctly Coldiron trait. *It can't be,* she thought. But even the woman's age seemed to confirm what her mind was suggesting. *"Annabelle?"*

The blood drained from her face as she rocked back and covered her mouth.

"Oh, my God!" Keith cried. "It's you! It has to be you."

"We were told you fell off a cliff, into the ocean," Maisey said. "That *you* were the one who died."

Keith must've been overwhelmed by relief as well as surprise. He hadn't hurt anyone, just as they'd both hoped. But Maisey couldn't focus on that. She was too stunned—and waiting for Annabelle's reaction.

"I never . . . fell off any cliff," Annabelle said.

"Then how . . . It doesn't make sense," Maisey

whispered. It *didn't* make sense. What had Gretchen done? How? And why? "Lindsay was right," she said. "Gretchen lied. Gretchen lied about everything."

Keith grabbed Maisey. "That's why they could never find her body!"

Annabelle lowered the hand that had been covering her mouth. "Then why would you believe it?" she asked. "Why would *anyone* believe it?"

"Because they . . . they found your doll, the one you took everywhere," Keith said.

Annabelle shook her head. "That can't be. My mother—Gretchen," she quickly amended, "told me she took the doll to the hospital and had it buried with my family. And now you're telling me that she . . . what? *Staged* the whole thing?"

"She had to have," Maisey said. "She told you we were dead, and she told us you were dead so we'd never look for one another. So she could take you and move on as if we'd never existed."

"You're saying she kidnapped me." Annabelle was growing angry. "*Why?* Why would she do something so terrible? She was a wonderful woman. A kind and loving mother."

Maisey had no answer. Keith didn't seem to have one, either. With Gretchen dead, how would they ever find out?

But then Maisey thought of Gretchen's son. "The only person who might be able to answer that is Paul, right? He was older than you by what . . . four years? Maybe *he* remembers something."

Tears began to stream down Annabelle's cheeks. "He's never mentioned my birth family. Neither did Sarah before she . . . before."

"I'm not trying to upset you," Maisey said. "But they probably wouldn't have said anything, especially if Gretchen swore them to secrecy. Maybe . . . because of Sarah's disease, she meant for you to be her daughter's replacement."

"No. She didn't know Sarah had kidney disease. Not back then," she said. But then a hint of clarity entered her expression and she wiped at her tears. "I think I know why," she said. "She *hated* my real mother. Said it was a blessing she was gone, that she wasn't taking proper care of me and I deserved better. But she felt bad about my father, who was a nice man."

"Gretchen thought our father was a nice man, and yet she was blackmailing him?" Keith said.

Annabelle's eyebrows flew up. "What are you talking about?"

Maisey jumped in. "She claimed *Keith* pushed you, and to save Keith from the stigma that would create, Dad paid her handsomely."

Before she could react, Keith slapped the counter. "Wait a second. *That's* why she claimed it was me! Without that, she wouldn't have had anything to hold over Mom and

Dad. There would've been no way to get money."

"She probably saw it as child support." Maisey could tell that Annabelle was getting defensive on Gretchen's behalf and wanted to appease her. "A way to give Annabelle—you—more than she could afford on her own."

"I don't understand," Annabelle said. "I can't—I can't believe what I'm hearing."

"We'll explain," Maisey told her. "We'll explain it all. And, hard as this might be to hear, we can prove it."

"But you're thinking Gretchen was an evil person," she said. "She wasn't. She wasn't evil at all."

"She took you away from us," Keith retorted. "And she blamed me and blackmailed Dad. Even if she thought of that money as child support, a way to insure that you'd have what you needed, what kind of woman does that?"

Maisey knew his remarks weren't helping, but he was struggling with his own emotions.

Fortunately, Annabelle seemed to understand, because the expression on her face grew more sad than angry. "Someone who thought she was saving me. She cried whenever I talked about my brother or my sister. But she said my birth mother was a cruel, cold woman who shouldn't have had children."

"In Gretchen's mind, Josephine deserved what she got," Maisey said, filling in the obvious.

"And you were the only one of the three of us worth saving?" Keith asked.

Annabelle must've recognized the bitterness in his voice. "Maybe I was the only one she felt she *could* save."

"She couldn't have pretended that we'd all fallen into the ocean and expected to get away with it," Maisey agreed.

The bell jingled over the door as another patron walked in. "I—I don't want to . . . continue this discussion here," Annabelle said, lowering her voice. "Can you come by my house in an hour or so? I'll call my husband, see if he can take over the store."

She was married. Maisey wondered if she also had children. "Of course," she said, and put Annabelle's address in her phone.

Rafe waited in the drawing room of Coldiron House. He'd been there before, but he'd never felt quite this nervous. He was afraid he might be meddling in something he shouldn't. Maisey wouldn't appreciate his getting involved. And yet . . . paying a visit to Josephine Lazarow was the only way he could possibly remedy the situation. He didn't want to be even *part* of the reason Maisey and her mother weren't getting along.

There was a noise at the door. He'd been too wound up to take the seat Pippa had offered him, so he was standing at the window when

Josephine walked in. As usual, she was dressed as if she was a senator or the first lady or someone equally important. The look she gave him was as imperious as ever, but he wasn't about to let her overstep her bounds where *he* was concerned.

"Raphael." She acknowledged him with a slight dip of her head. "What can I do for you? I hope you haven't come to revise the timeline you gave me on Smuggler's Cove. I've been assuming you're making great progress there, despite your other . . . distractions."

Was she referring to Laney or Maisey—or both? It was hard not to take offense, but he stifled the desire to defend himself and carefully modulated his voice. "Smuggler's Cove is going according to plan."

"I'm glad to hear it. I'd hate to have to break that contract."

He clenched his jaw when she smiled at him, once again battling his natural inclination to react to her nastiness with a sharp word or two. "I'll make sure you have no reason to even try."

"Wonderful. So then . . . why are you here? I can't imagine we have any other business. Your bungalow closed escrow two months ago. There's nothing I can do about selling you that, although I regret it now."

She was determined to keep jabbing at him, but he decided that his best defense was not to reveal how much it bothered him. "Why do you regret it?" he asked calmly. "The only thing that's changed is Maisey."

"My daughter? Isn't that enough? Sadly, Maisey's return was something I could not have foreseen."

"Have I ever done anything to make you dislike me, Mrs. Lazarow?" he asked. "Or are you acting on prejudice alone? A man of my background couldn't possibly be a good match for a Coldiron?"

She arched her eyebrows. "Don't tell me you think I should be more receptive. Do you even have a degree?"

"No," he admitted. "I had no money for college, and I was so busy acting out at the time, I'm not sure I could've settled down and studied if I'd been given a grant."

"Big of you to admit it at least."

The door opened and Pippa poked her head in. "Would you like me to bring some tea?"

"No. I won't be here that long," Rafe said before Josephine could respond.

Pippa looked between them and, when Josephine didn't correct him, backed out and closed the door.

"We were talking about the lost opportunities of my youth, I believe," he said, matching her more formal diction. "I think it's important for you to note that I'm not the same man I was then."

"Which means you can reclaim all those years?

Somehow make up for the education you never sought?"

"I've found a vocation that I'm good at, and I make a decent amount. There are worse ways to live." He didn't see Keith being any happier, for instance.

"You could never run the Coldiron empire, never take over for me."

"I don't aspire to that. You have two children, who will probably do just fine. So maybe that's where the misunderstanding comes in. I'm not after anything of yours. To prove I care about your daughter and not what she stands to inherit, I'll gladly sign a prenup, if my relationship with Maisey progresses that far. But I want something from you in return."

She smoothed her expensive slacks. "Of course you do. And what is that? Another bungalow? A hefty payment up front?"

He shook his head. "No. I would appreciate you staying out of my relationship with Maisey. No matter what you think of me, I know I can give her the love she needs and deserves. If I didn't care about her, it wouldn't disturb me so much that being with me is tearing her away from her family."

"And if I simply tell you to leave my house this instant?"

He shrugged. "I will have done all I can. But I would say this. Please don't make her choose. In case you're under any delusions—I'm not asking because I think *I'm* the one who'd lose out."

Her mouth opened and closed with no sound, as if she didn't know what to say.

"I will support you and respect you as her mother," he went on. "All I ask is that you give me a little respect in return."

"That's *all* you ask," she repeated. She couldn't seem to believe he'd come here just to make peace.

"That's it."

She clasped her hands in her lap. "You know you're not the only . . . bone of contention between Maisey and me."

"I do. That's part of the reason I don't want to cause her any more pain. She's been through enough."

She glared at him for several seconds. Then she said, "I'll have my attorney draw up a prenup. Might as well have you sign it while you're agreeable."

"I'll sign it anytime you want," he said with a slight bow.

31

Annabelle had three children—Zac, who was five, Chloe, who was eight, and Brooklyn, who was fourteen. Maisey loved her nieces and nephew almost instantly. And the same held true for

Annabelle's husband, Landon, a big bear of a man who, together with his father, owned the swamp tour business she'd visited earlier. He'd been out on the water with a group of tourists, and the employee manning his store hadn't recognized "Roxanne's" maiden name when Maisey asked for Paul Phillips. That was one of the things they discussed—and laughed about—once Landon had closed the video shop and come home. They also talked about how life in Lafitte compared to Fairham, how Annabelle had purchased the video shop from her brother, Paul, when he moved to Colorado to be closer to his wife's family, and Maisey's books. Annabelle was astonished that she'd never heard of them. But Maisey wasn't surprised. It wasn't as if she'd attained the status of a Dr. Seuss.

It wasn't until the kids went to bed that they tackled some of the harder subjects they were anxious to discuss.

"How much of that day do you remember?" Maisey asked Annabelle, referring to when she was supposedly pushed off that cliff. It was now just the two of them, and Landon and Keith. They were all sitting around the kitchen table with cups of coffee in Roxanne's comfortable, middle-class house.

"Quite a bit," she replied. "I remember Gretchen taking us all to the library, where a man called Ranger came and took me to some shack."

"That would be Ranger Phillips," Maisey said. "He's still alive, and he still lives in that shack."

"You're kidding," she said.

"I've been there." Maisey took the last sip of her coffee. "Do *you* remember that trip to the library, Keith?"

"Not at all," he replied, "but I don't remember very much from before I turned five and started school."

"And we went to the library all the time," Annabelle said. "He wouldn't have any reason to recall it. Nothing different happened to him. I probably only remember because it was the day that changed everything."

"Was Ranger nice to you?"

"He wasn't *mean*. I could tell he didn't really want me with him, though. They had a heated discussion—one filled with harsh whispering. Then he took me to get some ice cream and said Gretchen would pick me up later." She stared off into space. "It took her so long I was sure she'd forgotten me. I got so homesick. I cried several times, which made Ranger uncomfortable. He kept offering me candy to shut me up. I think junk food was about all I ate that day. When Gretchen finally came, she told me she had terrible news."

"That's when she said we'd all been killed?" Keith guessed.

"Yes. You can imagine what that was like. I felt completely lost and begged to go home with her, but she wouldn't hear of it. She said she couldn't let anyone see me because then I'd go to an orphanage, which was a terrible, lonely place. She promised if I was a good girl she'd come back for me, and that I could live with her."

"I can't believe Gretchen would do that," Landon said.

"Neither can I," his wife agreed. "I never once questioned what she'd told me."

"You wouldn't," Maisey said. "You were only six. And she'd been your caregiver. Of course you'd trust her."

"Did you get the impression that she lived with any regret?" Landon asked. "Do you think she was ever tempted to tell you the truth?"

Annabelle shook her head. "Looking back, I think she was convinced she was doing the right thing, that she was protecting me, making sure I was no longer in the hands of a cruel mother who would only abuse me."

"So you knew Gretchen, too?" Maisey asked, speaking to Landon.

He gave her a charismatic smile. "I did. Rocki and I were high school sweethearts, so we've been together for over twenty years."

"That's a long time," Maisey said.

"Wait a sec." Keith scooted his chair a few inches from the table. "How did Gretchen get you off the island?" he asked Annabelle. "Without someone seeing you, I mean?"

"I hid in the back of Ranger's truck, with all the boxes and furniture, when he moved her. I stayed down like they told me to because I was so frightened I'd be sent to an orphanage. She kept telling me how terrible my life would be without a family. I was willing to do almost anything so that she wouldn't abandon me."

"She certainly pulled it off," Maisey said, marveling at the ease with which Gretchen had kidnapped a child.

"You were telling us that you two were high school sweethearts." Keith directed Landon back to that subject.

"We were. Went to the same college, too—Louisiana State University—and stayed together that whole time. We were married as soon as we graduated."

Maisey had been wondering how Annabelle could accept a new name and a new life without ever coming back, when she was older, to find what remained of her old one—if only to rediscover the island and locate any distant relatives. But the more they talked, the more Maisey began to understand. Annabelle was too happy, too fulfilled in Lafitte, where Landon's relatives had embraced her, to look back for long, especially since she thought her immediate family was gone and everyone on Fairham Island would be a stranger to her.

"So now that you know the truth, what name

are you going to use?" Maisey asked. "I mean . . . Annabelle's your legal name."

"But Roxanne's the only name Landon's ever known me by," she said. "The kids, too, of course, and all my friends and family here in Lafitte. I can't see going back to Annabelle."

"Makes sense to stick with Roxanne," Maisey agreed. Maybe Roxanne hadn't grown up with the same wealth and privilege they'd known, but she'd received far more love. That was apparent. So was the fact that Gretchen had believed she was doing the right thing by "stealing" Annabelle —had believed she was rescuing a child.

Annabelle took another sip of coffee before addressing Keith. "You said that Gretchen blackmailed our father, and you have proof."

"Maisey does."

As soon as they'd explained about the letters, Annabelle asked for the dates they were written and it soon became clear that those dates coincided with the worst of Sarah's illness, which made Gretchen's actions understandable if not forgivable.

They decided it must've been Ranger who'd mailed the letters, so the postmark wouldn't give away Gretchen's location. He was probably the "friend" who'd collected the money for her, too.

They talked for several more hours about Gretchen and Sarah and Paul—and Ranger, and whether or not he should be brought up on charges. Maisey felt he should, but Annabelle said she preferred to let it go. "He's an old man now," she said. "What good would it do to put him in prison? For the majority of my life, I've been happy. Otherwise, maybe I'd feel differently."

"So . . . here's the *big* question," Maisey said. It was nearly three in the morning by this time, and they were getting tired despite the adrenaline that'd kept them going so far.

"There are a lot of big questions," Annabelle—Roxanne—joked. "But I bet I can guess what you're going to ask. Whether I want to see . . . Mom."

"Yes." Roxanne's response would form the basis of what Maisey told everyone, even Rafe. She hadn't called him since leaving Fairham, but he'd attempted to reach her. She knew he had to be worrying about her; she'd check in tomorrow sometime, since it was too late now.

Roxanne tucked the wisps of hair that'd fallen around her face behind her ears. "I think I do. I remember her as . . . austere, but not all my memories are bad. She certainly smelled good."

They laughed at that. Then they talked about how beautiful Josephine was—how that hadn't changed—before growing serious again. "A visit to Fairham could be traumatic," Maisey said. "Are you sure you're up for it?"

She nodded. "I'd like to see how she reacts to

my husband and my children. But confronting her will definitely be weird."

"It can't be too bad if I'm there with you," her husband said, and she covered his hand with hers as he squeezed her shoulder.

"When do you think you'll come?" Keith had been more animated tonight than Maisey had seen him in a long time, and that felt good. Now Maisey would have help in loving him and trying to support him. Maybe it would be enough to make a difference.

"We're running two businesses, and the kids have school, so it's not easy for us to get away," Roxanne said. "But going to Fairham for Thanksgiving would be nice."

Maisey covered a yawn. She wouldn't be able to keep her eyes open much longer. "That sounds perfect. If Mom lets me through the door, I'll come back, too."

Keith nudged her with his knee. "Come back? You're not really leaving Fairham, are you?"

"What else can I do? She kicked me out of the bungalow and fired me from the flower shop. I have no job and no place to live." She got up and put her cup in the sink. "Fairham was only a temporary stop, anyway—just someplace where I could lick my wounds and spend time with my brother. As it turned out, I only made matters worse for you. So I should move on, get back to my career."

"*I* made matters worse for me, Maisey," he said. "Not you."

"Where will you move?" Roxanne asked. "Back to NYC, even though Jack's there?"

"The city's big enough for both of us. I love Manhattan. I just need to create more of a life for myself. I let him define who I was before. I won't make the mistake of letting another man do that."

"Come on," Keith argued. "No one loves Smuggler's Cove more than you do. You belong there."

She rinsed her cup. "If I were independently wealthy, things might be different."

"You said you have enough to last for a while."

"It wouldn't be wise to use up the rest of my savings."

"What about Rafe?" he asked.

Roxanne twisted around to face her. "Keith was telling me about the new man in your life."

"When?" Maisey asked.

"When you went to the bathroom after I kissed the kids good-night."

Maisey scowled at Keith. "Big mouth."

"Oh, come on," he said. "Admit it. You like him."

"I *do* like him."

Keith brought his own cup over. "No, I mean you *really* like him. Don't let Mom split you guys up. Fight back—by staying."

She rinsed his cup, too, since she was already

at the sink. "I can't stay on the off chance that Rafe and I can make a go of it. I have to start rebuilding my life somewhere that's a little more conducive to a fresh start."

"You could always come here," Roxanne said.

Maisey smiled. "I'll consider that."

"But if you move . . . maybe what might've happened between you and Rafe never will," Keith said.

She dried her hands and gave him a hug. "And maybe it's not meant to. It's hard for me to say what's best. I was so sure, once upon a time. Now? I realize that life is uncertain."

"You'll get it figured out," Roxanne said. "And we'll be there to support you in whatever you do."

Maisey smiled and hugged her older sister, too. Finding Roxanne was like suddenly being given a best friend.

Keith was sleeping on the couch, but Chloe had been asked to bunk in with Brooklyn so Maisey could have a room to herself. She appreciated the privacy. Although she was exhausted and emotionally drained after all the highs and lows of the past two weeks, she felt restless as she sat on the bed, staring at Rafe's last text.

Haven't heard from you today. Everything okay?

Judging by when that had appeared, he'd sent it right before bed. Now that she was alone and wasn't so overcome by shock and disbelief at finding her sister *alive,* she wanted to call him back. She felt she'd sleep better if she could only hear his voice—which was as crazy as everything else going on in her life right now. They hadn't been seeing each other all that long.

You can't *be in love with him,* she told herself. But it sure seemed like it. That was part of the reason she was convinced she needed to leave Fairham. The island was even less hospitable for her than she'd expected. She'd finally realized that she'd never be able to have a relationship with Josephine, at least nothing resembling the kind she'd always wanted. And if what was going on between her and Rafe turned out to be nothing more than a brief affair? She'd be making herself too vulnerable if she stayed.

So where was she going to go? And what was she going to do? Ever since Ellie died, it was as though she'd been tumbling down a mountain, slamming into one rock after the next. But if her life hadn't taken that *exact* path, if she and Jack hadn't divorced and she hadn't returned to Fairham Island, Rafe never would've brought her those pictures. He would've taken them to her mother, as he'd originally planned, and Josephine would've destroyed them. Then no one would've learned that Annabelle still existed.

"Compensating blessings," she muttered as she thought of the fun they'd had together this evening.

A soft tap sounded on the door.

"Come in."

Keith poked his head inside the room. "It's me. You got a minute?"

"Of course. Everything okay? It's been a wild night."

"No joke. But I'm happy. Hopeful. And more determined than ever to get myself turned around. I mean it, Maisey. If you two can lead successful lives, so can I. I let Mom get into my head and undermine my confidence. She doesn't *intend* to do that. She just has a way of . . . making me feel like she's the only one in the world who's capable of anything."

They'd talked about this before. Maisey nodded. "You have to make up your mind— make up your mind and fight to stay clean. It'll get easier with time, but the first few weeks and months will be difficult. You know that."

"God, yes." He sat on the foot of the bed. "But I'll do it. I promise."

"I believe you."

"Thank you. No matter what I've done, you've always been willing to forgive me, always been there to encourage me."

"Because I love you," she said.

His smile hitched up on one side. "I love you, too," he said, and hugged her again before he left.

As soon as the door closed, Maisey returned her attention to her phone. **It's very late, so I hope this doesn't wake you,** she wrote, **but you're not going to believe what's happened. It's huge. Shocking. Exciting. But this might surprise you even more: considering how badly I want to be with you right now, I think I'm in love with you, Rafe. Is that possible after so short a time?**

Her stomach knotted as she read and reread her own words. They'd scare the hell out of him. She could easily imagine him telling her that they should take their relationship more slowly, maybe date other people *if* she decided to remain on Fairham. He had a daughter to consider, after all. Blah, blah, blah . . .

But once he said those things, once he bailed on her, she could move off the island without feeling she was leaving something important behind.

Taking a deep breath, she hit Send.

The following morning, Laney had to tap Rafe's leg several times to draw his attention away from Maisey's text. His heart was beating so hard and fast he thought his daughter could hear it. He hadn't received one word from Maisey all day yesterday, not even to let him know she'd landed safely in New Orleans. And then to get a response like this?

It was the last thing he'd been expecting . . .

"Daddy, what are you doing?" Laney asked. "Why are you so quiet?"

"I'm . . . reading something, Laney-bug," he said, still so distracted he could barely manage a response.

"Reading what?" she asked. "Will you read it to me?"

Could he trust what Maisey had written? He almost wondered if someone else had gotten hold of her phone. She'd put so much effort into shutting him down and pushing him away.

What had made her change direction so abruptly? Could she have talked to her mother? Was it that he'd agreed to sign a prenup?

No. He was willing to bet his whole life's earnings that Josephine would never tell her what she'd soon have in her safekeeping.

So "I love you" was "I love you," and it excited him so much that she'd suddenly declared herself he could hardly breathe.

"Daddy?" Laney tapped him again.

"Maisey sent me a message," he said.

"Is she coming back?"

"Yes."

"When?"

"Soon. I hope."

"Is that what her message says?"

He felt a goofy smile coming on. "No. It says she might be in love with me. What do you think of that?"

"Does that mean she wants to *kiss* you?"

He tweaked the end of her nose. "I would guess it does."

She gasped and covered her mouth. "Our dinner worked! Wait till I tell Grandma!"

He laughed as he scooped her up and twirled her around in his arms. "What should I say to Maisey?" he asked.

"Tell her you love her, too!" she cried. "Then see if she'll marry us!"

"What's wrong?" Roxanne asked.

Maisey was sitting at the breakfast table when Rafe's response came in. Even though she'd had only a few hours' sleep, she'd gotten up the moment she heard movement in the kitchen to help Rocki get the kids off to school. Being an aunt was new to her, and she wanted to take advantage of every minute.

When she didn't answer right away, the kids looked up from their food.

"You're turning red," Chloe said.

"That text must be from a guy," Brooklyn added with an insider's smile. Maisey guessed, since Brooklyn was a teenager, she had her own share of interest in the opposite sex.

Zac shoveled another spoonful of oatmeal into his mouth and spoke around it. "Do you have a boyfriend?"

"She does," their mother replied. "His name's Rafe."

"Is that Rafe who's texting you?" Brooklyn asked. "What's he saying?"

Maisey shook her head. "I can't . . . I can't believe it. This was *not* the response I was expecting."

Rocki's eyebrows drew together. "Tell us!"

She put a hand to her chest as if she could control her excitement. "I think he's asking me to marry him."

"You said it wasn't serious with this guy!" Rocki cried.

"This does sound pretty serious, doesn't it," she murmured, still shocked.

"Let me see." Rocki scooted closer. "Oh, my gosh!"

"What are you going to tell him, Aunt Maisey?" Brooklyn asked, her breakfast forgotten.

"I'm going to tell him we need to take the time to get to know each other properly before we have a wedding, but . . ."

"But it's a possibility," Rocki finished.

The smile that spread across Maisey's face came from somewhere deep inside. "It's *definitely* a possibility."

Chloe drummed her fingers on the table to create more urgency. "So answer him!"

Maisey's hands were shaking, but after several fixes she managed to write. **I'd love to be Laney's mother.**

A ding alerted the whole table when he

responded. "What'd he say now?" Rocki asked.

"Are you only interested in my daughter?"

Everyone hopped out of their chairs to crowd close so they could witness the exchange first-hand. **I'll put up with you to get her,** she wrote back.

"That isn't nice," Brooklyn complained.

"He knows I'm joking."

Another text arrived. **Then you'd better hurry home before I start auditioning other women for the part.**

"He's funny," Chloe said.

Maisey chuckled. **Don't you want to hear my good news?**

Far as I'm concerned, no news could be better than this, he wrote back. **I was expecting it to take months to convince you to open that stubborn heart of yours. But go ahead and bring me up to speed.**

"You're going to tell him about Mom," Brooklyn guessed.

"That's exactly what I'm going to do," Maisey said.

My sister didn't fall off a cliff.

What happened to her?

Maisey used the camera in her phone to take a picture of Rocki, which she sent to Rafe.

Meet Annabelle aka Roxanne. Happily married with three children in Lafitte, Louisiana.

Holy shit! Does your mother know?

No, but she's about to find out.

Maisey and Keith spent three days with Roxanne and her family—three days without contacting Josephine or telling her what they'd found—before they were ready to go back to Fairham. It was hard for Maisey to leave her sister and her sister's family, but she missed Rafe and Laney and was excited to see them. Rafe claimed he'd made peace with her mother, which was completely unexpected. While Jack had never tried to bridge that gap, Rafe insisted it was important for her to feel comfortable on Fairham Island, even if she moved out of the bungalow and into town until they decided to proceed with the wedding.

Maisey was grateful that he cared enough to take that into consideration. She was becoming more and more convinced that, even though Rafe wasn't making the kind of money Jack was, he'd take better care of her. They'd take better care of each other.

He had Laney with him when he picked her and Keith up at the airport. They all had dinner together in Charleston. Then they drove to Coldiron House to drop off Keith.

When Maisey unfastened her seat belt, too, Rafe seemed surprised. "I assumed you'd come back tomorrow for the big talk. As far as we know, your mother's in bed."

Even if Josephine was in bed, Keith would wake her up. No way would he be able to keep their secret until morning. And Maisey wanted to be there when Josephine learned about Annabelle, wanted to see if she could discern any relief or tenderness or gratitude that Annabelle was alive. Somehow that was important to her—probably because *she'd* lost a child and would give anything to have her back.

"No, I can't wait that long." Maisey also couldn't feel comfortable returning to the bungalow unless she knew her mother didn't mind. It was a question of pride more than anything.

"Then do you want me to wait in town so I can come and get you when you're done?" Rafe asked.

"No need for that," Keith said. "I'll drive her over."

Rafe pulled Maisey toward him for a kiss. Then she kissed Laney. "See you later, bug," she said, and climbed out.

"Do you really love my daddy?" Laney asked before Maisey could shut the door.

Maisey laughed. "It's pretty impossible not to love him, wouldn't you say?"

Laney grinned and Maisey ducked inside the car to kiss her again before trailing her brother to the grand entrance of the mansion where they'd been raised.

Keith let them in, although Maisey felt so much like a stranger, or an unwelcome guest, that her immediate instinct was to knock.

"Mom?" he yelled. "Mom, where are you?"

There was no response, not until he called several times. Finally, Josephine appeared at the top of the winding staircase, dressed in a silk robe. Even now, when they'd caught her while she was lying in bed, no doubt watching TV with her little lap dog, there wasn't a hair out of place.

"What's going on? Why are you yelling like that?" she asked. "Whatever you have to say, I don't want to hear it. I told you to leave the past alone."

"Because you think something terrible happened, and it's so dark and upsetting you don't want to deal with it," Keith said. "What happened back then *was* wrong, and upsetting, but it's not what you think. I didn't push Annabelle, Mom. I didn't hurt her at all."

She gripped the railing. "Who told you that?"

"Annabelle did," he replied.

She didn't say anything. She just stood there.

"Annabelle's alive, Mother," Maisey added.

She didn't move, didn't flinch, but Maisey could see her shock in the stiffness of her posture.

"Can you believe it?" Keith asked. "No one pushed her. She didn't even fall. We found her! We stayed with her. That's where we've been all this time. We met her husband and her kids. She's beautiful and happy and well."

"That can't be true," she murmured.

"It is," Keith insisted. "We'll prove it to you."

Josephine started to speak but had to clear her throat first. "But how could that . . . how could she have disappeared without—"

Keith beckoned her toward them. "Come down, to the drawing room, and we'll tell you."

As she descended the stairs, her hands were shaking. She clasped them in her lap once they reached the drawing room—she hated anyone knowing she was vulnerable even more than she hated being vulnerable—but Maisey wasn't fooled. Josephine cared about the child she'd lost. Maybe she didn't have the same feelings most mothers did, but she felt . . . *something*.

"Is she going to come and see me?" she asked when they'd told her everything and she'd had some time to digest it.

"She wants to come for Thanksgiving."

"And will she bring my grandchildren?"

"Yes. You have three of them," Keith said. This was repeated information, but no one cared. "Five, eight and fourteen."

"They're already getting so big," she mumbled.

"They're wonderful," Maisey said.

Suddenly, her mother's knuckles whitened and her eyes narrowed. "How dare Gretchen do what she did!"

"It's no excuse, but she thought she was protecting someone she loved," Maisey said. "Ranger thought the same thing."

"From who? From *me*? As if *I've* ever done anything to hurt a child!"

Maisey and Keith exchanged a glance. Apparently their mother was living in denial. Maisey was tempted to call her on it, to make her admit the truth as she would've made anyone else admit it. But then Maisey realized there was no point in continuing to let those days ruin these. Josephine no longer held the power she once did. They were all safe.

Keith must've been thinking the same thing. "At least we've got her back," he said. "At last. And that wouldn't have happened if Maisey hadn't continued to push. I'd still be here, thinking I must be some kind of psychopath to have done something so terrible. And you'd still be angry at her for digging into this and feeling you had to protect me from myself."

Her nostrils flared. "It could've gone differently."

"But it didn't."

Josephine stared at the carpet for a moment. "Your father loved her so much. He was never the same after we lost her."

It was a miracle Josephine had stayed the same. But her mother was nothing if not resilient. She was a survivor, a woman who never let anything defeat her.

"I'm exhausted," Maisey said. "Now that you know, I'm going to have Keith take me home—as long as it's okay if I continue to stay in the bungalow."

Josephine raised her eyes. "Of course it's fine."

"Thank you."

"Rafe came by while you were gone," she said before Maisey could leave.

"I know," she responded. "He doesn't want any animosity between you and me. He especially doesn't want to be the cause of it."

"He loves you," she said simply, and Maisey couldn't believe it but she got the impression that her mother didn't mind.

EPILOGUE

Maisey had spoken to Roxanne every few days since they'd been together in early October, but she was still excited about seeing her and the rest of the family for Thanksgiving. Keith had arranged to meet them at the ferry and bring them to Coldiron House, just as he'd done for her when she'd first returned to Fairham. It seemed appropriate. And they couldn't have fit everyone into Josephine's Mercedes if anyone else had gone along.

"Are they here yet?" Laney asked.

Maisey was standing at the window, holding Laney's hand. Laney couldn't see the drive, but she could feel everyone's excitement. She was so good at picking up on the emotional subtleties of what went on around her. Maisey had decided she was very smart—and very intuitive. "Not yet, honey."

"I can't wait!" She squeezed Maisey's hand. Being with Vera all day, Laney didn't get the opportunity to play with other children as often as Maisey would've liked, so she was looking forward to introducing her to her new "cousins" —and Laney was just as eager to meet them.

"Neither can I," Maisey admitted.

"Don't bunch up your dress like that," Josephine said to Laney from her perch on the sofa. "You'll wrinkle it."

"It's okay if she wrinkles it," Maisey said, but there wasn't much conviction in her words. She was too preoccupied to let her mother's obsession with beauty rile her today.

Rafe had gone to the kitchen to get a glass of water, but now he came up behind them. "Watching for their car isn't going to make them arrive any sooner," he told her with an indulgent chuckle, obviously charmed by her vigil.

Keeping that vigil was certainly easier than

focusing on her mother. Although Josephine had allowed her to continue living in the bungalow, Maisey had insisted on paying rent. And she'd stopped working at the flower shop. She'd started writing again, was fairly certain she'd have her next Molly Brimble book finished by Christmas. Being around Laney inspired her, made her think of all kinds of things she could have Molly Brimble do. She only wished Laney could see her drawings. Rafe told her they were wonderful, but then he told her everything she did was wonderful.

"Can't you two come and sit down?" Josephine asked, but she seemed nervous, too. Although she'd spoken to Roxanne a few times on the phone, it still seemed as if she hadn't adjusted to having Annabelle—as Roxanne—back in the family.

"Laney, Grandma Josie is serious," she said when they ignored her. "You're ruining your nice dress, and if you do that you won't look pretty when they arrive."

Feeling her jaw drop, Maisey turned to stare at Josephine. It wasn't the admonishment that surprised her. Her mother had said many, many things like that to her over the years. It was the fact that she'd called herself "Grandma Josie," which would've been remarkable enough if she and Rafe were married, but they weren't. They'd set the date for April 15.

"What?" her mother said when Maisey raised her eyebrows.

She knew what, but Rafe nudged Maisey before she could comment. He didn't want her to put Josephine on the spot, even though Maisey felt Josephine deserved it. After everything she'd had to say about taking on the care of a special-needs child, it was damned ironic that Josephine seemed to love Laney even more than her little Yorkie.

"I'll stop, Grandma. I want to be pretty," Laney said. But then she started to hop from one foot to the other to relieve her anxiety.

Her mother might've said something about that, too—if Maisey hadn't seen Keith pull into the drive with Roxanne, Landon, Brooklyn, Chloe and Zac. "They're here," she cried, and rushed out of the house with Laney.

"God, it's good to see you," she said as she threw her arms around Roxanne.

"Same here." Her sister lowered her voice. "Keith looks great. Healthier than when he was in Louisiana."

Because he'd been clean since then. "He's taking better care of himself. It was a good decision for him to move to Charleston. He's working as an IT guy for a friend of Mom's, and it seems to be just far enough removed to give them each the space they need."

That was all the time they had to talk because

Landon swept her into a big hug next, and there were introductions all around, with Rafe and Laney and the kids.

It wasn't until they'd gotten through most of them that Maisey realized her mother hadn't entered the fray—and turned to see her looking out from the doorway, as if she didn't quite know how to join in the excitement.

"Roxanne." Maisey turned her so that she could see Josephine.

"Mom?" she said.

When Maisey heard the break in her voice, she knew her sister was about to cry. But that didn't surprise her. Roxanne expressed emotion freely. What shocked Maisey were the tears streaming down their mother's face as the two of them embraced.

AUTHOR'S NOTE

I got the idea for this story from a *Dateline* episode I watched years ago. It was about a brother and a sister who got together as adults and began to rehash old memories of a third child they both dimly remembered but hadn't previously been convinced even existed. Fortified by their unity, they decided that they'd once had a younger sibling and set out to learn what happened to her.

That episode, coupled with my love for a mysterious, gothic feel to a story, so captured my imagination that I wanted to write a book about two siblings in a similar situation. This is that story. I hope you'll enjoy seeing Maisey defy her powerful mother to fight for a child who no longer has a voice—and that you'll be intrigued by what she finds.

For a full list of my novels, and the series and trilogies in which many of them belong, please visit brendanovak.com.Feel free to email me from my website, too. I enjoy hearing from readers. And check out my latest endeavors to raise money for diabetes research (my youngest son has Type 1). To date, I've raised $2.7 million and currently have a cookbook on the market— *LOVE THAT! Brenda Novak's Every Occasion Cookbook*—that contains all my healthiest recipes (which have really come in handy over the years since I have five kids). All proceeds will go to the Diabetes Research Institute, because I believe they are currently our best hope for a cure.

Here's wishing you many hours of reading pleasure!

Brenda Novak

Reader's Guide

1. Many people would say that parenting has changed a great deal during the past two or three generations. Do you agree? If so, what do you feel are some of the most significant changes? What positives result from these changes? Do you see any negatives?

2. Quite a few children seem to carry resentment because of the way they were raised, while others seem to escape the damage from poor parental behavior—and the resentment it causes. Why is there such a drastic difference, often within the same household?

3. How can people who hang on to resentment, especially against friends or family members, begin to let it go? What might happen if they don't?

4. Do you feel that Keith will be able to change his life? Do you think it was his mother's behavior that caused him to act out? Does his relationship with Maisey make a difference, give him a better chance at recovery?

5. Josephine has never been a nurturing parent, and yet she always made sure her children were safe and supervised, and that their physical needs were met. What do you think compels her to act as she does? Would you say she loves her children in spite of her sharp edges?

6. Do you blame Gretchen for doing what she

did—even though, because of her actions, Roxanne/Annabelle lived a happier life?

7. If you were Roxanne/Annabelle, how would you feel toward the woman who raised you?

8. According to Robert Frost, "Home is the place where, when you have to go there, they have to take you in." Would you say Fairham is a safe haven for Maisey? Or another challenge?

9. How does the love Rafe shows Laney affect Maisey?

10. What impact did Malcolm, Maisey's father, have on her life? How did his death change her—and her family?

11. Do you feel that Maisey and Rafe are a well-matched couple? Why or why not?

Center Point Large Print
600 Brooks Road / PO Box 1
Thorndike, ME 04986-0001 USA

(207) 568-3717

US & Canada:
1 800 929-9108
www.centerpointlargeprint.com